A GUILE OF DRAGONS

JAMES ENGE

A GUILE OF DRAGONS

A TOURNAMENT OF SHADOWS | BOOK ONE

PYR®

an imprint of Prometheus Books
Amherst, NY

Published 2012 by Pyr®, an imprint of Prometheus Books

Cover illustration © Steve Stone
Map by Rhys Davies
Cover design by Jacqueline Nasso Cooke

Inquiries should be addressed to
Pyr
59 John Glenn Drive
Amherst, New York 14228–2119
VOICE: 716–691–0133
FAX: 716–691–0137
WWW.PYRSF.COM

16 15 14 13 12 5 4 3 2 1

Library of Congress Cataloging-in-Publication Data

Enge, James, 1960–
A guile of dragons : tournament of shadows I / by James Enge.
p. cm. — (Tournament of shadows ; bk. 1)
First published: London : Gollancz, an imprint of Orion Publishing Group, 2011.
ISBN 978–1–61614–628-3 (pbk.)
ISBN 978–1–61614–629-0 (ebook)
I. Title.

PS3605.N43G85 2012
813'.6—dc23

2012013638

Printed in the United States of America

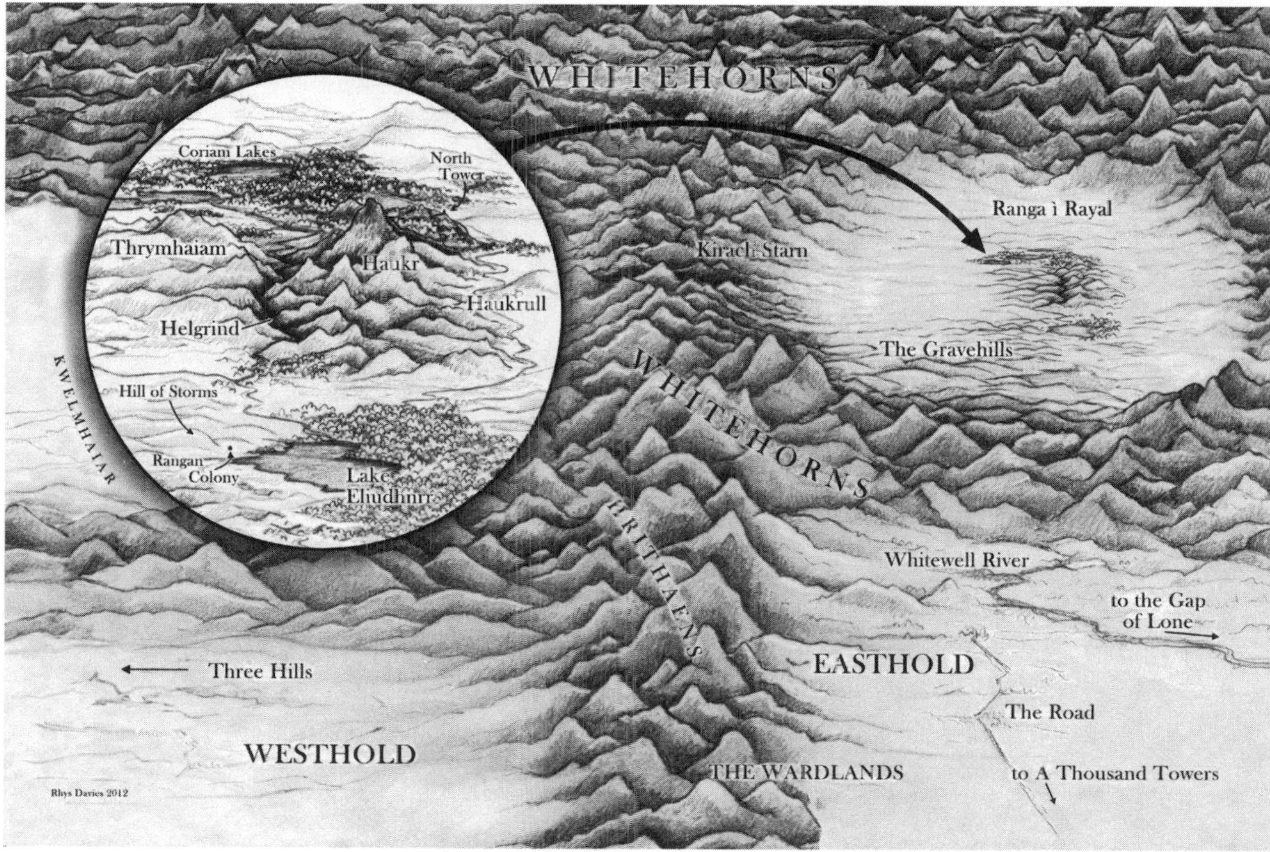
WHITEHORNS
Coriam Lakes
North Tower
Thrymhaiam
Haukr
Haukrull
Helgrind
Hill of Storms
Rangan Colony
Lake Eliudhnrr
KWELMHAIAR
Kirach Starn
Ranga i Rayal
The Gravehills
WHITEHORNS
HRITHAENS
Whitewell River
to the Gap of Lone
EASTHOLD
The Road
to A Thousand Towers
THE WARDLANDS
Three Hills
WESTHOLD
Rhys Davies 2012

To Patrick,
who deserves a book of real history but instead gets this.

Laudato si, mi Signore, per frate Focu,
per lo quale ennallumini la nocte:
ed ello è bello et iucundo et robustoso et forte.

ACKNOWLEDGMENTS

Kierkegaard's *Either/Or* is quoted from the translation by David F. Swenson and Lillian Marvin Swenson (revised by Howard A. Johnson) (Garden City, NY: Doubleday/Anchor, 1971).

The quotation for Dostoevsky's *Notes from Underground* is from David Magarshack's translation (*Dostoevsky's Best Stories* [New York: Modern Library, 1955]).

All translations from the Dwarvish and Wardic in the text are from H. N. Emrys' magisterial commentary on Von Brauch's *Liber Glaucus* (Musopolis: Euphemia State University Press, 1952). They are used here by gracious permission of her estate.

Contents

The day of wrath, that day
will shatter the centuries in fire.

—*Dies Irae*

PART ONE

ALL SUCH ENEMIES

I have the courage, I believe, to doubt everything: I have the courage, I believe, to fight with everything; but I have not the courage to know anything, not the courage to possess, to own anything. Most people complain that the world is so prosaic, that life is not like romance, where opportunities are always so favorable. I complain that life is not like romance, where one had hard-hearted parents, and nixies and trolls to fight, and enchanted princesses to free. What are all such enemies, taken together, compared to the pale, bloodless, tenacious nocturnal shapes with which I fight, and to whom I give life and substance?

—Kierkegaard, *Either/Or*

Chapter One

In a Dark Wood

The Two Powers hated everything, each other most of all. When Torlan said, "Yes," Zahkaar said, "No," and when Torlan said, "I meant no, ha ha ha," Zahkaar said, "I meant yes," and did not laugh. It made their conversations tedious, but they were not aware of it: tedium was not something they could experience.

The Two Powers pervaded the universe; so it was written in the holy books of the Anhikh sorcerer-priests. Those-who-know, the fratricidal fraternity of magical adepts, gave them a more local habitation, in the accursed forest of Tychar, Laent's dark-blue poisonous heart.

This is the history of the universe, according to the Anhikh religion of the Two Powers. In the beginning, there was nothing. Then one of the Two Powers came into being (some say it was Torlan, the power of Fate; some say it was Zahkaar, the power of Chaos—wars have been fought over this important issue). Its being naturally summoned its anti-being into existence, and they began to struggle. Time and the universe and everything in it is a consequence of that struggle. In the end, one of the Powers will vanquish the other, and time and the universe and everything in it will be swept away in that unending victory.

Those-who-know do not generally believe this. But there was no denying the existence of the Two Powers, nor their dreadful if ill-defined abilities, and sorcerers of every stripe of opinion generally gave them a wide berth. "Being an atheist is no protection," as Guelph the Many-Minded remarked on his scaffold, "if a god decides to believe in you."

Today, on the first day of the new year, the two gods had decided to believe in someone.

"Ambrosius," said Torlan, the power of Fate.

"Ambrosius," disagreed Zahkaar, the power of Chaos.

"We hate him," Torlan said.

"Hate," agreed Zahkaar reluctantly, then added, "I hated him first."

"Liar. Liar."

"You're the liar."

"All my decrees are true and eternal."

"True and eternal *lies*."

So the long day wore on. They enjoyed, insofar as they could enjoy anything, when they could disagree about something they agreed on. It made the inevitable cooperation less repugnant to their natures.

But the new quarrel, added to their endless ancient quarrel, did not stop them from executing the resolution arising from their clashing wills. They both hated Ambrosius. He would suffer for inspiring them to agree on anything.

Chapter Two

Conversations in Broceliande

Worlds away, in another time (because we travel through time as well as space when we traverse the Sea of Worlds), Nimue Viviana was also thinking about an Ambrosius. More precisely, she had learned that she was pregnant by Merlin Ambrosius, and she was just deciding to expose the child as soon as it was born.

The decision was a painful business, but only the first of many. She still had to face the crisis of the disaster: tell Merlin she was pregnant, face his fury, and be driven away like a thieving servant.

That was the way things were. She knew it well enough. Merlin was a mysterious figure in young King Arthur's court, but he was (as she had found) a man like other men. He had chosen her as his mistress, but she was not anywhere near his rank, just a Coranian peasant whose parents were dead. When a man picks a mistress like that, as Nimue had observed, he does it so that he can dispose of her when she becomes inconvenient. And there could be nothing more inconvenient than a pregnant mistress. If he were a peasant, he would leave her. As a noble, he could make her leave him.

Thinking this way, she felt she was waking from a dream. They had been happy; they had loved each other. But those were just feelings; they would vanish like mist at the squalling rise of an unwanted son. (By certain arts she had determined that the child was a boy.) She must anticipate this and act now, against her feelings. It was the sensible thing. Merlin, above all others, would understand that.

She'd met the stranger Earno a little more than a week ago. She was out riding in the forest Broceliande and passed by a tall man in a red cloak, standing in a clearing, watching her. She should have known better than to stop. But he called her by name as she passed, and spoke to her in the secret speech. She rode on at first, but then drew rein at the clearing's edge. In the end, she went back to him.

And when she returned to Merlin that night she said nothing of the stranger.

Earno knew so much! That, in the end, was what counted with Nimue. Hungers of the body could be fed, satiated, soothed, but this hunger of the mind never rested content. She reveled in it, hated it, served it. Her hunger for knowledge was what attracted Merlin to her, so he said. Her continuing delight in learning was one reason their affair had been so harmonious. He had taught her much—too much, or not enough. For the thing was over, she was still hungry, and who could she go to now? Mistress Aldwyn who grew poisons among the hedges? Or some semiliterate bishop? Or Sir Kay, who counted the bushels of flour in the kitchens of Camelot and never got the same number twice? There was no one. No one but Merlin. And now: Earno.

So she asked Earno, when it was obvious what he had in mind, "Will you teach me, as Merlin has taught me?"

Earno answered slowly. He was as tall as Merlin, but heavier in build and in mind. He was balding and his beard was a reddish gray. Everything about him suggested slow care and deliberateness. No one could have been more different from the quicksilvery Merlin. He acknowledged as much, saying, "There is no one like Merlin Ambrosius. In my country, which is also his, he is called the master of all makers. He is a great seer also and walks in spirit through the future and the past."

Nimue shrugged restlessly. She hadn't come to Earno to hear him sing Merlin's praises.

"Nevertheless," Earno continued relentlessly, deliberately, "Merlin has not, I know, opened his mind to you fully. He has denied you knowledge of many things, especially regarding his homeland. I can guarantee an answer to every such question."

She listened to all he proposed and agreed to nothing. The decision lay in her hands and she wanted it that way. He seemed to accept this. He also seemed to know she was pregnant, though she never told him. He left her alone in the woods, finally, to return to the man he had asked her to betray.

A week later, the decision was still in her hands, but it would not be much longer. Her body was changing, and Merlin was at last beginning to notice that. If he realized she was pregnant, she would miss her chance.

So that night she made the decision. She lit a blue lamp and set it in her window before she went to Merlin in his chambers. This was the sign Earno had asked for. The next morning she invited Merlin along on her daily ride into Broceliande, to investigate an ancient tower she said she had discovered in the woods. She was sure he would not refuse her, and he didn't.

As they rode under the eaves of the forest, Nimue had a sudden impulse to tell Merlin she was pregnant. The resolution was conceived in an instant, struggled to be born into action, and (evil omen—or was it?) died without seeing the light. She literally could not speak. It would be throwing her life away. Earno obviously felt no interest in her physically, but he had promised to look after her and teach her, and she thought she could count on that. Merlin was unknowable. With her future at stake, she needed something she could count on. When she found she could speak, she chose not to.

There was little chance of her being heard, anyway. Merlin was discussing his favorite topic. He never cared for digressions from it, unless he introduced them himself.

"Because power," he was saying as they cantered along, "is what matters. That's what your local theologians tend to miss. To do good or evil one must first have the power to *do*."

Tangled in her own thoughts, she didn't say anything to this, though she realized Merlin expected some answer. There was a slight rasp in his voice as he continued, "You can't imagine what it's like."

"I've tried to," she said at last. Would Earno kill Merlin? she wondered. He'd promised not to. If he did . . .

"You miss my point," Merlin swept on, slightly mollified. "Imagination has its limits. This must be experienced. And you will experience it: the thrill of power over the lives and dreams of others. Dragons have a name for it in their language: *khûn tenadh*, the game of power. A master dragon plays the game to keep control of his guile of unruly followers. A man or woman can play the game on another level."

"You say: a man *or* a woman."

"Such as myself," said Merlin, pleased. "Or yourself. Yes."

Nimue was annoyed. Once she had believed these sly little hints of Merlin's; perhaps he himself believed in them still. But she had long ago noticed he found a way to keep the upper hand, and there was no reason to believe things would ever be different. Otherwise she would not have begun the game that (unknown to him) was in play.

"Someday," Merlin continued, "when matters are settled, we may even have an heir."

The dreamy wishful tone of his voice was more than she could bear. "'May have'?" she said bitterly. "Surely it's just a matter of time?" *And less than you think,* she nearly added. For an old man, Merlin was relentless in bed, as hungry for her body as she was for his mind.

"Not altogether," Merlin admitted. "Ages ago when my wife . . . died, I decided . . . I decided I did not want an heir. I would be the last of the Ambrosii. So I had a friend set an infertility spell on me, a very powerful one."

"Could it have worn off?" Nimue wondered, and was appalled when she realized she'd said it aloud.

But Merlin simply smiled with a horrible smugness and said, "Virility and fertility are different, my dear. No, this spell will never *wear off*, as you say. It would take a good deal of trouble to undo, and someone else would have to cast the counterspell: a magician's attempt to reshape himself is almost always disastrous. I've lived without even the hope or desire of a child for so long. But now . . . Well, not *now*, obviously. But I begin to think that soon I may revisit that choice."

Someone else would have to cast the counterspell. Nimue thought of Earno and his knowledge of her pregnancy that was too obvious to need stating. Her thoughts were bitter and almost moved her to speak. But he had said *not now, obviously*. She was pregnant *now*. Again, she didn't speak.

The woods became too dense for riding; they dismounted their horses and, leaving the reins tied to a branch, walked deeper into the woods and Merlin's doom.

"I know it may seem strange to you," Merlin was saying, "but the game of power I am playing is different from Morgan's, or Arthur's, or Emperor Lucius'—that sad, bereft little man. All these—the king, his knights, the nations—are no more than a part of the chessboard, a few of the pieces. Some of the problems are here, but the opponent is elsewhere."

"Who is your opponent?" she asked, guessing she knew.

Merlin smiled. He was always smiling, and whatever he said, he hid something unsaid behind that smile. "I play against my old master, the summoner Bleys, and against his rival and peer, the summoner Lernaion. And, I suppose, against the entire Graith of Guardians that they lead and guide. None of these is yet aware that the game is in progress, so it has been a little one-sided so far. Things will get a bit thicker presently."

"What of the third summoner? You said once there were three."

"There is a third, the Summoner of the Outer Lands." Merlin's smile broadened. "You might say he is my ally."

Nimue wasn't smiling. "I wish you'd explain it to me clearly. I don't want power. I just want to know."

"That is how it begins, for such as you and me."

"This says nothing." Desperation gave her words an edge. Soon Merlin and all he knew would be beyond her reach. "When you were young, you found Bleys to teach you. Now you must teach me."

He laughed. "I've taught you much already. If I make you always aware of what you have left to learn . . . Well, in part that's because I don't want your hunger to disappear."

"That could never happen."

"It does, though. I've seen it happen to so many of those-who-know. It's easy to get tired, to say, 'I know all I need,' or '—all that is important' or even '—all there is to know.' It is difficult to sustain the hunger for knowledge."

"That's just an excuse. I've heard others before."

"No, believe me, Nimue Viviana. Nothing that I know will I deny to you forever. But if I gave it all at once, you could not receive it."

"Teach me, then. Tell me something worth knowing."

"Impatience. All right. I'll tell you about this mysterious tower you've found."

"You will?" For a moment she was simply afraid. Merlin was Merlin! Who could tell what he knew, or how he knew it?

"Yes," he said, unaware of her distress. "From your description, it's a relic of your ancestors, the Coranian exiles. Exiles, that is, from my country, the Wardlands. In the last stages of their decadence, they conquered Ireland and they nearly conquered Britain."

"What stopped them?" asked Nimue, more at ease now (or at least less frightened).

"I did. I had uses for these islands; I still do. But as to your tower: it will have a cave underneath it, I expect, which you did not find. Within this will be a grave and a treasury. Yes, if it hasn't been broken into, it might be interesting."

"You knew the Coranians well?" Nimue asked. Earno had spoken of them also, but she wanted to know more. She always wanted to know more.

"In a way," Merlin replied. "Hereabouts, and elsewhere, too, they talk about the Coranians as if they were a different breed of humankind. But they weren't, really—just some people with . . . with a common idea. An idea with certain merits, I've come to realize. Someday I'll bring you to the Northhold of the Wardlands. There you can still see the graves of the Corain, the high kings of the Coranians."

"Are they so impressive?" Nimue wondered.

"In a way. At night." There was an odd tone in his voice—pride mixed with shame or grief.

They were nearly at the tower; it loomed over the nearby trees.

"Who is Earno?" The question, so often on her mind, was out of her mouth before she was aware of it. But she decided, belatedly, that it was only fair that Merlin have a warning, however oblique, of his imminent danger.

But Merlin was serenely, stupidly unflappable. "Have I mentioned him to you? That seems odd. He's a vocate, a member of the Graith of Guardians. He killed a dragon once—his chief claim to fame."

"Many knights have done as much." Despite her words, Nimue was impressed. *Imagine old Earno with a mailcoat and a longsword!* she thought, and smiled.

"So they say," Merlin agreed dryly. "But this was no sickly Scandinavian hole-dweller. Kellander Rukh was his name, full master of a guile of dragons. To defeat such an enemy is something to boast about, and to give him credit, Earno never does. Not really. Earno was a man to watch at one time, but he missed his chance somehow. Not a player, just a piece; he follows Lernaion's faction on the Graith. He has some cause to dislike me."

"Then you're in danger from him."

Merlin stopped walking and took her hands. "No. He had some suspicions, but Lernaion reined him in. I am perfectly safe."

"But the Third Summoner—suppose—"

"Be at peace. *I* am the Third Summoner. There. Now you know something worth knowing." He squeezed her hands once more, let them go and walked into the green shadows at the base of the tower.

Nimue followed silently. There was nothing more to say. And if there were, she would not.

The tower spiraled, hornlike, above the green-gold tops of the nearby trees. It was set on a gray rock carven with strange letters. There were no stairs ascending the sheer rock, but Merlin wasn't concerned.

"'Venhadhur,'" he read. "A king's name. The epitaph is mere bombast. He must have been very late, a semibarbarian petty king of mixed Coranian ancestry. Otherwise he would have been buried near the Hill of Storms in the Northhold."

"You taught me to read the secret speech, but I can't read this."

"Yes, yes. It's a Firbolgi script, if I'm not mistaken. But I beg you to remember, my dear, it is not 'the secret speech,' nor 'Coranian.' It is the language of the Wardlands—Wardic, some call it. Aha. Look at this, now."

He had made one of the carven words recede, revealing a small lever.

"This is very clever workmanship," he said, "but it won't last. Look at the cracks in that tower! Much of the foundation is based on spells that are now fading. In a century, no one will know this tower was ever here. The Coranian makers could have learned something from their enemies, the dwarves."

He pulled the lever and stood back. Part of the stone split open and moved aside, revealing a curved stairway that led deep under the rock.

"That's strange," Merlin remarked. "No treasury; no coffin. There is something on that bottom step, however. Wait here; I'll just go see what it is."

She had no intention of going down. This was the very moment of betrayal, and she didn't want to be near him when he discovered it.

"It's a summoner's cloak," he called up to her, "the long white mantle of office. How odd." He bent down to examine the cloak. His own cloak, which he kept wrapped over his shoulders to conceal the crook in them, fell away. He ignored that. Gingerly, almost as if he could not help himself, he reached down to touch the white cloak.

Abruptly the white cloak rose of its own accord and fell about Merlin in tightening folds. He began to cry out some words, perhaps some sort of counterspell. She might have gone to him then, in spite of everything, but Earno was at her side, holding her arm in an unbreakable grip.

The stone began to grate shut over the stairwell. Soon the rock was a single piece again, and Merlin had disappeared underneath it.

She turned on Earno, venting on him the shame and rage she felt for herself. "Liar! You said he wouldn't be harmed!"

"He hasn't been," the stocky red-bearded man replied patiently, deliberately. "Give me a moment and we'll speak with him."

He took a piece of silvered glass and a diamond stylus from a pocket in his cloak. He scraped a few symbols on the mirror and muttered some words latent with power. She could feel the spell activate, and the mirror went dark. Somehow, although there was no light in the glass, she could see Merlin in the darkness, struggling with his bonds in the underground chamber.

"Merlin!" Earno called through the glass.

Merlin's swaddled form grew still. "It is Earno, isn't it?" he replied, his voice rising through the glass with an odd echoing ring.

"Yes."

"This trap has been ingeniously prepared."

"I only had to change the cell slightly. It *was* a Coranian tomb at one time."

"And now it is mine. Ironic."

"On the contrary. I suggest you induce a withdrawal trance until I return with the Two Summoners. It may take some months, as time runs here, to navigate the Sea of Worlds."

"And if I choose to starve, or die of thirst, instead?"

"Then the partisans of the Ambrosii will mourn, and a terrible danger will have been removed from the Wardlands."

"Earno! Listen. The Wardlands are in danger. That's why we need unity. The realm will need to use all its . . . resources with . . . with efficiency—"

"Merlin," Earno interrupted, "when I was a child my rhetor made me spend a full day justifying the notion of setting a monarch over the Wardlands."

"And?"

"I liked my arguments. But I didn't convince my rhetor or myself. Don't flatter yourself that *you* will."

"I am impressed, Earno. I'm sorry now I mocked you."

"No doubt you are. That woman is here."

"I don't wish to speak to her."

"You should. You will not have another chance for some months."

"Ah. Of course. She will provide your evidence that I have broken the First Decree."

"Yes."

"But . . . I don't understand. Why did she agree? Can you tell me . . . How did you *know* she would agree?"

Fear and pain vibrated in Merlin's glassy voice. Nimue had never heard him speak that way before. She took the mirror from Earno and, ignoring him, told Merlin everything: about her pregnancy, and her fear, and Earno's promises. They talked a long time, till the sun was westering and a red light filtered through the green trees. Finally, she found herself saying, "But I never promised to testify against you. And I will not."

After a long pause, Merlin responded, "I can't say it doesn't matter. But, of all people, I should understand. This is not the end, not for such as you and me. So." Another pause. Then, "As to testifying, they will place you on the Witness Stone. It will place you in rapport with the assembled Graith. The questions you are asked will raise memories the Graith can read. Don't resist. It's dangerous and will do no good."

The concern in his glassy fragile voice wounded Nimue deeply with love and anger. "But we must fight them!" she cried fiercely.

Merlin laughed—it sounded as if it hurt him, and it surely hurt her. "Nimue . . . I think we will. With all our strength and sight. At another time. But now you should go. Go away!"

She handed the mirror to Earno and turned away while he broke the glass and the spell.

"We'll take your horses to the coast," he said presently. "I have a ship waiting there."

They turned their back on the tower and walked in silence for a while, as shadows rose around them.

"What has he done that is so terrible?" she asked, finally.

"Many things. But it amounts to one thing: he has conspired to rule the Wardlands. That is not permitted."

"Your king forbids it, I suppose. How did he get *his* power?"

"There is no king—save One."

She guessed this was some sort of religious statement and changed her approach. "Your governors, then. This Graith he spoke of."

"The Graith are not governors. We simply defend the border."

"Well . . ."

"I can't explain," he said impatiently. "People govern themselves in the Wardlands. No one is permitted to have unrestricted power over anyone else. There is no governor, no class of rulers, as you have in the unguarded lands."

"I can't believe that. It must be chaos."

"This Europe of yours, this is chaos."

"Not Britain."

"Britain is closer to chaos than you might think. The Britain you know is a creation of Merlin Ambrosius. He distorted the history of your world with a power focus I found myself unable to influence, or even fully comprehend. Sages from New Moorhope may be needed to counter-inscribe it. Once that is done, history will begin to resume its natural shape."

"Arthur's kingdom will last. It's been foretold."

"Maybe. Maybe so. But the French knights have had more than one quarrel with Arthur's relatives that Merlin had to smooth over. Then there are the Saxons and, for that matter, the Grail cult. Merlin tried to suppress it, but he never quite succeeded. Possibly it was an inevitable side effect of the focus, or there may have been other powers in play—"

"What does any of this matter to your Graith of Guardians? Your Wardlands are far away, across the sea, you said."

"Across the Sea of Worlds," he said, correcting her. "Yes, it is far away, worlds away. But Merlin was creating an alliance of warriors and seers that the Graith might have been unable to defeat. Now you understand, I suppose."

"Is he so evil for this? Will you put him to death? He said—"

"His motives don't matter. His actions threaten the realm I swore to protect. I don't judge; I defend."

"So you will kill him."

"No. If the Graith finds he has broken the First Decree—and they will—he will be sent into exile. He must leave the Wardlands and never return."

They didn't speak again until they had almost reached the horses. Then Nimue turned to Earno and said, "What did he mean when he said, 'I'm sorry I mocked you'?"

Earno Dragonkiller shook his head and did not answer.

Chapter Three

The Sea of Worlds

Nimue tried to escape from Earno fifteen times on the ride from Broceliande to the coast. Each time she failed. Earno didn't seem to resent it; he explained he had been a ship's officer for many decades and he was used to chasing down men who had jumped ship. He wasn't ill-tempered, but he was relentless. The next day they reached the stony pink shores of Bretagne where his ship was waiting, and the reluctant Nimue was still in tow.

It was an odd ship indeed to Nimue's eyes. The wood of the hull looked blue and shiny like glass; and it was smooth and cold like glass under her fingers when Earno helped (or forced) her to climb aboard. The interior of the ship was just ordinary wood, as far as she could tell, so she guessed the exterior was like paint or glaze applied to decorate the ship. She didn't know how one could do this with glass, but she added it to her list of things she was eager to know.

The single sail was pale and translucent, as if it was woven from glass. It moved in the wind, as sails will, but when Earno hauled it high and cast off from the shore, Nimue noticed that the wind that moved the sail was not the wind she felt on her face. The world's wind was from the northwest, and should have driven Earno's shining blue craft back onto the rose-pale rocks of the Breton coast. The shining sail felt the wind from some other quarter, some other world, and carried them westward, straight into the Ocean.

She wanted to ask about the boat and the sail and the wind, but Earno brushed her off. "I will answer all your questions in time," he said. "But now I have a course to lay out. I prefer to travel with a navigator, but that wasn't possible on this trip." He sat on a bench outside the little ship's single cabin and fiddled with a slate and a spidery sort of compass which had a number of legs that moved independently.

Nimue solemnly watched the coast fade behind her, then turned to look ahead. She had never been on a long sea voyage, and she wondered what it would be like. Ahead of them was a clot of darkness and fog, strangely out of place in the bright clear afternoon.

"Earno," she said, "there is a dark patch ahead of us."

"Excellent," he replied.

The patch grew larger as they grew nearer—actually larger, not just apparently larger. Soon it stretched from horizon to horizon. The mist covered sun and sky like a curtain. She felt her heart fall suddenly, as if she were losing something she could never regain.

Earno got up from time to time to adjust the tiller or the sail, but apart from that he was absorbed in calculations. She moped at the rail of the ship, idly staring into the fog.

As she did so, strange notions began to grow in her head. Ordinary fog veils sight by putting something in the way of everything else, but this fog seemed to be too full of things for any one thing to be seen clearly. But if she concentrated, she could see things in it: faces, and human forms, and inhuman forms, and dark shapes like islands, although they moved past very quickly, much more quickly than she thought they were sailing. She heard voices, too, a mingled chorus of ghosts and shadows like a crowd on tournament days, everyone saying so much that none of it made any sense.

Then another ship passed quite near them. It was only a boat, really. But it was quite clear in the darkness and fog, because of an orange lantern hanging on the stern. A ghostly pale old man was pulling the oars, singing a sad song in a happy voice. Nimue didn't know the words, but they moved her inexpressibly. In the prow sat a dark-skinned child or dwarf. The boat came into view, passed alongside them, began to vanish in the mist.

Earno was wrapped up in his calculations. If he didn't notice the splash when she struck the water, she might reach the other boat and be well away before he saw she was gone. And, with escape attempts, perhaps the sixteenth time was the charm. Hoping that was so, Nimue jumped from the blue craft into the sea.

Except she never did strike the water. She found herself adrift in the dense mist alongside the blue craft, the other boat quite gone. She felt strange; she could suddenly hear all the voices sighing in the mist. And now they did make sense. It was she who didn't. Didn't make sense at all, would never make sense again. The blue craft began to get rather vague and indefinite, as if it were farther away in the foggy sea-that-was-not-a-sea.

Then Earno was there, bending over the rail. He grabbed her by the hair and dragged her back into the blue craft.

"You must not do that again," he said to her. "Please believe this for your own safety: the time for escape has passed. This is like no worldly sea you may know; it may transform those reckless enough to pass through it. Our course and the magical intentions sealed into the hull will protect us, but if you leave the ship you may be changed or destroyed."

She did believe him, but she guessed his warning came too late. She already felt different. The voices she had heard in the mist were still in her head, and her belly had changed size and shape; she was more pregnant than she had been this morning.

She lay on the deck, her head sodden with alien dreams, a strange life moving tentatively within her, and waited for her next chance.

Chapter Four

The Witness Stone

There were voices in Nimue's head all the time now. Only some of them were her own, and those weren't the most interesting ones.

People, she found, were like choirs of singers, not all of whom were singing the same tune. Very often the same thought, the same words, were sung very differently by the mind's many mouths.

She was standing once on a street in A Thousand Towers—a city much greater than any she had seen. And a woman was saying to a man, "I will see you at Three Hills House when Trumpeter sets." That was what she was saying with the mouth in her face, the least important of her many mouths. But inside her, she was screaming it with fear. She was crooning it with desire. She was gnashing the words angrily like broken teeth. She was grieving over them like dead children.

And the man said nothing, but smiled at a woman who wasn't there at all. They walked off in different directions, unaware that they had never really been in the same place, would never be.

But Nimue stayed, and watched, and listened to the things that people said, and the things that they really said.

She never tried to escape anymore. She had no idea where the Wardlands were, what part of the map they were on, if they were on any map. But she knew she didn't know how to get from here back to where she was from, and she had a thin frosty feeling from the future that she would never see the old places again.

She wasn't terribly upset about that. She had seen the spires of Camelot and the walls of Paris. She had even seen Rome, where fingers of broken stone accused the uncaring sky and a frightened baron and his knights crouched behind a curve of the dirty green river and called themselves the kings of the world. She had heard wilder tales of the east with its many cities and silken roads. But she didn't believe there was any city on Earth like A Thousand Towers.

The many towers that gave the city its name were mostly very old, from a time when the city was bound by its walls. But they were all in excellent repair, working homes for the ancient families that lived in them. She herself was housed in one: Tower Ambrose, ancestral home of Merlin and his notorious kin. Every morning she climbed to its height and watched the sun rise out of the west, over the steep ragged ridge of the Hrithaen Mountains.

The sun rose in the west here. That's how far from home she was. She said to Earno, "If the sun rises there, that's the east." But he replied, "East and west are not arbitrary directions. The worlds are linked by the Sea of Worlds, and they radiate from the anchor of the Rock Probability in non-random fashion. The points of the compass, like Probability, are fixed. Our sun rises on the western edge of the world, as it faces the Sea of Worlds."

"A globe doesn't have an edge. If I were on the other side of the globe—"

And then he explained to her that the world was flat. That was a very long strange conversation, in which she learned and unlearned many things.

The great city center bristled with its many towers, but the city spread far beyond its ancient walls now: long ages of peace had made the towers relics, those that had not been dismantled. On either side of the river Ruleijn the long twisting tree-lined streets ran, speckled with markets and bookstalls and smithies and wineshops and schools and open-air refectories and dancing greens and gymnasia where people wrestled as naked as seals and buildings that clearly had some function but Nimue didn't understand it.

And she never got lost. It seemed as if part of her had always lived there, or had waited to live there. She had walked the place in dreams, never remembering them until she woke to find herself there.

One evening she was coming home to Tower Ambrose, the sun a smoky red eye sinking beyond the blue wrinkled line of the Grartan Mountains in the east, when Earno met her on the street.

"You shouldn't walk so much," he said gruffly, not bothering to greet her.

"Pregnant women need exercise too," she pointed out, amused. She knew that he was worried about her trying to escape again, and that he was angry at her because she was associated with Merlin, and that he despised her because she had betrayed Merlin, and that he was frightened of her because her swollen belly reminded him of his mother in her childbearing youth, and that he felt a faint dark trickle of desire for her, which in turn disgusted him because he was primarily attracted to younger men. All these were voices in his chorus, but underneath and overtop of all them was this: she was in his charge and he was concerned for her well-being. That was the strong harmonizing note in his internal chorus. She found his inner self in great harmony with his outer self, more so than anyone whose heart she listened to. She had grown to like him a good deal, though the reverse was not true.

"Ah," said Earno's face. *Pregnant women: bad luck on a ship*, said his heart.

"We're not aboard the *Stonebreaker* now, Earno," she replied, to his thought rather than his speech. *Stonebreaker* was the ship he had commanded in his youth, the one where he had fought and killed a dragon. He was usually thinking about it, even when he wasn't talking about it, which he seldom did.

"Are you reading me now?" he asked, alarm coloring his face and all his thoughts.

She laughed at the question. She could remember when she, like Earno, would have had to go into some sort of trance to reach the level of sight that she experienced continuously, without effort, since her swim through the Sea of Worlds. She could remember it, but she didn't really believe in it. Everyone walked in all realms simultaneously; most could not bring themselves to notice it, but they garnered knowledge from it unconsciously, as Earno now did, speaking in harmony with her unspoken thought, "I am afraid that the Sea of Worlds did you harm."

"You think of the hole in my mind as a flaw. Why not a door?"

"In any castle wall, a door is a flaw," he said solemnly. "Our minds are more like castles than like open cities—there is a danger to us if any stranger, any enemy can come upon us and enter our selves." He said this partly because it was true and partly because he was afraid his farmer-mother would find out that he hated slaughtering animals. His mother had been dead for a century, and it had been more than two centuries since he'd fled the family farm and begun to work on the merchant ships that sailed the Sea of Worlds out of Anglecross Port. But the fear still jangled the song of his thoughts. Also, there was a stone there, weighing heavily down on the notes.

"You're thinking of the Witness Stone," she said.

He nodded. "There is danger for any witness on the stone, anyone who undergoes a forced rapport in any circumstance. But I fear this will be worse for you. I wish—" He wished there were some way he could protect her, she saw; he also wished there were some way he could hide from the contempt of his dead mother. "There will be seers of great skill and power present," he said aloud. "They will not seek to harm you. But neither will they really try to protect you. Their goal will be to learn what you know of Merlin's deeds in your world. If the inquiry harms you, they'll shed no tears."

She was strangely moved at his cold concern, the sympathy he betrayed when he said *they* instead of *we*. But she was not afraid, not until it was too late to do any good, if it ever would have done any good.

They came for her before dawn. The west-facing window of her bedroom was still dark when she found herself shaken awake by the grumpy doorwatcher. (He was not one of Merlin's people. He'd been hired by the Graith to tend the tower while Merlin faced his trial, or whatever they called it—hired with whose money she had no idea. The sole comfort of being a prisoner is that money is someone else's problem.)

She threw the doorwatcher out and dressed at a leisurely pace, keeping her eyes on the strange stars out her window. When she was ready, she threw a shawl over her head and went to meet her inquisitors.

There were eight Guardians waiting for her in the dooryard of the tower. Four wore long bloodred cloaks like Earno did. She knew (now) that this marked them as vocates—full members of the Graith of Guardians. The others wore short gray capes—that meant they were thains, mere candidates to the Graith, really. They were the most soldierly of the three ranks of Guardian, and these ones carried spears taller than themselves. They might have been mere ceremonial weapons; the shafts were ivory-pale and the gores glittered like ice. But the thains carried them lightly, as if from long practice, and they looked sturdy enough to do some damage at need.

"So!" laughed Nimue, pointing at the points. "You'll poke me with those until I talk, eh?"

"Be quiet," said one of the vocates, a furious white-faced, white-haired woman. "We don't need you to talk."

"God Avenger, Noreê!" uttered another vocate, a dark-haired man who moved with catlike grace and wore a sword at his side. "Please ignore my colleague's ill-temper, Nimue. Talk as it suits you—though it's true that it doesn't matter what you say. The real questions, and answers, will not involve words."

"They never do. Naevros," she added impishly, reading his name floating on the surface of his mind. He had been thinking of introducing himself but then thought better of it.

His pleasant face didn't twitch, but inwardly he recoiled violently when he realized what she'd done.

The gray-caped thains weren't as self-controlled and moved farther away, as if that made their thoughts safer from intrusion. Since they were taking her to have *her* thoughts intruded on, Nimue found this amusing and laughed outright.

"Well, Guardians," said a tall, bendable, fair-haired vocate, "she's either got nerves of stone or she has no idea what's ahead of her. Or she's crazy. Or maybe there's something I haven't thought of; it's just barely possible. Madam, I'm called Jordel. Naevros you know, and he has introduced Noreê to you. It remains to me to introduce the brooding silent craglike figure yonder, known with bitter irony as Illion the Wise."

Illion's wry jester's face grinned a little wider and he said, "Ignore him, Nimue. We all do."

"Except when you *need* me."

"We never need him. Shall we introduce the thains, too, Jordel, or should we be off?"

"First, *you* should be off. Second, she already knows their names. Third, I can't remember their names. Fourth, I don't want to know their names, because I don't anticipate needing the services of these quivering custards in gray capes on any future occasion."

Sullenly, the thains closed in again, their clenched determination to do their duty like heads of barley on the long wavering stalks of their fear.

Jordel and Illion led the way with two of the thains while the others followed. As he walked Jordel chatted with her, the thains, Illion, and stray passersby—either to set her at ease, or to pass the time, or because he couldn't bear to do otherwise. Underneath he was like steel—so guarded in his thoughts that she wondered if even he could hear them.

They came finally to the old wall of the city. It had long since fallen into ruin through disuse, but the Chamber of Stations was there, where the ruined wall met the river Ruleijn. There the Graith of Guardians had met since before there was history (so Earno said). The chamber was faced and domed in red marble, a beautiful if somewhat sinister shade, reminding her of dried blood. A single thain stood on the steps outside the chamber, spinning her heavy spear idly in her fingers as if it were a stylus. Her hair was mingled red and black; her eyes were amber; her skin was pale; her mouth was like a wound. She frightened Nimue more than anyone she had met in the Wardlands.

"Maijarra, my dear—" Jordel began.

"I'm not your dear."

"Thain Maijarra, then. We want to return these thains for the money back, please. They were quite useless."

Maijarra's yellow eyes scanned the abashed thains. "Oh?"

"Yes. Fortunately, Nimue came along quietly. Otherwise Illion and I would have had to subdue her with bare fisticuffs."

"What's a fisticuff?"

"How should I know, and me being a man of peace?"

"I'll talk to them. The others are inside."

The thains stayed behind and spoke with Maijarra in low voices while Nimue and the vocates mounted the gray steps to the door of the red dome.

The others, many others, were indeed there. The barrel of the dome was ringed with windows and there was plenty of light, but still Nimue felt a darkness and a chill in that chamber. There was a round table on a dais, and standing at the table were many red-cloaked figures: the vocates of the Graith of Guardians.

Earno was not standing with them. He stood at the foot of the dais along with Merlin, whose wrists were bound with golden cords. Earno was speaking passionately about something. The First Decree, or monarchy, or freedom, or something. But he was thinking about slaughtering season on his family's farm, how he used to run and hide, how they always dragged him there to watch the killing and, on one nightmarish occasion, to actually kill a beast: an old ram with scraggly wool. In Earno's mind, Merlin was that ram, which Nimue thought was quite amusing. She was less amused to realize that her face was on one of the dead beasts in Earno's submerged, distorted memory—one of the beasts whose death he had watched and had been unable to prevent.

He turned and looked at her. "Here is my witness," he said, looking at her but still speaking to the Graith. "She will tell you of Merlin's deeds in this other world. Then you, my peers, will speak his fate."

Earno stepped forward and took her by the hand. He walked her over to a gray marbled chunk of rock in an apse of the chamber. He said no word to her, nor needed to: she knew this was the Witness Stone, and what he would do. He put her hand on the stone and she was suddenly not herself.

Not only herself, anyway. She was still there, floating in the center of her own awareness, but now circling her in every dimension were these other minds, briefly hers and forever not-hers, joined for this moment in the rapport of the stone.

They remembered her memories and understood them in ways she never had. For instance: when she assisted Merlin in moving the Giants' Walk from Ireland to Britain. It was the feat of making she was most proud of. They had anchored the stones so securely in the green plain of Salisbury that they seemed to have grown there. As the vocates remembered her memories, she slowly realized it was even more marvelous than that. Merlin had used a power-focus that anchored the stones in time as well as space, rewriting the history of the world so that the stones had been there for ages, had never been in Ireland at all. This the vocates understood, and so she understood it. That was interesting to her.

But not as interesting as *their* memories. While they were riffling through her fragmented selfhood, she found herself free to explore theirs. This one, named Vineion, lived in a tower with a hundred dogs. He thought rather like a dog, mulling over feeding times and runs along the river and games and loyalty and fear. Jordel was remembering a time when Merlin had sewn up a wound in his side, but was regretfully deciding that the old man would have to be exiled. Callion the Proud, a tall marble-faced vocate, was detached from the inquiry, having already made up his mind. He was watching Noreê with cool patient longing.

Noreê herself was the strangest mind of all. Her self was like a crystal shell on which played simulacra of feelings or thoughts, but that wasn't what she was really thinking or feeling. Nimue had never sensed so harrowingly complete a personal defense. She wondered idly what was going on behind it.

Merlin was in the room, but apparently the rapport of the stone barred her from joining minds with him. He looked concerned. Really, she had never seen him so concerned.

Another presence she couldn't feel was the life in her own womb. It was odd to her, alien indeed since their passage through the Sea of Worlds, but she had grown used to feeling it and the not-feeling was unpleasant, like the numbness of a frozen limb. Why would they bar her from contact with her unborn child? It made no sense.

She explored the barrier with her awareness . . . and was trapped by it.

Her selfhood divided. Part of it was as unconcerned as ever, if diminished. Part of her was trapped in the barrier wrapped around her own womb.

Her child was dying. Anyway, it was fighting for its life, helplessly struggling against a more powerful, endlessly malefic entity: Noreê. That was the secret behind the vocate's shell: she had somehow used the Stone to create a separate rapport between herself and the fetus and she was launching attack after attack on it, trying to kill it with her mind. Nimue knew she should stand between her child and the murderous seer, but her heart quailed as she even thought of doing so: Noreê's hate was raw, desperate, dangerous. It would kill Nimue as readily as her child.

She wondered if she could disrupt the separate rapport through the Stone. . . . Noreê was fearfully powerful, but she was doing three things at once: sustaining the separate rapport, maintaining her facade for the Graith, and striving to kill the child. If Nimue could strike one of those things off balance . . .

The rapport that was killing her child was also a passageway. Things can move both ways through a passage. . . . She tried sending thoughts past the volcanic torrent of Noreê's hate. The seer was intent on her task, and hardly noticed their passage.

The thoughts percolated through Noreê's facade, appearing on the surface of her shell. *Help*, they said, in Latin and Wardic. *Noreê is killing us.*

Callion was the first to notice. He broke rapport and spoke sharply to Noreê with his mouth. He called to the other Guardians. They shifted their attention to batter at Noreê's facade.

The barriers broke. The tide of hate receded and Nimue was alone in her own mind with her wounded weeping child.

She would have spoken then, said something to the frost-faced witch who hated her child so much with so little reason. But something was wrong. There was a pain in her, merely physical, but demanding all her attention. Noreê had succeeded in convincing her body to reject the child.

She slipped in a puddle of amniotic fluid and blood pouring from her own body and fell speechless from the stone.

Or was it the child rejecting her? She thought of that as she swam in and out of awareness over the next few hours. The child seemed fighting to be free of her, struggling to climb out of her. She wanted to let it. She had never felt pain like this before. This could not be normal. Or maybe it was. Old women talked of childbirth and looked wise and said poetic things . . . and all the time they knew it was like *this*. Lying whores. She'd do the same to them one day. Christ, oh sweet Christ, it *hurt*.

And in the end, there it was, a boy, and the pain was receding like a fiery red tide, and Merlin was there holding the child, cutting the cord and wrapping the baby with a grayish cloth. He said a funny thing as he handed the child to her: "The blood may fume a bit, but the cloth won't burn, at least for a while."

She took the child and tried to feel for it what you were supposed to feel. It looked funny. And it watched her, oddly intent, with slate gray eyes. It had long fingers and its head was hairy—she'd seen some newborns, but never with heads of hair like this.

"What do we call it?"

"In the Wardlands, the first name is the mother's privilege, the last name the father's. I'll call him Ambrosius, if you don't mind."

"No, that's right." Names. She should have been thinking of names. Only she'd had no one to talk to about it, really. "Aren't you mad at me?"

"Some," Merlin admitted. She'd seen him lie like a fiend, but he never did to her; she wondered why. "But," he continued, "the thing is done. This part of our lives is over. We have a chance to start again."

"With our. With our son." She wasn't sure how she felt about that.

"Not necessarily. The Graith have given me permission to leave him behind. He can be raised in the Wardlands."

"Is it really so wonderful here?" She thought resentfully of Noreê but couldn't say anything, not yet.

"He'd be better off. But we can take him with, if you'd like."

She didn't want to. She wanted someone to take the pain and the strangeness of him from her. It was a relief to think of someone else bearing that burden. "All right," she said weakly.

"Then you had better name him and we'll be off."

"You can't be serious," she said weakly. "I'm still bleeding."

"I'll find you some healing on the way. But half the Graith are outside, waiting to see us to the border."

Borders. Marches. Moors. That lake on the moor where she and Merlin had met . . .

She told him the name she was giving the boy, and Merlin laughed. "Your family and its Mor-names—Morgause, Morgan, Mordred . . ."

"It's what I want. It's the last thing I'll give him."

"You never know. You may meet again someday. Just a moment while I write a note to my friend."

He scribbled something on a sheet of paper and handed it to a thain standing nearby. "You'll take this to my old friend, won't you, Thain Maijarra?" he said. "I can't command you anymore, but I hope you'll do me the favor."

"As soon as you and the lady leave."

"You are implacable, young Guardian."

"I know my duty. Sir. If you knew yours, mine would be easier today. I don't enjoy this kind of work."

"That is your mistake, young woman. Relish your life to the last bite. Even if it's bitter, it has a kind of savor if it's your own."

She didn't answer him at all, and the old wizard turned to help his young trembling wife from her bloody bed of childbirth. They left the room together, hand in hand, not looking back.

The child remained on the bed. His swaddling clothes were, in fact, smoldering slightly, but he wasn't distressed by it. The room began to grow dark. The child cried out, giving tentative crowlike coughs. No one came. The child's crying grew louder and less tentative. The room grew darker. Still no one came.

Chapter Five

Tyr's Grasp

On the one hand . . .

Tyr syr Theorn's face was gray as a piece of northern granite, and some people said it was about that expressive. Other Ilk, non-dwarves: they said that. Dwarves knew what each other were feeling well enough without winking and smirking about it. So when the news came to the Northhold that the Graith had arrested Merlin Ambrosius (hero of Tunglskin and *harven* kin to the Eldest of the Seven Clans under Thrymhaiam, *that* Merlin), Tyr only needed to say, "I think I'll take a trip south," and everyone knew what he meant. Everyone who mattered: those of his blood, both *ruthen* and *harven*. They brought weapons: weapons and tools to sell, for the dwarves of Northhold could sell anything of that sort they had made at any price they cared to set in any market in any world within sailing distance. Naturally, they brought weapons. And if they planned to use them, that was their business.

It would be a fearful treason to draw blades against the Graith. They had been under the Guard for centuries now, and the long peace was welcome, welcome. But even before they were under the Guard, Merlin was their friend. He stood with them against the Dead Corain and their living armies. Merlin was their blood: *harven coruthen*, chosen-not-given. Those who harmed their blood would pay in blood. Blood for blood. It was their law, their way.

But Merlin never called on them for help. His trial or whatever it was went on in the Station Chamber of the Graith, and the dwarves cannily bought and sold in the marketplace, and they waited patiently for any sign that Merlin wanted their help, but he never gave it. Maybe he didn't want to enfold them in his troubles. Maybe he had forgotten them and their loyalty: it was long years since he had walked in their mountains. It didn't matter. Their loyalty remained and so did they, buying and selling in the marketplace. And waiting.

Then, in the evening of a certain day, a message came. It was addressed to Gryr syr Theorn, Tyr's father. Tyr read it.

My old friend, I am sorry to bring you in the shadow of my troubles.

Tyr shook his head grimly at this. It was generous, but it wasn't a dwarvish generosity. Merlin's troubles were theirs by right, and he was denying them their fair share. Also, he had not bothered to learn (or to remember) that Oldfather Gryr had been dead and standing among those-who-watch for two hundred years. Never mind. He wrote now, and calling one of them by name he called them all. That was the dwarvish way.

I am sent into exile—justly, I might add, so forego your thoughts of vengeance. But my son has just been born and the Graith allows me to leave him behind and be raised under the Guard. Few, if any, will actually take him into their home, of course. So I thought of you. If you will raise him for me and teach him something of the arts of making, I will be grateful. We must leave him in the birthing chamber in old Tower Ambrose, as the Graith is forcing me to leave the Wardlands this instant. The child's name is Morlock Ambrosius, as mine is,

MERLIN AMBROSIUS

Tyr shook his head again. Grateful? He didn't understand the word. Merlin's blood was his blood; that was all. If Merlin didn't understand that, Tyr sure as Canyon did.

"Vetrtheorn," he said, calling his eldest son to him. "I have an errand in the city. Band our folk together and pack up everything; we leave for the north when I return."

Vetrtheorn never spoke two words where none would do, so he nodded. Tyr, who would have enjoyed a conversation every now and then with one of his sons, shrugged and walked away into town.

Tower Ambrose was dark and empty when Tyr reached it. For centuries its retainers had been dwindling; Merlin seemed determined to be the last of the Ambrosii, and he had spent much of his life roaming the face of the world or strange byways in the Sea of Worlds. Now those last few retainers had fled, their loyalty blasted by the decree of Merlin's exile. Tyr spat into the street, ritually cursing their unknown names. Loyalty that was conditional, that could be broken by ill fortune or ill fame, was mere treason-in-waiting as far as Tyr was concerned.

Tyr had never been in the birthing chamber of Tower Ambrose. He took a coldlight from a pocket in his left sleeve and tapped it against a wall to activate the lumen. By its cold grayish light he proceeded to search the tower room by room.

He was well into the fourth story before he found Morlock at last. He almost missed the child, who had fallen asleep among the blankets. But there was smoke and the scent of blood in the room, and Tyr remembered what his father had told him about the blood of Ambrose: that it was latent with fire. Coming near the childbed, Tyr saw the still shape of the child. On his first approach Tyr thought it might be dead. But then the child opened his eyes in the gray light and croaked wearily.

"Well, then, youngling!" said Tyr. "You've had a long day, no doubt, and I see you're tired. Hungry and thirsty, too, I guess. God Creator. What do babies of your Other Ilk eat, I wonder?" He thought about the provisions they had back at their lodgings: travel-food mostly—flatbread, smoked landfish, gnurr-sausage. That would never do. Maybe they could buy some milk in the city? He believed Other Ilk children ate milk, or perhaps it was cheese. He would get some of both and see what worked.

In the meantime there was a bottle of water handy, so Tyr soaked a twisted cloth in the water and offered it to the child. The baby seized the cloth in his long strong fingers and eagerly squeezed the water into his mouth.

"That's the boy!" remarked Tyr approvingly. "Canyon keep us, have you got teeth in there, already? And hair all over your head like a rug. Either everything I knew about babies is wrong, or you're an odd one." The dwarf offered his new son another rag drenched in water and watched him drink.

"Well, little Morlocktheorn, *harven coruthen*, we had better go meet your brothers. They'll be surprised and glad to know you, I've no doubt. I am myself." He tucked the coldlight into a buttonhole of his jacket, picked up the baby, and twirled him into a blanket. The baby squawked with surprise and dismay, but didn't otherwise complain. Tyr guessed that the boy and Vetrtheorn were destined to have some long, mostly silent conversations: here Tyr was acquiring another taciturn son in his garrulous old age.

When he turned to go, he saw that they were not alone. A tall red-cloaked figure stood in the door: long ice-white hair falling past her shoulders, ice-white scars seaming her face, ice-blue eyes stabbing at Tyr through the shadows.

"You'd be the vocate Noreê, I guess," Tyr said. "I greet you."

"Give me that child, whoever you are."

"Who I am is Tyr syr Theorn, Eldest of the Seven Elders under Thrymhaiam. This child is my son *harven coruthen*, chosen-not-given. I do not unchoose my children."

"That child is an Ambrosius, and I will see them expunged from this realm. The old one is gone; Earno will see him over the border. When I realized the child was left behind I came for it. Give it to me."

"No."

"You say you know who I am. Then you know I do what I set out to do."

"A noble deed, then—the death of a child."

"For the safety of this realm I would kill armies of children."

"Then the Canyon take you and your realm, madam."

She took a step into the room. "It's the child that must go to the canyon at the world's dark heart, and you will join it there if you don't surrender it to me."

Tyr backed away as she stepped forward. "You're wrong to do this," he said. "Your peers on the Graith of Guardians will be displeased."

"When the thing is done, they'll find a way to live with it. So will you. So will I. Let it go. Give it to me."

"Blood for blood is dwarvish law. There is no price for blood. If you want peace in your realm, leave the dwarves alone. We fight for those of our blood, whether given or chosen."

"But the child is *not* of your blood. It is—what do you say? It is of the Other Ilk. Let it go. It must sicken you to be near it."

"Like all fanatics, madam, you suffer from the delusion that everyone secretly shares your opinions. You may be sickened and frightened by this child, but I'm not. He's an ugly little monster, I admit, but look at those hands! He'll be some kind of maker, if he has half his father's talent. Anyway, he is my blood, chosen-not-given."

"Are you trying to talk me out of this? You can't talk me out of it. Are you hoping that someone will come to save you? No one is coming to save you. The partisans of the Ambrosii have fled."

"No, madam. One remains."

"I am Noreê of the Gray Hills. Do you understand? I killed two of the Dark Seven with my own hands, a third with my blade. I will have that child." She was halfway into the room now, and Tyr stood with his back to the wall, next to the window.

"No," he said simply. "You will not."

"I think I can take it without killing or maiming you. I would rather do so. It is true that the dwarves would avenge any harm done to you. But not to that thing. Give it to me, or fight for it: I'm done talking."

The dwarvish Elder shook his head, reflecting that Noreê, had, as fanatics usually do, overlooked several options, including the one he'd had in mind from the start of this confrontation.

Tyr jumped through the open window beside him and fell four stories down to the street. He landed on his feet, of course, and the pavement shattered beneath them. But none of his bones broke: he was a dwarf, and he had made his shoes with his own hands.

The child was crying. He was badly jarred, and it wasn't impossible that some of *his* bones were broken: the Other Ilk were strangely fragile. "Listen, young Morlock," Tyr told the weeping child. "If that's the worst thing that ever happens to you, count yourself blessed."

Morlock's new father tucked him into his elbow and ran off at a wolf's pace through the darkness to the edge of the city where his kith were waiting. They would leave for the north instantly. Even Noreê would not dare come as an aggressor to the Northhold. And the child would never leave the north and return to these soft child-killing holds of the south ever again, not if Tyr had anything to say about it. Young Ambrosius could live out a long quiet life among his *harven* people and all would be well. Tyr believed that. He insisted on it. All would be well.

On the other hand . . .

Twelve years later he was still insisting that all would be well, but the insistence had grown a little weary. The night Morlock blew up his workroom, the insistence nearly gave way.

First there was the explosion itself. Tyr awakened groggily to the sound of glass trumpets and screams. He jumped from his nest as soon as he recognized the call. He hadn't heard it in hundreds of years, not since he was a child learning the words and songs from his father's father's brother, Oldfather Khust. But he had never forgotten it: it meant, *Dragons are attacking.*

He threw a blanket around himself, ran out into the halls, and turned down into the corridor vomiting out the loudest noise. There he found Underguide Naeth presiding over a full-blown riot of his kin, screaming, "They're coming! They're coming! They're *here*!"

"Naeth, stop that noise and talk to me," Tyr said. He did not raise his voice, but somehow everyone present heard him and fell silent, waiting for the Eldest's word. Fear of the ancient enemy was blood-deep in them, but loyalty was their bone.

"There is a fire, and the inner walls are breaking. That Other Ilk is part of it. I saw him there, basking in the fire like a dragon. I saw him."

"Are you speaking of my *harven* son—your kin, chosen-not-given?"

"*I* didn't choose him. And—"

"But I did. His *ruthen* father saved our people from the Dead Corain before your grandfather was born. If you slander his-son-and-mine again, you will pay the price. I have spoken." Tyr's right hand clenched into a fist before his chest.

Naeth bowed his head, abashed at the mention of his grandfather, a dwarf whose sons were all *harven coruthen*.

"Can anyone talk sense to me?" Tyr demanded.

"No," said a brassy voice. "But I saw it. I can tell you what happened."

Tyr's eyes focused on the downy-bearded dwarf who had spoken. A youngster—perhaps not even thirty. One of his maternal uncle's great-grandsons: Deor was the child's name.

"Tell me then, Deortheorn."

The young dwarf bowed, flattered that the Eldest had remembered his name—but not overwhelmed. He started right in talking.

"Your *harven* son and Naeth had an argument about a seedstone he was working on. I didn't understand what they were saying, but I stayed around to listen because he never talks that much about anything, so I figured it must be important. Morlock, I mean: he's not one to talk. Anyway, Naeth dismissed us to the sleepbenches for the midnight nap, but I noticed Morlock get up and sneak off. I figure he's going back to work on his seedstone, so after a while I get up and follow him, because, you know."

"You like to know things," Tyr suggested.

"Right! Anyway. I was spying on him, I guess, so I didn't want him to know I was spying on him—"

"That follows."

"—so I followed him, but not too close. Back to his workbench he goes, and he's talking to himself all the time in at least three languages, none of which was ours. He spent some time at his bench—I think he was inscribing something on the seedstone. When all of a sudden it blossomed."

"The seedstone blossomed while he was at the workbench."

"He was holding it in his *hand*."

"Sustainer." Tyr was envisioning a funeral and a very difficult letter he would have to write to Morlock's *ruthen* parents.

"It lifts him up—whoosh! like a tidal wave—and smacks him against the wall. There was a lot of fire and smoke. I tried to reach him, but it was too hot."

"He's probably dead anyway."

"Oh, he's not dead. I heard him talking to himself. He said something like, 'How can I draw a shape without any lines? What if the ur-shape moves like water over time?' And other stuff I couldn't understand. Actually, I can't understand any of that stuff."

"Hm." Neither did Tyr, but there was no point in saying so. "Take me to him, or as near as you can."

The young dwarf led the old one deeper into the earth, to a corridor filled with smoke that was slow to disperse. The air was hot, and as they came to the portal of the bachelors' workroom the blast was like a furnace.

"Eldest," said Deor hesitantly.

Before the youngster could say anything more, Tyr said, "Wait here. If I don't come out with Morlock soon, go get Vetr and tell him what has happened."

"Eldest—"

"There is a time for talking and a time for doing. I have told you what to do." Without waiting for a reply, Tyr stepped into the burning room.

The pattern of the fire was wild—like snakes on the ground, like cracks in the earth. It was not spreading, except in one corner at the back of the room where the walls were crumbling as the fire crept up them, blood-bright ivy. The Eldest sidled along the walls of the chamber and avoided the worst of the fires. It was not as bad as cave-leaping over the lava rivers of the Westway underroads. Tyr had done that often in his reckless youth. Now he was not reckless: he never took a risk without a reason.

Soon he saw, through the red murk, his *harven* son hunching over something. He was holding whatever-it-was still on the floor with his feet, working on it with a diamond stylus held in his left hand. His right arm hung at his side, limp as liver-noodles—which the fingers of his right hand, in fact, strongly resembled: liver-noodles that had been smashed with a hammer.

"*Harven* Morlock," Tyr called, when he had approached as close as he could. "Come here. We must leave this place."

Morlock shook his head and muttered.

"There is danger," Tyr insisted. "The walls are giving way."

"I know! I know!" the boy shouted. "Unpatterning doesn't eat the fire, so I'm rescripting the pattern at the gemstone's core."

"We can take care of that later. Your hand needs tending to, by the look of it."

"There is no later. The fire won't stop unless I stop it. Shut up, won't you shut up? I have to hold the shifting ur-shapes in my mind!"

Tyr suspected the boy was irrational, although he found it hard to tell with Other Ilk in general and Morlock in particular. He thought about throwing something to knock the boy out and then dragging him out of there somehow. On the other hand, there was some chance that Morlock, crazy or not, knew what he was doing.

His decision was still taking form when it became irrelevant. The fire vanished with a kind of thunderclap. Tyr crouched, bracing himself against the icy shock that rode the air, re-echoing in the crumbling room. When it passed he looked up to see Morlock slumped against the wall. His right hand and bare feet were frost-blue.

There were still some small fires burning in the suddenly freezing room: Morlock's Ambrosial blood setting fire even to the stones it dripped on. But the terrible blaze was gone. Where its center had been, Tyr saw a small dark gem with a fiery red heart: the bloom from Morlock's seedstone, repatterned—whatever that meant. Tyr pocketed it and went over to Morlock. The boy's clothes and limbs were in rags. There was a medallion around his neck that Tyr thought he recognized. He looked at it solemnly for a few moments and then reached down and snapped the chain, putting it with the medallion in his pocket alongside the stone. Then he grabbed his bleeding, burning, *harven* son under the shoulders and dragged him away to the Healing Chambers.

Vyrlaeth was an unpleasantly lizardlike dwarf with a long gray tongue that he rested thoughtfully between his gray lips when he wasn't speaking—sometimes, even when he was. He shaved his face, and he knotted his hair like a female. But he was the best healer under Thrymhaiam, and Tyr was glad he was tending to Morlock.

"Yes, yes," Vyrlaeth was saying now. "The burns are slighter than one would expect. The heritage of Ambrose. Indeed, the blaze must have been fierce to raise any blisters at all. Most troubling are the blast impacts on his hands and feet, and the frostbite here and there. You must explain to me sometime how the injuries occurred."

"As soon as I understand it myself," Tyr promised.

"Well." The gray tongue glistened between the gray lips. A shrug. "It's the injuries themselves that concern me, of course."

"Can you save his hands? He's a fine maker."

"Oh yes. Yes, indeed." The tongue again. "We will weave the bones, the blood vessels, the tendons and muscles together again. The flesh is wounded, but nothing has died." The tongue. "Death itself is an interesting problem." Tongue. "Not unsolvable. Partial death, anyway—tissue death. Necrosis . . . necrosis . . ." He whispered the word as if it were the name of his firstborn daughter.

"Can I speak to him?" Tyr asked, eager to escape from the sight of the healer's tongue and his sentimental daydreams of necrosis.

"Surely." A gray smooth-skinned smile. "In his moods, he might even answer you."

Morlock was lying on a stone sleepbench stripped of its blankets; there was even a stone pillow. The healers were taking no chances with the fires that might arise from Morlock's burning blood. Tyr couldn't blame them; the bandages on Morlock's hands and feet were smoking slightly, even though they were laced with so many fire-quell magics that they made Tyr's beard bristle like an unhappy badger.

He sat down beside his strangest son and said, "Morlock. I know you're awake."

"How can I sleep, thinking about the ur-shapes?" Morlock muttered.

His moods. Some of Morlock's *harven* kin thought him insane; Tyr had never agreed, and not just out of loyalty to the boy's *ruthen* father. Trying to trust that feeling, Tyr observed quietly, "I don't know what you mean by ur-shapes, Morlock. What are they and why are they bothering you?"

Morlock reached out his bandaged hands to take a stylus and slate from a stone table next to his rocky bed.

"Should you be using those?" Tyr asked anxiously.

"Vyrlaeth says it doesn't matter for the reweaving," Morlock said. He paused and stared off into space for a moment. "Healing is a strange art. Bodies are so unclean. But the patterns are so complex. I think that is a making I will never master."

"Ur-shapes," Tyr reminded him, but Morlock had already turned back to his slate. The shattered, bandaged fingers sketched three elegant shapes with the stylus: a square, a circle, a hexagon.

"This," Morlock said, "is three pictures of that." He pointed at the coldlight lamp standing on the stone table.

"How so?" Tyr said. Although he thought he understood, he also thought it was a good discipline for Morlock to express his ideas in words.

"What if we were on the surface of the slate?" Morlock said after a while, "as flat as the slate itself, and could see nothing except what was on the slate?"

Tyr's eyes crossed a little; then he smiled and said, "Suppose we were."

"Yes, and suppose the lamp passed through the slate somehow. This"—he tapped the slate—"is what we would see: not the true shape, but a series of sections. The square base. The round ring securing the light to the base. The long six-sided coldlight. We might think these were all different things, or that the object was changing shape over time, but it wouldn't be true. The true shape of the thing would be an ur-shape for us. We could deduce the true shape using our minds and memories, but we could never see it."

"And you think . . ."

"I think we do live on a slate. Or maybe: in a box. There are measurements and dimensions that we don't see, and, and, and when those shapes pass through our senses we don't truly see them. We have to understand them. I am saying this badly."

"No, I think I follow you. This is the scholium called *multidimensional geometry*"—he spoke the phrase in Wardic, as there was no exact equivalent in Dwarvish—"by those-who-know."

"Oh." Morlock blinked and shrugged. "I thought I invented it."

"You did, it seems. Someone else just did so first. But I don't see what this has to do with your explosive seedstone."

"Oh. That." Morlock's face twisted with unhappiness, anger, shame. "We were drawing matrices for seedstones and—Does Naeth know about *multidimensional geometry*?"

"Doubt it."

"Well. I was trying to explain to him about the ur-shapes. Because it matters for the matrices. The matrices apply power to the focus in the heart of the seedstone, creating the bloom of matter, but if you used ur-shapes you could draw different types of matrices. They might apply new levels of power, create new kinds of stone. He—he—wouldn't listen. So I. So I. So I."

"So you completely destroyed the work-chamber and the structural integrity of several walls."

"I guess. I need to know more about *multidimensional geometry*. Can you teach me?"

"No," Tyr admitted, "or at least not much. And as far as I know, no one has applied it to seedstone-crafting, so I ask you to tread carefully there. That runaway exothermia was like nothing I have ever seen."

Morlock nodded, visibly storing away the new words for later use and thought. "What a disaster," he reflected, after a long stretch of thoughtful silence.

"Not altogether," Tyr said, drawing out the gem from his pocket. The surface was dark red, like a garnet, but there was a deep golden flaw running down to its heart.

Morlock's gray eyes glared at the thing with distaste. "You should get rid of it. It is ugly, ill-made, possibly dangerous."

Tyr looked mildly on his ugly, ill-made, possibly dangerous son. "I collect such things, though," Tyr said, "and I don't lightly get rid of those I've become attached to. I'll keep this, if you don't mind."

"Everything that's mine is yours," Morlock said unhesitatingly. Then he hesitated. "But that thing . . . the core may fail. I scripted the repatterning recklessly, not knowing what I was doing. If it is unstable there might be another runaway exothermia . . . or . . . what is the opposite? When things grow colder?"

"Endothermia, I think."

"That, then."

"Well, you will study, and someday perfect the design. I'll keep this against that day."

"Who will teach me?" asked Morlock. He hardly needed to say, *Not Naeth, I hope*: it was written on his usually inexpressive face.

"I think to send you south, to New Moorhope. You can learn much of geometry there from those-who-know, and healing, too, if you choose, and many other things."

Morlock's face lost all expression again. "I am to be sent away."

"Morlocktheorn. This is an opportunity, not a punishment. You have talent, but not skill. You could have both. Think of this."

Morlock nodded in acceptance.

They talked of some other things, and Tyr rose to go without ever mentioning the other thing he had in his pocket, the medallion he had removed from Morlock's neck.

On it was an image of Morlock's *ruthen* father, old Ambrosius. Morlock had said something disrespectful about the old man last year, and Tyr had ordered the boy to make this reminder of his first father and wear it for a month. Nothing cast more shame on a *harven* family than raising a child who scorned their *ruthen* parents. At first, when he'd seen the medallion still about Morlock's neck in the burning chamber, Tyr had been relieved: perhaps the lesson was taking root. Then he looked closer.

The image was defaced: the eyes were gouged out and the rest of the face was slashed into a blur by a thousand or more savage strokes with a variety of tools, blunt and sharp. MERLIN AMBROSIUS had once been inscribed under the face. MERLIN was completely scratched away: a ragged trench took its place on the medallion's surface. AMBROSIUS was still there, each letter standing alone in a deeply incised square. Tyr's lesson of respect had been transformed into a talisman of hate.

The obverse bore an image of Morlock's mother. It remained untouched. Was that a sign of reverence? Indifference? Tyr could not be sure.

In fact, the matter was beyond Tyr's reach and he knew it. In New Moorhope, the greatest center of lore and learning in the Wardlands (perhaps the world, or many a world), there were mindhealers as well as geometers. Should he send Morlock to them, as well?

But the boy never *spoke* of it. Whenever he spoke of his *ruthen* father nowadays, it was with measured respect for old Ambrosius' achievements, never a word of disrespect. And he rarely spoke of the old man at all. Whatever Morlock felt, he knew it was wrong, and he kept it locked up inside himself. That was good, wasn't it? It showed he was learning.

Tyr walked away and went about his work as Eldest of the Seven Clans. He had many things to think about, but Morlock was often on his mind, if never quite in his grasp.

PART TWO

UNDER THE GUARD

Does the eagle know what is in the pit?
Or wilt thou go ask the mole?
Can wisdom be put in a silver rod?
Or love in a golden bowl?

—Blake, *The Book of Thel*

Chapter Six

Earno Goes North

Years later, in the hour before dawn, Earno Dragonkiller lay dreaming.

From his bed he seemed to see red light on the clouds outside his window. He heard the roar of a high wind and the unmistakable crackling of an open fire. He rose from his bed in the dark red light and went to the window. He saw, without surprise, that the city, A Thousand Towers, was burning. The river Ruleijn ran red as blood with reflected light. Turning away from the window, he noticed that beside his bed stood a spiraling stairway, where none had been before. He ascended it without hesitation, and it led him to the roof of his house.

Casting his gaze about as he reached the roof, he saw instantly that the fire had gutted Tower Ambrose, ancient home of the Ambrosii. He watched with some satisfaction as it collapsed into a smoky glowing ruin. But as it fell the horizon itself gave way and he surveyed all the Wardlands at a glance.

And it was all burning; fire devoured not just A Thousand Towers but the whole realm. An arc of fire swung through the Easthold down to the islands of the south; looking west, he seemed to be able to see over the Hrithaens, the tallest mountains in the world, and he found that the narrow plains of the Westhold also blazed, bright with death. At last he looked north, where he saw the Whitethorn Mountains, belying their name, black as cinders surrounding the red coals that had been the Northhold. Seeing that the flames had died down in the north, he realized that the fire must have started there. For the first time, fear struck through his dreaming calm. For the first time, it seemed more than a dream.

"Lernaion!" He awakened to the harsh croak of his own voice in the midnight darkness of his room. Sleep did not return to him that night.

The summoner Earno went to Illion's house the next morning before dawn. Illion, already known as Illion the Wise, was a vocate, the second rank of Guardian. Most of his peers belonged to one of the three factions that followed each of the Three Summoners. There were some free voices heard at Station, though, who spoke their own words and adhered to no faction; notorious among these was Illion. For that reason he was no obvious ally to Earno. But when the summoner looked for advice, he not infrequently went to his neighbor and opponent Illion.

The vocate, who was having breakfast, invited his senior in, but Earno sat sullenly at the table without eating anything; he spoke hardly more than he ate. Illion, seeing his mood, waited until he was ready to speak his mind.

"Vocate Illion," Earno said finally, "I must leave this morning."

"I'm sorry," Illion said. "I'd hoped we could work together on the Kaenish matter. If the Two Powers are reaching westward—"

"Yes, well, that's dead and buried now."

"I'm afraid it's not, though. I'd hoped we could discuss it with those who sometimes speak along with me at Station."

"This Station is over, as far as I'm concerned."

"I don't see why. There's much that can be done; there's much that needs doing."

"You misunderstand me. I must leave A Thousand Towers. I must . . ." Earno seemed to hear the almost hysterical compulsion in his own voice and concluded curtly, "I am going north."

"Oh." Illion thought about this for a while. The summoner Lernaion had gone north early in the year, to set the protective wards about the Northhold. That had been in late winter, on the twenty-second of Jaric. It was now the twenty-sixth of the Mother and the Maiden, well into fall. Perhaps two hundred and eighty days had passed, with not even a message from the north. People were beginning to talk. "You are concerned for Lernaion?" he said finally.

"Yes." Earno met his eye with a glare.

Illion recognized Earno's defensiveness on the subject of Lernaion, whose faction he had followed when he was a vocate. But, for himself, he respected Earno's insight and was troubled.

They rose from the table and walked out of the wide open doors of Illion's house. The sun had just risen, red on the western horizon. Earno silently saluted Tower Ambrose, unruined, brooding over the river Ruleijn. They turned their back on it and walked down toward the old city walls where the Station Chamber stood.

"After the Station ends," Illion said, "I will be going up to Three Hills. There will be some other vocates with me."

Three Hills was in Westhold, just south of Northhold's border.

"For how long?" Earno asked.

"Three or four of us will always be there, until I hear from you."

Earno nodded. They walked the rest of the way in silence.

Earno returned home and gathered some things together. Just as he was mounting his horse to depart, a young woman wearing the gray cape of a thain rode up and handed him a message.

It was unsigned, but written in Illion's tall, tangled script. It said only: *Morlock syr Theorn, thain, guarding at the Lonetower in the Gap of Lone. He served me well as guide in the north, five years ago. He has also walked some of the unguarded lands, including Kaen.*

"My regards to Illion," Earno said curtly to the thain, who was waiting for a response. "I find his advice good."

"When isn't it?" she replied brashly.

He waved her away and rode off down the street.

"The Road," as an Easthold proverb boasts, "runs." It links A Thousand Towers with the densely populated manors and port-cities of the south; it penetrates the Hrithaens to communicate with Westhold; it spans the long arc of Easthold, north to south.

The Road runs—but not forever. Earno came to its northernmost point as darkness was falling on the thirteenth day of the month of Bayring. The stone paving simply came to an end without so much as a signpost or a milestone. But, Earno reflected, a signpost was hardly necessary. Travellers who came this far north surely knew where they were going . . . or didn't care where they went.

There was an inn at the end of the road, but Earno didn't enter it. The Lonetower was only a short ride north of here. But he dismounted to give his horse and himself some rest.

Chariot, the first moon, was standing halfway down toward the eastern horizon. In a month and a half it would set and the first month of the new year would begin: Cymbals, named for the characteristic instrument of the Winter Feast. The second moon, Horseman, whose rising and setting marked the months, would rise again on the first night of Borderer, the last month, to finally set on the last night of the year. Now Earno watched the western horizon for the rise of Trumpeter, the third moon. It, too, would set on the last night of the year, but it was faster as well as smaller than its two companions: it would cross the sky three times before then.

Now it rose, fiercely radiant as it ascended from the west. Small though it was, it shed twice as much light as somber Chariot, sinking in the east. Earno watched Trumpeter clear the horizon (crooked with the Hrithaen peaks), then remounted his horse and rode on through the dim blue landscape. Not much later he arrived at the Lonetower in the Gap of Lone.

A sentinel in the gray cape of a thain greeted him at the gate of the tower, taking in his white mantle of office. "Hail Summoner . . . Earno?" he said, somewhat tentatively, peering in the light of the moons.

Without dismounting, Earno nodded in acknowledgement. He said, "Hail in turn to you, Thain. Bring Thain Morlock to me."

"What for? Has he done something?" demanded the sentinel, with undisguised eagerness.

Earno frowned. "Bring him to me."

"Beg your pardon, sir." The sentinel was embarrassed.

"Don't call me 'sir.' You have my pardon. Bring Morlock to me."

"Beg your pardon, s—Summoner Earno. He is on patrol." The sentinel gestured vaguely east.

Earno turned his eyes to the moonlight-colored gap. This was a flat grassy plain set between two mountain ranges: the Grartan, marching southward, and the Whitethorns (second only to the high Hrithaens) running from west to east. Looking at the Gap of Lone one always felt the unnaturalness of it, as if someone had pressed flat the region where the mountains ranges joined, or as if the plain had somehow stayed as it was while the bordering regions crumpled upward into mountains.

"Which post?" Earno asked. "The Grartan? Or the Whitethorn side?"

"Neither, sir," said the sentinel, forgetting himself. "He's in the Maze itself." He gestured again at the colorless open plain of grass.

In that case, Earno knew, he might be hours or days in returning to the Lonetower, and it would be fruitless to go out seeking him. Earno considered lodging at the Lonetower, imagined dozens of gray-caped thains goggling at him and calling him "sir," and rejected the idea. "When Morlock returns, send him to me at the inn by the end of the road. You know it?"

"Yes, sir."

"Have him bring two horses," Earno added, and rode away.

The next day, about noon, the landlord came to his room and told him that the Thain Morlock was awaiting him in the courtyard of the inn. Earno donned his mantle and gathered up his belongings.

The thains were the third and lowest class of Guardian, more candidates to the Graith than Guardians proper. Unlike vocates who could (if they chose) jealously guard their independence, or the summoners, who had powerful prerogatives and influence, thains were obliged to obey their seniors in the Graith, even senior thains. Their life resembled the military castes of the unguarded lands—but not too closely. Their discipline was to prepare them for radical independence, not unthinking obedience.

In general thains did not impress Earno; this Morlock was no exception. The summoner had expected him to be a dwarf. (The Theorn were a dwarvish clan.) He was not, though. He was of middle height for a man; his hair was dark and tangled; his skin was grayish—or perhaps it only seemed so, since all of his clothes, not just his cape, were gray in color, down to his unpolished boots. His eyes were an alarmingly pale shade of gray also. There was something awkward about him—the set of his shoulders, maybe. The expression on his face was sullen and dull.

"Thain Morlock," said Earno, greeting him pleasantly, "I am the summoner Earno."

"I know," said the thain, after a long pause.

Earno looked at him sharply. Was he being insolent? Earno had spent half his life as the officer of a merchant ship, and he had an ingrained dislike for insolence. "I'm told you're a northerner," he continued more briskly.

Morlock stared at him. "I was fostered by Theorn clan," he said slowly.

Becoming impatient, Earno said, "I wish to go north. What road do you recommend?"

Again a pause. "That depends," Morlock said.

"On what?"

"On where you intend to arrive."

Earno was about to reply harshly to this when he realized that the question had not occurred to him before. To him the north was almost entirely unknown, and Lernaion's location within it was entirely unknown.

"How would you go?" he asked, trying to be less insistent.

Morlock shrugged. "When I go I travel to Thrymhaiam, my clanhome. Or to Northtower—thains' tower east of there. Same route. So. Along the Whitewell—river with its source in the 'Thorns. Then. Down past the gravehills. Ah. A network of valleys, you have to know them, leads to Thrymhaiam. From Thrymhaiam you can travel all around by . . . tunnels. Except to the west. The Fire is too hot there. . . . I mean, the mountains, they're volcanic." His hands clenched suddenly, and apparently involuntarily.

Finding this broken recital deeply irritating, Earno interrupted. "Very well. You will guide me to Thrymhaiam."

Morlock nodded. He looked apprehensively at Earno's pack.

Noting this, "We leave immediately," Earno said.

The thain nodded again and turned to his horse. He mounted with deliberate speed. Earno saw a cloud of dust shake loose from his clothes, and realized they were not, in fact, gray (except for the thain's cape), but had been coated thick with dust.

Feeling his face grow hot, Earno realized what had happened. The thain had returned from his patrol and had been instantly dispatched by his overzealous seniors. Possibly he had not slept in days; he had brought no pack.

Earno knew he should tell the thain to dismount, to get some rest, at least to wash off and find some of the things he would need before they set out.

He did not. He mounted the horse the thain had brought for him. Then Morlock led the way across the courtyard and across the Road, west and north, toward the Whitethorns.

Something bothered Earno all that day. It was Morlock's name. Somehow, it was known to him, but he couldn't summon the memory.

It occurred to him while he was sleeping, and he awoke at once. He sat up in the darkness, pulling his mantle around him. The embers of the campfire still cast a dim glow over the area. He saw the outline of Morlock's shape, sprawled in a pile of leaves. Behind him he dimly heard the roar of the Whitewell River.

He got up and took a few hot coals in a metal cup. He walked over to where Morlock lay and dropped them among the leaves.

Almost immediately, fire leapt up and spread through the dry leaves. Presently the light woke Morlock. His cold gray eyes opened, and they looked through the flames at Earno. A long eerie moment passed, and then Morlock set to beating out the flames with his bare hands. In a few moments they were extinguished.

"You've burnt my cape," Morlock observed shortly.

"But not *you*."

"No," Morlock admitted, "not me."

"Then you are Morlock *Ambrosius*—the son of the exile." All the Ambrosii had it, this immunity from fire.

"No."

"You deny it, do you?" It was what Earno had waited for. Once before an Ambrosius had called him a liar to his face . . .

"No," Morlock said flatly. "Merlin was my father. But I was fostered with Theorn clan when my parents went into exile. My name is Morlock syr Theorn."

Earno was taken aback. Something of the matter was lodged in his memory, confirming Morlock's story. He had supposed that Morlock had become a Guardian under false pretenses, that there was some sort of plot.

. . . Now he saw that there was no plot. Abruptly (he was a person of abrupt emotions, though he struggled against them) he felt sorry for the young thain, glaring up at him from a bed of ashes.

"You know I exiled your father—" Earno began.

"It was the Graith of Guardians that exiled Merlin!" the thain said harshly, as if he were offended.

Again Earno was taken aback. "You are right," he said. "I misspoke." He had forgotten what he was going to say.

Morlock shrugged and stood up.

Earno turned away and went back to his sleeping cloak. As he fell asleep he heard Morlock gathering a new bed of dry leaves.

Chapter Seven

Knife

The next day they stopped at a large farm on the bank of the Whitewell to get the supplies they would need in their trip over the mountains. Morlock knew the people well; he often stopped there for provisions when he took the road home. Usually he only needed food, though. Now he wanted heavy clothes for the summoner and himself, food for both, and some kind of weapon. He was no good with a bow, and swords are useless, unless you expect to run into a duelist. An axe would have been best: good for defense, and useful, too. Morlock never felt that it was trouble for nothing when he carried an axe over the mountains. The farmer only had one, though, and was unwilling to part with it. Morlock settled at last for a knife. Decent metal, but terrible work: his fingers itched for the tools and time to set it right. But the time, at least, he didn't have; the summoner had stamped away from the haggling with unconcealed impatience.

There was a problem with the farmer, too. He had assumed that Morlock would stay and work for the knife, as he usually did for his provisions. "The horses are more than enough for the clothes and food," he explained. "But the knife is different. Metal's scarce. On this side of the mountains, I mean."

Morlock understood. "I'll bring you a knife from Thrymhaiam."

"Bring two."

"One," Morlock said flatly. They could do without the knife, if need be.

The farmer saw it in his face. "A real working knife, now," he insisted, conceding the point. "None of these silver showpieces."

Morlock stood. "Northern steel. From my hand or my father's."

"I don't want better." The farmer stood and they struck hands. Then they went to make packs for the provisions.

Fifteen days later the two Guardians were high in the Whitethorns, at the source of the Whitewell. This was a hot spring, running out of a steep snow-clad mountainside. The banks of the stream were anything but white: black mud, gray stone—even green with life at spots. But it was striking to see water running in the deep snow of the high mountains.

"This is rather high in the mountains for a hot spring, isn't it?" Earno asked the thain.

Morlock shrugged. "Northhold is new." It seemed to be a proverb.

"When will we get through the mountains?"

The thain glanced at him in surprise. "It's mostly mountains, in the 'Hold."

"But not like this."

"No. In . . . Dwarvish we call the Whitethorns 'the Walls.' Or maybe 'the Shields'; Dwarvish doesn't distinguish. We are in South Wall, now, a low part. You could almost cart goods along the Whitewell."

Earno felt differently. But he was no mountaineer.

Morlock led the way up a nearby ridge and pointed. "Look."

Earno was already looking. For long days the horizon had been narrowing—deeply oppressive to him, who had grown up on the wide plains of Westhold and spent much of his life upon the sea. The nearest mountains had become the limit of vision, and although these were gigantic Earno had begun to feel as if he were spending day after day in the same frigid closed room.

But now, between two nearby mountains, there was a break in the horizon. He could see deep into the north, many days' travel: hills and smaller mountains, blue with distance, some topped already with snow, like still white flames in blue smoke.

"Those low hills you see before us," Morlock was saying, "extend over to the west, past what we can see. Beyond them, ahead of us, you see a group of snow-covered peaks."

"Yes."

"That is Thrymhaiam, home of the Seven Clans."

"Then we go through the hills."

"No. It is not a good idea to travel through the gravehills."

"Ah. The Dead Corain. Now I shall see their graves."

"You see them now. If it were night you would see the banefires."

"They still burn, then?"

"Yes. We will see them as we travel west around the hills. It will take more than one night."

"Why don't we turn east? I can see the end of the hills; it must be the shorter way."

After a moment Morlock said, "We might do so, if you wish. There is a settlement of the Other Ilk that way."

The phrase "Other Ilk" struck Earno strangely. He wondered what it meant, but he felt he should know. Then at last, he dragged up the memory, from when he was trading with many nations in the unguarded lands: it was an expression dwarves used to refer to non-dwarves. Earno was of the Other Ilk—as was Morlock himself, really.

"We must go east," Earno said. He was thinking that he might hear some news of Lernaion that way. "I'm sorry," he added. He never cared to overrule a subordinate, unless it was necessary.

The thain nodded. "The Hill of Storms is near there," he observed, almost conversationally.

This caught Earno's interest. "Why would they settle there?" he asked as they began to descend the ridge's far side, "these . . . Other Ilk?"

"It is only a colony, really, from Ranga í Rayal, a settlement beyond Thrymhaiam to the north. Ranga has good farmland, but they don't have as much metal as they'd like. There are rich deposits near the gravehills, though, so they established a mine there."

"Couldn't they trade for the metal?"

"Yes. They get most of their metal from us—that is, from the Seven Clans under Thrymhaiam. And we get food from them. But it's good to have a choice, you see. So the Rangans develop mines where they can. And Thrymhaiam trades with others for food. Your people, for one."

"My people?" Earno was surprised.

"Westholders. They are great sea-goers, the people of Westhold. The trading ships come as far north as the Broken Coast, and beyond."

"I once worked on a trading ship," Earno observed.

"Yes, I know: the *Stonebreaker*, to the unguarded lands. They still sing that story on the ships. A guile of dragons attacked the convoy, and you killed the master dragon, Kellander Rukh, in single combat."

Earno looked at him and smiled. "A sailor's first skill is lying, you know. They learn it before they tie their first knot."

Morlock smiled a little, too, but said seriously, "You can tell when they're lying. They're too proud to lie about you, or Illion."

"Well . . . Your line, too, is very famous," Earno said generously.

Morlock paused, then said, "It's true. Naevros syr Tol carries a blade from Thrymhaiam, and would never use another. They say he's the best swordsman under the Guard."

"The Hill of Storms—That was a great victory of your father's, wasn't it?" Earno insisted.

Morlock said nothing. He shifted the pack on his crooked shoulders and continued to lead the way down.

"Can it be you don't know the story?" Earno asked, following him. He thought it strange that Morlock could tell a tale of his father's greatest enemy, Earno himself, but none about his father. Had they failed to tell him about the heritage of the Ambrosii at Thrymhaiam? As much as Earno hated Merlin, this seemed wrong. He continued, "It was before the Northhold came under the Guard. The peoples of the north appealed to the Graith for aid against the Coranians, who were invading them. Merlin was a vocate, then, and when the Graith refused to act as a body he went alone over the mountains and fought the Dead Cor on the Hill of Storms. He defeated him with his own accursed blade, the sword-scepter Gryregaest—"

"I know all that!" shouted Morlock furiously.

They did not speak again for the rest of that day.

Presently Earno decided that he had made a mistake. Morlock must hate him for what he had done to Merlin. And Earno, for the first time, realized he felt guilty because of that. He had injured Morlock terribly, without knowing or intending it, years ago. He would do the same thing today, if it were needed to maintain the Guard. But he felt guilty all the same. And he wanted Morlock to forgive him for what he had done. He saw now that he had been trying to ingratiate himself with the thain—he, the Summoner of the Inner Lands!—so that he would be forgiven. And Morlock had dismissed him with contempt.

And rightly so. The boy had earned his hatred. It had been ungenerous of Earno to try and take that from him, too. He would not try again.

The next day they walked into the mining settlement after dark, just as the banefires on the crown of the Hill of Storms began to burn. The hill stood high, dark and threatening over the settlement, and the intense blue fire obscuring its height cast no radiance into the town. You could sometimes see shapes moving in the banefire light, but as Morlock had told Earno the night before, it was not a good idea to look for them deliberately. "Because then the voices may follow," he muttered, when pressed for an explanation, and Earno did not ask further.

Without saying what he expected, he had stood guard all night with the knife in his hand. Though obviously exhausted, he had pressed the march all the next day, trying to reach the settlement before another nightfall. Now that they were finally there, Earno noticed, he did not look noticeably relieved. But what he felt was his business.

"Is there a head man?" Earno asked the thain.

"There will be an Arbiter of the Peace. Her house is the high one, at the end of the street."

"Very well. Stay here and watch over the packs." Earno supposed it might have been useful to have the thain with him at the meeting. But he was tired of Morlock's sullen company.

"A moment," Morlock said, and fumbled at his belt. "Take this, please."

Earno found the knife in his hands. The extent of Morlock's dwarvish prejudice struck him speechless. Did he really think that a village Arbiter would attack the Summoner of the Inner Lands? Or that Earno Dragonkiller lacked his own methods of protecting himself? After a long look at the impassive thain, Earno placed the knife under his white mantle and silently walked away to the Arbiter's house.

The Arbiter was a tall woman, her hair as dark as Morlock's, her skin nearly as pale. There was nothing crooked or dwarvish about her, though. (Earno had begun to fear that everyone was like that in the north.) There was nothing hidden about her, either. Earno was announced while she was sitting over the remains of her dinner, and she leapt up to greet the summoner. By that time Earno had entered the room, and the Arbiter suddenly stopped and stared. Obviously she had been expecting his peer, but Earno (with his red-gray beard and stocky build) cut quite a different figure from the dark-skinned knifelike Lernaion. The Arbiter laughed, confessed her surprise, and led her guest to the seat of honor as the remains of her meal were borne away.

Earno tried not to follow these with his eyes, but his host noted the effort and said, "Yes, it's poor stuff. But we're not starving, nor need you while you're with us."

"I'm surprised," admitted Earno, "since it's past harvest, and Ranga í Rayal is said to have rich farmland."

The Arbiter flushed, pleased, yet somehow embarrassed at the compliment. "It has," she said. "And harvest is long past. So's slaughtering, in fact, or should be. But we have had no drudgings—you would say 'shipments,' I guess—from Ranga for nearly a month."

"That seems strange."

"It is strange. But we have stores to rely on. Any throw, we expect relief . . . soon. Perhaps the slaughtering held them up there. It can be tricky, sometimes."

Earno nodded and smiled politely. He had run away from his parents' farm in Westhold when still young; it had been slaughtering season. After some more talk about Ranga and its colony, he said, "I've come to consult with my peer, Summoner Lernaion. I take it you've seen him."

"Keep you! Many times! He's been in the 'Hold for months, setting the Wards. He left here the last time less than half a month ago."

"Bound for where?"

"Thrymhaiam. Where else can you go? All roads up here lead to the wormhuggers, since they made them. Fortunately all roads lead away from them, too, if you understand me."

Earno thought he did. "Wormhuggers" must be some local slur for dwarves. Earno felt as if he should object, but really could not bring himself to. "Did the summoner seem disturbed?" he asked.

"Well, the summoner never showed his feelings, not to me. But there were plenty among his escort who were worried sick. And I've seen the Wards set before; never have I seen it take so long."

"Did he mention what was wrong?"

"We hardly spoke, not as you and I are doing now. But, again, I heard from his escort that he was worried about the banefires. They are burning brighter and higher this year than ever before."

Earno nodded. Things were not as bad as he had feared, but he was glad he had come. "We will not trouble you long. Tomorrow we will follow Lernaion to Thrymhaiam, and thence probably to Thains' Northtower. But if we could find lodgings for the night . . ."

The Arbiter looked welcoming and apprehensive at once. "Your escort is . . . ?"

"One thain only," Earno reassured her, realizing that she must be thinking of her limited store of food. "And—"

At that there came a knocking on the door, and sounds of shouting rang in the entryway. Arbiter and summoner rose together and went to investigate.

They found a pair of the Arbiter's servants carrying an unconscious man while another servant struggled to close the door against a crowd of angry townspeople. At the entrance of the Arbiter silence fell immediately. Earno recognized the unconscious man as his thain.

The Arbiter turned to one of her servants. "Tell me," she said curtly.

"The man was selling food, Arbiter. It's that one—the wormhugger from Thrymhaiam. He had two packs of food, and he was selling it, and the crowd formed, and things got out of hand. We came and took him into sanctuary, or were trying to."

"He said he'd sell me flatbread for some dried meat," shouted a man at the doorway. "He wouldn't take money. I haven't had meat for fifty days! It's *them* that stopped the drudgings! So they could do *this* to us!" Others began shouting behind him.

Earno stood forward and spoke one of the Silent Words. Everyone clapped their hands over their ears except Earno himself, who was braced at the shock-center, and the unconscious man, who was unceremoniously dumped on the floor. As their ears were still ringing Earno spoke into the silence, saying, "This man is a thain and a Guardian of these lands. He came north from the Easthold with me and knew nothing of your troubles. That he was selling the food we would need on our journey I will not believe; your own accounts give you the lie. You have also accused yourselves of assaulting the inviolable person of a Guardian. The penalty for that is exile."

"How could we know?" demanded one of the townsmen.

Sternly, Earno pointed at the thain's gray cape of office. With irritation he noted that it was soiled, torn, and even burned—hardly recognizable, even in the lamplit hallway. His gesture was ruined.

"Go now," the Arbiter said to her people. "And keep the peace!"

Without further dispute, they went.

The thain was carried to the dining hall and laid on the bare table. Wine was sent for. The summoner and the Arbiter looked at his wounds, but these were hardly more than scrapes and bruises. It was surprising he was still unconscious.

"It is a bad time," the Arbiter was saying. "They are just barely hungry. But they are, well—farm people, used to feasting when fall comes. And a month with nothing from Ranga, no message, even . . . They're frightened."

Earno said nothing. He cleaned and bound the more serious of the cuts, then stepped aside to wait for the thain to regain consciousness.

"The . . . He's well-known around here, of course," the Arbiter continued. "He . . . well, you can understand the wor—the dwarves being the way they are. But it's a little grotesque to see . . . well, another kind of person act that way. A little unnerving . . ."

Earno motioned her to silence. Morlock had begun to stir, and then suddenly his eyes opened. But he was not awake. Earno, even standing some distance away, was amazed at the intense clarity of his gray eyes, the pupils contracted almost to invisibility. Himself a master of Seeing, he recognized the rapture of vision.

In a voice taut with urgency Morlock cried out, "Regin and Fafnir were brothers!" He laughed aloud, an ugly sound. Then he fell silent.

"Those names—" the Arbiter began, but again Earno waved her silent.

Quietly, so as not to interrupt the vision, Earno prompted Morlock, "Tell your tale. What news of Regin and Fafnir?"

But the spell was broken. Morlock regained consciousness. Watching the wakeful expression settle down on his face, Earno thought of a series of gauze curtains descending before a light. When the last one descended, the light disappeared. His face sullen and suspicious, Morlock sat up.

"What was your vision?" asked the summoner.

"I don't remember," said the thain.

Then Morlock and the Arbiter eyed each other coldly. Earno, watching them, decided that prejudice was a knife with two edges.

Thinking this, he suddenly remembered the knife hidden under his cloak. He thought of Morlock confronting the angry mob on the dark street, and for the first time realized why Morlock had surrendered the blade. That, too, was like a spell breaking.

Chapter Eight

Settlement

The two Guardians slept that night in rooms of the Arbiter's house. Earno's room faced the Hill of Storms, and he did not sleep well. Though the shutter was closed, he could still see the eerie blue light of banefire around the edge of the window. When he finally fell asleep he dreamed of that stormy Station of the Graith when he had convicted Merlin of impairing the Guard, and in doing so had defied almost every Guardian in the Graith, including his patron Lernaion. But in the dream, as he made his accusation, Earno saw that Merlin wore the cape of a thain, ragged and singed. He was also holding the accursed sword-scepter Gryregaest in his hands. Suddenly, nothing Earno said seemed to mean anything, but he could not stop talking, making the same speech he had made a generation ago. (He had not forgotten a word of that speech, nor would he ever.) Finally, Ambrosius cast the sword onto the Witness Stone standing between them; the blade shattered like black glass, and Earno's dream with it.

It was just before dawn when he awoke. There was still a blue light seeping through the shuttered window, but it was the natural gray-blue of gloaming. He went to the window, unbarred it, and opened the shutter. Then he sat on the sill and drank in the electric air of those mountains.

The Hill of Storms frowned upon the settlement. Earno could pick out few details of the surface. But in silhouette against the brightening sky he could see a sharply angled object on the crown. He supposed it was the Broken Altar, if there was such a thing. (There was no better authority for it than *First Merlin's Song*, the tale of Merlin's struggle against the Dead Cor.) Earno thought of Merlin as he looked at the hill, and of his strange dream the night before. He noted, from his second-floor window, that there was a high wooden fence encircling the hill at its base, apparently designed to keep people out rather than anything in. He wondered what it was for, and his speculations did nothing to settle his mind.

As he sat on the sill, he realized he could hear voices coming from below him. Walking back and forth, Morlock and the Arbiter were speaking intently to each other behind the house.

"In return," the Arbiter was saying, "I want you to persuade your father not to take revenge against the town, or Ranga."

The summoner could imagine Morlock shaking his head (although the eaves of the house hid the speakers from him). "I cannot speak for my father," the thain's voice said. "I have no authority there."

"A dwarvish answer. What *more* do you want?"

"Nothing." Morlock stopped walking. "Keep your horses! But I tell you this: I am a Guardian of the Wardlands, all these lands. Even Ranga."

"A dwarvish answer! It costs you nothing; it sounds well. And Ranga will still pay the penalty."

"It *is* a dwarvish answer. I was taught to say what I mean. That is why you will not trust me. You never mean what you say, so you must always say more than you mean. Dwarves are not like that." He paused, and continued more slowly. "They are unlike you in other ways also. They took me in, they gave me shelter, and no one else under the Guard would dare to do it. For that alone, I would give *dwarvish answers* as long as I live." Earno heard his footsteps as he strode away.

Turning back to his room, Earno thought about the conversation he had overheard. In a way he was pleased that Morlock could feel and express as humane an emotion as loyalty, and it explained much in his manner. But in another way Earno was deeply disturbed. If Morlock and Merlin were in contact ("persuade your father," the Arbiter had said) then Morlock had broken the First Decree—the decree forbade contact between those in exile and those under the Guard. But if Merlin was able to frequent the north so much that the Arbiter feared reprisals for having harmed his son . . . that was bad. If Morlock had, as a thain, aided him, it was treason. Ambrosius the son could easily follow his father into exile, both denounced by Earno.

While part of him whispered that the prospect was right and inevitable, the rest of Earno felt weary. How could he condemn a man for speaking occasionally with his own father? Yet such a thing put the whole realm in danger, if the father was Merlin Ambrosius. Who knew his purposes? Now Earno wondered if the trouble with the Wards was Merlin's doing. If so, Morlock's exile was already a certain thing.

When Earno descended to the main hall of the Arbiter's house, he found the Arbiter herself awaiting him. They greeted each other, and then she spoke.

"I sent my servants to recover your packs, but I'm afraid they were carried off by the crowd. They can probably be recovered, given a few days."

"That's unfortunate. My business is urgent."

"So your thain informed me. I have taken the liberty of preparing two of my finest horses for you and your thain. Please do me the honor of accepting them, for you *and* your companion." The emphasis in her last phrase was oddly insistent.

"I do so; thank you." Earno wondered about the flourishes; in the Westhold no high-minded host would think twice about giving an honored guest a horse. But perhaps they were more valuable here. "That is . . . Thank you very much. When our packs are recovered, please send them on to Thrymhaiam."

"It will be done," said the Arbiter, with an air of concluding some sort of deal.

They walked together to the front door of the house. Morlock was standing in the street outside; not far away two horses were tethered, already saddled. Morlock looked at the Arbiter warily. With almost equal wariness, Earno noted an Arbiter's servant on either side of the door. Set to keep Morlock from entering?

"Ride well, Morlock syr Theorn," said the Arbiter pleasantly. "And good fortune to you, Summoner Earno."

Morlock looked once at Earno and then away. He walked over to the horses, untethered one, and mounted it. When Earno had done the same Morlock rode off down the street, looking neither right nor left until the settlement was far behind them.

Later that day, after hours of silence, Earno asked, "What's wrong?"

Morlock shook his head, but answered, saying, "The Arbiter will look on these horses as a binding settlement—for my beating. Horses are valuable in the north."

"And so?" Earno said sharply, thinking of the conversation he had overheard. "Were you thinking of revenge?"

"*No.* That is the point."

"It's one I don't understand."

"Dwarves do not accept wergild. It is not our way. Injuries . . . you revenge them or forgive them. You do not accept payment for them."

Earno had heard differently of dwarves, but kept silent. It was, however, as if Morlock had read his mind.

"When you go through life with people saying of you . . . that you would buy and sell everything . . . you become careful of what you will buy or sell."

"We need the horses," Earno said.

Morlock nodded.

Earno thought of saying that they could send the horses back from Thrymhaiam. But he was not sure they would not need them still. He said impatiently, "What would you have of me?"

Morlock replied, "Do not speak of this at Thrymhaiam. They will have to know, but let them know from me."

"Very well," said Earno, who was prepared to concern himself with other matters.

Among these were the location of Lernaion and the present condition of the Wards. Since he had word of Lernaion's well-being as recently as a half-month ago, long after his concern had begun, he gave his thoughts mostly to the Wards. They had always been difficult to set around the North; that was why Lernaion had come north with a company of thains and vocates to assist him. Since Merlin's exile, Lernaion was the member of the Graith most skilled in protective magic such as the Wards. If Lernaion was in difficulties, it was something to be concerned about. And Earno's concern now had a name: Merlin.

Who else but Merlin could defeat, or even hamper, Lernaion in an exercise of this sort of power? And now Earno had reason to believe that Merlin was again a presence to be feared in the north.

The summoner shook his head. It was not unheard-of that one determined person, moving alone, might make it through the Wards and return to the Wardlands. This was rarely a matter of great concern. One person could hardly be a danger to the Guard, living in secret. If they revealed themselves, then the Graith dealt with them. Most exiles who made their way back did not reveal themselves: instead they took up private lives in the lands. Some in the Graith (Illion, for instance) argued that, by doing so, they had renounced the unrestricted ambition that had earned them (or their ancestors) exile, and so deserved pardon. The Summoner of the City, Lernaion, held a stricter view: that exile was a permanent and irrevocable sentence, not to be suspended or ameliorated in any case. Otherwise, said Lernaion, the First Decree would cease to carry any weight, since the exile that it mandated was the only punishment the Graith could inflict (except in the case of armed invasion, which it was the Graith's purpose to prevent).

Earno was inclined to take the stricter view himself; otherwise the fertile disorder of the unruled realm would slump into chaos. But there could be no disagreement about a consciously malefic intruder such as Merlin. His action in disrupting the Wards (if, Earno reminded himself faintly, he had actually done so) proved his malice, and his danger. And, Earno added thoughtfully, it underlined the potential threat of all the individual exiles that had returned to the Wardlands.

Suddenly, impulsively, Earno began to hope that Merlin had returned, and had done some terrible crime. Then Earno could face him again. And if he defeated the exile and brought him before the Graith . . . It would be a great deed. It would silence many of his critics among the vocates. And it would help settle a more vigorous policy toward returned exiles; this would win him new influence with his peers, Bleys and Lernaion.

Perhaps roving bands of thains could be set up, to investigate rumors of returnees. They had similar things in the unguarded lands, Earno knew. It would be childish naiveté to forego them here under the Guard, where they were most needed.

Then perhaps something could be done about intensifying the Wards themselves, to choke off the slow permeation of returning exiles. Then the seacoasts would be the only way for outsiders to enter the Wardlands.

Slowly, and in great detail, he began to review methods of tightening the Guard along the coasts.

As they rode on in silence, the shame of having his injuries bought and sold by others faded from Morlock's mind. The unstained familiar wonder of his homeland stole over him. Wherever he looked he saw the narrow horizon pierced by mountain peaks like pale thorns. The sky above was chill and blue, with storm clouds approaching from the west. The slopes they rode among were rolling and green with life, in sharp glorious disharmony with the steep dead gravehills on their left.

He saw that the blue-gold autumn flowers were already dying, and that a blackiron maijarra tree was already in its darkest bloom. Both of these things meant a long winter and an early one. And it had been unseasonably cold every night since they had entered the Whitethorns; the passes would soon be closed.

He looked back up at the clouds to see if they brought snow, guessed that they did, but kept on looking. The sky of the Northhold fascinated him. Half-filled with clouds, it seemed deeper and higher than when it was clear. You could measure it then with your eyes, finding it immeasurable. While clear it was just a narrow water-blue dome; when covered with storm clouds (vast, whirling, mountain-sized shapes) you could see how much space the sky enfolded. And, glimpsing a field of blue between parted clouds, you knew its distance was more than you could know.

Morlock exhaled slowly and only then realized he had been holding his breath. He lowered his gaze to the horizon and saw with surprise what looked like smoke over the mountains east of Thrymhaiam.

Earno returned to himself when he heard someone speaking to horses. Shaking loose from a consideration of possible harbor defenses for the southern coast, he realized that the voice had been Morlock's. For a moment he had thought himself back in Westhold.

"That is western dialect," he said, when the horses had turned in the required direction.

"Yes," said Morlock. "The horses understand it, though they have never been west of Kirach Starn. Illion taught me it, when I was guiding him in the north."

"Ah, Illion." Earno had thought about Illion a good deal in the last half-month or so, and his possible motives in saddling him with this particular guide. "You know him well?"

"He commended me to the Graith. Otherwise . . . I would not be a Guardian."

Earno wished he were not. The Graith would be unlikely to banish one of the Guarded for harboring his exiled father; a Guardian was another matter. But Earno did not mention this, of course. Impulsively he asked, "What do you think of the Other Ilk—the Rangans, for instance?"

Morlock considered. "The Rangans have many good metalworkers," he said, "but . . ."

"Yes?"

"They don't build well." Morlock's expression was unreadable.

The summoner shook his head irritably and resumed his distant thoughts.

He became conscious of the outer world again when the horses left the path for a stone road. He looked at the thain.

"We are very near to Thrymhaiam now," Morlock remarked. "Look!"

Earno, looking, saw a cluster of snow-topped mountains blotting out the horizon to the north. The stone path led directly into them through the steepening hills. To the right he saw a higher range of mountains, proceeding from the southeast to the north beyond Thrymhaiam. "Is Ranga beyond those?" he asked the thain.

"No," Morlock replied. "Those we call the Haukr. There is a very ancient settlement in one of the valleys beyond, called Haukrull. The Thains' Northtower is north of there. Ranga is beyond Thrymhaiam to the north and west; we cannot see it."

"I have been in mountains before," Earno remarked, "but none like these."

"Yes. Northhold is new. They say the Wards are responsible, raising the mountains along the southern border, before we came under the Guard, and disturbing the lands beyond. Now the Wards are on the northern border, and the lands are being disturbed again."

"It sounds a dangerous place to live," Earno remarked.

Morlock shrugged. Earno waited, but he said no more.

Presently they came to a high stone gate, set into the base of a steep slope. "We have come to Southgate of Thrymhaiam," Morlock said.

There were five dwarves sitting at a stone table outside the gate, discussing something with heat but without hostility. One looked up at the sound of the thain's voice and cried out, "*Harven* Morlock!"

"*Harven* Deor," responded Morlock, smiling.

The dwarves leapt to their feet and rushed to the two Guardians, helping them to dismount (which they evidently considered an act of desperate danger) and greeting their kinsman with voluble and, to Earno, unintelligible words, while Morlock responded in the same language.

"*Lar arsamnen san guardiansclef iddornin, Morlocktheorn*," the dwarf called Deor remarked, when the ceremonies were evidently completed.

"What Guardians were those, Deortheorn?" asked Morlock in Wardic, the speech common to the southern holds.

"*Hurs?*" responded the mystified dwarf, then continued in Wardic, "Ah, yes, I grasp it." He turned toward Earno. "Summoner, I welcome you to the Deep Halls of Theornn. The companion of our *harven* kin, you shall have the seat of honor. I beg your leave to bring you to the Eldest of Theorn Clan, first of the Seven Clans under Thrymhaiam."

"You have my leave readily, Deor syr Theorn," Earno answered. "Also my leave to respond to your . . . *harven* kinsman's question, which you may consider my own."

They walked together through the stone gateway. Two of the dwarves, without being instructed, led away the horses, and the other two remained to watch the gate . . . and, no doubt, to conclude their argument.

Deor was saying, "We have seen so many senior Guardians in the past season or two that I wonder I lowered myself to speak to such a junior thain. The summoner Lernaion, with five vocates and a passel of thains—"

"An entire passel, Deor?" Morlock asked, smiling one-sidedly.

"—a *passel* of thains (you can't embarrass me, *harven*; I know I speak this tongue better than you do), has been in the Northhold for some months. Setting the Wards, you see. I assumed you knew this, Morlocktheorn."

"No. But as you say, I am a junior thain."

"Hmph. Well, by any door, they have passed through Thrymhaiam several times, the last less than two calls ago. They were headed for Northtower, by way of Haukrull."

The gateway turned into a short tunnel that ended in dimness.

"You know," said Morlock, his voice falling curiously dead in the narrow tunnel, "I thought I saw smoke in the Haukr mountains as we were riding today."

"Well, I expect it's blown east from Ranga. They had a terrible fire there: the whole crop burned, most of the animals killed. The valley is still smoldering."

Earno found this interesting and disturbing. "Is that common?" he asked.

"Well, it has never happened before," the dwarf replied. "But it was a very dry summer. It is very bad in Ranga, now; they have some sort of plague. Haukr is helping with food, and of course we've cancelled their debts. But you can't eat metal, so we haven't been able to do much for them."

"Deortheorn," Morlock said, "Ranga's mining settlement has had no news of this. Word must . . . I should say, perhaps word could be sent to them. . . ."

Morlock had apparently committed some gaffe, and his kin laughed at him for it. "Very well, Elder Brother, I hear and obey—"

"Hear, anyway," Morlock interrupted him. "They are very short of food, too."

"Well, the Eldest will have to approve any drudgings of food. It will be a hard winter for the Deep Halls as it is."

They had entered the dimness at the end of the tunnel, now, and passed into the great terminal of Southgate. From the outside this had seemed an imposing arm of the mountain, impregnable by force. Inside, once his eyes grew used to the light (there were lamps set into the wall at various points, crystalline cylinders full of some pale glowing fluid, but their light did not compare to the open sunlight) Earno saw that the entire arm had been hollowed out to form a vast chamber into which many brightly lit tunnels opened. The walls of the terminal chamber were honeycombed with what appeared to be storerooms. Earno guessed that a great deal of trade came through the Southgate, in given seasons. Now everything seemed to be fastened down for the coming winter, though.

Glancing over his shoulder, he saw a battered shield hanging over the bright exit of the gate-tunnel. He thought he could see markings on the shield's dented surface.

"What is that?" he asked, halting.

Morlock said nothing. Deor, glancing at him, said, "A shield."

"Yes, of course. But it seems to have some significance. Aren't those heraldic markings on the surface?"

"Yes," said Deor slowly.

"I wasn't aware that dwarves used them," Earno remarked.

"We don't," Deor replied, smiling.

"It's a riddle, then?" Earno replied, smiling himself (rather wryly: he had never been good at riddles). "May I take a closer look?"

Deor seemed pleased, but for some reason he looked at Morlock again. The thain's face was impassive. "Yes, indeed," said the dwarf at last.

Earno retraced their steps and stood below the shield. It was coated with dust and had taken a severe beating before it was set up for display. In addition the daylight echoing from the gate-tunnel made it difficult to see the shield, in the dimness above the lintel. But the images were broad, in the manner of heraldry. Earno thought he could see a bird in flight . . . a branch sprouting small sharp leaves—or thorns . . . It was a peregrine falcon, in flight above a branch of flowering thorn.

"It is the crest of Ambrosius," said Earno in dismay.

"Yes," said Deor, with unmistakable pride. "It was Merlin's shield. He carried it through the night of Tunglskin . . . that is, he carried it to the combat at the Hill of Storms. (You know *First Merlin's Song*, of course.) After his victory he came here for healing and rest. The shield was his gift to Oldfather Lyrn, who was then Eldest of Theorn Clan. Oldfather Lyrn decreed that it be held here in honor until . . . until it is needed again."

Earno was conscious of Morlock's gray eyes, almost luminous in the dimness, fixed on him. "A fitting honor," Earno said stiffly, "for a famous deed."

Deor laughed good-naturedly and said something in Dwarvish. "I beg your pardon, Summoner Earno," he added. "I can see that you are going to prosper in these halls."

He led the summoner and the still-silent thain away, across the shadowy chamber of the Southgate terminal. He passed into one of the bright tunnels issuing from the far wall, and they followed him.

Deor led them through a maze of tunnels, deeper and higher as they walked. Earno seemed to feel the weight of stone accumulating above them—an oppressive feeling, and one hard to separate from the shock of seeing the Ambrose crest in this unexpected place. But, for all his mood, he had to admit that the stone hallways were large, well-lit by the flameless lamps, and well-aired. They met many dwarves on their journey, who greeted them courteously but did not delay them.

Finally they arrived at a large wooden door, at the top of a long flight of staircases. Outside it a very young (and beardless) dwarf was in waiting.

Morlock turned abruptly to Deor and took him by the shoulder. He went down on one knee unself-consciously, apparently to meet the dwarf's eye. "Deortheorn," he said, "a drudging must be sent to the Rangan settlement by Tunglskin, equal at least to the value of the two horses we were riding. I say this not as my father's son or your *harven* kin, but friend to friend. Do you understand?"

"I can guess," Deor said quietly. His mouth twisted behind his beard, as if he would have preferred to speak in Dwarvish. But after looking directly at the cuts and bruises on Morlock's face he said flatly, "If it were not for Ranga's trouble we would pay them in blood."

"No. It is better this way."

"Well. Because it's you that's asking. There is a group of Westhold traders in the Kirach Starn. I will send one of my mother's cousins to buy from them with my own treasure."

"I will repay."

"You. Will. Not. But you might help me with my gems. I'm not growing them well, lately, and no one grows them like you."

"Agreed."

"Then."

Morlock stood up and the dwarf-lad (or lass?) opened the door. Deor entered first, and Morlock stood back, allowing the summoner to pass ahead of him. Earno heard Morlock enter and shut the wooden door behind him.

The room was in sharp contrast to the halls they had travelled through. The walls were faced with white marble, the ceiling was covered with incised panels, and in the wall a deep-set window had been driven through the mountainside. Beside the window sat an old dwarf in a polished, intricately carven chair of dark wood. He seemed to be shorter than Deor (who was over four feet tall). But his shoulders were broader and his hands looked as if they could crush stone. His hair fell to his shoulders, and his beard flowed over his chest; both were iron gray. His eyes, too, were gray, a darker and earthier color than Morlock's. Here was, clearly, the Eldest of Clan Theorn, first of the Seven Clans under Thrymhaiam. Earno supposed he had outlived five centuries. Beside him on a table was a small oil lamp, whose flame provided the only light in the little room. But the Eldest was not looking at the room. Even after they had entered he kept gazing resolutely at the blue twilight deepening outside his window. From a heavy silver chain around his neck hung a pendant stone: a blood-colored gem scarred by a deep golden flaw.

"Tyr, Eldest of Clan Theorn," Deor said formally, "I bring you guests, a summoner and a thain of the Graith of Guardians."

"Deor, great-grandson of my mother's brother," Tyr replied without moving his head, "how shall I thank you for such a service? Word has preceded you, though, and I am prepared. Wait outside."

The younger dwarf left.

"Thain Morlock," said the ancient dwarf, not removing his gaze from the window, "when you last left Thrymhaiam you forswore all authority and seniority in our clans, not by our custom but in accord with the First Decree of your Graith. Now! Shall I receive you as kin or as guest? Choose."

"Eldest," said Morlock defiantly, "I am a Guardian and subject to the rigors of the First Decree. But Theorn is my clan, and no other. I claim from you the rights of kin, which neither you nor the Graith can deny me here."

Finally the old dwarf looked into the room. He did not smile, but he seemed pleased. "You will find it rougher than usual in the bachelors' warren, Morlocktheorn," he said. "But tonight you will sit at my table. This is because the summoner, who must sit there, is your guest. Also: because it is my will, which neither you nor the Graith can deny me here."

"*Harven*, I never would."

"*Harven*, you—your memory is short. Go with Deor now, my son, and let him see to your needs."

Morlock bowed and left.

Earno was briefly annoyed that Morlock obeyed the Eldest's command without so much as a glance at Earno. But the annoyance was swallowed by a vaster feeling of surprise. The Eldest had called Morlock "my son." It might be just a manner of speech, but such a casual use of a kinship term seemed unlikely among this kin-obsessed people. What was it Tyr had called Deor? *Great-grandson of my mother's brother*. It was less a term of address than a pocket genealogy, but perhaps the dwarves made little distinction between the two.

He turned to the Eldest with a question on his lips, but he found himself speechless as he encountered the old dwarf's angry glare.

"No, don't trouble to introduce yourself, Summoner. I know you as well as I need to. And if anyone but my youngest son had brought you here I would have had the gate thrown shut in your face."

That answered Earno's question, at any rate: Morlock was clearly the foster son of the Eldest himself. That put the Arbiter's comments to Morlock, back at the Rangan colony, about "your father" in an ambiguous light. But he had no time to think of these things now.

"I can't guest here under these terms," Earno said, and would have continued.

"Yet you will," the Eldest forestalled him grimly. "You can reach no settlement in a day's walk, you have no provisions or steeds, and in simple fact, I will not allow you to leave."

"You are an imposing host," Earno observed, confident in his ability to leave if he chose. "But we have horses."

"*They* are not yours," the Eldest shouted. "I know the Ranga breed, horses and lower animals, too well."

Then Earno understood the Eldest's puzzling attitude, at least in part. Somehow Tyr had heard of the events at the Rangan colony. He was simply venting his anger at Earno—whom, however, he seemed to resent for other reasons as well.

"I've promised not to speak of this matter to you, Tyr syr Theorn," Earno said. "But I can at least say that Morlock has a plan for settling it which may meet with your approval."

"Eh. Morlock always has ideas. You have not seen how badly some of them work out." The dwarf's gray hand went to the red stone on his chest, then fell away. "Don't mistake me; he's clever, my youngest son. But he will never be wise. This idea he had of joining your Graith—look what has happened there. I could not believe my eyes when I saw the thains in Lernaion's escort, with their silken cloaks, their soft manners and their hard words. May my son never be like them! But still: what has he gotten for his faithful service but rags on his shoulders and bruises on his face? To say nothing of the shame of serving the enemy of his *ruthen* father."

"*Ruthen*?"

"Given. Natural-born. However you say it. I mean old Ambrosius, of course."

"He is honored in these halls," said Earno, remembering the shield at Southgate.

"Except by Morlock, who defends the Graith (and *you*), greatly to his own disgrace. Oh, I grant him his integrity. But I disagree with his choice. And in any case it does not look well. His *ruthen* father . . ."

"The north is one of the Wardlands, now. When Merlin impaired the Guard, he betrayed the north as well."

"Well, you must be content with your victory, as we must be with our dissent. The end of this matter is that you are welcome here, Summoner, even if you are disliked." Tyr paused, as if steeling himself to something. "Moreover, since you may need to return many times, as your peer Lernaion has, you should know that you will always be welcome here, with or without my youngest son. But if you had come, this time, without him—it would have been otherwise!"

"You're not very generous."

"I might have been, had my son been better treated in your service."

"He is not in *my* service—"

"Put that aside! He is under obedience to you. Hereabouts, that means you have obligations to him."

Earno saw it differently. "He must take care of himself."

"That is very true, but also not very generous. Think on it, Summoner. The lass outside will take you to your rooms." Then the ancient dwarf turned his face and looked out the window, into the darkness of full autumn night.

Chapter Nine

Fire and Thunder

The meal that night had a festive air about it. It was held in the High Hall of the East, a tremendously difficult place to reach, at least for Earno. He found himself disturbingly prone to be out of breath, even after many days of travel through the mountainous north, and there were many stairs to climb in Thrymhaiam. When he finally reached the hall, trailing his little dwarfling guide, he felt as if he had climbed a mountain. As, in fact, he had. For when his guide led him to the Eldest's table he saw that, just beyond it, was a bank of high windows.

Delighted, Earno went to them immediately. He had not realized how high they had climbed. Far below them he could see the tops of clouds. The steep dark sides of Thrymhaiam's mountains disappeared in a deep valley filled with mist. Across the narrow valley another range of mountains lifted up, their peaks miles distant and already crowned with snow. Above them, the somber moon Chariot glowed. The whole scene, however, was lit by the second moon, Horseman, which had risen eight days ago. It was invisible from where he stood, since he had no view to the west, but it caused the high range opposite to glow with a thin bluish light. Coming after hours spent in the corridors and staircases of the Deep Halls, the view gave him a heady sense of breathing room.

"Is that the Haukr yonder?" he asked his guide. But, in turning around, he found that the little dwarf-lass had gone and it was Deor standing beside him.

"Yes," the dwarf replied. "That is the Haukr. Magnificent mountains, those. You were missing your guide, little Ny, I guess."

"I was," Earno admitted.

"She's gone to stand as gate-guard with the other cwens. Then she'll have to get something to eat. But she'll be back later, I expect. A quiet lass, not like some."

"How high are we, really?"

"Not so high. That valley down there is actually a gorge several miles deep. We're not even at the peak of this mountain, which is one of the lowest of Thrymhaiam. It's the gorge that gives the sense of height. We call it Helgrind—'deeper than the sea,' in your language."

"That sounds familiar, for some reason . . ." the summoner said slowly. Then he heard a voice behind him chanting:

"O what is higher than the tree?
And what is deeper than the sea?

"Or what is heavier than lead?
And what is better than the bread?

"Or what is sharper than a thorn?
And what is louder than a horn?

"O heaven is higher than the tree,
and hell is deeper than the sea.

"O sin is heavier than lead,
the blessing's better than the bread.

"O hunger's sharper than a thorn
and shame is louder than a horn."

The voice was Morlock's. He joined them at the window, smiling a rare crooked smile.

"You are in peerless voice tonight, Thain Morlock," said Earno, almost inclined to like him. "But in the Westhold we sing: 'the thunder's louder than a horn.'"

"Well, perhaps your horns in Westhold are louder than we have here," Deor suggested. "Then, too, some people are afraid of thunder, which is a great shame."

"Why?"

"It's the lightning that kills. Thunder is just noise."

The meal began shortly thereafter with the entrance of Tyr. Many of the Eldest's immediate family had already settled at the long black table, and the rest did so as he appeared, resplendent in blue clothes, that odd fiery-red gem still on his chest. The summoner was guided to a low-slung seat on the left hand of the Eldest's chair. On the summoner's left sat Deor, and there was a succession of younger dwarves, some almost beardless, farther down. Facing them was a line of considerably older dwarves, all densely bearded. From the fact that Morlock was placed with them and for some other reasons Earno guessed that these were the sons of Tyr. This guess proved to be correct. They were a grim lot, hardly saying a word after they gruffly introduced themselves. The younger dwarves (guests? descendants?) were much more talkative; Earno wondered why this was so.

The exception was the Eldest, who plied him with questions about the new religion of the Kaeniar—the Way of the Two Powers.

"It is not really new, as I understand," Earno said. "It is a sorcerer-cult of the Anhikh. They believe that the universe is the accidental by-product of the conflict of the two primal powers, Fate and Chaos."

"Yet Morlock tells me these shrines are springing up all along the shore of the Narrow Sea—in Kaen, not Anhi."

"Morlock knows a good deal," conceded Earno. "He may have been talking with Illion, who was in Kaen this past summer."

"Morlock was there himself, I think. But he does not know what his Graith intends to do about it, anyway. I won't ask you, since you'd obviously rather not talk about it. I'm glad to know you're aware of this, though. From all I hear, the Kaeniar are bad, but the Anhikh are worse. I'd hate to be facing them across the Narrow Sea."

Earno nodded. "The children of Kaen have never been our friends. But we must think long and hard before we permit a conquering power in the east."

"And they actually believe that these primal forces live—where is it?"

"In Tychar," Earno recalled, "the winterwood."

Tyr grunted incredulously. "Astonishing what some people will believe." He turned away to make a libation before his father's deathmask, which was on a stand beside him.

Next to Earno, Deor was leaning over the table, reminding Morlock of some cousins of his—some *harven* cousins.

Morlock nodded. "I remember them."

"The ones that were always setting you on fire?"

"Yes."

"They took over the trading house on the Broken Coast. In five months they had doubled our best trade year."

"I'm not surprised," Morlock said. "They were very convincing. I was just short of adulthood, you remember, and they had me believing it was my own, um, fluids that were causing the fires."

A couple of Morlock's *harven* brothers laughed belatedly at this, surprising Earno. Morlock turned to the one beside him and said, "Vetr, do you still oversee the Ranga trade?"

The one called Vetr nodded wordlessly. Deor said, "Ah, here it comes."

"Deor and I looked in on the travellers back from Ranga."

Vetr shook his head gloomily. "You should not have done, Morlock-theorn," he said with difficulty. Earno realized belatedly that he could barely manage Wardic, the realm's common speech. "They are diseased, badly diseased," he added, after some thought.

"They are sick, yes, but . . . It reminds me of an illness I've seen in the south, along the Narrow Sea. It comes from a poison that the Kaeniar use."

Vetr smiled. "No Kaenish here, Morlock."

"The lizards the poison comes from might be. The traders say they saw none, but they ate mostly stored food and I was thinking . . ."

Vetr nodded. Slow in speech, he was far from slow in thought. "The stores. Haukr stores, our stores. They must be checked."

"I don't think much of your idea, Morlock," Tyr interjected. "Thrymhaiam has been eating stored food since summer. The only dwarves that fell sick were in Ranga when they did so."

Morlock shrugged.

"Has anyone else caught the disease?" Earno asked "Anyone in Thrymhaiam?"

"No—unless we have," said Deor.

"They were poisoned," said Morlock, not stubbornly, but as a matter of fact. "That's their disease. We won't fall sick from talking to them."

Earno thought of Lernaion and his escort being poisoned by stored food in Haukr. Or: a plague fever sweeping out of the north to decimate the Wardlands. That was a kind of destruction by fire he had not anticipated. But the conversation around him was turning in different directions, which was just as well.

"Naeth couldn't bring himself to finish the shaft," a young dwarf called Laen was saying, "because it cut through this 'lovely' formation. The work still isn't done. He should be a farmer!"

"No, no," said Deor, as if this were too harsh a criticism for anyone. "Not a miner, though, you're right."

"I learned lode-seeking from Naeth," Morlock observed.

Deor was at once impressed and defensive. "Yes, but he has no practical skills. You remember what a thumphead he was about—I mean, when he was our tutor for gemstones."

Morlock shrugged. "I think he cares more about metal or crystal within living rock than any use they might be put to."

"It's lunacy."

"He knows a great deal."

"But he makes no use of it," Deor insisted.

Morlock nodded slowly. "I asked him about the Ranga blaze. He thinks it was the Fire . . . that is, vulcanism," he added, glancing at Earno. It was only then that Earno realized that they were speaking Wardic, and even censoring their use of it, for his benefit alone.

"Ranga has no Fire, Morlock," Elder Tyr said, forestalling a reply from Deor.

"Naeth thinks that might be changing."

"Naeth wants it to change," Tyr replied. "It would suit his notions. But I have been listening to the land for months, and I have heard no Fire in Ranga."

Earno found Morlock's presence disconcerting. He resembled his father, his *ruthen* father, greatly just then: with his crooked shoulders and his crooked smile, a crooked kind of confidence among people he knew. Earno thought about his notion that Merlin was the cause of the northern troubles and was intuitively convinced of its truth. Old Tyr would shelter him at Thrymhaiam, certainly, and perhaps there were others in the north who would do the same. The summoner had been fitting the details he knew into a consistent pattern, and he found it worked admirably.

The second course, roasted fungi stuffed with some sort of diced meat, was brought in. When he resumed his train of thought he felt himself feverish and distracted, with a strange ache inside his head. Something was wrong. He could lie to himself or face it: something was wrong.

He stared out of the windows, trying to lose his thoughts in the magnificent view. But there were more lights in the room now, many of them torches, and he could see little except reflections of himself and the rest of the company in the dark glassy surface.

". . . it was not the summoner Lernaion who bothered our Eldest," Deor was saying mischievously. "No: it was those splendiferous thains."

Vetr grunted. "One spoke dozen languages. Not ours, though."

Morlock was looking uncomfortable. "They're senior thains. Seniority gives privileges in the Guardians, just as it does in the Seven Clans. Is this news? Thains' Northtower is on our very border."

"Well, you didn't see them," Deor replied. "They weren't much like those peasants in Northtower. How they whined. Roughing it in the newest hold!"

"Their fingers were as soft as feathers," one dwarf recalled with amazement.

"One had a tear in his silken cloak," another dwarf recalled. "Didn't want it mended—that'd make an ugly seam, he said. He wondered if we could get him another."

"Another tear?" said Deor. "Easy enough!"

There was laughter. Part of it was real amusement; part of it was local or racial prejudice. But part of it was anger. Morlock's ragged and burned cape would linger in the clans' memory alongside that torn silken cloak. Earno thought of Tyr's words to him earlier: *May my son never be like them! But still . . .*

"It's no great honor to be a senior thain," Earno found himself saying, into a silence that formed around his words. "It is honorable enough, and perhaps very comfortable. But the real honor is to be elected vocate. Younger thains have that honor more often, and with some reason." He paused, concerned that he had said too much or not enough.

But it wasn't so. The dwarves were nodding solemnly. Apparently something he had said had checked their anger without giving them the impression that he had personally elected Morlock to the rank of vocate.

Which would be far from the case. For, if Earno's deductions were correct, he would soon be sending their *harven* kinsman into exile. He felt anxiety suddenly descend on him again, and his head ached. He looked at the windows again, almost yearningly, longing for solitude and escape. But all he could see was the red light of the torches glittering on black surfaces. Watching them, he swiftly became dizzy; he felt that he was seeing two levels of reality at once, as in a Sight. There was no Sight, no revelation. Yet the illusion continued.

He heard Tyr speaking in his ear. "Summoner Earno, is anything wrong?"

"Do you see anything outside?" he responded tensely. "In the chasm?"

Everyone stood and looked out the windows. They glanced at each other, but Earno found the dwarvish expressions (including Morlock's) unreadable.

"Extinguish the lights!" the Eldest commanded, and it was done.

There was red light glowing diffusely in the thick blue clouds of Helgrind chasm. The light moved and dimmed and brightened, flowing like water. Presently it could be seen that there were many brighter parts of the light, as intensely red-gold as separate flames or coals in the murkily glowing clouds.

"The Fire?" Deor demanded of no one in particular.

"No," said the Eldest Tyr firmly. "Not as you mean."

They waited.

The dragons broke through the clouds in groups of three, casting distorted shadows behind them by their own light. There were perhaps a dozen groups. Most of them soared steeply out of the range of sight, but three dragons flew directly to the windows of the High Hall of the East. One roosted directly before the windows (the mountain shook beneath them) and peered within: smoke and fire trailing from his jaws, his bright scales shedding red light at their edges, his slotted eyes as red and gold as molten metal.

Eldest Tyr moved to take a coldlight and lit it. Then he walked to the windows so that the dragon could see him clearly.

The Eldest spoke. "I know you," he said quietly. "I know you and I deny you. In the first days of the father of my father's father my kith defeated you and drove you from this land. You have come again. You will be killed again. Let all of you come, all our ancient enemies together. Let them come to steal our homes and the things our skill has made. Let the Longest War flare up again in every mountain valley, in every cave beneath the earth. These mountains have stood and will stand. If we cannot live within them we will die beneath them. We will *deny* you our homes, and the things our skill has made!"

Earno wondered if the dwarf was in rapport with the dragon somehow or whether he spoke for his people's benefit or for other reasons. But it was as if the dragon understood him. He rose up on his hind legs and roared flame down on the bank of windows.

Earno flinched (was it the mountain, or the deck of *Stonebreaker* shuddering beneath him?) but the Eldest stood motionless as the wave of fire broke like water on the slabs of dwarvish crystal. The sound of all three dragons roaring penetrated dimly into the hall.

"Father," said Morlock, after some moments, "*yedhra harven coruthen*, the Deep Halls are under attack. You must lead your people."

Tyr turned to him quickly, as if startled, but there was no surprise on his face. "Morlocktheorn, you are right. I have been wondering why . . . But that does not matter, not yet." He turned to his other sons and spoke to each of them briefly in Dwarvish.

Earno stood motionless, not daring to move or think, lest he make some new error. He was the chief Guardian here. But he had no authority over anyone save Morlock. And he wondered if Morlock would obey his commands, rather than Tyr's, and if it would be right to do so. He had foreseen so much! Somehow, visions had come to him, warning him of this danger. But foreknowledge had been wasted by folly. He waited, not thinking, not moving, and the red light moved about him like a sea of blood.

The dragons began to batter the mountainside with their tails; the stone walls and floor shuddered with the repeated attacks, and the mountain above them rumbled disturbingly. Tyr still stood, defiantly, before the windows, issuing commands to his kith.

Earno felt a touch on his sleeve and moved instinctively toward it. Morlock was there, his expression at once concerned and eager. The summoner felt it was unusual for the thain to be so unguarded, and it would have been interesting to watch if he were not so reluctant to meet Morlock's eye.

"Summoner Earno," said the thain, presenting to him a very young beardless dwarf, "this is Olla, a messenger stationed at the Helgrind Gate, that faces the Runhaiar . . . the tunnels which pass under the Haukr."

Earno nodded.

"She says that an hour ago a woman crawled over the threshold out of the Helgrind and collapsed. She was wearing a vocate's cloak."

Earno nodded again. As moments passed he realized painfully that he must also speak and move.

"Lead me to her, then."

The sound of the dragons' attack faded like thunder as they descended under the mountain.

It took much less than an hour to descend to the Helgrind Gate. Arriving there they found the vocate still lying on a bed of rags before the great cave of the Helgrind Gate. The portcullis was down. The dwarf guards beside it were armored and carried long spears with metal shafts.

Morlock greeted them in Dwarvish, and they responded in kind. He spoke with them for a few moments and then, seeing that Earno had made no move toward the vocate, went and knelt by her.

"Vocate Almeijn," he said to her, and she started.

"Who are you?" she demanded thinly. She moved her head as she spoke, and only then did Earno recognize her. Her gray hair was stained and torn, and there were venom burns on her face and hands.

"Morlock syr Theorn, a thain. I must know what happened to you and your company."

"Yes. You must tell the Graith . . . I can't. I'm dying. I can't. I won't. I won't. God Sustainer, I'm so hungry!"

"They'll bring food. They should have done so already."

"No." Her throat clenched visibly, the neck muscles moving like fingers beneath her slack wrinkled skin. "No! It doesn't matter. Listen! There are dragons!"

"I know," Morlock said patiently. "How many?"

"How many? *How many?* How do I know how many? But they are a guile together; they have a master. . . . I saw him. . . . The sky was full of fire. I ran. Crawled . . . underground. Lost in the tunnels. So hungry. But there was water."

"What happened to Summoner Lernaion?" Morlock asked gently.

"He was fey. A dead man! So proud, so . . . wise. I told him, before we left the tunnels. I told him about my dream. I told him I was afraid of the sky. *He* said . . . about old people, eager to be buried. It was clever. It was cruel. But he was tired of being underground. I'm not *angry* anymore. But when we came out into the light . . . I was still angry. I could taste the smoke, the tang of venom in the air. I should have said. . . . I didn't say anything. Waited for them to notice. They were fey. They didn't notice.

"Then we came over the rise. The town was there, all ashen, with bodies burning in the streets. No dragons. But that feeling. Then we looked up. There they were on the mountain, watching us. They leapt up into the air. So many! Like birds in the winter. You see them in the Southhold. Blackbirds. In troops. And they fly together and turn all at once, the light flashing on their black wings and bodies. Then they all roared and the sky was red and the air stank of poison. I was too afraid to move. We were all afraid.

"Then one fell out of the guile-in-flight, dropped like a hawk, stalled over us, stretching out his claws. Roared. Like red fog, the poison and the fire. I saw the collar about his neck, the sign of the master, like in *Earno's Song*. The guile master: that was too much. I ran. Not back. Two tried that; he burned them, breathed right on them. Aside. Away in the valley. He didn't care. Hunt me down later. I thought so too. Found a cave, crawled inside. Kept on crawling. It went on and on . . . Into the tunnels. I. I. No. No. No! The Graith . . . yes, of course. Tell *them*. The summoner. *I won't! I won't!* The summoner. Oh, yes. Yes. I will. But I failed. . . ."

"No, Vocate Almeijn!" Morlock said urgently. "The summoner is here, Earno himself; he has heard all you have said. The Guard is maintained; be at peace."

"It. It wasn't so important. And I'm not *angry* anymore. He was fey. Maybe I was fey, too. . . ."

As her voice trailed off Almeijn's face turned toward Earno. He could not tell if she recognized him. He caught one glimpse of deep fiery redness in the blacks of her eyes—like the flash of a cat's eyes. Then her eyelids closed convulsively.

Morlock rose and spoke to the dwarves in their own language. Two of them covered Almeijn's hands and carried her body away. Morlock spoke for a few moments with the other guards and then crossed over to Earno.

"Did you notice her eyes?" the thain asked.

"Did you look in them?" demanded the summoner, suddenly alarmed.

"Only for a moment. Then I looked away. I've heard . . ."

"Yes," said Earno. "You're right. It was a dragonspell."

They stood there in silence for some time. Earno dimly sensed Morlock's impatience, but he could not bring himself to move. He hoped his inertia made him look as if he were deep in thought. But he was not. His thoughts were embroiled in a cloud of deep red light, the color that had flashed from Almeijn's eyes.

"The gate guards tell me that Elder Tyr has gone to Southgate, which is under attack by dragons," Morlock said finally. "Shall we bring him this news?"

Earno nodded. As wordlessly, Morlock took a torch from the wall of the gate chamber and led the way into the corridors.

They arrived at Southgate after several hours of travel. Earno was bone-weary, but determined to keep pace with his thain-attendant.

The battle for Southgate had ended long before their arrival. The roof of the terminal chamber was stove in, and a great part of the mountain above had fallen down in avalanche. But dwarves were already at work, bringing order out of the ruin. Passages had been cleared through the rubble to many of the corridors that had converged at Southgate. Thus Earno and Morlock came abruptly to the ragged end of their corridor and found themselves in the darkness and bitter cold of the autumn night.

Earno paused gratefully, drinking in the refreshing night air, at first not recognizing where they were. Then he looked with amazement on the wreckage of what he had seen whole just an hour before sunset. In the light of the major moons (Horseman was standing radiant in the western sky while somber Chariot loomed above the eastern horizon) it appeared to be nothing but a vast heap of broken stones.

Turning to make some comment to Morlock, Earno saw the thain's face graven with shock and grief. He was pressing a hand against the side of the trench in which they were standing, as if it were the stump of a severed limb. He shook his head and walked swiftly away through the trench leading out of the corridor, forcing the summoner to follow before he had quite caught his breath; Earno's comment, if it had ever been made, would certainly have gone unnoticed.

As Earno's eyes grew used to the moonlight he saw that a legion of dwarves was at work amid the vast rolling hills of broken stone. Above them the dragons moved like red stars of ill omen, occasionally setting behind the black mountainous silhouette of Thrymhaiam.

"*Hurm strakna?*" came a challenge out of the darkness above them.

"I am Morlock syr Theorn," the thain replied, "conducting Earno Summoner, called Dragonkiller."

"Welcome Dragonkiller! *Rokhlan!*" cried the voice, and a chorus of assents echoed him. "*Ath! Ath!*"

"*Ath rokhlan sael!*" Morlock replied, somewhat perfunctorily. "Is Eldest Tyr at Southgate?" he continued.

"He is just before the gate-that-was, with the slain *rokhleni*."

Morlock shouted into the darkness. "*Hurs?*"

"Your pardon, Elder Brother," another voice replied. "*With* the slain—not among them."

"Your pardon, rather," said Morlock, clearly embarrassed. "To die a *rokhlan* would be no shame."

"To wish one's father alive is certainly none," said yet another voice from the darkness above, this one known to Earno. "I notice, though, you do not ask about any of your lesser kin. Perhaps in a month or so you would have gotten around to asking, 'What ever happened to *harven* Deor?' only to be told I had died heroically under a load of rubble, while taking a valiant nap behind the rockpile—"

A chorus of shouts drowned out Deor's self-lament.

"Then you can haul the rest of these stones by yourselves," Deor said, sparking off a new outburst of good-tempered abuse. "Stand aside, Thain and Summoner!" he hollered over the voices of his mates. "I'm rolling down this rock-slide!"

Earno and Morlock backed away to the far side of the trench. Deor appeared suddenly in the sphere of light cast by Morlock's torch, picking his way swiftly down the steep slope of rocks. Surprisingly few of them shook loose under the oblique impact of his heavy dwarvish boots, and Earno realized that the rocks in the trench wall had been fitted together to form a solid, though temporary, construction. It was anything but a rock-slide; Earno would have called it painstaking salvage work. For the dwarves, taking such pains was apparently a matter of instinct.

"A dark morning for us all, Guardians!" Deor said in greeting. "But perhaps not so bad as it might have been. Come along, if it suits you; the Eldest would no doubt like to hear your news."

They followed him down the trench, toward the site where the gate had been. Deor was an interesting study to Earno. He seemed to be as hurt and grieved by the destruction about them as Morlock was. But he was challenged and invigorated in a way that Morlock was not. His eyes dripped tears he did not even attempt to hide. But he moved with a quick decisiveness, cracking jokes like nuts. From what Earno could see of the other dwarves—and hear, as the air above them resounded with the ringing consonants of the Dwarvish language—they were reacting much as Deor was. Morlock, in sharp contrast, seemed to become more silent, if that were possible, and more somber with each step.

Finally they reached a space beyond the rubble. Earno spotted the stone table at which Deor and his companions had been sitting the previous evening. It looked strangely isolated, without the slope of the mountain above it. The whole area had been burned with fire and stank of blood and venom.

In the middle of the bleakest space stood the Eldest and Vetr, his eldest son. They carried long spears, virtually twice their own height; beside them on the ground lay three dead dwarves, one of them a beardless child. The child, Earno realized, was Ny, the wordless dwarf-lass who had been his guide. Beyond them, asprawl over the small hill that stood above the road leading south, stretched the torn fuming corpse of the dragon they had slain at the cost of their lives.

The Eldest was drawing on the venom-stained ground with the butt-end of his spear, twirling the long metal shaft in his fingers as if it were a stylus. He looked up at the approach of the newcomers. "*Khuf!* Douse that torch!" he commanded. "No fire at the vigil of *rokhleni*!"

Morlock ground out the torch without a word.

"A moment from you all," Tyr requested curtly, and turned back to Vetr. "So: you see it. We can only begin to build the new gate out of the wreck of the old. We will need more stone. The gate, which should have been the strongest point in the perimeter, had become the weakest. In recent centuries the fortifying stone had all been hollowed out for storerooms and guest chambers."

Vetr grunted. He seemed dismayed. "Same must be in other gates."

"Not all," Tyr corrected him. "The Helgrind Gate, certainly: much trade with Haukr has gone through the Runhaiar. Northgate, too: the Ranga trade led us to weaken ourselves there. But the High Gate over the Coriam Lakes must still be strong enough to stand, among others."

"Then?"

"Those chambers, in the weakened gates, must be cleared out, of course. Then: filled up with stone, gravel, debris from the mines—anything that can give weight to a wall. But the new Southgate will be different. We will cut down to bedrock and rebuild the shoulder of the mountain, fusing stone to stone. And we will timber the new terminal chamber with a web of maijarra wood. Let there be no honeycombing of the walls; we have already spent too many lives with such economy."

Vetr said nothing. But his shadowy face turned toward the dark mountainside above them. There the dragons still wandered, spreading fire among the black pine forests.

"Let them come," said Tyr, understanding Vetr's gesture. "I mean it, Vetrtheorn! The work must be done as it ought to be done. To work in a panic, to content ourselves with a flawed job that would fail us when we need it most—this would be to hand the dragons their victory. They watch us, even now. They understand the choices before us. So must we, also. It is all or nothing. Either we rebuild the gate as it ought to have been, or we seal the southern corridors and carry on the Longest War with our backs to a solid wall."

"Seal the corridors!" Vetr was truly dismayed.

"Yes. All or nothing, Vetrtheorn. The Longest War has returned—*they* have returned: to plunder, to kill, to destroy. That is the nature of dragons. Very well: it is our nature to defend, to build, to make. To remember and forget. The more they are dragons, the more we must be dwarves."

"*Akhram hav!*" Vetr said thoughtfully. "It will be done."

"It will be yours to do," the Eldest replied. "I misdoubt I shall see the Seven Clans at peace again." He turned back to the others and said, "Your pardon, Summoner and my kin. Yours, especially, Morlock. I should have remembered you were never taught how to stand a death-vigil over *rokhleni*. It was thought a rather obscure ritual, even when I was young."

"No offense, *yedhra harven*. I hope it is obscure again before I am old."

"Who can say, Morlocktheorn? The hero labors to slay monsters, that heroism will become unnecessary. The thinker labors to systemize thought, that thinking will become unnecessary. The worker labors to amass treasure, that work will become unnecessary. Softness, stupidity, and sloth inevitably follow; have any of the three really benefited their children? Yet we work and work and work. . . ."

Morlock shrugged; even in the darkness Earno sensed his discomfort. "Surely there are other monsters to slay . . . other thoughts to think . . ."

"And other treasures to amass? Yes. That last thought smacks of greed, of course. And we both know scholars, as greedy of knowledge as a miser is of coins. In my old age have I grown greedy of monsters, unwilling to turn away from the darkness in which I see myself most clearly?"

"For our sake, *yedhra*—I hope not."

"My mother's shadow! I am well-answered of my earlier rebuke—Morlock, you have chided me twice."

"I meant no harm, *yedhra harven*; all this is strange to me, like an epic of the Longest War." He gestured abruptly at the dead unbearded dwarf. "But surely that is—"

"Whoever she may be, Morlock, it would be unwise to say the name. That, too, is part of the vigil. To say their names would be to call them back from their journey to those-who-watch; that would be dangerous for them and for us. We watch until sunrise. When the gate in the west opens they can depart the world as the sun enters and take their places among those-who-watch."

Earno recognized the name of the ancestral almost-gods who, in dwarvish belief, mediated between the Creator and Creation. The notion had always struck him as primitive before. Now he did not know what to think.

Meanwhile Morlock, like Vetr before him, had glanced up at the dark fire-written mountainside above them. The Eldest understood the impulsive motion. "A *rokhlan*'s vigil is stood where he has fallen," the ancient dwarf said flatly. "In any case, my place is here, to direct the work. Necessary business does not defile the vigil. Go, now, Vetr; send the message to the gate-leaders and the Elders of the Lesser Clans."

The Eldest's eldest son bowed and vanished into the darkness and the dust clouds drifting from the wreckage of the gate.

Morlock knelt down by the fallen dwarves and looked long at each one of their beardless faces. In the midst of his contemplation he glanced up and said to the Eldest, who was gazing fixedly at him, "Is this fitting?"

"Certainly," the ancient dwarf replied. "Look on them. Remember their deeds, good and bad, and, in your own heart, praise their names. After the Praising of Day we will bury them"—and he gestured with the point of his long spear—"there, where the old gate opened up."

Morlock nodded, then glanced sharply down at one of the fallen.

Earno, following Morlock's eye, saw that one of the dwarves lay beside a battered shield . . . the one bearing the Ambrosian hawk and thorns.

"Yes," said the Eldest, who had apparently been waiting for Morlock to notice this, "she seized it at the dragon's first approach and bore it through the whole battle. She won the honor of *rokhlan* under its protection. Let none say the Ambrosii have brought bad luck to Thrymhaiam!"

Morlock did not say so. He said nothing at all.

"Will you bear it now," the Eldest asked quietly, "since danger has come again to the north?"

"No!" said Morlock sharply, and stood up.

The Eldest turned away for a moment. Earno dimly understood that the exchange had some awful significance. But in his weary bewildered state nothing was clear to him. Why should the Eldest, Morlock's *harven* father, wish Morlock to take up the shield of his *ruthen* father, the disgraced and exiled Merlin? Why was the Eldest not pleased when Morlock refused to consider himself an Ambrosius at all, with what Earno was inclined to consider as a laudable shame? Of course, he *was* an Ambrosius: his very stance, the trick of his expressions gave him away. But at least he tried to overcome his heritage, to deny it, to hate it. That was good, wasn't it?

Eldest Tyr had turned back to the group. "Then," he said matter-of-factly. "The shield will be placed as a marker over their tombs. Let it remain there until someone arises who can bear it. I have spoken."

There was a tense brief silence. The Eldest broke it, saying calmly,

"What word do you bring of your comrade Guardian? I heard a message that she died."

With Earno's permission, Morlock told the Eldest and Deor the whole story of the encounter with Almeijn at the Helgrind Gate. Vetr returned in the course of the telling, and what he had missed was recounted to him in the Dwarvish language. All three dwarves appeared very disturbed by the story.

"This is troubling, Morlocktheorn," Tyr said, when the thain was finished. "We had discussed this before your arrival. It is obvious (now!) that the dragons have been in the north for months—because of the fire and the poisonings at Ranga, the trouble with the Wards, some other things. Why, then, did they wait till now to show themselves?"

"We guessed that they didn't want to, even now," Deor explained. "It would have made sense for them to wait until winter had closed the passes southward. Then they would have had all winter to deal with us alone and to settle into dwellings through the north, and the southern holds would know nothing of it. But we supposed the vocate had escaped them, and that for some reason they felt they must pursue her, even at the risk of showing themselves."

"Now, though," Tyr continued, "you tell us she was under their spell. That undermines everything we had thought we knew."

"Well," said Deor, "we don't know what the spell was for, or whether it was effective. Maybe her story was the simple truth."

"I couldn't tell," Morlock said. "I'm no adept at dragonspells."

"Few are," Tyr acknowledged, "save the dragons themselves. I must say for myself that I don't understand this guile business. Or those collars: our dragonlore says nothing of them. But the dragonlore is not what it was: we have striven to forget what we no longer needed to know."

The other two dwarves and Morlock seemed embarrassed, reluctant to explain. Because of himself, Earno realized. So he explained to the Eldest that the guile was what the dragons of the Blackthorn Range had for a tribe or a clan. Each guile had a varying number of members and was invariably led by a powerful male, the master of the guile, who wore a collar of office.

"I understand that well enough," the Eldest answered patiently. "That's the point, isn't it? Since they all wear collars—"

For a moment the remark did not penetrate. Then they all turned with renewed interest toward the Eldest.

"You saw them, Eldest Tyr?" Deor asked.

"Not every one. Don't be a fool. But the three dragons who attacked the High Hall of the East all wore collars. You must have seen them."

Earno closed his eyes and tried to remember, but all he could call to mind was the small black silhouette of the Eldest against a bank of fire-bright windows.

"Our view was maybe not so uncluttered as yours, *yedhra*," said Morlock, with his peculiar half-smile. "Could you describe the collars?"

"Some sort of metal," said the Eldest, disgruntled and pleased. "I could sketch them, I suppose. But I don't need to. Yonder dragon has one. Vetrtheorn, Deor—go, bring the collar and lay it at the feet of our *rokhleni*."

Vetr looked reluctant. "Two of the five gate-keepers live," he said, after a moment. "Despoiling the *rokh*—it is their right."

"Yes," agreed Tyr, "but they lie in the Healing Chambers where we will, I guess, be standing their vigil in a few days."

Vetr continued to argue, more fluently, in Dwarvish.

Tyr lifted his free hand in a commanding gesture, and his son fell silent. "Vetr!" Tyr said. "Be at peace. Those-who-watch do not forbid what is needful. Bring me the collar, that I may see it."

Vetr lowered his head in submission. He and Deor hurried away up the slope where the fallen dragon lay. Soon they returned, bearing between them a long heavy chain. The links were as long as a man's arm and as wide as a dwarf's body. The chain was made of iron, and looked to Earno to be the sort of thing that might be used to seal a harbor. But it was partially covered with red gold, as if it had been dipped in precious metal like dye. Deor and Vetr had severed a link to remove the collar; in another place it looked as if two loose ends had been fused together by draconic heat.

Earno examined the chain very carefully, down on one knee at the feet of the *rokhleni*. When he glanced up he saw that the others' eyes were upon him, as if they were awaiting his verdict.

"It is very unlike the collar of Kellander Rukh, whom I slew," Earno said slowly. "It is cruder. And yet . . . there is a likeness, too; I cannot deny it. It would be very strange if the members of a guile were all permitted to wear such collars."

"Do you suppose there could be different collars," Deor suggested, "as for different ranks within the guile?"

When Earno said nothing, Morlock responded, "It seems hard to believe, from what I've heard. As if the dragons could form a military cohort . . . How could they cooperate so closely? The guile—from what I've heard—is just a group dominated by fear of a single individual."

"What else is any army, Morlocktheorn?" Deor countered.

"Morlock is more or less correct," Earno said reluctantly. (He would have said nothing, but the others were turning to him to settle the matter.) "That is the reason the guile invariably scatters when its master is killed."

"Then. Maybe there is no guile here," Deor suggested. "Perhaps it is just a group of dragons who have come together to raid the hold."

Vetr muttered in Dwarvish, then said, "The difference? If they pretend to cooperate . . . they must cooperate to pretend. It would be worse than a guile."

"Well, if it seems worse let's drop the notion at once!" Deor replied, laughing. Vetr did not join in or reply.

Earno took no part in the ensuing discussion. The sky in the west was turning a deep radiant blue—the abrupt gloaming of the Wardlands had begun, and the light of the second moon was suddenly pale. Earno saw the red stars circling the black fire-scarred outlines of Thrymhaiam's peaks rise up and pass over the high crooked horizon to the east. The dragons were retreating over the Haukr.

Many among the dwarves laboring in the ruin of Southgate also noticed the departure. Cries of victory and defiance rose up from the broken stones, pursuing the dragons on their storm-swift wings.

"Now they return to Haukrull," Tyr said. "If we knew just a little for certain we would know a great deal besides. But we know nothing for certain, except that they are here."

Tyr's remark oddly echoed the thoughts whirling in Earno's mind. Morlock might be a traitor (loyal to his natural father) or he might not. His hostility toward Merlin might be feigned—or it might not. Tyr had testified to that hostility, expressed concern about it. Tyr might be honest . . . or he might not be. Tyr would be inclined to aid Morlock, no matter what, and he clearly held Merlin in high esteem. That last, in a way, argued for his honesty: he did not hesitate to display a bias that might give rise to suspicion. But if he knew the suspicion had already arisen he might display the bias to, paradoxically, allay the suspicion with the appearance of honesty by being honest. Earno might be able to trust them all completely. Or he might not.

In any case, and this was the crux of the matter, Earno had to *seem* as if he trusted them completely, especially if he did not. Therefore he must do exactly as he would have done if he had been able to trust them. But he would preserve his distrust within him, bury it like treasure in his heart to keep it safe. That way he would do two things while seeming to do one, and at least one of him would be preserved. Yes.

"The course is clear," he said aloud, and for the first time that night his voice was strong and decisive. The others all turned to him in surprise.

"The course is clear," he repeated. "I will issue a challenge to the master of the guile. My thain will carry the challenge to Haukrull. Pride, and the need to maintain prestige before his followers, will force the master to accept the challenge, if there is a guile. Also, pride will compel him to respect the embassy of a challenger. And if there is no guile, if this is just a crowd of equals . . ."

"Then," Morlock said, "I should learn what I can and return as I can."

"Yes," Earno agreed. He did not add what they all knew: that, if there was no guile, Morlock would be unlikely to return at all: there would be no master to enforce restraint on the ravenous dragons. But if Morlock did not return, that itself would answer the question they needed to answer.

But (and Earno realized this too late) it would not answer *his* questions. If Morlock did not return, it might only mean that he had stayed with his natural father's allies, the dragons, to give Earno the wrong impression. Or it might mean what it seemed to mean. . . .

He began to suspect that, from now on, everything would have two meanings for him—one possibly true, the other certainly false—and he would never have a way of choosing between them. He would have to learn to live with both: betraying the enemy in his friends, befriending the ally in his enemies.

For if Morlock was a traitor, he deserved the treachery this mission would be if he were not a traitor. Similarly, if he was not a traitor, there was no treason: Earno was merely requiring the self-sacrifice Morlock had sworn to give. Earno was satisfied, and would have been completely satisfied, if only it were not so difficult to meet Morlock's eye. Nevertheless he began to speak aloud the cold clear unambiguous words of his challenge.

Before he was finished, sunlight struck the smoke still rising from the mountains and the dwarves began to sing.

PART THREE

ENVOY TO DRAGONS

He entered the doors of hell, the deep gates of Dis,
the forest shrouded in fear's shadow.
He stood before the dark gods and the dreadful king—
those hearts unable to pity human prayers.

—Vergil, *Georgics*

Chapter Ten

The Deep Roads

In the utter blindness beneath a mountain's roots, Morlock paused to consider his way.

He had left Thrymhaiam two days ago, an hour after sunlight touched her western slopes. He had gone alone through the Helgrind Gate. It was dark as he crossed the narrow, terribly deep chasm of the Helgrind. But the mist carried only the clean rocky smell of mountain water; there was no taint of venom in it. He reached the high unbarred entrance to the Runhaiar easily, although it was impossible to see in the darkness and fog; his feet knew the way across the shallow Helgrind stream. As a youth he had lived for more than a year beyond the Haukr, working at the Seven Clans' trading house there. He'd often travelled between Haukrull and Thrymhaiam. That had been a fine and troubling time for Morlock. He wondered what Haukrull looked like now. Almeijn's words returned to him as he walked through the resounding darkness: *The town was there, all ashen, with bodies burning in the streets. . . .*

Almeijn. At the thought of her he stopped moving. He had long ago learned to walk in the dark of the Runhaiar without fear, and his reflexes had found the Pilgrims' Way to Haukrull almost without seeking it. But they had played him false after all. He had an idea about Almeijn, and to pursue it he must take a different route through the darkness. He had to find not the familiar road that the Guardians must have taken to Haukrull, but the mysterious path on which Almeijn had returned alone.

As he stopped he realized he did not know exactly where he was. If he gave it some thought he might have reasoned it out (he had not been moving wholly unconsciously), but there was no need. He walked back to the last junction of tunnels he'd passed, trailing his right hand along the wall a little higher than his shoulders. Presently he found what he wanted: a pattern of warmth and coolness inscribed in the smooth stone. He moved his hands over the pattern, and as he did the pattern took shape in his mind. The shapes were not precisely intelligible, an apparently arbitrary mixture of abstract swirls and slanting lines. There was a similar pattern in every tunnel at every junction in the sprawling extent of the Runhaiar. They had obviously been placed by the Runhaiar's builders as signposts. Although they recorded no known language, experienced guides could make some sense of them.

Morlock could not read the signs as well as some of his *harven* kin, but he was no novice. The pattern under his hands told him clearly that the High Arches (a major landmark on the Pilgrims' Way to Haukrull) were at the far end of the tunnel where he stood. It also told him that the Drowned Arches (a vast, partly underwater chamber) were to the south of him. Morlock had never been to the Drowned Arches, but it was the only place in the Runhaiar where water ran. He guessed that Almeijn's path had led there, or near there. She'd said, *There was water.*

He stepped out of the tunnel; the echoes of his footsteps and the motion of the air told him he was in a junction-chamber between three or more tunnels. He turned to the one immediately on his left. Stepping inside it, he breathed deeply. He'd hoped that the air would be moister or warmer than normal. It was the usual air of the Deep Roads, though: dry, cool, stale. But the way led south and (he found, advancing a few steps) downward. He walked onward into the dark.

Much later, Morlock paused in an open area between tunnels. He regretted now that he had never visited the Drowned Arches; he felt lost in the darkness. The patterns on the walls were strange; he could not tell if he had come too far or not far enough. If he had taken a wrong turn he doubted he could even retrace his steps. Certainly he had never even heard of a place like this.

He cleared his throat and called out, to judge the chamber's size. On impulse he used his clan name. "Theorn!" There was no echo.

He took three steps and called out again. He waited a few seconds and called out a third time. Finally he heard an answering *Theorn!*, but with so strange and muffled a sound he didn't know what to make of it.

Walking farther he reached the wall of the chamber. He reached out and touched it; the stone was crusted with dry filth. Morlock drew his fingers along the surface vertically, tracing out a flat arcing rib carved out of the stone wall. Less than a hand's-breadth away on either side his hands encountered others. This was like the walls of the High Arches, except that those were clean. . . . Moving his hands vertically along the wall he found a level, higher than his head, where the filth ceased. It was an old water line. Plainly, he stood in what had been the Drowned Arches.

"There was water," said Morlock, consciously echoing Almeijn as he walked about the chamber. "Where is it now?"

The floor of the chamber (which seemed to be oval) angled sharply down toward its the long end.

Where did it go? asked the echo.

The water must have sunk down the angling floor as it receded. Perhaps there was a passage down that way, through which Almeijn might have passed. But Morlock doubted there was any water; he'd sensed no moisture in the air from the moment he'd entered. In fact . . .

Morlock crouched down and put his hands on the floor. It was coarsely textured and clean, free from watery filth. He guessed that he stood on some vast stone lid, and that the true floor of the chamber lay below. Its angle suggested that it had been lowered from the upper wall by means of its weight. If dwarves had built it there would have been a counterweight system to draw it back into the wall as needed. Morlock leapt toward the upper wall to investigate.

Soon his hands met what they were seeking: a recess in the upper wall almost as broad as himself, which contained a heavy block of stone with a horizontal bar carved out of it. The stone was angled sharply back, away from Morlock. As he ran his fingers over the block in the dark (very carefully, so as to avoid tripping the mechanism) he guessed that the work had been done in haste, but not recently. There was no weathering in the underground corridors of the Runhaiar, of course, but Morlock guessed that long ages had passed since the crumbling surface of the stone had been severed from its native rock.

The design of the lever was so familiar that it made Morlock remember the claims that the dwarves had built the Runhaiar, in the age before the Longest War began. Tyr did not believe the claims (never saying why), and Tyr knew more of his kith's history than anyone. Yet here was this lever, like many Morlock had seen in Thrymhaiam. But if dwarves had made such a lever to draw back a floor, they certainly would have also made a ledge for the person operating the lever to stand on while the floor moved. Here there was none.

He shrugged. Probably the floor did not recede entirely. He readied himself to shift his footing as the floor drew back up and pulled the heavy stone bar toward himself.

The floor vanished beneath his feet as the massive slab of stone roared its way down into the mountain's roots. Only Morlock's reflexes saved him from death—the primitive instinct of a cave-dweller and a stoneworker who is always mindful of the danger in a precariously balanced rock. As soon as he felt his footing give way he let go the stone bar and reached out frantically, as he fell, for the gap out of which the slab had descended. He just caught the ledge with his right hand as he fell past it; the weight of his body hung from four fingers as his feet swung far to the right. He threw his head to the right as well, and the heavy lever-stone hardly grazed his left shoulder as it swung ruinously down. He heard it carried high again, as he desperately halted the swing of his body by applying his boots and his free hand against the slick, ribbed wall. Clenching his teeth he felt the breath of the stone's passage as it swung down again, drawn by its own weight. It continued to swing back and forth for some time as the grating roar of the descending slab died away in the half-darkness.

And it was a *half*-darkness, not the absolute blindness he had become accustomed to. In that instant, as his footing gave way, his whole world had changed. Hot steaming air surrounded him; the wall he clung to was slick with moisture; from somewhere beneath him there was a dim source of reddish light. As he hung there gasping he heard the echo speak.

Come down, then, come down. You must come down.

It was no illusion. He could smell the poison in the air, reminding him of Almeijn's stained hair and haunting spell-lit eyes. The voice kept on speaking, calling him downward, inviting him to enter the den of a dragon.

You cannot go back. There is no other way for you, now. Come forward. Come now.

Morlock took in his surroundings. What the rumbling insidious voice said was untrue. He could go back. He saw that the ledge ran back under a tunnel entrance. . . . It must be the tunnel by which he had entered the Arches. He could edge around, hand over hand, and climb up there—go back the way he had come.

But he had not come here simply to *go back*. He'd guessed that at least one dragon from the guile had been stationed in the Runhaiar. He was only a thain; he had been sent to carry a message and to gather news. He could go back; he would not.

He looked, then, for ways to go down. The wall was sheer, except for the carven ribs. The drop to some kind of surface was something under twice Morlock's own height. It gleamed wetly, but the light was dim and the surface seemed dark and motionless; he could not tell if it was water or wet stone. His skin crawled at the thought he might plunge over his head into water that had been stagnant underground for centuries. But it was the only way. He braced his feet for a solid fall, but took a deep breath as if he were diving; then he let his aching fingers relax.

The breath proved unnecessary. The surface splashed as he struck it, but the water was only a foot or two in depth. Morlock slumped against the wall for a few moments, taking deep breaths of the moist sickening air. Then he started as he felt a drop of cool water touch his face. He heard others fall in the water around him. When he concentrated he could see drops falling, red streaks against darkness in the dim light.

Rain under the mountains! He guessed that the cold walls and ceiling of the Arches were sweating in the hot moist air and that the drops were returning as rain. Not so wonderful, when you thought about it. But it still seemed wonderful as he watched it fall. Rain under the mountains. It was like a portent.

Slowly, reluctantly, he directed his eyes toward the source of the dim light. It was a ragged hole in the wall of living rock, which seemed almost to have been gnawed. Its threshold was concealed under the black water. Beyond it lay the source of the red light, the heat, the poisonous reek that troubled this once peacefully dead place. It spoke to him as he hesitated.

Come forward. Come now. I command you.

He had already decided to go forward. But suddenly the dread of a dragonspell came over him. Would he even know if one took hold of him? Almeijn apparently had never known.

He moved forward. He had been sent; he had already decided. (But was this how it had happened to Almeijn?) He moved toward the rough circle of dim red light.

Saijok Mahr smiled the long lipless smile of wrath when he saw the pride-sickening little animal they had sent against him. He considered killing it for that reason alone as it sloshed through the hole in the wall. But a feeling peculiar to dragons stayed him, *sterch*: a kind of affection for himself. This creature's advent was proof that his gamble in sending that other creature on to Thrymhaiam was still paying off. Perhaps he could use this one as he had that one. . . .

That one had already paid off, very satisfyingly. (*Khûn tenadh!* The game of power! There was nothing like it.) He had known of his success when Vild Kharum came, howling and crawling, before the gate to his den.

A creature had escaped, Vild had moaned. The Softclaws at Thrymhaiam had been warned. The guile had been compelled to show itself while hunting the creature down, had failed anyway. It must have passed through Runhaiar. Vild "suspected" Saijok.

"Suspected" him! How he had laughed!

"Suspect me, then!" Saijok had replied. "And when you feel claws in your eyes and teeth in your throat you can 'suspect' me, then, too! Come inside my den, Vild, and I will lay your suspicions to rest. It must be terrible to be so afraid."

"Come out!" Vild had snarled. "Come out, worm, and challenge me so!"

"*Kruma kharum*," he sneered then, "lord of lords! I still have scars between my wings from the last time I challenged you . . . scars you never made. Your slaves are with you, now, I know. They'd tear my wings off before I could reach you. But I haven't given up. You *have* something that's *mine*."

No insult could be more deadly. Vild had barked at his door for hours and gone away hoarse. Saijok Mahr gloried in the memory as he lay, half-submerged, in the deep end of the pool.

He kept an eye on the creature as it sloshed forward at the shallow end.

He could not do so without noticing that the pool was almost deep enough for him to drink again. After his last sleep he had almost drunk enough to drown his thirst. . . . Almost, almost. That was long ago. Now his thirst tormented him, almost unbearably. Almost, almost. But he would not drink again until it was time, though he lay half-buried in water. He could subordinate his desires to his needs, serving them both ruthlessly. That was what made him a master of his kind.

He watched the creature as it found the gray corpse of the mandrake floating in the pool. That amused him, even as the memory hurt him, and he let it continue. He knew the creature would think the body was one of its own kind. The mistake was natural: for the corpse was vaguely manlike in shape, and Saijok had mauled it badly in killing it.

The creature turned the body over in the water. He watched the newcomer suddenly recoil from the blunt snout and heavy platelike scales of the corpse. With pride he noted that the dead mandrake would have grown into a likely dragon, had there been time. That was precisely why he'd had to kill it, of course. . . .

Time to speak. He reveled in the fine calculations of this game, *khûn tenadh*, the game of power. This was not even a particularly difficult problem—although, like a master, he took pleasure in every exercise of his skill. He had presented enough marvels to astonish and bewilder a better mind than this creature could possibly have. The main thing now was to speak first. If it spoke first, he would have to answer, and even if he answered by destroying it (which Saijok did not intend to do) the creature would have won a kind of victory. The cardinal rule of the game of power (of which the rest were merely variations) was: allow your enemy no victories, only concealed or open defeats.

He raised himself from the dark glittering water in a cloud of steam.

"You came at my command," he said, with some benevolence. "You have learned your first lesson well."

You have trespassed against the Guard, it said dimly, then something else, then, *Summoner Earno.*

Saijok threw back his head and laughed, letting fire trail from his jaws. He was disturbed and intrigued. He had heard of Earno Dragonkiller. He knew, of course, that a summoner and a set of Guardians was part of the hoard of Vild Kharum. If he could obtain a summoner of his own, and a dragonkiller at that, he might use it as a stake to tempt Vild into a real and final challenge . . . without his slave-guards, winner take all.

He saw the creature eyeing his collar of power. He was pleased and surprised. But it was a drawback as well. If the creature had seen members of the guile, he knew they all wore collars.

It was saying something— . . . *challenge of the summoner Earno. No member of the guile may stay my embassy.*

He snarled. "I am Saijok Mahr; I am no *member* but master of the Ghân guiles." Then an idea took him and he laughed. It emerged, complete to the last wriggle, in his mind. Vild Kharum was as good as dead. "Yet I will allow you to pass," he continued. "You will be *my* envoy to the guile."

The creature raised its face in defiance, as Saijok had guessed it would, and he caught its eye. And the thing was done; the dragonspell was placed.

Except . . . it was *not*. Saijok fixed the thing's eye with a fire-bright glance and waited for that moment, that pause, that snap that was like biting through bone. Yet it never came.

As the echoes of the creature's shouted defiance faded away, Saijok shifted thoughtfully in the pool and pondered the creature. The dragonspell seemed to surround it like a dark red cloud. He found the phenomenon interesting. It more than made up for his failure in placing the spell. Let this creature go to Vild and deliver his challenge; let Vild see the strange effect and wonder at the powers of Saijok Mahr.

He laughed. "Go now!" he said, gesturing with a foreclaw. "Take the tunnel yonder."

The creature said something. Saijok paid no attention to the words, but he tasted insolence in the tone. So he said, "You are my ambassador whether you will it or not." He laughed again; fire and steam floated through the chamber. When they began to dissipate the creature was gone.

Saijok was content. Then his thirst overpowered him and he lowered his snout to drink.

Morlock crouched, gasping, in the rough tunnel beyond the dragon's den.

You are my ambassador whether you will it or not! Each word had seemed to make the stones tremble. But perhaps that was just the spell working.

"You looked in its eyes! You looked in its eyes!" he raged at himself uselessly. For a few moments he had been sure it would kill him. Now it did not need to, though. And that was worse. His mind felt free and might even be so . . . except as the dragon wished it. There was a taste of venom in his mouth; he turned his head and spat.

He sat down and put both hands over his face. He felt the same; he felt no control on him. He remembered everything that had happened (or so it seemed). Would that be so, if the dragon had placed a spell?

There was another thing the dragon might have meant, he realized. Morlock's mere presence in Haukrull might mean something to the other dragons there, he realized. If Saijok controlled the ways through the Runhaiar, and the guile was aware of this . . . The fact that he had let a thain pass might mean something. It might be a gesture of defiance or a token of alliance. That did not matter. What mattered was that he might be as free as he felt; he *might* not be under control.

He was unpleasantly aware that these thoughts might be symptoms, not a disproof, of the spell working within him. But he could not turn back because of doubt. Perhaps the spell (if there was a spell . . . he *hated* thinking like this) was meant to take effect back in Thrymhaiam. Better, in that case, that he go forward and perhaps die in Haukrull. And if he was not under a spell . . . he had already learned much; he would surely learn more in the valley.

He got to his feet and went down the tunnel, which seemed to be the passage of an underground river recently gone dry. Presently he felt a draft of cold clean air and looked up. He saw nothing, but reaching up, he felt a passage leading straight up from the roof of the tunnel. Perhaps it had been a well when the tunnel was a river. His hands could not tell him whether it was made or was a natural formation. But it was a way out.

Lifting himself up into the empty well, he managed to inchworm up it, as if it were a chimney in a rock-cliff. Finally his hands, reaching up, spread out on a surface of dry sandy earth. He drew himself out of the well. Free air flowed over him in the bluish darkness.

As blind with weariness as with the dark, he drew his cape about him and lay down. A single doubt clung to him: that dragons might see him as he slept. But he shook loose from the thought and there was no other.

When he awoke he found he was in a narrow cave with a sandy floor. The cracklike opening of the cave was blindingly bright. Morlock ate the last of the flatbread in his pack as he was waiting for his eyes to grow used to the light. Then he rose to his feet and, leaving the empty pack and the Runhaiar behind, he stepped out into the light.

Chapter Eleven

Challenge

The summoner Earno woke to find the Eldest of Theorn Clan sitting beside his bed. He sat up, somewhat apprehensively. "I happened to be here last night," he explained, "so I settled down rather than return to my rooms."

"I know why you were here, Summoner," said Tyr. "I've come to apologize for my cold welcome to you."

"There have been many misunderstandings," Earno said slowly. "None of them seems to matter now."

"No," the Eldest agreed, "now that we have something really important to worry about." He stood. "Would you be wanting breakfast?"

Earno rose also. He'd slept in his clothes, with his mantle drawn about him; before that he'd had a long working night. "Not yet, thank you," he replied. "I should see how matters are prospering here."

"Here" was the Healing Chambers of Thrymhaiam. Earno had been there, almost since the first attack on Thrymhaiam two nights ago. He had spent most of those hours treating those bound in dragonspell.

"How are matters on the outside?" he asked the Eldest.

"There have been many deaths," the Eldest said grimly. "The huntress and farmer clans over Thrymhaiam have suffered the most. But the dragons have not launched an all-out attack since the first night. We have been sending messages to the Other Ilk throughout the hold. It is hard to say whether any have gotten through. None have yet returned."

"What have you lost?" Earno asked.

"In looting? Some. Not very much. They kill rather than steal. Yes, they've shown a kind of discipline. . . ."

How bad that was neither of them needed to say.

Tyr accompanied Earno on his rounds. Earno had no skill with wounds that was greater than that of the dwarvish healers, who were an efficient if pitiless lot. Vyrlaeth, in particular, was having a fine time: whenever he met Earno he mentioned with sinister delight how many bodies (living and dead) he had been privileged to cut into with skin-saw and bone-chisel. Earno, in contrast, treated only the poisoned and spellbound. There were many of these, though.

"The poisoned are simple enough," Earno explained. "A purge will clear them of venom, at least enough to keep them from dying. They can recover from the rest, given time."

"And they take a long time to die, in any case," Tyr remarked. "I have seen enough of it this fall. The skin and muscles contract, until they can neither move nor breathe. Then the joints snap and they are torn to shreds by their own bones. It is terrible to think that we might have saved our Rangan traders, and many of the Other Ilk as well, by simply . . . well, sticking a finger down their throats. . . ."

Most of the poisoned dwarves had been dosed and given into the care of their families. This was too dangerous a method with the spellbound, though: it was impossible to know what commands had been laid upon them until the spell was loosed. Also, the spellbound could pass their compulsion to others like a plague, by means of the dragonlight lingering in their eyes. They were kept in the Healing Chambers—along with those who tended them.

The summoner and the Eldest arrived at the first patient.

"Ah, Vendas," Tyr said. "I knew his father well. Has he improved, do you think?"

Earno inspected the dwarf's stiff motionless face, the eyes clenched shut like fists. "No," he finally answered the Eldest. "He hasn't. I am concerned about this dwarf. A command may have been laid upon him. He was a hunter?"

"Yes, one of the few males. His companions were all slain; he alone was left alive and unwounded."

"He should be separated from these others and a guard placed on him, one who knows the dangers."

"Very well."

The next patient was Deor.

"That herbal goo of yours," he told Earno, "gave me really foul dreams."

Earno smiled tentatively. "No," he replied, "it merely released them. And I'm glad to hear it." He passed a mirror before the young dwarf's eyes, watching his reaction, and nodded. "You are dismissed, Deor syr Theorn; the spell is loosed."

"I never felt spellbound, you know. Just a little strange."

"There was no command laid upon you. I guess you looked into a dragon's eyes last night, when they struck at the workers around Southgate-ruin."

"Well, I did. Just for a moment."

"Last night you wouldn't admit it."

"Wouldn't I?" Deor looked surprised, then disturbed. "That's true!"

"Don't worry. There never was any real danger. A spell unfocused by a command simply fades with time. But until it has faded it makes one liable to suggestion."

"Eh. That was how you got me to drink that stuff."

Tyr laughed. They were about to move on when Deor said, "Is there any news about Morlock?"

"No," said Tyr.

"Ah, well. He can have only just reached Haukrull by now."

After the rest of the victims were examined, and most of them released, Earno walked with Tyr to his chambers to have breakfast.

"It is a good thing you were here," Tyr told him. "Our dragonlore is out of date, and much of it has been lost. Even in my youth it was considered a useless and somewhat morbid study. No one of us would have recognized the threat of spells."

Earno didn't wish to say how the idea had come to him. So he said, "I thought some still studied the subject for its own interest."

"There are always antiquarians. I sent a few to you yesterday, when I heard what you were doing. I hope they didn't get in the way."

"They were helpful. Without them I would never have known an infusion of maijarra leaves could loose the spell."

"Helpful, were they? Frankly, I'm surprised. I spent half the night, or maybe it just seemed that long, arguing with one of them. He had a notion that dragons were actually extinct. That was . . . before. You understand. Now he insists that the dragons we face today are a different breed than those we fought ages past in the Longest War."

"Um. Interesting."

"But useless. The definition of an antiquarian."

Earno shook his head. "They say you are an antiquarian yourself, Eldest Tyr."

"They just mean I'm old. But I'm not useless, not yet."

They arrived at the corridor leading to the Eldest's chambers. Tyr pulled open a door and waved Earno in. "Just wait in here a moment, until I've seen about breakfast. It'll be nothing fancy, mind you. The feasts are over for Thrymhaiam, for a season." Then he left.

In the room where Earno found himself there were workbenches, where restless dwarves could work with their hands while they waited to see the Eldest. This amused Earno (he would have preferred a pitcher of warm water, a basin, and a dish of soap), but he recognized the compliment it implied. He wondered if Tyr actually expected him to while away the time by polishing a few stones he might (but did not) have in his pocket, or by cutting glass for mirrors.

This last bench drew his eye, though. He went to it and found a few scraps of mirror. He raised one and looked into his own eyes.

Yes. The flash of deep bright red was still there. He had hoped it would be gone by now. He was sure, he was almost sure, that the dragonspell had not been focused by a command. Perhaps looking into the eyes of so many spellbound had reinforced his own spell. It was unfortunate.

Perhaps he should take some of the maijarra infusion. But maijarra trees were rare in these parts. (The tree had been extinct on Thrymhaiam for centuries, although, ironically, it was extremely common in Haukrull, beyond the Haukr mountains, where the dragons now reigned.) He, as a summoner, had many other ways of countering the spell. Best to leave the herbs for those who had none.

He was uneasily aware of the danger, that his reluctance to take this most direct step toward lifting the spell might be an effect of the spell itself. But he also knew that, for the moment, he himself was in control and that the spell would only grow weaker in time, since it had not, could not have been fixed by a command. His wild suspicions and fears seemed to have passed with Morlock into the darkness under the mountains. For now, the danger was no danger. He heard Tyr approaching and hastily put the mirror fragment down.

Morlock lay in the dark among the ruined timbers of a burned building. A few stray fumes floated upward in the darkness, until they were brilliantly lanced by the crossed light of the major moons. But it wasn't the building smoldering; it was him.

He tried to remember things but could not. Had he delivered the challenge? He remembered the sound of his own voice screaming hatred or defiance, then the rush of flames that swept him off his feet. . . . Had that been Saijok Mahr? Or Vild Kharum? Then he had to ask himself: who is Vild Kharum?

The master of the guile, he answered himself immediately. It seemed as if he had known this for a long while, but he couldn't remember when he had learned it. He had not known the name that morning (which morning?) when he stepped into the light and Haukrull vale. He remembered walking slowly up the valley . . . after that it became confused. He didn't want to remember. There was something horrible in those events, something he refused to remember.

He clenched his teeth and retook the journey step by step.

At first it was as if nothing had changed in the valley. He saw scattered maijarra trees in bloom. There were blackirons and brightirons, the ashen glow of the brightirons radiant amid the unpolished ebony of their darker cousins. There was even a line of rare coppers, crookedly following a vein of ore, their leaves alive with unearthly colors in the autumnal light.

"Maijarra are weeds," the Eldest Tyr had told him long ago, "and enough of them can ruin a mountain, plowing through the underpinnings for veins of metal."

"They're pretty weeds, though," Morlock had remarked, to which the Eldest responded with an incredulous grunt.

There was a maijarra forest along the northern edge of Haukrull vale where the Eldest's statement was proved literally true: maijarra roots had dug into the fabric of the range and collapsed an entire mountain. The Other Ilk in Haukrull were always taking up a campaign to exterminate the maijarra in Haukrull, as the Seven Clans long ago had done on Thrymhaiam. They had not advanced very far, however. A mature maijarra is very difficult to kill.

Topping a rise, Morlock saw for the first time evidence of the dragons in Haukrull. In the deep depression between two outflung arms of Mount Gramer he saw a long, torn, burned space, dead black against the dying gold of the grass. He advanced cautiously down the slope, but he was sure the ruin had been wreaked some time ago: there was no smoke, no flower of steam opening in the air, no feeling of heat from the jagged black earthen scar as he approached it.

Before he had reached it (it sprawled unavoidable across his northward path) he saw more signs of the dragons. A hole had been blown out of Gramer's side, so that the two arms of the mountain formed a sort of sunken road leading to this door. And it *was* a door: great slabs of stone formed the threshold, doorposts, and lintel. The door was large enough to admit a giant—or a dragon. He had to think of Saijok Mahr, dwelling in the depths of the Runhaiar, and he guessed this was the entrance to his den. He would have gone no nearer, but he saw there was writing on the doorposts.

He went halfheartedly, reluctantly, expecting at any moment the appearance of Saijok's flaming wolflike head in the dark doorway. The air flowing from it carried a poisonous stench. But it was cool; the poison had been exhaled long ago. There was no dragon near, or so he guessed. Holding an edge of his cape over his mouth to screen out the poison, he went forward.

The left-hand doorpost was covered with carven words and crudely executed reliefs. The right-hand post bore nothing but a crooked line of runic letters, too far up for Morlock to be able to distinguish them. But much of the writing on the other post Morlock found to be readable. The lettering was Dwarvish, and so, too, was much of the language, though of a strange and archaic kind. The script was thick with non-Dwarvish words, also. Some of these he recognized; others he did not. There was the word *kharum*, for instance: the Anhikh word for "ruler of a city" or "king." Yet it always appeared, in the inscriptions, beside another word, *vild*, which Morlock did not recognize.

In the bright empty morning, he stood before the written stone and read it through. The inscription told of a battle between Saijok Mahr and this *vild kharum* who, from the reliefs, was also a dragon. The battle had been interrupted, according to the reliefs, by a horde of batlike creatures. Although the inscription at this point became unreadable, Morlock guessed that the bats represented lesser dragons, allies or servants of the *vild kharum*. In contrast, the blankness of the right-hand stone now seemed more than a little ominous—as if it represented a yet-unwritten revenge against the *vild kharum* and its allies.

He was disturbed that these creatures, who clearly hated each other as much as or more than they hated the rest of the world, should use a language so clearly akin to that of his own people. Perhaps they had stolen it: clearly they were all born thieves and marauders, taking what they were unable to make. This could be true for words, he supposed, as well as anything made from silver or gold. Perhaps it could.

He turned back to the inscription for a moment. Studying the runes, he found them crookedly carved. The reliefs were indeed coarsely imagined and poorly executed. But he was convinced that the work had been done by tools held in hands: he could see the marks where a hammer had missed its stroke, where a chisel had gone astray. The tools might have been obtained in Haukrull, but he did not think any of the Other Ilk had done the carving; it was too inept and outlandish. He thought of the manlike beast that drifted dead in the dragon's pool. But how had such an outlandish creature come into the Wardlands? Astride a dragon's back?

Buried in thought he climbed the long hill before him. Before he reached its height he heard a loud roar and the rasp of wings on the air. A shadow fell between him and the sun.

There were three of them: a mud-colored dragon with a collar of iron and two great golden dragons with bronze collars. When they fell on him he raised his cape as a token and cried out that he had an embassy to the master of the guile. Each one flew over him, and they landed forming a triangle around him. The wind from their wingbeats knocked him to the ground, but he leapt up again and demanded that they take him to their master.

And they did. The mud-colored dragon was sent ahead as a messenger while the two great golden worms walked on either side of Morlock. Somehow he expected them to be as graceless on the ground as they were lithe in the air, but it wasn't so. He was always conscious of their weight as they strode beside him, yet it was not because they lumbered. They were agile, glittering, silent and swift. The earth shuddered beneath their feet when they walked, but he felt his own footfalls were louder than theirs. It was his own gasps that broke the silence as he struggled to keep pace with them.

They passed by the Pilgrims' Gate to the Runhaiar, where Lernaion and his companions had walked, but in his exertions Morlock failed to notice anything that would have confirmed or disproved Almeijn's story. They passed by the town Haukrull—as ruined as Almeijn had described it, or worse. He saw that there were dozens of open fires in the upper valley even now.

Morlock had just noticed this when the dragon on his left turned and spoke its first words to him.

Go through the guile, it said, in Wardic. *Vild Kharum you will know by the Triple Collar that he wears, and that he lies upon the hoard.*

Then both dragons leapt into the air. Their wingbeats struck Morlock off his feet again. He watched them trail arcs of smoke through the evening sky and settle down in the upper valley, adding two more fires to the many (fifty? a hundred?) already burning there.

He got to his feet and walked on. He took his time. He didn't suppose the dragons would be patient, but he had walked all day at a bitter pace; he must not arrive out of breath. *Shallow breath means a broken message,* went the thain's axiom; he must deliver the challenge.

Walking into the fields afire with the guile of dragons, he found the air increasingly thick with smoke, steam, and the taste of venom. The sound of the dragons' massed breathing was like the earth sighing in the Firehills of the northwest: not loud, or itself dangerous, but an omen of sudden dangers.

He heard them speaking with each other as he walked among them. At first the harsh resonant words were so much noise to him. But as he advanced he realized he could understand bits and pieces. Their spoken language was also a kind of Dwarvish, even more outlandish and corrupt than the script on Saijok Mahr's doorpost. In the language of his *harven* kin, Morlock heard the dragons making wagers for his bones.

I will take the left leg from Kharum.

Not. Not.

Stake me! I have twenty; give me twenty.

Not. The bone for the gold, only.

I will show you the bone and take your gold.

Done. But it will not be.

Morlock walked on, wondering. This was not what he had imagined a guile to be. He had never really imagined one, he realized, except as a submissive band of acolytes following their master. The flight of batlike creatures on Saijok's doorpost was hardly less lifelike than the image in Morlock's mind.

The Triple Chain. I would not wear it.

Yes: not. As I live, not.

You claim it? You? You sang a different song at Ghânfell Assembly.

I claim nothing, not. But I am a master and no member. . . .

It was almost what Saijok Mahr had said. Morlock saw then that they were indeed all masters. They all wore collars of power. There was no mystery about Saijok now. Clearly he was a rogue who refused to accept the overlordship of Vild Kharum. And there seemed to be many in the guile who were almost as openly rebellious.

. . . the Softclaws at Thrymhaiam.

Runshav King, you fear the Little Cousins.

They killed Gharlan Jarl. I saw them smashing his teeth by the southern gate.

He was a red. Reds breathe hot, but their bellies are soft.

Vild is a red.

I saw his belly bleeding after we had driven off Saijok Mahr.

Morlock walked on. It was as though he were invisible to these hulking smoke-wrapped figures. He walked though their fires and was not burned. He heard their words and understood them, although they did not know or care. As he approached the pile of treasure on which the master dragon lay, like a red lizard sunning itself in the day's last light, he understood something else. Earno's challenge was an error. If the summoner came here he would be taken captive or killed, even if he conquered this Vild Kharum. There was no real master to this guile of masters—not in the sense that

Earno knew. These followed a leader, but they would not be dismayed at his fall. Each would welcome its own chance at the Triple Collar.

The Triple Collar. He saw it now: lead-colored metal hammered into subtle links, wrapped around Vild's long serpentine neck. He advanced the last few steps toward the master of this guile of masters. The sun was on the crooked eastern horizon; its light faded with Morlock's every step. But in the light that remained, including the dragons' own fire, he examined the Triple Collar.

It was, he saw at once, as different as could be from the collars of the other dragons. Those were badly formed adaptations; some, like that of the dragon slain at Southgate (Gharlan Jarl?), were merely iron chains crudely fused and partly coated with precious metal. But Vild's collar was no mere chain; its linkages were subtle, and he could see the gleam of etching on its flat dull plates (though whether images or symbols he could not tell). He was certain that no dragon could have made the Triple Collar. But it had been made for a dragon; that was also obvious. By whom? And why?

He drew to a halt, his head bowed with weariness and frustration. Then he raised it, drew a breath, and opened his mouth, Earno's death sentence on his lips. He didn't speak it. Everything seemed so futile. Earno had counted on their unity, and it was their division that would give them victory. It made them seem invincible. All his life he had been taught that division was weakness; it was hard to grasp that it could be a kind of strength as well. But when he saw this, he also saw (madly and irrelevantly) it was the strength that guarded the Wardlands. Division guaranteed that everyone would be strong.

But the guile of masters was different from this. They were like his *ruthen* father. They settled for division, but each one dreamed of unity, longing for the unity of its own undisputed dominance. Those dreams of unity were the weakness in their division. The thought lightened Morlock's heart. He spoke at last. He spoke from his heart to theirs. He was inspired.

"Masters of the Blackthorn Range!" he cried in the Dwarvish language. His thainish training was not wasted: the upper valley rang with his voice. "I bring a message from your peers and enemies, the Graith of Guardians—"

The rumble of draconic voices behind him rose to a tumult.

Silence! the master dragon roared. And silence fell. They might hate him, but still they feared him. Why? It would be worth knowing, but Morlock felt he would never know. He raised his eyes and deliberately met those of Vild Kharum. He saw those red-gold slotted eyes narrow and intensify to fire-bright clarity. *Silence,* Vild repeated, exerting his power of fascination. The word hung in the steam-thick darkening air, creating the thing it named.

Morlock waited, until he was sure every dragon in the guile knew its master was attempting to place a spell on him. He hoped it would fail, as Saijok's had failed in the Runhaiar. When he knew it had, he raised his voice and cried out, "Go forth from this land, now under the Guard, or prepare to be hunted down one by one for your crimes against the Guarded—"

He got no further. From the moment the master dragon saw his spell had not taken he began to prepare his answer—an unanswerable one. Vild rose to his crooked hind legs and threw back his wings, drawing air deep into his fiery lungs, the sunken serpentine chest expanding to three times its normal width. Finally the wolflike jaw lowered, and he roared down flame on the thain.

Morlock's last word crumbled to an unintelligible scream of defiance as he saw the flames lance forward between Vild's dark fangs. The flame swept forward and hurled itself about him, carrying him off his feet, throwing him backward. Wrapped in red light and poison, Morlock lost consciousness.

That was all there was. That was all that was necessary to take him from the Runhaiar to the wreckage of Haukrull, where he now guessed himself to be. He supposed he had fallen among the remains of an outlying house. That was all there was.

Except . . . (he admitted it reluctantly to himself) there was more. It was impossible, as if he had grown new memories, like mushrooms, as he lay unconscious in the dark. Perhaps they were just dreams. Certainly they were quite strange.

He remembered standing in a faraway place, having an insane argument with a voice that spoke to him from a cloud of bright unburning flames, demanding recognition. It was as if he had to explain something to the flames. He felt he should explain, but he couldn't think of what. And every now and then the flames would suggest something but when he eagerly began to respond dismissed his statement imperiously.

Morlock!

"Morlock is dead, I think. He was dying when I last saw him—" He felt a sharp stabbing relief that Morlock's problems were not his own.

Merlin!

"There is no Merlin."

Ambrosius!

"From the Unspoken tongues—the surname of a famous family of Eastholders—now extinct."

Syr Theorn!

He knew this name of course. Theornn, in Dwarvish legend, was the eponymous ancestor of the group of clans that excavated and still inhabited Thrymhaiam. It was an easy question to answer; he could have answered without shame. But he didn't answer. The thought of Thrymhaiam suffused him with guilt. Earno was at Thrymhaiam, and he had failed to deliver his challenge. Worse than failed: had chosen not to. Indeed for reasons that seemed good. But that made it worse than ever: who was he to disregard the commands of the Dragonkiller? He was a worthless thain. Or was that Morlock? Surely it was Morlock who had done that? Still, obscurely, he felt responsible, as if he ought to explain for Morlock who was, after all, surely dead now.

"Earno . . ."

He was cut off by a burst of wordless anger, more painful than Vild's fire, dissolving his fragmented sense of identity. *What was Earno to him? That fool. He had tried to warn him, but it had done no good ever since that summons to Tychar—*

Shocked by the alien thoughts coursing through his mind (but *were* they alien? this anger had a familiar feel to it) he was most troubled by the fact that he could not remember the summons to Tychar. The very thought of it was charged with importance, but he did not remember it. He tried to remember and met resistance. He brushed this aside and seized the relevant memories. They rushed down on him, like an avalanche through the bright unburning flames.

. . . because she was useless: there was a madness in her from her mother.

He went in underneath the trees, the densely intertwined boughs with their sparse blue-black leaves covering his white mantle with darkness. That made him think (again!) of the day Nimue had betrayed him to Earno. Much had begun and ended on that day!

For a long time he walked north through the winterwood. From the slope of the rugged ground and occasional glimpses of the dim horizon in clearings, he knew he was coming closer to the Blackthorn Range.

*Finally he came to a clearing where the sky was not visible, only a high dome of dimly glowing white mist. A lake of the same lay before him. He sat down at the edge of the clearing, resting his crooked shoulders against an only slightly more crooked tree trunk. He found his thoughts turning not to Faith, or Ambrosia, or even Nimue, but to his son who—*there came a part he did not wish to remember, that he refused to remember.

His legs gave way and he fell to his knees before the Two Powers.

"Our war makes the world that you know," said the white Presence on the black throne. (Torlan? Or Zahkaar?) "Your disbelief is as irrelevant as your belief would be. Our existences do not require your belief."

"Our power can, however, in some measure descend to yourself," said the black Presence on the white throne. (Zahkaar? Or Torlan?) "Only that power, believe in it or not, can give you victory over your enemies in the Wardlands."

"Your enemies," he replied absently, pondering the spell that bound him. It emanated from a place between the two thrones, shifting back and forth as the Powers exerted their tension on each other. His Sight could trace the spells' invisible patterns in the stale air. His staff was with him, and his crystalline focus was bound up in a corner of his cloak. He could break the spell. But he waited. The two voices spoke on, in careful inimical alternation.

"We require your consent," asserted one, and paused.

"To consent, you will require proof," said the other.

He found himself able to rise. He did so more slowly than was necessary, leaning heavily on his staff. When he had risen he put his hand under his cloak, as if to press against his heart. He wheezed loudly. His fingers closed on the cold smooth surface of his focus.

"Go back as you came. Go back."

"Go back."

He turned and went slowly—not exactly as he had come, but in the manner of an old beaten man. He went from the place of pillars on the high dark island in the glowing mist. He went down the white-and-black, black-and-white stone stairway to the edge of the mist. The Two Powers stayed where they were (if that was where they were), but their voices followed him.

"The two greatest masters of the Blackthorn Range. Saijok Mahr—"

"—and Vild Kharum. They were extending hegemonies . . ."

"It was natural law, the conflict of our wills. The guiles would unite."

"The function of this development was clear."

"They would move to settle their ancient grudge against the Seven Clans under Thrymhaiam—since passed under the Guard."

"This suited our opposing purposes."

"It was not even necessary for us to summon them."

"They had already sought us out."

He descended toward the mist, which opened like a tunnel before him.

"Imagine, Ambrosius, the powers that can be yours—"

"Remember, also, the vengeance your pride requires—"

(The memories were becoming painful. Morlock, lying in the wrecked house, wondered dimly why he had not told them he was not an Ambrosius, had never been an Ambrosius.)

He walked down into the dark hole in the mist and passed along the tunnel beyond.

"The kingship will finally be yours."

"And not only of one land."

"You need not fear us."

"We need no kingship."

"Yet natural law, the conflict of our wills, informs us—"

"The growing influence of the Two Powers in Kaen threatens the Wardlands."

"The Guardians are already grown curious; soon they will act. . . ."

The mist grew red, before and above him. Still he walked on until the mist rolled back like a curtain, revealing two dragons drifting in midair above him. One was greenish black. The other was a red, and he recognized this one instantly.

"Vild Kharum," he muttered. Long ago, when he was still only a vocate, the people of Aflraun had offered him a tithe of all they possessed to fend off an attack by Vild and his ruin. He had done it, too—and, like a fool, refused the money. A capable maker could make his own money, of course, but he later learned how much people valued what they had to pay for—and how little they valued anything else.

"How are the spoils of Aflraun, Vild?" he called out mockingly in greeting.

The dragon roared. He did not move to avoid the flames but stood, bracing himself with his staff. His bravado was wasted, though; the flames never reached him. They turned back and engulfed Vild.

Soon he realized why. Both dragons were surrounded by a net of fine fiery lines.

The net narrowed in its middle, as if it had been twisted to make separate chambers for the two dragons. But the situation was more complicated than that. He traced one line from Vild's end across the narrow separation to the stranger dragon's side. He saw that it looped back to join itself, forming a continuous double loop—the symbol for eternity or infinity in many cultures, especially those under the sway of the Two Powers. He wondered how many lines there were, and tried to count a cross-section. He found he could not. Between every two lines there was another; another, too, between that one and either of the adjacent lines. . . . An infinite series of parallel lines. But if he stood back and looked at the whole he found the dragons clearly visible, as they should not have been.

The two dragons reacted differently to their imprisonment. Vild was roaring again, trying to break through the fiery lines with fire. The lines about him were vivid and distinct. The stranger dragon was doing otherwise; he waited, almost quiescent, smoke trailing from his distended nostrils. Around him the lines were dim, almost invisible. It suggested the stranger dragon was more subtle, and therefore more dangerous, than the red-gold rival master.

Perhaps the green-black dragon had simply realized what he himself had known almost instantly: those mind-bending lines of fire were merely an illusion. The real containment spell came from elsewhere, a variation of the one that had held him earlier. It proceeded from the same source: the shifting point of balance between the thrones of the Two Powers. Still holding his focus, he could trace the web of force back through the misty firelit air.

The voices were speaking again in his ear, but he didn't listen to them. He was weighing in his mind the consequences of cancelling the spell and releasing the dragons. And, since he was who he was—(the memories became painful here; Morlock put his hands over his face)*—Ambrosius, the pause was a brief one. He put his thumb, second finger, and forefinger around the focus and let an image form in his mind. The image formed also in the focus. A lesser maker would have had to see the focus to know that the image was forming: to concentrate on the details, execute the lines. But he was who he was. The image formed; he knew it; that knowledge was simply a recognition of his own strength.*

When the image had fully formed in the crystalline focus, he exerted his will through the focus and the image appeared in the mist above. It was an image of the two dragons, coiled and writhing in midair, mirror-perfect reflections of Vild Kharum and Saijok Mahr.

The mechanism of the spell perceived its objects and wrapped itself around the images, leaving the real dragons free. For a moment he wished he had Gryregaest in his hands again: this would have been a battle to equal that night on Tunglskin!

Vild fell on him, breathing fire. The voices behind him called out, "Merlin, you are twice a traitor—"

The memories became too tormenting to bear. Morlock shook free of them, shouting that it was a lie: he was no Ambrosius, no traitor, no Merlin. It was only when the echoes of his own voice returned to him, as he lay in the ruined house, that he realized he'd been a fool. Soon afterward, he heard the speech of dragons.

Chapter Twelve

Maijarra

One day it occurred to Deor that Morlock was dead. The thought came to him suddenly. It was too quick to be painful. He was polishing one of his gems. It was new work . . . and poor stuff. But better than he had grown before. He remembered that Morlock promised to help him with his gems, but never had the chance. *Ah, well*, he thought, *the promise is at peace*. The phrase was a ritual formula, referring to unkept obligations of the dead.

It surprised him a little that the idea did not surprise him. Yes, Morlock was almost certainly dead. The thought had a dense black finality to it, but no pain, not yet.

He finished polishing the stone and looked at it. Yes, it was bad. The color was not what he had wanted, and light passed through it milkily. He fell to thinking of the gems Morlock had grown: how fine they were, how large and full of light. Morlock had been incredibly gifted at that kind of making. Clever at it. It was a game. Once he had grown a gem with Deor's name in it, written in runic letters. It hadn't looked well—they both admitted that—but who else could have done it at all? Then there was that night he had blown up the work chambers, making the freakish flawed gem that Tyr still wore as a pendant. Deor laughed about that whenever he thought of it, and he laughed a little now.

There was some pain, now, though. Once Morlock, before he had reached his full growth, had burst into Deor's workroom. "I need air!" he shouted. Deor dropped his tools and, an hour or so later, found himself following Morlock out of the unglazed window in the Eldest's audience chamber. They crossed the ice lake atop Thrymhaiam, went through the

Firehills and on to the Broken Coast, where the Whitethorns ran into the northern ocean.

They didn't return for more than a year, because Eldest Tyr sent a message after them, commanding them to work at the trading house the clans had set up on the Broken Coast, to deal with the ships that came north from Westhold. Perhaps it was a kind of punishment, an exile, and perhaps it was something else. Perhaps the Eldest had already realized what Deor and Morlock himself learned more slowly: that Morlock would never be at peace under Thrymhaiam.

Now it would never be like that again. No one would ever stand outside his door at midnight shouting, "Air! Air!" It would never be the same. Or rather: it would *always* be the same now. Morlock had been a brief flash of light in Thrymhaiam's caverns. Inevitably he had flickered and gone out.

"I need air," muttered Deor, in a kind of rebellion. But it wasn't true. The greatest part of him was content, even in grief, in the niche that the countless ages of Thrymhaiam's history had provided him. For a time, though, he had shared the senseless painful freedom of one who did not know his place, who did not belong. He could not forget it.

He wondered how Morlock had died. Suddenly he could no longer sit still. He got to his feet and moved restlessly about the room. Then something occurred to him. It was a bizarre thought, against the rules, and none of his business anyway. So he decided to do it. He would do it for Morlock.

He left his workshop and went to the Healing Chambers. There he met strange Vyrlaeth with his lizardlike smile, and they had a brief discussion. Deor left with a small tightly wrapped packet of maijarra leaves. Deor returned to his rooms and made a triply powerful infusion of the stuff, as if it were tea. Then he poured it into an empty bottle and plugged it with wax. He carried this with him as he returned to the Healing Chambers.

Seven full days after the first assault on Thrymhaiam there was only one dwarf still subject to dragonspell. This was Vendas. He lay in a separate chamber, a guard with him at all times. Deor went to the chamber and entered it.

The sick dwarf lay on a bed with no coverings. He was fully clothed, except for his boots, which stood beside the bed. The guard was sitting glumly on a stool against the far wall. The set of his shoulders was patient, but his hands were restless. He looked up without hope as Deor entered.

"Go home, Orn," said Deor.

Orn leapt to his feet, then hesitated. "You mean it?" he asked. "I was to stay all night."

"I mean it. My family has gone to the Deep Shelters, and I don't seem to sleep the same without them. "

Orn nodded. It was a common complaint. "I would stay . . . except I left something unfinished at my bench. I would have brought it with me, but they told me not."

"You know what I usually do? Bring wax tablets and a stylus. That way you can at least sketch out what you're working on. It helps."

"Ach. I can't work that way. I never know what I'm going to do until I heft the stuff with my hands."

"Well."

"Besides, you don't have any tablets with you. I'll wait until you get some."

"Never mind. I've got this." Deor showed him the bottle. Dwarves are beer-drinkers, as a rule, but Deor was known to have picked up southern habits.

Orn laughed and said, "Well, I'll leave Ven to you. Pour some of that Southhold wine down his throat and see what he does."

"I just might do that," Deor said. "How has he been?"

"Just nothing. For seven days nothing. He'll die soon, of thirst if nothing else."

It would be ironic if someone dying slowly of thirst were to suddenly drown. That was Deor's chief concern about his plan. He bid Orn good night and sat down on the stool.

When the sound of Orn's footfalls had died away in the corridor outside, Deor stood and went to the bed where Ven lay.

As he unstoppered the bottle he wondered what he ought to do. He supposed he should pull back Ven's lips and hold his nose, pouring the liquid between his teeth. The problem was that this would almost certainly result in him breathing it in. He had come to cure Ven, not kill him.

The thought re-formed itself in his mind, and at last he knew his own intent. He had indeed come to cure Ven—or kill him. Ven was the only, albeit unwilling, agent of the dragons under Thrymhaiam. Reclaiming him, or killing him if it happened that way, would be an act of revenge, the first act of a revenge that would become famous.

True, Ven was essentially innocent. But it was part of the ethic of revenge to make the innocent suffer. This was something Morlock had never understood. The logic of revenge requires an insane and unbearable punishment for the most sane and thinkable offense. It makes the next offense less thinkable and besides . . . it was simply necessary.

Ven's eyes opened. It was shocking, not only because he had been unconscious for seven days, but because of the eyes themselves. They were red. The "blacks" fairly glowed a deep fiery red, dimly coloring the once-gray irises. Even the whites were bright and bloodshot.

"You," Ven croaked.

Deor wondered what had caused him to finally stir. Perhaps only now had he realized he was not alone. Perhaps he had suddenly given up resisting the dragonspell. Perhaps he had been told to wait just this long before awaking. It didn't matter.

"You," Ven croaked. "You will be the first. I bring a song without words. I bring the Consolation of the Two Powers—"

Deor deftly put the neck of the bottle between Ven's teeth and held his patient's nose. The subsequent gargling explosion was indeed a song without words.

Left leg. Left leg. The left leg: you will have it . . .

Not as it was. Not. Where is Vild now? This is no victory—

You are a tonguer and a Softclaw. I sold you the left leg for twenty.

Morlock lay in the ruined house, listening to two dragons track him down. They had heard his cry and were coming for him. They were searching already, apparently, even before his involuntary shouts. A trophy of the Guardian whom the master was unable to spellbind would be a valuable and sought-after possession in the guile, or so Morlock gathered from eavesdropping on the dragons. Vild had been forced to three challenges in succession after Morlock's embassy.

Like old Ambrosius in Aflraun, said one. This stray comment struck Morlock like a fist. For a moment the gathering strength of his sanity vanished in a flood of anxiety and self-hatred.

Yet Vild is still crowing like a rooster on a dung heap, the other dragon grumbled in reply.

The two fell silent for a moment. Morlock found that he could indeed hear a dragon roaring repeatedly in triumph. That could mean only one thing: Vild had won his duels and killed each one of his self-styled rivals in combat. The fact hung in Morlock's awareness for a moment without carrying any weight. Then he realized: those dragons had rebelled because of *his* words. They were three dragons who would fly no more to Thrymhaiam to plunder and kill his *harven* kin. How many more might be drawn down the same path?

Then Morlock knew he had found a weapon to destroy the guile. Crazed or not, his mind held the secret of victory against the invaders. He must return to Thrymhaiam, so that wiser minds could put his knowledge to use.

He listened to the two dragons (apparently there were only two) approach from the north to the sound of crushing and splintering wood. (There must be other buildings nearby, then. Perhaps the house had been part of an outlying farm.) Their search went slowly. Morlock guessed that, like most serpents, they heard poorly. Their fiery venom-laden breath would also prevent them from having much of a sense of smell. But Morlock did not doubt they must have unusually clear eyesight, in day or night. That was what he must guard himself against.

Keeping his own ears attentive, he rolled over and crept on his hands and knees past blackened and fallen timbers to the collapsed doorway of the building. Cautiously he peered out.

Beyond the broken doorway he saw the hundred fires of the guile of dragons, with Vild Kharum above them on the hoard nestled into the side of a mountain. The master dragon was still roaring in triumph. Morlock could see several smoking heaps before the hoard, from which the light was fading. The scene was perhaps five hundred paces distant to the southwest.

Morlock pulled back until they were out of sight. He was confused. He had clearly heard the two dragons approaching from the north. Regardless of that he himself was north and somewhat east of the ruin. This was bad. He had hoped to make his way through the ruins of Haukrull town to the Pilgrim's Gate of the Runhaiar, and from there go to Thrymhaiam easily enough. Now that was obviously impossible; he could not hope to creep past the guile without any of its members noticing him. He would have to head north and try crossing the Haukr range overland, by way of the Thains' Northtower.

He looked out again. He didn't think he would have survived if he were thrown this far by Vild's fiery blast; the fall would have killed him. Probably he had fallen some distance away and crawled instinctively toward cover. It was strange that he didn't remember, while he did "remember" things that surely never happened to him. Yet between fire, blows to the head, and poison he was lucky not to be worse off than he was.

But it was insane to put it like that, with a hundred dragons between him and safety. He could go the other way, over the mountains . . . except that his clothes were singed rags, he had no food, and there were two dragons between him and the mountains, waiting for him to raise his head.

He shook his head and tried to think. That last was the real problem. It wasn't the hundred dragons burning the fields of Haukrull, or the fact that he would freeze or starve in the mountains, should he ever get there. It was the two dragons lumbering about outside. The problem was insoluble, but *that* was it; the others would only matter in the unlikely event that he solved this first one. He was safe from them.

A wild thought occurred to him. If the situation had been less desperate he would have ignored it. But he had no time to reason with his wiser self. The two dragons were approaching the ruin where he was hiding.

Morlock slipped out of the wrecked doorway, crouching down by the crumpled wall. He hoped none of the dragons still in the assembled guile could see him. Then he spoke, in a penetrating yet directionless tone. (A thainish skill. But he was a worthless thain.) He spoke in a twisted Dwarvish that he hoped would pass for the dragons' own language.

"Only one can take the trophy," he said.

Their soft shuddering footfalls ceased. Neither spoke. Morlock knew they were trying to judge his location with their indistinct hearing. They were terribly close; he could smell their fire. But he knew they would not act on what he had said so far.

He spoke again. "Buying and selling—*bargaining* like Softclaws." (He wondered what a Softclaw was.)

One snarled, a terrifying sound: like a tree splintering in a storm. But neither one did anything else.

Morlock gave it up. His device was too obvious. No doubt the two would quarrel—over his bones. In the meantime he could do nothing that would cause them to fight each other.

He could only try, then, to make them think he was somewhere else. He picked up a charred rafter-end and hurled it at a nearby building. (Had the dragons already been there? he wondered too late.)

The ploy was instantly disastrous. The two dragons' radiant eyes spotted the flying fragment before it reached the top of its arc. One, with a happy roar, leapt into the air, hurling himself into Morlock's vision like a fiery star leaving the zone of eclipse. The other struck directly through the building, shrugging aside the charred beams like a cloud of ash.

In desperation Morlock turned and fled. The flying dragon knocked him off his feet as it landed. He went down spinning and saw its long narrow head lunge forward for the kill. It snapped once, prematurely, and the other was upon it, fitting fiery jaws about its neck.

Fire outlined the serpentine figures as they struggled. Morlock, dazed though he was, understood that this was his chance; there would be no other. He rolled to his feet and ran upslope.

In the bleak light of Chariot and Horseman, he could see a dark swathe cut out of the glittering mountainside before him. That had to be the maijarra forest that spilled over the valley's northwest edge. It had to be.

He heard a dragon die under the claws of its rival. His time, too, was nearly at an end. As he closed on the forest his eyes began to pick out details from the general darkness. The trees looked like withered oaks: the boughs were twisted, ash-strewn, leafless, though this was the maijarra's growing season. He kept on running, but he had no real hope now. He heard the roar of the victor dragon as it took to the air. Gasping in the thin air he wished that his course was not uphill; years of living in the south had softened his lungs.

He looked over his shoulder and saw the sky, half-covered with clouds, lit up by a fountain of red stars, increasingly many of them, stark and brilliant against the blue-black night. Alerted by the struggling dragons' roars, the guile was rising to join the hunt. And, shedding bright smoke as it flew, the victor dragon hurtled down toward him.

He ran under the eaves of the forest, and the boughs threw a sheltering cloak of darkness over him. The sensation was pleasant but brief. The descending dragon roared, and the darkness rolled back. In the red light Morlock saw his shadow caught in an endless distorted web. He ran over the heavy roots and red-barred shadows, dodging tree trunks as he went. The dragon was over his head, above the branches. It was among the branches. It was upon him. It roared, and the blast, though less powerful than Vild's, threw him headfirst against a tree. Dazed and unable to move he lay beneath the clouds of steam and venom, awaiting death.

It did not come. When he was able, he raised his head and looked back. The dragon was struggling, suspended between heaven and earth like a character in the old songs. It was trapped in the dense web of branches—branches that did not burst into flame around it.

Maijarra! They were all around him. Fire had withered their leaves and flowers, but maijarra wood did not burn, even in the deep furnaces of the dwarves.

Morlock got to his feet. He watched the dragon writhe among the branches. Then he turned away. The maijarra forest stretched for miles into the mountains. If he lost himself in it the guile would be unlikely to find him. It seemed altogether likely that he would live long enough to starve or die of cold in the mountains.

He laughed out loud and ran uphill, deeper into the woods and darkness.

It snowed heavily that night, dimming but not altogether silencing the sounds of the pursuing dragons. The snow was, perhaps, lucky for Morlock. If it weren't snowing, he might have been tempted to sleep no matter how cold it seemed. But the discomfort of the wet flakes in the cold air forced him to recognize that sleep would be pleasantly fatal.

Although the trees protected him from the wind, the seemingly endless night was cold indeed. It was an achingly long time since he had eaten, also, and for long moments he found he must stand shivering convulsively, in a senseless outburst of misdirected energy. But when he was able he kept moving over the slush-covered root-crossed ground.

When the light began to return to the sky, the snow ceased. Shortly after that he reached the crest of the long steep slope he had been climbing, which on the far side descended more gradually. The slope now angled down to his right, still more gradually. To his left, through a screen of white-etched black branches, he saw the peaks Gramer, Groja, Wyrtgeorn, Jess, and Fell: the mountains of Haukr. They stood almost mystically clear in the deep blue predawn air, snow lying far down along their shoulders. Ahead of him, he guessed, was the Ruined Mountain—the place where maijarra had collapsed part of the mountain ridge. The forest did not extend any farther than that into the mountains. Nevertheless Morlock felt he would find any cover he needed among the rocks and twisting passages of the Ruined Mountain, until he reached the Thains' Northtower. He did not suppose this would still be standing, but he hoped to find some provisions (and perhaps some clothing) amid the rubble.

As he walked downslope the trees began to grow farther apart. Although this, like the growing light, increased his danger, he could not fail to welcome the open spaces. It was invigorating to see the peaks of the crooked close horizon blaze with white light. The light filled his eyes and his heart; he felt he could go on forever.

As the day grew warmer and the cold loosened its painful numbing grip upon his limbs, Morlock found himself increasingly bored and irritable. It was a little surprising to find himself cursing tree roots that he stumbled over and dimly hating the trees they belonged to when a half a day before (that is, one long dark night before) the forest had certainly saved his life.

Toward afternoon the forest began to grow more dense again, and the slope turned slightly uphill. Perversely Morlock's mood changed, and he began to feel exhilarated. Everything he saw was outlined in light, even the shadows. Little of last night's snow was left. The next snow would surely last, he predicted to himself happily. They were on winter's threshold, and winter never kept the north waiting long. A fragile but intense feeling of strength filled him, and he leapt up the root-woven slope with new eagerness.

In the late afternoon the slope fell away jaggedly and the forest ended abruptly at the verge. Morlock stepped out cautiously into the unbroken sunlight, making his way down the ominously unstable slope of broken stones. The hulk of the Ruined Mountain rose before him as he descended. It would not be wise, he felt, to attempt to scale it after last night's snow and today's thaw had loosened the rocks.

Fortunately he could turn west here. He saw a crooked path leading away from the base of the slope, south and west, through the stones. Yes, he could take that.

Not yet, though. He was not sleepy (fortunately, because he could hardly afford to sleep yet), but he was a little tired. He'd been walking all day and all night . . . and all the previous day, too. And then, he observed hazily to himself, there was everything else.

He sat down on the edge of a flat stone that caught the eastering sun. He was a little surprised that he was not sleepy. He was surprised, too, by the warmth of the sunlight. It was extremely warm. The contrast with last night was welcome, but a little cloudy along with everything else. Still.

He slept.

He awoke to gnawing hunger, darkness, and deadly cold. For a moment he thought he was still in the woods, or even back in Haukrull, only having dreamed his escape. But he felt the flat stone under his hands, now numbingly cold in what must be (a glance at the stars told him) the second hour after sunset. Reality returned to him swiftly. He noted that both the major moons were visible in the eastern half of the crystalline clear sky.

There was a swift, almost noiseless movement on the dark slope above him. Morlock rolled to his feet and saw an equine silhouette, darker than the sky itself, standing over him. He saw the translucent spiral of the single horn, radiant in the light of the major moons. Its eyes, too, seemed to emit a silver light. Morlock met that gaze and lost long moments in strange timeless communion that was not communication.

At last the contact was broken and Morlock stepped back on shifting ground. He looked downward while regaining his balance, and, when he looked up, the unicorn was gone. Off in the night he heard a few light noises, as if rocks were rattling against one another briefly in the windless night. These soon ceased.

Morlock was left wondering. He had rarely seen one of the Swift People so close before, although they lived in the Northhold, as in all the mountains of the Wardlands. But he had heard that blacks were as rare among them as albinos were among the lower animals. He wondered if the meeting was accidental or purposeful, and whose purpose . . .

The Swift People were dangerous; he knew that much. Not so long ago he had seen the corpse of a unicorn hunter in the thickly wooded slopes of the Grartan Range. In ancient days, when the Wardlands and the land of Kaen were contiguous, unicorn-hunting had been a high adventure for the Kaeniar—all the more adventurous for being routinely fatal. And tradition was so powerful in that sun-drenched rocky land that even now a few young aristocrats would cross the Narrow Sea to hunt unicorns among the Grartans. So it had been with this one, whose body Morlock had seen on a patrol from the Lonetower. His poison-tipped lance had been shattered and his chest riven by the beautiful deadly horn he had coveted.

Yet Morlock's pulse was racing not because he had sensed danger. He felt a kind of exhilaration in the apparition's strangeness and, paradoxically, almost a sense of kinship. Unicorns were formidable, and he guessed they might be enemies of dragons. The thought, a comforting one, was new to him.

That comfort didn't alleviate cold or hunger, though. He set off through the dark stone path he had spotted in sunlight, taking his bearings by the stars and his memories of the place. He expected it to be difficult, but in fact it was easier than negotiating the Runhaiar.

He had just left the rubble surrounding the Ruined Mountain when he looked up to take a sight on the stars and saw the Thains' Northtower before him. It was not, as he expected, a dark ruined silhouette; it was whole, and the many windows glittered with lamplight.

Astonished, he made his way toward it, trying to keep either moon from casting his shadow on open ground. He moved toward the tower by a twisting laborious route through rocks and stunted bushes. He was half convinced that this was an illusion or a trap.

There was someone standing slumped against the doorpost in a stance that Morlock knew well. It was one way to catnap on a night watch. When your knees gave way under you, you woke up. It was hard on the knees, though.

Morlock walked up to the door, still believing it was all an illusion. At that moment the thain on watch slumped down farther and then leapt tall in sudden wakefulness. "Who's that?" he cried. "Watchmaster? I—"

Then he bit off his explanations and bent his head forward to peer at Morlock. He was only a shadow in Morlock's eyes, but in the light of the open doorway he could see Morlock well.

"Oh! So it's you, Crookback. With Bleys, were you?"

Then Morlock knew it was no illusion. He almost wished it were.

Chapter Thirteen

Voices

"Come in, Crookback. You look a little chilly!" The watch-thain was someone Morlock had known slightly when he first came to the Lonetower. Morlock did not remember his name, nor he Morlock's apparently.

"How many people are within this tower?" Morlock demanded. "Don't you know the Guard has been broken?"

"Dragons. We know it well enough. We knew it before most." The thain's expression, like his voice, was fatuously self-congratulatory.

"You might have shared the news," Morlock observed bitterly. He thought of Almeijn, of the dead *rokhleni* at Southgate, of the huntresses trapped and killed on the mountain heights when the dragons attacked.

"We've been busy enough without that. Like the Watchmaster says, it's not easy to organize a response to a crisis of this magnitude."

Morlock frowned. He was hungry and tired—perhaps he wasn't thinking clearly. The other thain didn't seem to be making any sense. Response? Crisis? Why hadn't they raised the alarm? Why weren't they hiding in the woods or fighting the dragons in the valley? What were they doing in this indefensible place?

"You'll have to see the Watchmaster, Crook. He wants all refugees to report to him in person."

"Watchmaster? Who's the senior thain?"

"The Watchmaster. It's a handier title. Wait a moment."

The watch-thain pulled a whistle from under his tunic and sounded it three times: two long blasts and a short one. The stones rang with echoes. Morlock fought an impulse to crouch down in hiding.

The watch-thain looked at him and laughed. "A little . . . nervous, eh? Don't worry. You're out of it now. The dragons haven't dared to attack this tower, you know."

"What?" Morlock said sharply. But another thain had come down the entryway, and the door-watch explained to the newcomer that Morlock was to be taken to the Watchmaster. Morlock was suddenly struck by the fact that both thains had green straps sewn into the shoulders of their capes.

"And it's petitioning day, too," the newcomer was lamenting.

"Prioritize it. Watchmaster's special orders override Watchmaster's standing orders. Don't let those silverbuttons get in your way."

The newcomer smiled nervously. "Yes, sir!"

Beneath Morlock's weariness and hunger a dark anger was kindling. He wordlessly allowed the guide-thain to lead him down the lighted corridor within. They went up several flights of long winding stairs. They passed a great number of people sitting on the steps. Everywhere there was the sound of voices, drifting down the access corridors and air shafts, speaking in many dialects of Wardic. The Thains' Northtower was thick with inhabitants. All the survivors of Haukrull must have gathered here, along with any survivors from Lernaion's party.

They finally came to the top of the tower. The corridor at the head of the stair was crowded with people, most of them townsfolk from Haukrull with a few thains mixed in. The heat and smell of the crowd were like body blows to Morlock, already dizzy with weariness and hunger. The guide-thain glanced at Morlock with distaste, seized him by the arm, and began forcing his way through the crowd as if they were sheep, shouting "Make way, petitioners! Priority! Watchmaster's orders!"

There were a few muttered comments at this, but the air in the corridor was as thick with despair as with moisture. Few even complained; no one tried to bar the way.

Suddenly a clear familiar voice spoke out. "Morlock, Tyr's son, or it's not? Hey, Elder Brother—that your face, ugly?"

Morlock turned toward the voice. It belonged to Trua, oldest of Haukrull's Women Old. "Trua Old!" he laughed. "I thought you must be dead!"

The old woman laughed in turn. "You look as if you went to find out! You've come from where? With Lernaion you were not."

"Come along," the guide-thain said impatiently. "No time for talking with petitioners."

"Yes," said Morlock, "come along Trua Old. I'm going to talk to the senior thain. You must have a thing to say to him."

"As you say, Elder Brother," the Woman Old agreed.

The guide-thain began to argue against this, but Morlock and Trua simply left him behind in the suddenly uncooperative crowd.

"Why did you come to this death trap, Old?" Morlock asked.

"We were hungry, Morlocktheorn." She shook her head toward Morlock, suggesting that he shared the condition. "Food the Guardians had; none had we. But the townsfolk's rations again now have been cut—to less than a quarter a watch-herald's. Live for long on that we will not."

They had come to the door that closed off the end of the corridor. A thain, with a rough silver circle pinned to the left shoulder of his cape, was standing before the door, holding a long wooden pole with his hands.

"Stand and wait, petitioners," he said, barring the way.

The guide-thain came up behind them. "Priority, Lieutenant Sel. The special order on refugees."

"Acknowledged, Watchman. Dismissed."

The guide-thain turned and made his way back down the corridor. The "lieutenant" rapped his pole on the door behind him, and it was opened from within.

Morlock reached out and touched the insignia on the thain's shoulder. "What's this?" he demanded. "Rank?"

The "lieutenant" looked offended and nodded stiffly.

"First Decree!" Morlock's voice was low, but penetrating.

"The Watchmaster—"

"Then," Morlock interrupted him brusquely. "Old, precede me."

"After you, Elder Brother."

"I'm no one's elder now."

Trua nodded thoughtfully and went ahead into the airy many-windowed chamber that now lay open before them.

The senior thain sat behind a long table, flanked by two "lieutenants." A golden triangle hung around his neck on a light chain. There was a row of green-strapped watch-thains around the wall of the large semicircular room. They were unarmed, but their presence was threatening; probably the threat was intentional. Morlock clenched his teeth.

All in the room had heard the exchange with the door-ward. Some of the subordinates looked concerned, but the senior thain was unruffled.

"Make your report, Thain," he said briskly. "You're young Ambrosius, aren't you? Go on."

After a pause, Morlock replied carefully, "I am not under your authority."

"Never mind that; there's precedent. A number of Lernaion's party have accepted my authority."

"I was not with Lernaion." Morlock paused again, then continued reluctantly, "I speak for the summoner Earno."

For the first time the senior thain looked disturbed. "Nevertheless . . ."

"Put that aside!" Morlock broke in. "Why have you put Guardians in authority over the Guarded? Why have you created badges of rank for your peers? Have you invented oaths of allegiance to go with them?" He saw from the open fear among the watch-thains that this guess had struck home. All these things were violations of the First Decree.

He pressed on, quietly but with increasing anger, "Why have you compelled people in flight from disaster to inhabit this death trap, under pain of starvation? When did you first learn of the invasion of dragons? And why did you fail to raise the alarm throughout the north—throughout the Wardlands?"

His emotion had gotten the upper hand of his breath control; he had to pause to draw in air, then continued. "Answer all of these questions or none of them. I am not your superior. But I go on to Thrymhaiam, where the summoner awaits my return."

Now the senior thain looked confident, even smug, again. "You won't find that an easy journey. But, although I admit some of my procedures are novel, all that I have done I have done to guard the Guarded. Indeed, if the crisis is of prolonged duration, I hope to—that is, it may be necessary to institute similar reforms throughout the Wardlands. No one is kept here under duress, you see. Those who choose to stay are allowed to present their petitions, in an orderly manner, every fifth day, time permitting. Further, I could hardly have done better than to, well, encourage these townfolk to take refuge in this well-guarded fortress. As a newcomer I think you can hardly appreciate the difficulties involved in organizing a response to an emergency of this magni—"

Morlock felt his anger breaking through its restraints. "The Northtower is not a fortress. It is a farmhouse and a training station. It was built a century after the north came under the Guard and has never faced an enemy—until now."

"Then how do you explain—"

"I am not here to explain anything. But I tell you that a single dragon in its fury could lay this building's foundations bare to the sky."

"The tower has protected us so far," the senior thain insisted. "The dragons do not even dare to attack us!"

"Dragons do not eat flatbread and dried meat. To them it is chicken feed. And this is their henhouse. Like chickens you eat and strut and fight among yourselves and maintain your strictest protocol. And one day, when you are sufficiently fat, the dragons will smash your walls and pluck you, wriggling, from the rubble—"

"Take them out," said the senior thain in an iron voice. "Put that thain under restraint with the others—for the safety of the Guarded."

"Out? Out?" Trua muttered. "Out or in, this is land of me and mine. These stones were quarried from Thrymhaiam's sides, and bought or sold they were not ever. This fellow and I have the voice to claim this tower back. Decree of the Graith, you wand-wavers!"

Morlock gripped her by the forearm. "Trua! You are half-right."

"So much? I think you're getting soft, Elder Brother."

"I can't speak for Thrymhaiam. But you can reclaim the land for Haukrull. So you must."

"What? Morlock, I was just talking. Father of yours would forgive me never, if I let them lock you up."

"Locks are nothing. You must take the provisions from the tower and go into the maijarra woods. Otherwise you'll die."

"So what? Morlock, I'm tired. The people are tired. Toron my own is dead. So are half of the Women Old. We don't want to fight folks of our own."

"So what? So what?" Morlock said wearily. "So Toron died like a hero so you could live like a slave?"

Shock lit up Trua's faded features like lightning. They became tense with grief and anger as the shock wore away, finally settling into a look of calm suspicion as she regained control of herself. "Strike me," she said, "for forgetting you, Elder Brother. You were the trader worst that Thrymhaiam ever sent east of the Haukr. But you got people's attention, and your goods, they sold themselves."

"Then."

"Your slang Dwarvish! Toron died in his bed, Morlock, because I was too afraid to go back into the house and warn him. Instead I ran away. Now, though, I am tired of running."

Morlock shrugged and looked away. The public nature of Trua's confession embarrassed him more than its content. Anyone with any sense would run from a dragon.

"Mind it, don't," Trua said. "Too long I've let that hobble me. Go back to Thrymhaiam, Morlock; tell them you sold the goods."

Morlock took this literally as a dismissal. He did not suppose she would ever forgive what he had said to her; he found it hard to see why she should. But there was one more thing he could do before he left. He went to the door of the room and opened it. To the expectant crowd outside he cried in full voice, "Trua of the Women Old has words for witnesses."

In the moment of silence that followed this traditional call to a Haukrull town meeting Morlock saw that the door-ward had taken off his silver circle of rank. Then the members of the crowd began to well forward through the door, their voices clashing like spears against shields.

Morlock made his way through the crowd around the door and down the suddenly empty hallway. The refectory was in the basement, he knew; he had often travelled between here and the Lonetower. The stairway leading down was full of voices, some of them very angry now, but he met no one as he descended.

Morlock had a bad night. He drank a good deal of water—his throat burned with an incredible thirst—but when food was brought to him he found he could eat almost nothing. He drank some broth, but even that felt like stone in his stomach, and finally came back up glistening dark with venom. After vomiting he felt better, but he decided against eating again.

He bedded down in the storeroom with the provisioner's blessing. His sleep was troubled with ugly dreams, but he awoke only once, when Trua's people came to take charge of the stores.

Awareness took hold as he recognized the provisioner's sweaty face hanging over him, like a ceiling tile about to fall.

"Morlock, tell them!" he pleaded obscurely.

Morlock propped himself up on one elbow and looked around blearily. The small room was full of townfolk. At least he recognized some of them from the old days in Haukrull; none wore thainish gray.

"They've come to take me away," the provisioner said. "I had no rank. I gave out the rations as I was told. I'm just a provisioner."

"What is it?" Morlock asked, of no one in particular.

"Trua Old has reclaimed the Northtower for Haukrull and Thrymhaiam," said one, a woman in a brown cloak. "All stores raised on Haukrull land revert to the care of the Women Old. One of us will take over here. Meanwhile, the Women Old wish to speak with all the thains."

Morlock began to sit up. "Except you," the woman in brown said hastily. Morlock was perversely tempted to insist. But he was very tired, and equally reluctant to identify with these renegades.

"Go with them, Rhume," he said. "Trua Old won't let you be hurt. Remember me to her. . . ."

He must have slept then; he remembered nothing else. The next morning the townwoman in charge of the storerooms willingly issued him a change of clothes and a water bottle. She was more reluctant to surrender a thain's cloak, but Morlock pressed the point and she gave in.

Later that morning Trua met Morlock at the tower door. She was wearing the senior thain's golden triangle.

"Spoils of the hunt," she said curtly, when she noticed Morlock glancing at it. "So you're going to Thrymhaiam really?"

Morlock nodded.

"As walks go, a longish," she remarked.

It was, perhaps, a full day's walk. Morlock suspected, however, that she was referring to the fact that every step of the way was over open ground. Or did she simply mean it would take the rest of his life to complete it? He grunted.

"Stop that. Talk to me, you convert to dwarfhood."

Morlock laughed. "I'll tell those who wait in Thrymhaiam about you, Old."

"You'll live so long; likely it's not. I think we should send the Watchmaster of yours instead still."

"Watchmaster of mine he's not."

"Mock me, then. Who taught you to talk like a souther?"

"Yesterday you said I talk like a dwarf."

"You do so. A dwarf souther."

Morlock shrugged, half smiling. His smile faded rapidly, and he said, "I'm going now, Old."

She stepped forward and embraced him quickly. "Bye, Morlock Thain. I guess we'll be dead soon both. But it's better to die like this—giving in, not ever."

"Good-bye, Old," he said into her thin gray hair. "Take to the woods. We'll come for you from Thrymhaiam."

"Fool. Go, now, or are you waiting for dark?"

Morlock turned and walked out the open doorway. It was a radiant forenoon; he could not believe the sky held anything but clean light and white clouds. Yet it did, of course. He circled around the tower and, as soon as he reached the stubbly fields on the west side, began to run.

It would have been wiser to wait until nightfall. But it would not have been much wiser, since dragons could see well enough at night. And any waiting was dangerous; the longer he waited the harder it would be to leave. Soon he would be calling himself by a new title and organizing a response to a crisis of this magnitude. . . .

The high fields were golden still in the noonday sun. But the ground had a hardness to it. Fall was ending in the Northhold. There were storm clouds building on the southern horizon; Morlock knew winter was in them.

On the western horizon, gemlike and clear in the distance, he saw the High Gates of Thrymhaiam. They stood above the Coriam Lakes, source of the stream that ran through Helgrind chasm. There was a footpath from the cliff-edge of these high fields down to the cold blue lakes of Coriam. Morlock rarely had occasion to take that path, but he knew it well enough by sight. He'd stood many a watch at the High Gate. Visitors never came that way, so the watch often made their way down to the lakes to swim or to catch the occasional surreptitious fish. (Very surreptitious Morlock had always found them, anyway, but he wasn't much of an angler.)

A rumbling sound, like slow-building thunder, reached him from the south. He threw himself down in the golden stubble, watching and listening breathlessly. The ground was cold, giving the lie to the dreamlike warmth of the golden fields. Likewise the innocent blue-white sky could be pierced at any moment by the red fire of dragons. They must be watching this way, to make certain their captives in the Northtower did not escape to Thrymhaiam. Still, as Morlock lay on the ground he realized they had not seen him yet. Slowly he got to his feet and continued his run westward.

He reached the border of the fields that the thains of Northtower kept under cultivation. He ran on into the narrow mountain meadows. The going seemed slow, and Morlock soon found himself out of breath. He continued walking when he could no longer run, then ran again when he had swallowed some water and caught his breath. Sprinting and walking in turn he watched the western horizon open up and grow closer.

He expected every moment the occasion he could not plan for. A dragon would appear on the horizon, a cloud of dark smoke in the clean afternoon air; it would see him and stoop like a hawk. He imagined it a thousand ways as he ran and walked toward his lengthening shadow. He refused to imagine what would happen next. After all, he would have to face it soon enough. But he couldn't prevent the images of danger from rising unbidden in his mind.

Consequently he felt a strange sort of apprehension as he, at the end of the day, began to approach the ragged edge of the high fields. Something was wrong; he should not have gotten this far. Not only was he still alive, the dragons had not even seen him.

He looked longingly at the High Gates, just across the narrow valley. They gleamed red-gold against the already blue-black western sky. A gradual slope lifted upon his right hand; he knew that the footpath down to the lakes began on the other side. The temptation was to dash up the slope and down the path beyond. His body, which had run this far, was unwilling to keep still. He attempted to placate it with a mouthful of water, only to find his water bottle was dry. Yet he forced himself to stand under the slope and think the matter through.

Since the dragons knew the refugees must pass this way, they would have put a guard in the valley itself. This would enable them to keep an eye on activity in the High Gates at the same time. He crept cautiously up to the edge of the cliff, soil giving way to bare stone beneath his feet. He looked up and down the valley. Nowhere in its cool dimness did he see the sign of a dragon. There was no fire, no smoke, no tang of venom in the air.

Trying to ponder the matter coldly, Morlock felt his heart rising within him. It would be just that easy after all. He would scramble down the steep footpath, cross the narrow valley, and climb up to the High Gates. In an hour he would be home. Perhaps he should try to catch a fish. It was a small enough risk, after all that he had run, and what a joke it would be when he handed it solemnly to the watch-dwarves in the High Gates. Against his will he smiled and looked up the slope he would climb to reach the path downward. There was a sharp crag just beyond, picturesque in the red evening light. Memorable. He didn't actually remember it, but he had never seen it from this angle, in this fiery light. It looked like . . . It looked as if . . .

Morlock threw himself on the ground, just barely out of sight of the hulking brown dragon perched on the cliff. He found himself trembling. It was perched directly over the footpath leading down the cliff, its color blending in with the native rock. Fortunately Morlock had seen its head move as it glanced back along the valley. He wondered if it had seen him. He wondered what he should do.

He saw a white dragon-lungful of cool steam puff upward in the air. After some long moments, another followed. The shadows had risen in the meantime so that the second appeared dark blue at first. But even when it reached the zone of sunlight it seemed darker, heavier, smokier than the first breath.

What was happening? Was the dragon waking up after a long period of sleep or inactivity? (Did dragons sleep? Heroes in the old songs who depended on this invariably came to a bad end.) Would now be the best time to dart down the footpath? He discarded that thought immediately. The best time for that, if there was one, had now passed. The dragon, no matter how sluggish, would simply reach down and pluck him like a mouse off the cliff.

He could jump. The idea sprang into his awareness fully formed. Coldly, he considered it. The dragon would certainly see him. But it was the quickest way down the cliff face, without question. If he lived, perhaps he would be able to make his way into Helgrind. He had an idea the chasm, at its deepest, was too narrow for a dragon's wingspan—probably the only reason Almeijn had reached Thrymhaiam before she died. He could ask for no more. And some of the very deepest of the Coriam Lakes came right up to the foot of the cliff. It was possible, distinctly possible. But it was not a very dwarvish thing to do: few among the dwarves claimed any skill at watercraft. He found himself struggling against the idea.

He looked up and saw the puffs of steam had become a continuous trail of black smoke, forming a venomous cloud overhead in the rising dusk. Then he knew the merits of his idea were not a matter of debate. Either the dragon had already seen him, in which case it was preparing to come get him, or it would soon take flight for other reasons. But as soon as it took to the air it would see him and kill him. To jump was his only chance. He would take it, or lie still to await death.

He took it. He leapt to his feet and turned sharply left, away from the dragon, running along the ragged edge of the cliff. His eye caught the dark glitter of water below him just as the dragon roared; it had seen him at last. His feet skittered instinctively toward the edge when the dragon roared, but he drew them back and ran on along the verge. The water below was still too far from the cliff.

The dragon roared again, and this time its breath took fire. The cool blue dusk was transfigured into a nightmare by the bloodred light. Morlock heard its wings whistling in the air and looked over his shoulder as he ran. The dragon was lifting itself off the stone ledge. Then the ground disappeared from under his own feet. His mouth formed an involuntary shout of surprise, but he hit the ground before his lungs could issue it. He had fallen only about an arm's length; so he found as he rolled to his feet. But he had wasted time. The dragon was approaching. He saw water below him. He jumped out from the cliff with all his strength.

He fell for four hundred years, light as a leaf in the evening air. That was how it seemed, anyway. As he turned, falling, he saw the heavy batwinged dragon sweep over and turn downward in a steep controlled fall. It roared a third time, and the light spread like burning oil across the dark water below. Morlock believed the dragon was gaining on him, driving itself downward with its wings. The glittering waterscape vaulted upward and struck him like a field of stone.

Morlock arced through the dark water, struggling to make progress toward the surface and the shore. Then the dragon plunged into the lake, and the dark water became redly opalescent with fire and turbulence.

He felt a powerful current drawing him backward and down as the water went dark again. He fought the water savagely, hating it. It was the water keeping him from the air he needed so painfully, the water that was pushing him back toward the dragon. And in the middle of his struggle to hold his breath he realized he was tormentingly thirsty. It became a terrible temptation to open his lips and let the killing water in. He clenched his teeth. His feet touched something solid and he kicked off upward, finally breaking the surface. Expecting the dragon's abysslike jaws to open up beneath him at any moment, he swam over the center of the turbulence and fought his way to shore.

With almost the last of his strength he drew himself up on the rock ledge bordering the lake and crawled into the surrounding brush. He lay there for a few moments gasping, then crawled out and tried hopelessly to take his bearings for the Helgrind. He had fallen to the ground and was struggling back to his knees when he realized the dragon had not followed him out of the water. He looked back and saw that the turbulence in the lake was slowly clearing. At its center a dark shape lay still.

The serpentine shape was sinking out of sight in the once-blue water. A heavy layer of fog diffused the light of the major moons—which, in any case, would have only lit up the surface of the lake, now greasy with expelled venom.

That gave Morlock, perched on the stone ledge above the water, his first clue as to what had happened. The dragon had been thirsty. That was all! With the heat of its body and the venom secreted in its mouth or throat, a dragon must nearly always be thirsty. When it landed in the water after its sleep, it automatically began to drink. Perhaps, at first, it was only trying to draw him back into its jaws. In any case, it had been unable to stop drinking. It gorged itself on water until it drowned, until the fire in its heart was quenched.

Morlock, his own thirst still burning in his throat, thought of his own struggle to hold his breath and was faintly sickened. The feeling was not dispelled by the voices of his *harven* kin, the watch of the High Gates, as they ran down the mountainside crying, "*Rokhlan! Rokhlan!* Dragonkiller! Dragonkiller!"

That night Earno dreamed of his victory.

Kellander Rukh again flew in the sky, his ruin surrounding him like a smoky many-winged halo. Earno again stood on the deck of the *Stonebreaker*. He heard the death-cries of the captain below. He saw the mainmast in flames, the crew abandoning ship on every side. Everything was as it had been.

Except that, when Earno stood forth in pride and despair to cry out his own challenge to the master dragon, his voice broke and he found he could not speak. The dragon paused, called out his name in a mocking voice, and fell like a golden thunderbolt. The dream was over.

He awoke in darkness, in the grip of the same ominous feeling that had dogged him since midsummer. He realized that little Shoy, his new guide, was at his bedside, calling out his name.

Shoy told him that it was after midnight and that Morlock had returned from Haukrull. There was some confusion at first, as Shoy kept referring to Morlock as "the Dragonkiller."

PART FOUR

AGAINST EVERYTHING

Now I have a friend, for instance—why, goodness gracious, gentlemen, he is also a friend of yours, and indeed, whose friend is he not? In undertaking any business this gentleman at once explains in high-sounding and clear language how he intends to act in accordance with the laws of truth and reason. And not only that. He will talk to you, passionately and vehemently, all about real and normal human interests; he will scornfully reproach the shortsighted fools for not understanding their own interests, nor the real meaning of virtue and—exactly a quarter of an hour later, without any sudden or external cause, but just because of some inner impulse which is stronger than any of his own interests, he will do something quite different, that is to say, he will do something that is exactly contrary to what he has been saying himself: against laws of reason and against his own interests, in short, against everything.

—Dostoevsky, *Notes from the Underground*

CHAPTER FOURTEEN

Control

Ven was restless. He didn't like the bed. He felt exposed there, unprotected. He got up and tried the metal door of his cell. It was still locked. That no longer bothered him; he was used to it. But now he began to want a lock on his own side—he had no way to keep anyone out.

He went back to bed. If he crouched down behind it he would see whoever came in before they saw him. He tried it once and immediately felt safer.

Suddenly he saw a stone bottle that had been filled with water. It was lying in the far corner of the room. It occurred to him that, if he happened to fall asleep, even for a moment, someone could unlock the door and take the bottle, without him even knowing. The event was quite clear in his mind—it was just the sort of thing they *would* do. He imagined himself sleeping, the opening door, a long arm appearing in the door, hand outstretched like a snake's hood as it fell toward the bottle . . . *his* bottle. The thought pained him inexpressibly. He envisioned the event again and again, gnawing the ends of his fingers in vexation and fear.

Finally he could stand it no more. They had pushed him too far. Choosing his moment carefully, he leapt over the barricade and dashed to the corner. He snatched up the bottle and plunged back over the barricade. Safe! Even if they had seen him it was too late to act. If they came at him now he would bite them, as he had the other time. He had seized the moment and its fruit was his. They must be frustrated indeed, knowing the bottle was now his, never to be theirs.

He added the bottle to his little pile of possessions. There was a ring, a wax tablet and stylus, the buckles from his belt and boots (polished to an unsatisfyingly dull gloss). It was not so much, he thought sadly, looking at them, but it was a start. The bottle was a significant addition.

The florid words and complex theologies that had been impressed upon his memory were fading. They would have stayed vivid and clear only if he had put them to use. But even now he could remember some of them.

He muttered, "Asserted unities generate their opposites, resulting in dualities of opposition. Unbalanced trinities degenerate into dualities of opposition. Trinities can only be balanced by opposing trinities, resulting in effective dualities of opposition. In this way we can see that duality of opposition is the fundamental principle of existence. There is no unity; there is only duality."

He licked his lips (he was so thirsty!) and thought about gold.

Morlock was vomiting outside the High Gates when Tyrtheorn and Earno arrived. Deor was already there, perched on a rock safely out of the way.

"I don't think you're really trying, Morlock," he was saying sardonically. "There! That was better!"

Morlock retched again; the splashing sound that followed was painfully clear in the dark quiet of predawn. He spat, coughed, spat again. He shuddered violently a few times. Then, after remaining still for a moment, he said carefully, "Thank you."

"Bah. Don't be so polite. Get that venom out of you."

Morlock cleared his throat and spat. "I need something to drink," he said.

They both stood up, and that was when they saw the Eldest and the summoner standing in the gateway.

"Morlock's been doctoring himself," Deor said, breaking the embarrassed silence. He jumped down from the rock and ran past Tyr and Earno. There was a cask of beer in the watchroom off the corridor within. Deor drew a couple of mugs, exchanged a few words with the dwarves on watch, and walked back.

". . . that you knew this treatment for venom," Earno was saying.

Morlock nodded. "They taught us at the Lonetower. The Kaeniar use a venom like that of the dragons—Ah, Deor. Thanks." Morlock took one of the mugs and turned toward the darkness. He could be heard gargling a mouthful of beer, then rinsing out his mouth with the rest of the mugful. He turned back to them. Deor silently handed him the second mug, accepting the empty one in exchange.

"The worst part of it was eating," said Morlock, after a long pull on the mug. "I had to give the purge something to work on, you see." He drank again.

"Morlock, you're making me sick," Deor complained.

"Oh. I'm out of beer."

"I thought you were going to drink it, not water your chin with it!" Deor exploded. "I could roll the cask out here if you feel the urge to wash your hair."

"Um. No, thanks. I am beginning to be hungry, though."

"That's really revolting!" Deor exclaimed. "How can you talk about food after . . . What about a decent interval?"

"Three days is interval enough," muttered Morlock.

"I agree," Tyr said. "Deor, you can wait decently out here. Come within, Rokhlan; I think I hear the watch making breakfast."

"There's only one *rokhlan* here," Morlock said, as he followed his *harven* father into the High Gate. "The sentinel-dragon killed itself—"

"*Athru rokhleni! Rokhleni! Ath! Ath!*" It was the watch of the High Gates, calling into the corridor from the watchroom.

"Kinfolk," said Tyr, "I understand that there are two opinions about Morlock's title—"

A chorus of shouts interrupted him, Dwarvish and Wardic mixing together.

Deor was following Earno through the gateway. "Canyon keep it!" the young dwarf swore. "Don't let Morlock tell the story. 'I was just standing there, and this dragon—'"

The members of the watch came out and gathered them into the watchroom. Earno felt as if he had stumbled into a family celebration—a family he did not know, but had mistaken him for one of its own. They called him Rokhlan and seated him at the third place of honor, on the Eldest's right hand, as they sat down to listen to the story of Morlock's victory.

It was a great thing, in the north, to be a dragonkiller. The Eldest had explained it to Earno as they had travelled north to the High Gates. It went back to the Longest War (as so many things did) that had been fought between dragon and dwarf in these mountains. But the last dragon had been banished from the north long before it came under the Guard. Thus no one for millennia had earned the high title of *rokhlan* . . . except for the five heroes of Southgate, who were all dead now. (To be a *rokhlan* was frequently a posthumous honor.)

So it was Morlock who (after he had thoroughly doused himself at the washbasin) was seated at the head of the stone table in the watchroom; even Eldest Tyr sat below, on his right hand. He ate the bread and cheese and meat that the watch pressed on him, drank water, and listened glumly as Deor and a few members of the watch retold his exploit of the Coriam Lakes as he had told it to them, along with certain observations of their own.

He seemed particularly crooked and Ambrosian to Earno as he nodded over his half-empty plate. Earno couldn't even see details; anger, like a dark red cloud haloing the thain, prevented him from seeing Morlock clearly. Morlock shook off his sleepiness or gloom enough to glance at Earno, perhaps hoping to see how his senior was taking in the story. Earno looked away hastily, before their eyes had time to meet. (Had Morlock seen the flash of red light in his eyes? If he had, what could be done to remove him?)

For a time Earno watched Deor tell Morlock's story. He was too busy with his own thoughts to pay much attention, but he vaguely noted that the young dwarf seemed both proud of and angry at his *harven* kin.

Only at the end did Morlock himself speak. The watch-dwarves were telling how they had found him at the edge of the lake, "preparing to dive in and cut the collar from the dragon's throat."

"Eh, no," said Morlock. "Spare me that, kinfolk! I was only thinking."

"Well," said one of the watch, "but you won't tell us what you were thinking about."

"He won't tell us much of anything," Deor explained to Tyr and Earno. "When I arrived they were just beginning to worm the dragon story out of him. But he won't tell us anything about his trip through Haukrull, nor even where he got his change of clothes. We've decided there must be some sort of Guardian's decree against it—"

Earno had been angered by the thought that Morlock had already told the tale of his embassy to his kin. Finding himself wrong, Earno was irrationally angered again, as if this were a new and separate injury. Had it not been for the compulsion to secrecy, to silence, he would have burst forth with angry denunciations. They took form in his mind, like dark red clouds, but he could not free himself of them by speech. He must not speak. He could not. *Silence!*

The summoner found Tyr looking at him curiously, and he avoided meeting the Eldest's eye. Tyr noted the action, and it obviously surprised and concerned him. But when he finally spoke he did not refer to it.

"There is a room above this one," the Eldest said, "where you can hear Morlock's full report in privacy. I am needed elsewhere, but Deor will remain to learn those things which may immediately affect the safety of the Deep Halls."

Afraid to do more, Earno nodded stiffly, rose, and left the room. (What did the Eldest know? What did he, at least, suspect? Was he, too, part of the plot? If he was, there might be some way to eliminate him also.) Earno heard Morlock follow him more slowly, and he clenched his teeth.

There was a window in the upper chamber, something Earno was inclined to view as a luxury after days under Thrymhaiam. He seated himself on the stone bench carved out of the wall beneath the window. Looking outward to the east, he saw a dim light reflected on the mountains, although the sky beyond them was still a dark blue. Without returning his gaze to the chamber, he made an imperious gesture at Morlock, indicating that the thain might begin his report.

Morlock, entering behind the summoner, had noted that there were no other chairs. He therefore seated himself on the floor, with his back to the southern wall of the chamber. Having settled himself, he began to speak.

He began by telling of his encounter with Saijok Mahr under the Drowned Arches. Earno was interested, in a distant way, but to Morlock's amazement he completely discounted the importance of Saijok Mahr's exile under the mountains.

"The young bulls," he said, deigning to explain the matter to his thain, "often go into temporary exile after an unsuccessful challenge to the master, if they survive the duel. Eventually they return to the guile. Any idea of independent action during their exile—it's simply out of the question."

This was so imperceptive and unexpected a remark that Morlock found himself unable to continue his tale. After a few moments of silence, Earno glanced at him briefly (there was something strange, even serpentine, about that swift look) and said, "This clashes with some idea of your own, I take it."

"Yes," Morlock replied. "The guile . . . if it is a guile . . . There is nothing typical about it. They are all . . . All of them are masters in the Blackthorn Range. And Saijok, he . . . it . . . It is not merely a discontent, but one of the two great masters of the Blackthorn Range who were chosen by . . . by the Two Powers to . . . lead this . . ." He was unsure whether to call it an invasion or a raid. He felt the halting, unconvincing nature of his speech very clearly and wanted to use the precisely correct word.

Earno said stiffly, "These are but speculations of Vendas."

Vendas? Vendas? Was that a title of Merlin's? Morlock wondered. He now dreaded trying to explain the source of his knowledge about the Two Powers. How could he explain it, when he didn't understand it? But surely Vendas was a Dwarvish name; Das was one of the Seven Clans under Thrymhaiam. "Beg pardon, Summoner," he said, "but I know nothing of Vendas."

"Vendas who was spellbound. Surely your kinsman Deor told you."

Morlock shook his head, forbearing to comment that Deor was not a man.

"Vendas," Earno said with an odd intonation in his voice, "was one of those left spellbound after the first attack on Thrymhaiam. Some days later, when Vendas failed to improve, Deor (for reasons he does not explain) attempted a very dangerous experiment, forcing Vendas to drink . . . an infusion of certain herbs. The spell was ultimately loosed, but its aftereffects appear to be permanent."

"I don't understand."

"I'll explain. The dragon who bound Vendas filled his mind with . . . preachings about the Two Powers, as you call them. He was commanded to be a missionary for them in the Wardlands, and promised great rewards if he was successful. He can think of nothing but obeying those commands."

"Then the spell is not loosed."

"You are unsubtle. There is no spell. But he remembers the vision of the power and the rewards that were to be his. That vision obsesses him. He will do anything to obtain those rewards, not because the spell lingers, but because the spell-that-was fit too thoroughly well into a flaw in his character. The pressure on that flaw has broken his mind, and his will is no longer his own."

Morlock pondered this in silence.

"So you see," Earno continued, finally, "there is no reason, no matter what your . . . kinsmen may believe, to suppose that the Two Powers, as you call them, have any real existence. The dragons have simply attempted to use that religion—which is common in areas south of the Blackthorns—for purposes of their own."

He went on for some time in this way. Morlock ceased listening almost immediately. To his mind, the story of Vendas confirmed his "memories" linking the dragons with the Two Powers. But he saw that Earno would resist the idea, if he mentioned that odd visionary experience in Haukrull. Still . . . perhaps he ought to try. . . .

Morlock abruptly became conscious of a silence that already seemed to have lasted a long time. He looked up and saw the summoner again staring out the window. This was the bitterest of insults to a dwarf, worse even than staring over one's head while talking. Perhaps Earno was unaware of this, or perhaps he was offended by Morlock's inattention. Now it seemed as if Morlock must explain his "memories" of the Two Powers, to explain his preoccupation.

Something held him back, though. It was something like resentment, or perhaps merely disappointment. This was not how he had imagined his conference with Earno would go. He had hoped he would be able to tell Earno everything that had happened. Then Earno would explain to him whatever was confusing: the strange corpse in Saijok Mahr's pool, the repulsive and frightening notion that dragons and dwarves were somehow akin, the ineffectiveness of dragonspell upon him. Perhaps, he had thought, Earno would even explain those nightmarish memories of . . . of *being* Merlin. Morlock had never once doubted that Earno could do all this. Earno was wise; what he did not know he could find ways to understand.

But things were going wrong. Earno would not even listen to what he knew for certain, much less explain to him what remained mysterious. Earno, indeed, was rich in explanations, but they meant nothing; they were intended to cover up facts, not account for them.

Morlock acknowledged his resentment, but strove to keep it in check. He had spoken badly, perhaps. Earno came from a different folk. The fault might be his own. There might be no fault. In any case, he would correct the situation now. He would make Earno (Earno that fool he had tried to warn him)—he would *make* him understand.

Speaking carefully, slowly and in detail he explained. He had much to say, but he began with the matter of Vendas. He told Earno everything that had passed between him and his *harven* kin at the High Gates before Earno's arrival. He demonstrated, with mechanical precision, that Deor could have told him nothing about the Two Powers, or else that he himself was an irrecoverable liar.

Earno seemed to believe him, becoming more receptive as he spoke. But Morlock did not relax.

He found his apprehension justified. When he concluded Earno remarked, "This confirms my impression. You must have been under a dragonspell—"

Morlock reflected gloomily that this was one more thing he could not tell the summoner. If he claimed at this point to be immune to dragonspell . . . well, he simply would not be believed. He reflected that if Earno was intent on disbelieving everything he said, there had been little point in sending him to Haukrull. Almost absentmindedly he remarked, "I am not under a dragonspell. You may test this, if you like."

"Nevertheless, you may have been—"

"If I had been and it had passed I would remember the placing of the spell." He was baiting the summoner, in a way—daring him to say the word *liar.*

Earno sensed the defiance without understanding it and let some of his own long-held anger loose. "I think I have more experience in these matters than you—"

"Summoner, it was I who stood before Saijok Mahr and Vild Kharum. That is my experience. It was what you sent me to do."

"Then make your report!" the summoner commanded.

It was the last chance, Morlock knew. If Earno learned, in this temper, that he had deliberately not delivered the challenge . . . it would mean he would no longer be heard. If only the summoner were not so suspicious, so reluctant to approach the truths Morlock had to tell him.

Again he began slowly, describing in detail the entrance to Saijok Mahr's den. Too much detail, it seemed; before long Earno broke in impatiently. "Get to the point!"

It was no use, Morlock decided. He told the rest of his story in five flat sentences. After concluding his narrative he added, "Trua and her people will need assistance before winter sets in, or they will die. If you permit, I will tell the Eldest of them."

Earno heard him through with obviously increasing anger. The summoner kept his face averted (scornfully, so Morlock thought), so he could be seen only in profile. "That confirms it, then," he said, when Morlock was finished speaking. "You willfully disobeyed my command. You must have been under control."

"I was not!" Morlock shouted, losing his temper at last.

"Don't be too eager to deny it, Thain. It may be all that stands between you and exile."

Morlock leapt to his feet, biting back an inarticulate cry of anger. "More than that . . ." he said, choking with anger, "there is more than that between me and exile. I had no absolute command to deliver a challenge. You said it yourself, you said . . . if we knew there was a guile in Haukrull there'd be no need . . . to send me there. I was sent, first, to . . . to find out. To learn—"

"You found a guile. You spoke to the master. The challenge should have been given."

"There is a guile and there is not," Morlock replied. "Why will you not understand? This is not a guile as you know them. It does not live and die by the fear of a single leader. Your challenge is a futile gambit—"

"There is enough despair being preached beneath these mountains—"

"I do not despair. There is a way. If you will listen—"

"I have been listening. That is your problem, Thain—not that I have not heard you, but that I have heard you all too well."

Morlock shook his head and tried to begin again. "Listen—that is . . . Listen, Summoner. Suppose what you say is true. What harm has it done—" He broke off, enraged at the weakness of his appeal, the pleading in his voice. Why should he have to persuade his senior to hear the facts he had been commanded to learn?

"What harm?" said the summoner incredulously. "Instead of awaiting my advent the master may have taken the guile hunting through the Wardlands!"

Morlock found this too senseless to even be infuriating. Clearly the dragons aimed to reduce the north to captivity first. If they had intended to attack the rest of the Wardlands they'd had the months of summer and fall to do it in. "Well. Has he?" Morlock demanded dryly.

"Who are you to make demands of me," Earno shouted, "as if I were the thain and you were the summoner? I no longer require your presence, Thain Morlock, here or anywhere in the north. Tomorrow I will send you south with a letter. In the meantime—get out!"

Morlock turned and left the room without speaking.

That night in dreams, Morlock was Merlin the exile. For a tenth of all they possessed the citizens of Aflraun had purchased his services. For that price, paid in advance, Ambrosius swore to defend them against Earno Summoner, the dragon who threatened their homes with his guile.

The accursed sword Gryregaest glittered darkly in Ambrosius' hand as the dragon swept in from the west and south. The towers of Aflraun were lit up by the dragon's blood-bright spell-haunted eyes, like the peaks of Thrymhaiam in evening light.

Traitor! Liar! Exile! the dragon snarled. *I know you, Ambrosius, and your kind.*

Ambrosius raised the sword Gryregaest in reply; the blue light of banefire still surrounded it. The deadly light flared in midair and tightened around Earno Dragon like a net of blazing blue wires. The dragon began to burn with blue light, and continued to burn until there was nothing left of the dragon but a pile of ashes, like a heavy white cloak in the blue light of the banefire. He laughed, with a terrifying sense of vengeance achieved, until something stirred under the white cloak, crying, "Morlock!"

Guilt was the hook dragging him to wakefulness. He *was* Morlock, not Merlin. Vengeance for him was neither attainable nor thinkable. He was sorry, now, that he had killed Earno. Nothing could atone for such a crime. He was sick with shame and guilt, yet his head rang with echoes of imperfectly suppressed anger, like voices calling his name.

"Morlock!"

He would have to go before the Graith and confess. Or perhaps it would be better to flee across the border and hide in the unguarded lands. He might meet his father there. . . .

"Morlock! Hey, Morlock! It's no use, Raev. Go tell the summoner it's as I told him before: he's too sick to travel."

"Wait," Morlock said thickly.

"Ach—Canyon take you, Morlock, go back to sleep!"

Morlock opened his eyes. Deortheorn and a younger cousin of his, Raev, were standing next to Morlock's bed.

"What is it?" Morlock asked heavily.

"Earno's sending you south. Here's a letter you're to carry."

Morlock sat up cautiously. He was in the journey makers' sleeping hall, which was always dimly lit, as travelling workers are apt to sleep at any hour. Apparently he had not killed Earno, or anyone. Yet. He took the letter from Deor.

"Morlock, you can't go," Deor said. He didn't have to say why. The dragons would be watching all travel south. Several messages had already been sent to warn the other holds. They had gone by relay parties, some of whom were to return at each stage of the road, so that the group's progress could be gauged. No one had yet returned from any group, and all were being mourned as dead.

Morlock shrugged. "I'll go. I'm a Guardian, Deor."

Deor looked him in the eye. "I don't much like the Guardians I've met, Morlock. So that says nothing to me."

Morlock shrugged again. He was in no mood to disagree.

In a matter of moments Morlock was dressed. He bid Deor and Raev good-bye. Then he went to Southgate, or what had been Southgate. It was noon by the time he arrived there. The dwarves on watch greeted him as Rokhlan. They had a horse standing ready for him, the one he had ridden from the Rangan outpost. He viewed it with disfavor and mounted.

As he rode out among the ruins of Southgate he saw that much of the rubble was cleared away, and the stone cut down to bedrock where the southeast edge of the mountain had run. Parties of dwarves worked steadily as he passed, laying the foundation of the new wall. There were no dragons in sight . . . except the slain one, of course. It had been burned on the little hill where it had died, but the bones remained, black and ominous, against the pale clear sky of late fall.

Morlock breathed deeply. The air was clean and cold; he could see his breath. In vague curiosity, he rode up the black hill to look more closely at the dragon's bones.

Coming upon the head of the dragon, he saw with surprise that every tooth in its mouth had been smashed. Deliberately smashed; he could see the lines of the mallet-strokes from where he sat in the saddle.

He turned away with a sinking feeling. So obviously purposeful an act had not been done out of mere malice. Were the dwarves, even now, drawing the sentinel dragon from the Coriam Lakes, and smashing the corpse's teeth in their sockets, one by one? The notion disturbed him. Dwarves knew more about dragons than he had ever realized—far more than they had ever taught him. After his journey through dragon-infested Haukrull their reticence seemed somehow sinister. He had been taught that the Longest War was a conflict between . . . well, alien races, totally opposed peoples . . . good and evil. Perhaps it had been something more complicated: civil war—or some conflict closer and bloodier still. A family quarrel?

Wishing they had told him, he realized sadly that he thought of them as *them*. He was no longer one of them, had never really been, and they (wiser than he) had known it long ago.

Feeling rootless, he sensed a loss of purpose. He knew he should rouse his horse and move south with Earno's message. Yet nothing moved him to do this. In fact, he reached for the letter, broke its seal and read it.

It was addressed to a member of Earno's faction. It requested that the vocate gather a few colleagues and come north "as soon as is convenient." In a postscript Earno suggested that they begin proceedings to accuse, "one Morlock Ambrosius, the bearer of this letter" of impairment of the Guard. It was a curt and matter-of-fact message. There was nothing in it that suggested the actual facts, however: that the north had been invaded by dragons, that these had captured or killed Summoner Lernaion and his companions, that Earno himself was preparing for mortal combat with the master dragon.

Morlock lifted his face toward the gray fire-broken mountains of the west. That was the way he would go to deliver the letter: west, then south. (Earno's partisan lived in the Westhold.) He would have to pass Three

Hills, where Illion lived. He felt, suddenly, that it would be wise, wiser than he knew, to simply do as he had been told. That way it would all work out, though perhaps not as Earno or anyone else had envisioned. Perhaps it would be wise.

But he did not feel wise. It occurred to him that he was still thain-attendant to Earno and that (if the battle with Vild Kharum was not to be utterly doomed) he would need a weapon. There were many of these under Thrymhaiam, of course, and if there was need of another, then another could be made. But in that moment Morlock remembered his dream, in which he had used the sword Gryregaest to slay a dragon—Gryregaest, which (so the songs said) his *ruthen* father had left upon the Hill of Storms a millennium ago.

Morlock tore the letter in half and dropped it beside the dragon's bones. As an afterthought he returned to the grave of the *rokhleni* and took the battered black shield of the Ambrosii from the marker. Then he turned his horse and rode away south, toward the dead gray border of the gravehills.

CHAPTER FIFTEEN

Guardians

The air was suddenly thick with the sounds of the Dwarvish language.

"*San ralem hedra mat*," the Eldest Tyr was saying urgently as the door to his chambers swung open. "*San ralem hedra hŷn—*" He was addressing Vetr, his oldest son.

Deor, standing in the corridor outside, drew back instinctively. His title-of-authority, *doron onedra* ("kin-councillor") was no mean one. But his actual seniority, based on his age and kin-relationship to the Eldest, was much lower. As a matter of course, he knew of the lack of sympathy that prevailed between the Eldest and his oldest son, who would one day succeed him as ruler of the Seven Clans. But, like others, he did not care to think of it, and he took care to avoid witnessing scenes that were none of his business.

"Remember my words!" the Eldest was saying to his heir. "Remember them well—"

"Those words are not for me," Deor broke in, in an agony of embarrassment. "Permit me to withdraw!"

The Eldest looked from his son to Deor in surprise, although the younger dwarf was here at his summons. He put out his hands and said words of welcome—even relief. If he had been speaking another language (he was fluent in several) he might have said merely, "Deor, I'm glad you've come." Dwarvish being a language rich in metaphor, what he actually said was, "*Resh tornet, Heimar ingranat lo.*" (Literally, "If the sun had risen, [or] the King had just been crowned.") Deor understood him well enough, although he preferred a plainer style himself, and stayed where he was.

Vetr was less welcoming and less formal. He curtly nodded at Deor and, not noticing his father in any way, walked off down the corridor.

"Never mind," said the Eldest, leading Deor into his chambers. "He has cause for his feelings. He's a good son; he'll be a good Eldest."

"An excellent son," Deor said mechanically, glancing around the room. He saw the summoner Earno seated at a table near an inner door, staring fixedly at a candle that provided the room's only light. "I beg your pardon, Summoner," he said, speaking in Wardic. "I didn't see you . . ." His voice trailed off. The summoner didn't seem to notice his presence.

Deor looked at the Eldest. "Does the summoner understand us?" he asked in Dwarvish.

"No, not even if we spoke their Othertalk. But let's stick to Dwarvish, eh? The words will come more readily."

Deor nodded slowly. He turned back to the summoner, who was still staring at the candle.

"Look in his eyes," Tyr commanded.

The Eldest was the Eldest—but all the same, "I would rather not," said Deor. "He is under a dragonspell?"

"Yes."

Deor was tempted to ask about the state of fascination that Earno was in and how the Eldest had established it. But the Elders have their secrets, and there were more urgent questions. "Since when?" he asked.

"I do not know. I suspect since the first night he was here."

Deor tried to remember when that was, it seemed so long ago. Then he remembered: that was the first night the dragons had attacked Thrymhaiam.

"Well," he said. "I do not like this, Eldest Tyr!"

"No more do I."

"How long have you known, if you choose to tell me?"

"Since this afternoon, when Morlock left."

"How did you know?"

"I guessed it when I read the letter. After that I took certain steps."

"'The letter'? Earno's letter? Morlock showed it to you?"

"Not exactly. It's on the table yonder."

So it was. Deor went and picked it up. It was torn in half. He held the pieces together and read it.

He turned to his Eldest. "How did it come to you?" he demanded. The question was blunt, brutally blunt from one so junior to one so senior. But he had given it to Morlock himself. The thing touched his honor; he had a right to know.

The Eldest was not annoyed. "Morlock read it and tore it apart on Rokhfell of Southgate," the old dwarf said. "I was watching him, although he did not seem to notice me."

"What did he say when you spoke to him?"

"I didn't. I was with the work parties, some distance away. By the time I reached Rokhfell he had ridden away."

"West?"

"South. I expect he means to raise the alarm in other holds. We think none of our messengers survived, you know—but he might, as he did in Haukrull vale. And he has his obligations to the Graith."

Deor nodded in agreement. "The very thing. Earno must be a madman Morlock a traitor!"

"Earno is spellbound. That is a kind of madness, an induced one."

"Let's *ex*-duce it. If we cure him perhaps we can send a message—"

"Cure him? How do you propose to do that?"

Deor was surprised. "Why—as Earno himself cured me. As I cured Vendas."

"Is Vendas cured?"

Deor was silent. He had looked in on Vendas that morning.

"I've thought on this, Deortheorn," the Eldest said. "I have thought too much, maybe. Why did Earno's suspicions take the form they did? Plainly: because, before the spell was placed, they had *already* taken this form. Before Earno arrived at Thrymhaiam he suspected Morlock of treason."

"But why?"

"Morlock is an Ambrosius. He is Merlin's *ruthen* son and only heir. You are young, Deor—almost as young as Morlock. You do not remember Merlin. But I do. When Merlin finished his apprenticeship with Bleys, there were few in the world who could teach him anything. Those few were the master makers of the Seven Clans. Long he dwelt here under Thrymhaiam, and many times he returned here thereafter to learn and to teach. I came to know him well. And Morlock is Merlin reborn—at least, no one could look at the one without constantly being reminded of the other. So it must have been with Earno."

"But—"

"Let me finish, Deortheorn. Morlock is now *rokhlan*, a *dragonkiller*"—he used the Wardic word—"and for some reason this infuriates Earno, that an Ambrosius should be acclaimed as a dragonkiller. Deep within his memory, too deep for me to read the matter clearly, dragonkilling and Merlin's exile are closely linked. Earno sees himself always as vocate and dragonkiller, Ambrosius always as summoner, traitor, and exile. But now we have an Ambrosius who is also a dragonkiller, and may one day be a vocate."

"I don't understand," said Deor. "Morlock is not Merlin. And no matter what Morlock achieves, Earno is still *rokhlan* and summoner."

"It is deeper than reason, Deor. Morlock and Merlin are both Ambrosius. And it is as if Ambrosius the exile has returned and is taking over parts of Earno's life. That is how he sees it, at any rate. That is why I say *dragonkiller*, and not *rokhlan*—that is the word Earno uses in his own mind; he is besieged by it, barricaded behind it, imprisoned in it. Thus he has identified himself from his first youth—as the dragonkiller. But now he must confront another, claiming the same title. If he does not prove his claim to it once again, and repeat his old achievement of exiling Ambrosius, then Ambrosius may complete his theft of Earno's life by exiling and supplanting a summoner—Earno himself."

"Nonsense."

"Madness," the Eldest corrected. "Like Ven's, an induced one. I think that, before the spell took effect, Earno's deeper feelings were under control; he was willing to treat Morlock at least fairly, though by no means generously. But now the spell has changed his mind. Who can say his sick belief, the madness infesting his mind, will vanish when the spell is loosed? Who can say that it will ever vanish? Its roots are very deep."

Deor was silent for a time. The problem seemed insoluble. But the Eldest had called him here for a reason.

"What command has been placed on Earno?" he asked Tyr.

"None, so far as I can tell. But it seems that his own latent compulsion about proving himself the sole dragonkiller has taken the place of an external command, fixing the spell in place. He insists on being allowed to go to Haukrull and challenge the master of the guile."

"Oh. Oh. I see," said Deor, for he did at last, and looked away.

"I was certain you would," the Eldest said. "Yes, it is a fearful crime. Earno is a summoner, *rokhlan*, and, more importantly, our guest. We cannot simply send him under the mountains to die. But Morlock is our *harven* kin, entrusted to us by his *ruthen* mother and father. We must defend him and we will."

"One of us must go with Earno, then."

"Yes. As squire, and guide, and also to ensure that he *does* go. Thus those-who-watch will see that we are no more sparing of ourselves than we are with Earno. Perhaps that will earn us forgiveness."

Deor doubted this. But he did not otherwise disagree.

"Only one may go," Tyr said. "As Eldest that is my word. The Longest War has come again to Thrymhaiam, and no one must be permitted to simply throw his life away. Beyond that, I must consider who may claim the right or obligation to go—"

"I claim both," Deor said desperately. He turned again to face the Eldest, who seemed as grimly determined as himself.

"The choice surely falls between you and me," the Eldest replied. "I saw that at once. We will settle the question now, for Earno must be permitted to depart before the sun returns."

He held out his fist and opened the fingers of his hand. On his broad gray palm lay a golden coin. "Shield or skull?" the Eldest asked. "You choose and I will throw."

There were times when Aloê, thain-attendant to the vocate Naevros syr Tol, didn't approve of the world. With all due respect to Creator, Sustainer, and King, she was inclined to view the world as a botched job—something that barely limped along because the best gave their best to make it work. Without any self-consciousness, she counted herself among one of those best who made sacrifices, and sometimes she wondered whether the world was worth the trouble.

At its best, Aloê had to admit, the world was very good indeed. A fair day's sailing, for instance. Or even sailing through a storm—there was a fine narrow excitement to that. Sailing was the way the rest of the world should be but rarely was. Conditions varied infinitely; no two days, no two stretches of water were really the same. But the principles of action never varied, though actions themselves had to suit the infinite variety of actual environments.

But, though parts of life were like this, life as a whole was different. Storms in life were usually inner storms—as if the principles of action were in constant flux, though the environment itself never varied. Life was always a bother, and no one really understood. . . .

The rough open bareness of her surroundings was depressing her, she guessed. Talk about an unchanging environment: you couldn't get a more monotonous landscape than the Long Plain of Westhold—outside a painting by Zavell, maybe. And, unlike a painting, the plain went on and on, day's ride after day's ride. . . .

Determination gave her, if not a way out, then a way to cope. She kept riding north, through the immense harvested fields of Westhold. Their rough blankness gave solid form to her mood. Her thoughts were like crows, finding some invisible sustenance in the bleak emptiness. Still, she rode on. She had a task; she would perform it, even if it meant leaving her beloved Southhold, and even the comparative civilization of A Thousand Towers, and passing into the far north, where the people were as squat and pale (and approximately as talkative) as mushrooms.

A village broke the blank emptiness of the horizon. Gratefully she spurred her horse toward it. The low walls of its houses, rising about her, were a welcome shelter from the blankness of the sky, the bare dead prospect of the empty fields.

There was a market in progress. She stopped at the tavern and bought a cup of wine. Having drunk this, she left her horse in front of the tavern and wandered through the market.

She stood for a while before a storyteller, listening to a version of *First Merlin's Song*. The crowd seemed to take it all pretty seriously: Merlin planting the banefire hedges around the Dead Corain. And if they were already dead, Aloê wondered, what was the fuss about? She had grown up on the southern coast and was inclined to think of *First Merlin's* as an inferior grade of ghost story. She was quite fond of *Second* and *Third Merlin's*—they were more her sort of story. And she thought Merlin's portrait (in the Hall of Guardians at New Moorhope) was a masterwork: crooked and cultivated, intelligent and imperious, Merlin had been the epitome of a

Guardian. The black cloak, betokening exile, which hung beside the painting simply added the air of danger inevitable in any high prospect.

Without taking her eyes off the storyteller, she began to feel unsheltered, as if she were out on the Long Plain again. Turning to go, she found a group of townspeople were gaping at her in something like amazement. A compliment, in its way, but somehow she was not flattered. One dark-haired pale-skinned heavy woman, standing close to her, was staring at her dark golden hair and darker skin with a dim astonished longing that was not even envy. She smiled at the woman, but suddenly, jarringly (it was the world again, the botched discordant world) she wondered what it would be like to be this woman: incontestably ugly, probably poor, scratching out a living in these dim gigantic plains.

Realizing that, with these thoughts, her expression had changed, Aloê smiled again at the woman and walked past her, leaving the crowd with a careful slowness. When she reached her horse she mounted and rode off northward.

She reached Three Hills at sunset. There really were hills—she had begun to fear that the maps lied, that the plain went on forever. In fact, though the three hills for which the estate were named stood somewhat apart, there were more hills beyond them and, farther yet, mountains piercing the horizon like pale thorns.

Turning back to bid an angry good-bye to the plains she saw that the overcast sky was breaking up: there were long stretches of mysterious blue among the rough gray pinnacles of cloud. Looking east, she saw the clouds part there, admitting the last rays of sunlight into the world. The light struck red and purplish blue tints off the undersides of the broken clouds, deepening in contrast the narrow blue canyons of empty sky. As light fell on the yellow-gray fields, transmuting them in an instant to coarse bristling gold, she felt a sudden pang of guilt, as if the plains were a person she had somehow misjudged. She turned away and rode on.

Riding up among the Three Hills, she saw what she supposed was the manor house built up to and into the side of one of the hills, the one farthest north and west. Descending from the house along an unpaved path was a coarsely dressed workman. She reined in close to him and said, "Greetings, good tenant. Can you guide me to the lord of the manor?"

"Not."

"Excuse me?"

"Not a tenant. Don't have your tenant-farming in this part of Westhold. Anyway, my family owns this place." The man's voice was brisk, but agreeable.

Aloê happened to know that the family which owned Three Hills currently consisted of Illion, whom she knew, and his brother Lorion. So this must be the master of the manor whom she had addressed so cavalierly. "I'm sorry," she said.

"Doesn't bother me. Some of the workers bridle at the term—just so you know."

"I'm sorry," she said again, and was instantly angry at herself for the inane repetition. She was relieved when he matter-of-factly ignored it.

"You're looking for Naevros, I take it?"

"Yes."

"We knew you were coming, of course. Glad to see you. The stables are over there." He nodded pleasantly and walked away.

"Thank you," she said, somewhat at a loss. She had thought he was about to tell her where Naevros was. But she could find out by herself, no doubt, and it made sense to stable her horse.

The abrupt lasting twilight of the Wardlands had risen by the time she had reached a large outbuilding beyond the southeast hill. She guessed it might be a stable. But half the walls were down and no horses were visible. The gray shapes of some workmen stood aside in a group.

The workmen were discussing whether they should bring lights and continue the job or leave it as it was until morning.

Aloê had a gift of breaking graciously into conversations. She had a way with clients and tenants generally. She practiced both of these to a fine pitch on her family's estate in the Southhold. Her family was an important one on the southern coast, and she had grown up under the halo of power. It was a pity, she had often thought dispassionately, that the estate would never come to her, except under the most disastrous circumstances. (There were two sisters and a brother between her and the primacy.) She really had the best knack in the family for exercising power for the general good. But it was fair, too, that capable scions of a noble house go out "into the waters of the world" (as her family said). Better that than to stay at home, become a threadbare member of the gentry, watching one's descendants fade into the client class.

"Gentlemen," she said to the workers (the word came somewhat stickily to her tongue, but she would not make the mistake of calling them tenants; for all she knew she was addressing half the gentry of the Westhold), "I had heard there was stabling in this direction."

There was a pause, then one of the workers said, "Why? Is your horse pregnant?"

"Shouldn't be riding a pregnant horse," another commented.

"I'm not," she replied icily. For a moment she thought they were making some sort of coarse joke.

"Southcr!" said one of them. "Look at her seat! Never mind it, Thain; let your horse run free. There's water and fodder, brookways, and the night rider's between here and Hunting Wood. We'll call her for you when you're needing."

"Will you?" she said, a kind of challenge in her voice. She knew it was senseless, but she could not help it. She hated riding, and she didn't like the Westholder's comment about how she sat in the saddle, if that's what it had been.

One of them held her stirrup as she dismounted. His clothes were encrusted with dirt and manure, and he was sweating considerably more than her horse. She was about to turn away when she noticed with quiet horror that he was Naevros syr Tol.

"Shall we have you pitch in, Aloê?" he said pleasantly. "I think we have a spare shovel here, somewhere." He had noted and understood her reaction, of course; their tense rapport could be embarrassingly intense at times.

But she was nothing if not game. "Sharpen the blade, Vocate, and lead me to it." She had long declined to learn sword-fighting from him; it was a sore point between them at one time.

A chorus of protests arose from the other workers. Men from the west and east were narrow-minded about working with women as equals. To keep her from carrying out her threat they decided to quit work for the day. That suited Aloê well enough: she was tired from riding and she hated dirt. But she insisted on tending to her horse herself, while the Westholders stood about and shuffled their feet; she carried the saddle up to the house, also. Naevros reached for the bridle, and she handed it to him without a thought.

She wanted to tell him about the business she had completed for him in A Thousand Towers. He had originally planned to stay in the great city for two or three calls of Trumpeter after the Station was dismissed, but for some reason had changed his mind and rushed off with Illion and Noreê to Three Hills instead. He had left Aloê, with virtually no guidance, to finish his affairs in the city. This sort of situation, which arose quite rarely, was termed by thains "carrying the cloak" of the vocate in question. It was supposed to be a mark of respect and trust—in fact, only a step away from receiving one's own red cloak and a place to stand at Station. The whole business had been challenging and exciting, and there were some things she felt she had carried off rather neatly.

Yet she couldn't speak. After the immensity of the harvested plains, walking among the gray heavy movements of workmen in the blue dusk, her thoughts had a hollow ring to them. She imagined speaking them aloud and shook her head impatiently. No. It galled her that all she had done for the past month seemed trivial among a group of men with sweat drying on their faces. She knew the feeling would pass, though. The time was not right, that was all. Restless, she stepped forward lightly, leaving Naevros a step or two behind.

Noreê was dreaming in the Healing Wood.

She sat beneath a maple that had lost almost half its leaves. They lay beneath it, a blood-bright carpet exactly the color of her cloak. Sitting with her back to the trunk, she looked on the fallen leaves as a flat reflection, in golden dying grass, of the real tree. Buried among them, then, would be an image of herself, Noreê. To that reflective Noreê the ground would be a kind of sky: troubled but beautiful with green and stretches of gold and black-brown veins of storm cloud. The ground beneath the reflective Noreê, though, would be a bright blue, faulted by the red-flecked branch-roots of the tree. She could survey the sky as if it were bounded earth, or let her gaze penetrate deeply into it.

A long time later there were deep piles of white leaves gathering on the bright blue ground. They blew into bright-veined gray drifts, and more collected about them. They piled higher and deeper/lower. Concentrating on them, but not really concentrating at all, reflective and actual Noreê vanished in the unconscious apprehension of the purity of the broken silence, the absolute emptiness of the air surrounding them.

At some indefinable point there was a release. There was no division of Noreê into reflective and actual. She was one. Her soul remained where it was, resident always of itself. Her body remained where it was, beneath the wondrous beauty of the dying tree. But her tal, the link between them, the agency by which the spirit works on the body and the medium by which the body communicates with the spirit, was set free. There was no separation. Their union persisted, soul/tal/body—metaphysical triangle circumscribing physical life, but it extended through space. Unburdened of the need to consciously control her body, Noreê's mind leapt directly into the sky, through the window of her own tal.

The sensation of visionary flight, if it can be called sensation, is difficult to describe. Often, in memory, the flight becomes wholly visual, random bits of colorless data striking light like sparks in the sensorium, whereas they were of a different order of perception in experience. As an adept, Noreê found it best to interpret the flight in a way that would not overwhelm her in the explosion of lines and colors that the mind generates to give form to an incomprehensible experience. She concentrated rather on the perception of motion—a partly visual, partly tactile sense. There were other senses involved, too: in the profoundest flight of her vision she could bend her awareness downward to hear the sap flowing in the veins of a tree, and the slow persistent thoughts that guided its growth.

So it was now, as she swept east from the Healing Wood over the Hunting Wood, she saw the swift forms of horses struggling slowly through heavy still underbrush. Over one was the dim deliberate shape of a hunting cat lying along a bough. Its thoughts (which, in the instant of her overflight, were clear to her) precisely matched its motions as it stretched its limbs in preparation for the kill. Not far off, sweeping through the underbrush like a vagrant breeze, were the swift, contradictory thoughts/motions of Jordel. She read as heat his bright but fading satisfaction at having freed seven horses from their dangerous predicament.

Killing, by a law that predated human occupancy in the Westhold, was permitted in the Hunting Wood, but not in the Healing Wood. The horses, though, were creatures of the plain; they knew nothing of the forest's laws. So it was not unusual for one of the half-wild band of horses that belonged to Three Hills to become trapped in a romp through the Hunting Wood and have several of its members killed. Most often it was because they were pursuing a unicorn that had come down from the mountains.

Noreê instantly understood that Jordel (and Illion, whom she perceived close at hand) were involved in a struggle to free the horses after just such a venture. She understood, but (circling over the scene) she felt no impulse to conclude her vision and go to aid them. She was not even conscious of making a choice. Understanding and volition were strangely altered in the rapture of vision. The flight, as the seer's axiom had it, must take its course. Noreê's awareness vaulted over Illion as he sprang between the hunting cat and its prey. She arced east and north and upward, facing the mountains that thrust through the broken roof of clouds.

She perceived the exquisite stillness of the mountains, for stillness itself is a relation of motions. She ascended beyond them and prepared to perceive the Northhold.

An awareness brushed against hers. It was a gentle motion, but shudderingly powerful. Noreê had no time to decide what this meant. Suddenly she ceased moving and also fell endlessly downward. The contradiction of motion/stillness was profoundly painful to embrace. She recognized in it the cruelly abrupt end of her vision. As flames leapt up around her awareness, she realized she was a prisoner.

Aloê was watching the night sky from the window-ledge of her room when Naevros entered. She knew, without turning, that it was him: by the rhythm of his footfalls, the fact that he did not knock, a certain feeling she had had before he entered . . . a number of things. She said, without turning, "The sky is marvelously clear."

He came up and leaned against the window frame opposite her. "Yes," he said. "More than likely it will be cloudy again tomorrow. That's a familiar pattern up here."

Naevros fit in everywhere, but it was hard to think of him as a Northholder, used to weather even colder than this, a mountaineer, a mushroom, speaking a vocabulary thick with Dwarvish slang—when he bothered to speak. No, he did not fit the image. Perhaps that was why he had come south and joined the Graith, so many years ago. His parents were Westholders who settled in the north after it came under the Guard. That much Aloê knew, but she knew little else. Naevros seldom visited them and never spoke of them.

"Have you met your peers before?" Naevros asked.

"You mean Baran and Thea?" They were the thains-attendant on Jordel and Noreê respectively. "Yes, we know each other well. I've been wondering . . ."

"Yes?"

Aloê said slowly, "Since he became a vocate, Jordel has never chosen Baran as attendant."

"They're brothers. There would be difficulties—that hint of patronage."

"Yes. But he has chosen him now, to come here."

Naevros nodded. "There is a chance, Aloê, that we may face danger here in the north. Illion thinks so, at any rate, and he is a fair judge. And this is bad news, of course. But for thains every danger is an opportunity."

"So you have all brought your particular protégés," Aloê observed. "Except Illion."

Naevros smiled briefly in turn. "In a sense, Illion's protégé is far north of here already."

"You don't mean Earno?"

There was no light except starlight in the room; the window faced south, away from the major moons. But, turning to look at Naevros as they talked, she could see his face harden at the mention of the summoner. "No," he said. "But Earno's attendant was commended to him by Illion. You bore him the message, you know."

"Was that it? I didn't read it, you know."

"Oh. Well, Earno's attendant is young Ambrosius."

"Young Ambrosius," Aloê repeated. She could not imagine Earno having an Ambrosius as his attendant. And Merlin was supposed to have been the last of them, anyway.

"The one they call Morlock syr Theorn."

"*That* mushroom."

Naevros laughed, understanding her private slang without trouble.

"But," said Aloê, "I made my first tour of A Thousand Towers with him. He never said a word as the senior thain took us by Ambrose. Surely it belongs to him now."

"Ah, so you were particular friends."

"Oh, no. But we were stationed at A Thousand Towers at the same time a few years ago."

"I remember. I almost thought to sponsor him at one time."

"You're joking?"

"By no means. It would have given Earno something to think about. But he never had . . . your subtlety, your instinct for situations. He will never be a great swordsman, either."

"Neither will I."

"For different reasons. He . . . well, you knew him."

"They call him Crookback."

"Not you, I hope."

"No. Why does Illion favor him?"

"Oh, he's by no means stupid. They say he is already a gifted maker. I suppose we both remember a few times when he displayed power as a seer. And . . . the very thing I mentioned, that may look different to some. Such an inability resembles a kind of integrity."

That gave her something to think about. If the absence of an ability resembled integrity, then the presence of the ability might indicate lack of integrity . . . at least to "some." Was Naevros warning her that Illion had reservations about her character? Or . . . Naevros' statements, however simple in themselves, often carried implications that were intolerably complex.

As she thought, she twisted her fingers idly in her hair. She was about to turn and look back out into the night when she noticed that he was unnaturally still. With her intense understanding of his nature, she realized that he was giving rapt and unguarded attention to her fingers moving in her hair. In turn, of course, he recognized that she had noted his attention. But he went on watching as if he could not help it.

Her breathing quickened. She knew, of course, that Naevros thought she was beautiful, nor was he the only one. She, in turn, found him attractive: he was tall, dark-haired, deliberate and graceful. She supposed he knew how she felt. The mutual attraction was a powerful element—perhaps the essential element, the sustaining one—in their rapport.

But one of the reasons that Naevros appealed to her so strongly was that he could recognize and acknowledge her beauty with a certain subtlety. He noticed everything and she knew it, but he did not clutter his conversation with compliments. He had the courage not to express the inexpressible, knowing she would understand. This implicit understanding was precious to her.

Still . . . love (was this love?) had to move from implicit understanding to explicit acts. And she hated men like that, the way they looked at you, their faces greasy with anticipation. If Naevros turned to her that way, what would she do? Then again, he might never turn to her. What would she do then? Would it make a difference? Did she need a man to become who she was meant to be? She didn't see why. But need and want were different things. . . .

The silence, the stillness, had gone on too long. No one was turning toward or away from anyone here. Abruptly, Aloê realized that she was tense, angry and bored. But something was about to happen, or had been about to happen. In deference to that she felt she could not move. She could not be the one to spoil things, to make things impossible. But things were already impossible. When a knock came at the door she rolled off the window ledge and moved readily toward the door.

But suddenly Naevros reached out and touched her arm, restraining her for a moment. "Meet me in the entryway after supper," he said. "We will talk."

She nodded, a little disturbed by the explicitness of the request. She went to answer the door. A housekeeper was standing in the corridor outside; he had come to tell them that supper was ready.

The vocate Jordel was almost a parody of the typical Westholder. He was improbably tall, lightly built, and his hair was a tangled mop of fair brown curls. He moved with a wiry comic grace and he was always in motion. And: he talked.

His brother Baran was almost as tall, but very different. His light brown hair was close-cropped, and he was of a heavier build and a quieter demeanor than Jordel. He moved slowly when he moved, but "strong as Baran" was already a proverb in the village where he had grown up. Jordel, in his opinion, never had grown up.

"Stop bleeding on me," he growled as Jordel's bandaged hand swung out in a grand sweeping gesture. Jordel took no more notice of his brother's modest exaggeration than a river does of the occasional raindrop.

"So I *leapt* through the screen of branches," cried Jordel, his every limb starting at the word *leapt*. "On the other side, what should I—"

"You should—" Baran tried to interrupt.

"—should I see but Illion wrestling with a snarling bloodcat—"

"Mountain cat," Illion observed.

"—(a mewling mounting cat, then) to the ground with the horse in question rearing and screaming over both their heads!"

"What was the question?" Thea asked.

"Thinking quickly, actually not thinking at all if you can believe it of me, I handsprung over the friendly pair (yon cat and Mount Illion there) and snatched the horse by one ear. I shouted . . . but I won't mention it here, you get the idea, and so did he. I braced him as he staggered in a quarter circle on his hind feet, letting his feet fall—"

"Feet? And feet again?" cried Thea. "What sort of monster was this? Did it wear shoes or sandals, now?"

"—letting its front *feet* fall to the ground when he was facing away from Illion and his catamite. Then I whacked him on the rump and told him the way to the safe path.

"Then I heard this scream, and the next thing I knew I was halfway up an oak tree and fighting to get higher. I heard something rustling in the foliage near me and, assuming it to be Illion, said, 'Was that the *cat*? What did you do to it?'

"Away down below me I hear Illion's voice say, 'No, it was me. Been experimenting with some of the Silent Words.' At about this time, the leaves part like a curtain, and the cat, with whom I am sharing the tree, says—" and Jordel threw back his head and roared, in inaccurate but spirited mimicry of a mountain cat. "I snatched my left hand from the branch just *after* the cat's claws had landed atop it. My hand I mean. It amounts to the same thing, hand or branch, and—Thea must you make those faces? To make matters worse, my other hand was holding air at the moment and my feet were swinging free—"

"As usual," Baran muttered.

"—but I caught a branch with my legs before I had fallen too far. Then I heard Illion squeak, 'There's a few more horses in the wood, Jordel, I—I'm just sure of it. You take care of that monster and I'll go find them!' And then the victor of Kaen runs like a rabbit for home!"

Baran grunted. "With the horse out of danger and you hanging upside down in front of a cat in heat, everything had obviously returned to normal."

"Normal—" Jordel began.

"The word seems inapt, I grant you," agreed Thea. "Now Baran, admit Jordel is not normal."

"Normal—" Jordel repeated, then paused.

"We seem to have run aground," said Illion. "But here are Naevros and Aloê to give us a tow."

Those Guardians had indeed entered the room, just as Jordel had last begun to speak.

"Have you noticed," Thea said to Baran, "how everyone in Jordel's stories talks exactly like Jordel? Can you imagine Illion screaming 'that monster'—?"

"Baran's imagination is not an inexhaustible resource," Jordel observed, with a shade too much force. "Ah, hello Aloê. How was your ride north?"

After the round of greetings Thea deliberately led Aloê away from the group. It was, perhaps, not so deftly done. It was clear to Aloê that Thea was acting with some sort of purpose in mind. From the expression on Baran's and Jordel's faces Aloê guessed that they knew what the purpose was. She herself had no idea, and the matter did not become clearer as Thea engaged her in drifting conversation.

Thea was tall and pale, with long strong limbs and dark hair. Like Jordel, Baran, and Illion, she was a Westholder. She was a great favorite of Jordel's; they were often together, laughing and joking. But when Aloê asked her how things were between them, Thea looked puzzled.

"What a memory you have, Aloê!" she said, smiling and frowning at once.

"Memory?" said Aloê. "But you were always together, during the Station."

"What a memory you have," Thea repeated, and Aloê could not but understand. She became a little angry on Thea's behalf. She hated the sort of man who chose and discarded women like cut flowers, and Jordel was just that sort of man.

By way of changing the subject she asked when Noreê would be joining them.

"She went to the Healing Wood this morning," Thea replied. "She didn't know when she'd be back. 'The flight must take its course.'"

"So they say," Aloê agreed. "Is it true? I've rarely ascended to rapture, never in solitary flight."

Thea looked troubled. "It's difficult to know, much less explain. I've only flown through solitary rapture once, and I am still remembering and forgetting things about the experience."

Soon they were deep in conversation, sharing what they knew about visionary flight and tal. Presently Aloê sensed that Thea was distracted, in the middle of a remark she was making. Glancing around she saw why. Jordel was standing next to them. An expression of earnest intellectual interest lay across his features like a mask.

"You'll forgive me for saying so, Thain Aloê," he interposed smoothly, "but I disagree with you. Tal is not wholly nonphysical. It is a metaphysical medium with physical effect. Therefore it is, in some sense, as physical as it is nonphysical. It exists as an instrument for awareness in the physical world."

"I seem to remember the vocate Noreê saying the same thing," Aloê remarked, "in somewhat fewer words." Why had he come over here? Simply to annoy Thea? It irked her.

"Oh, indeed, I learned all I know from Noreê," conceded Jordel, smiling. "I was her thain-attendant when she and Illion walked against the Dark Seven of Kaen, as you may remember."

This was the equivalent of a maker modestly admitting that he had been tutored by Merlin Ambrosius, or a swordsman reluctantly conceding he had been trained by Naevros syr Tol. The man was strutting like a rooster. Aloê opened her mouth to speak, but hardly knew what she would say.

Then Naevros himself was there—dark, graceful, somber. His very presence lit up Jordel's new seriousness as an outrageous affectation. "Yes, Jordel, perhaps," he allowed. "But your point of view had certain teleological difficulties."

Jordel's smile did not change. But in him, the ever-changeable, this was a sign of deep distress. "I don't see what you mean," he admitted, finally.

"You imply, when you say 'instrument,' that tal is a deliberate creation, an instrument, of awareness—like an idea, or a volitional act, rather than a necessary consequence of, I should have said a necessary condition for, self-aware physical beings. You see the distinction, I'm sure."

"Not quite."

"Then. Uncounted beings have lived and died without the knowledge of tal, the link between physical and spiritual planes. They never used tal to experience visionary flight outside the body, as we do. Neither did they exploit a knowledge of it to sustain physical life beyond its natural term, as the Dead Corain are said to do. But tal itself, without their knowledge of it, made possible their lives as physical beings who could think, feel, and know."

"Yes, yes, I see," said Jordel, unquestionably irritated. "Is anyone else hungry? I'm hungry. I'm a physical being."

"Champion Naevros!" Aloê whispered, as they followed the others to the dining hall. "Imagine him trying to inflate himself like a frog in front of Thea!"

Naevros glanced at her and, a measurable moment later, smiled. "Yes. What will irritate him most, when he rethinks the conversation, is that he will find the objection to be trivial."

"What do you mean?"

"I didn't actually disagree with the substance of what he said. I simply made an argument out of one of the possible implications of one of the words he used."

Aloê smiled in turn. "If the objection had been more substantial—"

"He might have answered it more easily. Yes. He will be *very* irritated."

"You speak as if you know."

"I do. I once quoted Noreê on tal to Morlock, using much the same words as Jordel did just now. He gave me the argument that I just gave Jordel. It was three days before I realized what bothered me about Morlock's objection; by that time your mushroom had left the city."

"He's not *my* mushroom," Aloê protested, and laughing, they went into supper.

Noreê was imprisoned in a sheath of flames. There was fire all about her. Yet—she sensed a presence, and spoke to it.

Who are you? The words fell dead, without sound.

But a response came, of a kind. It had no more sound than her own words, yet she could hear it. *That does not matter. Listen—*

It matters! she said, and exerted her will, the will of Noreê. The flames began to dim.

Listen!

She did not even bother to respond.

Very well. It really doesn't matter. I am Merlin Ambrosius.

Astonishment caused her to relax her effort. *What is . . . this?*

He replied, *You are where you were. But I have imposed my fetch, the talic projection of my self, upon yours. You can move and speak as you like, but these actions will not affect your body until I release you.*

She was bemused by the implications. *I had no idea such a thing was possible.*

She felt his pride in his skill, received an impression (like a quick glance down a long, dimly lit corridor) of the long process of invention, driven by purpose. *Knowing that it is, you will soon be able to practice it—*

She interposed: *That is not my desire.*

—or defend against it, he added placatingly, irritatingly. *I have told you much worth knowing already. All I ask in return is that you listen a little longer.*

Her rejection was more than verbal. *No! I do not intend to join you in exile.* She was reasonably intrigued, but she was not inclined to sit at Merlin's feet. She exerted her will, the will of Noreê.

You think to discourage me, the voice in the flames said. *But I have tried to address two other persons in this way, one of them more than once, and failed. You hear me and respond; that is victory in itself. I will speak. You will not be able to ignore what I say.*

Already she could not; she sensed a danger to the Guard. *Whom have you talked to?* she demanded.

Merlin laughed. She heard nothing but felt his amusement with painful directness. In a timeless time, he replied, *I reached the summoner Earno several times. He was not willing to perceive my identity—there is a weakness in that man, Noreê; you should see to it—but he received my warning, more or less. I have also tried to communicate with my son. However—it proved to be insurmountably difficult.*

From what Noreê knew of Morlock, this did not strike her as unlikely.

I have been in Tychar, the master of all makers continued, *at the Place of the Two Powers.*

Noreê mocked him, hoping to lessen his control: *So you have progressed from atheist to pagan, Ambrosius?*

Merlin was difficult to irritate, though. *They really exist, Noreê. Read it in my mind. But I am no devotee of theirs; you will read that, too. I will open my memory to you presently. They offered me the kingship of the Wardlands—*

—which you accepted. Mock him, she thought. Weaken his hold on her.

I refused! I come to tell you that the danger to the Guard . . . is very great, very near. I'm growing weary. Your awareness is powerful, difficult to contain in this way. . . . The Two Powers would destroy the Wardlands; their agents are now in the North. . . .

Why does this concern you? Noreê demanded coldly.

I am still a Guardian of the Wardlands! Merlin replied, defiant. *What I did, I did to maintain the Guard, not destroy it! Spare yourself the effort; I sense your disbelief more pungently that you could express it.* He paused, then continued, *Believe what you like: that I am corrupt, and seek only power. Even so, especially so, I would not seek to rule over a conquered realm as the viceroy of Torlan and Zahkaar.*

Almost unwillingly, and nonverbally (the mental equivalent of a nod) Noreê acknowledged the likelihood of this.

I am nearly exhausted, Merlin admitted. *I am going to open my understanding to you now. Brace yourself. It encompasses many deaths. . . .*

After the last toast (the traditional "Maintain the Guard!") had been drunk at supper, Aloê was guided back to her rooms by Illion. She was glad to have a guide. Three Hills was by no means a maze, but it was a large and rambling house, built differently than any she had seen.

"It's dwarvish work," he said, when she asked him about it. "This is the third house my family has had at Three Hills. The first collapsed in a year of heavy rains, and the second was destroyed by lightning. So the head of the family hired the dwarves of Thrymhaiam to build a house that would last."

"It must have been expensive."

"The cost was not so great as some other difficulties," he said, smiling. "The north was not then under the Guard, and the Graith was quite suspicious of Three Hills and its family for a time. And the dwarves are difficult workmen: too brilliant to be guided, too proud to explain."

They reached Aloê's door, and Illion bid her good night. Aloê went inside and took a heavy cloak from her pack. Footsteps approached her door outside, then halted. Aloê returned to the door and stood, listening. The pace had not been Naevros', and she did not think it had been Illion's.

She opened the door. Jordel was standing, indecisively, in the hall outside.

"Thea," said Aloê pointedly, "is not here."

Jordel laughed. "If she were, I wouldn't be."

Aloê finally realized how things stood. "That's not true," she noted. "You broke into our conversation before supper."

"You're right. 'Wherever you go, I'll follow, in—'"

"You will *not*," said Aloê, alarmed.

"I'm just quoting a poem which—"

"I'm not."

He looked at her appraisingly. "Is there something between you and Naevros, then? He said there wasn't. But you talk like a married woman, as if you didn't have to give a reason to say no—"

Stung, she cried out, "You forget yourself! I need no reasons! If I did there would be plenty in the thousand men like you I've known—"

Jordel smiled angrily. "Really, Aloê, what a confession—"

She would not be interrupted, went on shouting "—thousands like you, gentry of the estates, with rings on their fingers, swarming like flies around the women on Dancing Days, with kisses and compliments and sugarstick cruelty . . ." Anger choked off her speech.

Jordel was still smiling tensely. "Did you realize I have no name?"

"Nonsense."

"No, no name at all, at least no surname. I am Jordel, my brother is Baran, and that is that. Our mother was a peasant, you see, and so, by aristocratic tradition, our father might have been *anybody*. So we have no surname. If I had been born on one of your estates in the south, I never would have been allowed to come to your Dancing Day . . . except to serve the food, or mix the wine, or help the gentry into their gilded dungcarts after a hard night's prancing—"

"You mean—"

"I mean that *you* forget yourself. I was not born on an estate (thanks, Creator!) and you are not heir to one. I am a peasant still, I suppose. But I didn't become the rest of the things that I am by being indirect, or overmodest."

"I don't care about that," she said impatiently. "Be clever. Be . . . proud of your humble origins. But leave me alone. No. Say nothing. Go!"

Jordel shrugged and went, with an infuriatingly loose-limbed stride that spoke loud his absolute unconcern. Aloê threw the cloak she held over her shoulders and ran off to meet Naevros. He was not in the entry hall. She ran by without waiting for him. She ran into the darkness outside, toward the steeper hills north of the Three. She ran until she no longer had a thought in her head or a feeling in her heart. She did not return to the house until long after every person inside it was asleep.

The next morning, Aloê awoke late with the morning sun shining through the western window. She arose and washed in a tense unmeditative calm. She went down to the dining hall in the same spirit, deliberately not thinking.

She met Naevros in the corridor leading to the dining hall. They greeted each other without words; neither did they touch. The rapport between them was tense, intimate, eternal. What had happened last night . . . what had, in fact, not happened . . . that changed nothing. She was relieved. In a way, anyway, she was relieved. They went toward the open hall, together, without touching.

All the other Guardians except Noreê were there. They rose in greeting. Naevros and Aloê took places at the table.

It was a strange meal, almost silent, but not uncommunicative. Aloê sat next to Thea and took something from her hands to pass to Jordel. Thea did not quite smile as their eyes met—but Jordel nodded to her, quite amiably. Then, glancing around the table, taking in expressions, Aloê guessed that there was little she had said or done in the past half-day that was not known to everyone present.

For a moment she was almost horrified. She was accustomed to thinking of her life and her actions as her own, her property—not shared goods, like well water or open fields. Then something opened up within her, like a fist unclenching.

As she sat there among the warm domestic smells—the slices of ham, the warm bread, the steam from the great clay teapot at the center of the table—she felt it wasn't such a terrible thing to have part of her life belong to others. Her friendship with Naevros was indestructible; she knew that now. Thea, who might have been merely a rival, was now also a friend. Jordel, mindful of his rejection, might be less of a predator and more of a man for a time. Baran, at least, had been roundly entertained. And Illion—

Looking up, she met Illion's eye as he raised his bowl of tea. She had the sense that her own knowledge was being embraced by his. The world would never be perfect. But it could be better than it was, if the best gave their best for it. She raised her own bowl to acknowledge his toast.

"I drink to the Guard," said her host, half smiling. "May it be maintained forever!"

"Maintain the Guard!" they said together, raising their drinks. It was the seal of their common intimacy.

"There is no Guard," said a cold clear voice.

In the doorway stood Noreê. Her iron-gray hair was wildly disordered. Her skin was as pale as old ice. Her blue eyes held the suffering look of someone called from rapture. But her face was calm and sane.

"There is no Guard," she repeated to the thunderstruck Guardians. "A guile of dragons has broken through the Wards and invaded the north. The summoner Lernaion and his companions are all killed or taken captive. The summoner Earno is bound in dragonspell. Whole valleys of the Guarded have been laid waste, and the citadel of Thrymhaiam is under siege. There is no Guard in the north. *The Guard is not maintained!*"

As the other Guardians stood up and cried out their disbelief and dismay, Illion drank off his toast and put down the bowl. He frowned thoughtfully. Aloê, seeing this, wondered what he was thinking.

In fact, he was thinking of Morlock. But just then he said nothing.

Chapter Sixteen

Tunglskin

The red light of late afternoon was falling on Tunglskin, the Hill of Storms. Morlock struck a final blow at the planking before him. The wood splintered and fell; a wide breach had been opened in the wooden wall surrounding the hill. He turned away and walked over to the tree where he had left the horse. He untied the reins he had knotted around a low branch.

He looked the horse in the eye. There had never been any affection between them. But he had never mistreated the horse, nor did he do so now. "Go home," he said, and added a word of Westhold dialect, resonant with power. The horse turned and ran along the wooden wall toward the Rangan outpost.

Morlock climbed through the breach in the wall and walked a little way up the slope. He sat down on a convenient rock and waited.

It was not long before the Arbiter and one of her servants appeared at the break in the fence. They peered through and immediately saw Morlock on the hill. Having given them, in his own way, fair warning, he stood and walked up the slope. Presently he heard the sound of hammers on wood, sealing him in like a corpse in a coffin. He walked on.

He came across an ascending stairway of stone steps set into the Hill. They were very weathered; a path had been worn down through the middle of each step, as if many feet had passed there. The carvings on them were difficult to discern in the failing light, but Morlock knew better than to examine Coranian carvings too closely at dusk. There were stories about that. There were stories about everything, here.

The stair passed by a cave. The cheerful light of a fire was flickering across the threshold, incongruous against the dark hillside. Morlock clenched his teeth and stood indecisively in the dusk. He had heard about this place. . . . Finally he left the stairway and entered the cave.

Inside, Merlin rose to greet him.

It was a Merlin a thousand years younger than Morlock's father, without even a gray streak in his black hair and beard. It was a Merlin who wore the red cloak of a vocate on his crooked shoulders, the black-and-white shield of Ambrosius on his arm (the same shield, barring a millennium of aging and of careful repair, slung now across Morlock's shoulder). It was a Merlin who was not yet known as the master of all makers, one who was yet establishing his first reputation as a hero.

"I do not know you," said Merlin Ambrosius. "But I knew you would come here." He smiled. "I take it for granted that you know me."

There was arrogance in that smile—a measured arrogance. The smile and the statement claimed nothing, after all, but the truth. Morlock had heard of Merlin.

"Sit down, if you wish. Warm yourself at the fire. You'll welcome the memory, soon enough."

Morlock remained standing. The image of Merlin sat down on the opposite side of the fire and continued to speak.

"You have come here, drawn by stories—I might even say legends. You have come here to better my deed. When I made certain choices I knew you, and others like you, would come; to you, I guess, my work here seems incomplete. So I have remained here, in simulacrum, to assure you that the deed is not incomplete, and to warn you against meddling with my work."

Merlin smiled engagingly. "Those are harsh words for a proud champion. I don't speak them lightly. They are the best advice I can give to someone I consider my peer."

"Get on with it!" Morlock muttered, embarrassed and angry.

"I will explain," the image continued. "We stand (or sit) in part of the tomb of the Great Cor, now known as the Dead Cor. He, like his successors, had a means of prolonging his physical life far beyond its natural term. By feeding on the tal of sacrificial victims he strengthened his own grip on life when it was failing him, preserving life in his body even when that body began to decay.

"In fact, he never died. But the time came when he could no longer act as monarch over the unruly sorcerer-nobles of his kingdom; he required all his power simply to sustain the burden of his own life. Finally he was deposed and his successor did him the honor of burying him alive within this hill, which was then north of the border of the Wardlands. For you must know that the Coranians were descended from exiles, and like all exiles they hungered to return to the Wardlands."

Morlock nodded reflexively. His mother had been descended from Coranian exiles; it was one of the two reasons he knew more than he wanted about Coranians.

"The practice became a custom," Merlin's simulacrum continued. "When a Cor grew too feeble to rule he was taken here and a hill raised over him, in imitation of this one, now called the Hill of Storms (although its Dwarvish name is Tunglskin). But none of the Corain were wholly dead. In time, as their numbers grew, the Dead Cor found he could exert control over, and draw power from, the lingering tal of his successors and inferiors.

"That was a grim time. You have heard of it, or you would not be here. The Dead Cor asserted his mastery over the reigning Cor, who (after a few trials of power) proved willing to be led. The dwarves of Thrymhaiam found their land invaded by the Coranians, who looked to it as the staging ground for an invasion of the very Wardlands. The Eldest of Theorn Clan appealed to the Graith of Guardians to make common cause against the Coranian exiles. The Graith paused, deliberated, and chose to do nothing. I did none of these.

"I will not retell my deeds in the north; you have heard of them, or you would not be here. But I will say a thing to you: my choice was single; I could not have done other than I did. It was not in me to counter the massed sorcery of millennia of the Dead Corain. But I could separate them from each other and from their living successors. This I did, by planting a hedge of banefire around every living corpse that ever carried the sword-scepter Gryregaest. As long as they cling to life, the banefires—a spell I wove into the network of power that bound the Corain together and which they cannot cross—will burn about them. Nor can they reach through the fire to work their influence on others, except at a very low level. And they cannot league with each other, as they did before the north came under the Guard. If left to themselves they will lose their strength and collapse in final physical death.

"But others can go to them. That is the real danger. It gives them continuing sources of strength, to refresh their failing tal. It gives them new physical forms, when their own utterly give way to time. It gives them news of the great world beyond their open graves. It gives them a kind of hope. For as long as they persist the likelihood increases that some force will be able to quench the banefires and set them free, for some reason of its own.

"If you are victorious here, this night, your victory will add nothing to the safety of the Wardlands. But your defeat will hasten its destruction. Make the right choice while you still can. Go back; prove yourself in places where you are truly needed. Do not disturb the dead—lest you join them."

Then Merlin stood and looked Morlock in the eye. In the next instant the fire disappeared and Merlin with it. A wind blew through the cave.

"You're wrong," Merlin's son said to the darkness still inscribed with his image, flickering and fading as Morlock's eyes grew used to the dark. "A thousand years, and the Dead Cor is as powerful as ever. And there are powers moving in the land you never expected to return. Besides, I need the sword you left behind. And I think I can do what you chose not to do."

The darkness did not answer; the spell had exhausted itself, until another traveller came.

Night had completely risen outside. Morlock left the cave behind him and went up the dark stone way.

Morlock's footfalls rang out, regular and quick, in the darkness. He had little time before the banefire kindled. In fact, it occurred to him (belatedly) that the whole purpose of the illusory experience in the cave might be to delay adventurers from reaching the top of the stairway before the banefire came into being.

He began to leap up the steps, three at a time. The dark silhouette of the hilltop sank down toward him. Coming to the end of the stairway he continued to run across the broken ground below the crown of the hill.

When the ground changed abruptly under him he fell to his hands and knees in a cloud of dust.

Choking, he felt the gritty sharpness of the dust in his nose and mouth. This, he realized, must be the zone of banefire; a millennium of it had powdered the stone and the soil that had once been there. He wondered what fed the fire, what would quench it. He wondered what the fire would do to him if he lingered here until it kindled. Would his immunity from fire protect him? He doubted it.

He leapt up and began to slog through the heavy drifts of dust. He saw the angular outline of the Broken Altar against the blue-black sky. He saw nothing else. He felt cold. Sweat poured off his face, the dust that rose about him in clouds caked in it, but he was cold. He was cold *inside*, agonizingly so, and the cold was growing.

Blue light bloomed in the dead clouds of dust; it was all about him. He was hurling himself into a hedge of blue flames; they raked the bare flesh of his hands and face like thorns. He unslung the shield of Ambrosius and held it before his face as he ran. He burst through the last wall of flame and fell to his knees on the stony ground within the circle of fire.

Pain sank long cold teeth into his face and hands. He could hardly relax his fingers to let the Ambrosian shield fall to the ground. In the light of the major moons he saw ragged lines of black blisters rising on his hands. Elsewhere he was numb, colder than he had been the night he had escaped the dragons in the maijarra wood. The blisters were the coldest of all, like tumors of ice under the skin. He put his hands under his arms to warm them and bit back cries of pain.

When he felt his fingers might be able to move again, he got to his feet, clenching and unclenching his hands. He recovered his shield and, stumbling occasionally on loose stones, went to meet his adversary.

There were no legends to guide him now, no useful ones. No one had ever come this far up the Hill and returned—except Merlin. There was no one to tell him why the Hill was so dark, even though the summit was ringed with fire. Looking about, he saw that the banefire cast no shadows. Its magical light revealed nothing but itself. The only real light on the hilltop was that of the three moons: somber Chariot, hovering over the crooked eastern horizon; Horseman, more vivid and higher in the eastern sky; and Trumpeter, bitterly bright, just now clearing the western horizon.

"*Khai, gradara!*" Morlock cried, greeting the new moon. Some legends associated the three moons with the Creator, the Sustainer, and the King. Others linked them with the three ranks of Guardian, Trumpeter being associated with the thains. It was as Kingstone and Sign of Thains that Morlock greeted the last moon of the year, rising among the fiercely radiant western stars.

Lowering his eyes to the dark earth, he saw the glitter of reflected banefire. Advancing toward the Broken Altar, he saw the sword Gryregaest lying atop its slanted surface. In all that prospect, the deadly fire revealed only the cursed sword. He would have gone toward it, but he saw something beyond the Broken Altar.

The horizon had changed. Instead of standing against blank sky, the altar was framed by higher ground. Banefire outlined the new horizon without illuminating it.

The top of the Hill had opened. Between the risen slopes of stone and earth, a manlike form moved slowly toward him.

"Come no closer," he said. "Speak! Speak, if you can."

The figure continued to approach, but only for a few steps. It wore a heavy robe of grayish cloth, interwoven with bright metallic threads. Much of the fabric had fallen away, though. Over its head was a deep hood. It wore no crown. But in its left, sleeve-muffled hand it carried half a broken scepter.

"Speak!" Morlock said again.

It raised its right hand to its hood and drew it back, just far enough that Morlock could see its chin and throat. There was a swathe of destruction across the throat, as if a fire had burned fiercely there. The chin, too, had a black burn-scar on its dead white flesh; at one point brown bone gleamed darkly in the dim moonlight. Plainly the Dead Cor could not speak. Why had he thought it could? Morlock wondered suddenly. Why had he asked it to speak, when it was he who had something to say?

Then Morlock felt the rapport, a cruel rapport, as the Dead Cor tried to seize control of him. Morlock's will flared up at the attempt. He cried aloud and raised both his fists, as if he could use them to beat back the intrusion.

The Dead Cor actually did take a step back at that moment. It did not move, otherwise, but Morlock nevertheless sensed a kind of acknowledgement from his antagonist. Raising the Ambrosian shield, he spoke.

"I am not one of the enchanted, who come here to die in the banefire. Such a one, no doubt, gave you the body you now wear. But I am alive, not dead; nor I did come here seeking death."

The Dead Cor made no motion and uttered no sound. But Morlock understood a kind of question. He realized that there was still a rapport between them. He chose not to use it for his answer, though.

"I have come for Gryregaest," Morlock said. "I claim it. . . . I claim it by right of blood, for my father was—it was my father who bound you here." His Ambrosian blood burned in him like guilt as he spoke. He added hastily, "Also, there is need for the blade in the world. Leave it to me, and I will do you no harm."

The banefire leapt up to towering heights, roaring like a ring of animals, throwing out smoke and sparks cold as a shower of snow. But this was only the outward echo of the stunning assault of the Dead Cor, again striving to seize control of Morlock's will. Wild images flooded his awareness: a network of dragons woven like baskets into the sky; the sensation of Gryregaest, like unleashed vengeance, in his hands; faces he did not recognize (familiar faces, these) wearing expressions of hatred and fear as spadesful of dirt slowly blotted out his vision while maggots wriggled under his skin. There were no words; there was no voice. But there was the battering of alien thoughts, reshaping his own without explaining them, drawing him out of himself; a sense of long-delayed victory gripped him, and he knew it could be his, if only he would surrender, if only he would give in.

Staggering in the arena of dim blue light and black shadows, Morlock felt his mind light up with anger. His anger gave him shelter, a rallying point for his dissolving selfhood, amidst the tremendous psychic assault. He hid beneath his anger, as it were, but even as he did so he knew it was a failing resource. It was an almost-rational thing—the sort of resentment one might feel for a blow on the face—and could not stand up to the Dead Cor's ageless hunger for new life.

But the rage had deep and dangerous roots that were stronger and less sane than itself. As his awareness began to fragment under the Dead Cor's assault, this deeper, madder fury began to break through: redder than blood, more poisonous than venom, it scorched Morlock as no fire ever had. With the last shreds of his volition he summoned it up and directed it all against the faceless outline of the Dead Cor through the vehicle of their rapport.

Half-ascended to the visionary state he saw the lightless figure of the Dead Cor flare up with a succession of blindingly bright images. Or perhaps it was only one image, made up of characters somehow mingled, as often happens in a vision. He saw a dragon that (incongruously, impossibly) had dwarvish hands, clenched tight, in place of claws. He saw a twisted monster of a man, half-Merlin, half-something else. . . . With an abrupt access of shame he realized it was himself. All this passed in an instant. Then the violence of his response destroyed the vehicle of rapport, and he found himself alone in his own mind.

It was a mind in chaos. His victory was exhilarating, but dangerous. There were thoughts and memories loose in his awareness that he had never been conscious of. He saw a face looking down on him with no particular expression. Abruptly, he knew the face was his mother's. He had thought he remembered nothing of her, but now her image was part of him. He wondered if there were any other memories he had hidden from himself.

But the occasion gave him no time to sort out his inner world. His enemy was advancing toward him. He was still in its kingdom, and the battle with it was not over.

As it shambled toward him he awaited its attack with some confidence. Yet it did nothing but walk. When it came within arm's reach it dropped the broken scepter and, without further preliminary, reached for his throat.

He struck its hands aside and stepped back. But it followed him instantly; he had to brace his feet to keep it from rushing him over. It seized his shoulders and tried to throw him down. Braced, he pushed it suddenly, and it lost balance as well as its grip on him. Then he found himself seized by the waist as it fell toward him. He was lifted from the ground and carried toward the Broken Altar, where Gryregaest lay, glittering in the moonlight.

Morlock guessed that the Dead Cor, defeated in his attempt to obtain control of his living body, was willing to settle for one slightly damaged. Even slain by violence, Morlock knew, his body would support life more readily than the rotting monstrosity the Dead Cor now wore. His tal, though diminished, would remain for some time after his life had been quenched. . . .

He braced a knee against the Dead King's neck and threw himself to one side. It overbalanced and fell, dropping him. It rolled to its feet and stood over him. He kicked it with both feet and, as it fell back, recovered and rose. On impulse he leapt toward the Broken Altar, remembering from *First Merlin's Song* how his *ruthen* father had used Gryregaest itself to defeat the Dead Cor.

But this was a mistake. The Dead Cor was not even momentarily stunned by its fall; it jumped up and seized him by the neck. Then it hauled him back, past the altar and away from the banefire, in the direction from which it had first appeared.

Realizing that the place between the risen slopes was the Dead Cor's focus of power, as well as its grave, Morlock fought with renewed intensity. A horror of the zone between the slopes came over him. He thought of it as a dark womb, from which death and disease issued, and into which this shambling death was trying to draw him. But each time he tried to make it to his feet the Dead Cor simply pulled him off-balance.

He took the Ambrosian shield, still slung over his shoulder, and jabbed it into the Dead Cor's midriff. The Dead Cor staggered, and this gave him a chance to drag his feet in a quarter circle and brace them, so he could try to push it over. But it had noticed his action and braced its own feet in turn. They grappled for a moment, and then Morlock felt the oozing flesh of the Dead Cor's hands tighten in a deadly circle around his throat. It had wanted to bring him alive into its grave. But it would not risk his escape.

He broke the grip with his arms, pushing the Dead Cor's out and back. Grasping its left arm in his right hand he felt the fabric of the ancient robe tear apart and the flesh beneath it also. The metal threads woven into the robe remained as the fabric crumbled into dust; beneath them the long bone of the arm gleamed in the moonlight, torn strings of semiliquid flesh hanging from it.

Horror paralyzed Morlock. For an instant only—but in the dark heart of that instant the Dead Cor struck him on the side of the head. He fell, and as he fell, he crossed the threshold of the open grave.

Power unfolded like a burning flower within him. Almost before he fell to the ground he rolled to his feet and struck back at the Dead Cor, who was following closely.

He was burning, wrapped in black-and-white fire. The Dead Cor, too, was alight, but more dimly. Morlock could barely see the greenish tal-luminescence that bound unbreathing life to its stolen bones. He swept out his burning hand and struck one of the Dead Cor's shoulders. The bone there splintered, and the light woven through it went dark. But at that moment he felt everything around him change subtly; his own light grew dimmer, and he felt the power within him lessen. When the Dead Cor moved to stand just out of reach he did not pursue it.

The sense of strength was intoxicating. The fact that he could stand there and choose whether to renew the battle or not was amazing to him. He let it amaze him and did not renew the battle.

He looked around at his surroundings. He found that he could see clearly in the darkness, although it remained somehow a darkness where even the light of the three moons did not penetrate. Perhaps, he thought, he was seeing by his own light. The thought pleased him obscurely.

What he saw, though, was beyond doubt repulsive. There were heaps of trash everywhere. These, perhaps, had once been wealth, or food, or living persons, but now they were nothing but wreckage over which the silver lights flickered dimly.

And yet . . . those lights! Looking more closely he saw that over each object there was a dimly luminous distorted image of itself, drawn in silver light. Going toward a pile of rotten fruit that lay upon the ground, he saw that the silvery images had tenuous roots in their source-objects. But the images were not of corrupt fruit; they were of wholesome ones. As he approached the fruit the images became more definite and less distorted in shape. Holding his hands over them he saw that his light perfected the images, so that they were whole and healthy, all but real in his hand. The objects themselves, though, remained a heap of rotten husks.

Next to these was a pile of dusty wreckage that looked like gnawed twists of black bark. The image above it was a stack of silver coins. Morlock held his hands close and watched the image become clear and perfect. It was fascinating—like being able to create wealth from nothing. But again the object itself remained unchanged, although the faint threads connecting image and object nearly disappeared.

Nearby on the ground lay a long twisted skeleton. He saw the weblike frames of vestigial wings attached to the long distorted spine, the narrow wolflike skull. Above the skeleton was the pale image of a crouching clench-fisted dwarf.

He turned on it with fury. He held out his hands and directed all his strength toward the image. The beard grew longer, the face more noble; the fists opened in a regal gesture of giving. Morlock was seized with the desire to make the image real, or at least so vivid as to obscure the nightmarishly distorted skeleton beneath. Because *this* was the truth and *that* was a lie—a trick of his enemy set here to confuse him about what was true and what was false, what was good and what was evil. He swore he would not let his enemy deceive him, no matter what face it wore. . . .

The thought of his enemy swung around and struck him with renewed force. Looking up sharply, he saw that the Dead Cor was still standing, just out of reach. It held in its hands the Ambrosian shield, which Morlock must have let fall somewhere. It no longer stood like a fighter, but Morlock knew that a deadlier combat had begun.

"I know," said the dwarvish image. Morlock looked sharply at the silver figure and saw that its mouth was indeed moving. But the tongue behind the bearded lips was narrow and it flickered like a serpent's; silver smoke trailed after its words into the pestilential air. It spoke Wardic, and its voice was Morlock's own.

"I know what you have come to learn," the dwarvish image said. "Since you have given to me, I can tell it to you. Gift for gift and harm for harm: that is law."

"Not my law," Morlock replied, facing the Dead Cor. Morlock knew it was that one who moved the dwarvish image to speak.

"It is the only law I know," the image behind him said. "Never have I taken without giving; never do I give without taking. This is my realm and my law. Listen. Learn. Receive."

"I give you nothing," Morlock said harshly.

The shining, smoking dwarf behind him laughed. "Nonsense. You gave me your voice—or how do I use it now? You gave me your anger. You gave me more news of the world than you know. I intend to make use of all these things. You will hear what I have to say, not by my will but your own. It was to hear these things you came here."

"I came here for the sword Gryregaest," Morlock insisted.

"Gryregaest?" The dwarvish image laughed again. (The twisted hulk of the Dead Cor was motionless throughout this.) "No, I think not. What use is Gryregaest to you in your troubles? It is not as if you need another curse on your blood.

"But I can answer your questions, Morlock *Ambrosius*. In the last long age of the Longest War I was already buried here. But I was not then hedged in with banefire. I walked long and far in search of souls to eat. I killed many a dwarf in the emptiness of my heart, and once, for a long rotting lifetime, I wore a dragon's flesh. There is nothing that can be known about what you wish to know that I do not know. Listen. Learn. Receive."

"No," Morlock croaked.

"I speak with your own voice. Do you think I know nothing of your mind? You have come here because I, too, am your kinsman, furthest ancestor of your mother's people, enemy to both your *harven* and *ruthen* fathers. You are half an Ambrose—maker, Guardian, servant. But you are also half-Coranian, half-monster, half-king. It is my blood in you that hates both your fathers. Each of them would lie for the other; I will tell you the truth about both. Regin and Fafnir were brothers. Listen. Learn. Receive."

Morlock was trapped. He wanted to deny, to respond, to defend. He could not. His anger and his hate were real. He had given them to the Dead Cor, little guessing how important they were. And their roots were still within him. Any words he might have spoken died in his throat, clenched like a fist with the rage that now came flooding back. He remembered the old story about the treacherous maker Regin and his hated brother, the dragon Fafnir. He dreaded and longed to hear what the Dead Cor would say next.

"Dragon and dwarf are blood-kin," the dwarvish image whispered behind his back. "This much you have guessed, and it is the truth. The ancestors of the dragons were mandrakes, two-legged serpents who lived in tunnels under the Whitethorn Mountains. They grew wise and their works were great: the Runhaiar was but one of many, most of which were destroyed in the Longest War. The mandrakes broke through to open sky and learned to love the light. By choice or by the destiny of their blood they grew wings, striving to reach the sun. Legends say they knew the name of your King when he was still in the world.

"As the world worsened, they mirrored it. Always greedy, they became lazy and bred slaves from their own blood to plunder what was left in the land's flesh. These slaves were weaker and lesser than their ancestors, and the fire in them was hidden deep within their hearts. These were the first dwarves. They labored underground and in their workshops while their masters brooded over vast hoards of treasure and learned only the art of stealing from each other.

"It was in this age that the mandrakes became dragons. Whether by choice—because, for stealth or force, a dragon is the perfect thief—or else by the destiny of their blood, mandrake after mandrake suffered the metamorphosis to dragon. They lost their hands. Their genitals remained but were useless; they could only give birth in death. Their fire burst forth uncontrollably, and the venom in their throats tormented them with eternal thirst. But they were strong: to fight, to steal, to keep. The strongest of them were nearly invulnerable, and they tested that strength in constant combat with each other. In this age their civilization fragmented, but it had not completely fallen: the dwarvish slave-race kept it alive.

"Then the dragon-plague began to spread among the dwarves. By choice or by the destiny of their blood, slave after slave underwent the metamorphosis and became a fire-breathing serpent. These were either killed or allowed to wander free, but in either case the wealth they produced was lost to their masters. The civilization of the dragons began its final collapse.

"Then Theornn arose and established a code of laws among the dwarves under him. Instead of greed they were taught hospitality. Instead of rage, justice. Creation, not possession; service, not mastery. The new dwarvish law placed blood above money: it was not to be bought or sold. To shed blood for money, to steal, to lie: these were made unthinkable crimes, punished with swift justice. The love of kin was also fostered, as antidote to selfishness. The dwarves of Theornn were taught to revere their ancestors, who had not undergone the metamorphosis; they came to believe (because Theornn encouraged it) that their ancestors watched over them, and their dearest wish was to join those-who-watch after death."

This description of dwarvish law (accurate, in the main) gave Morlock the voice to speak in defense of his *harven* kin. "Then I say Theornn was a prophet, who brought his people words of life and hope."

The silver dwarf behind him laughed, loud and long. "*His* people?" it said finally. "They were *his* people—his property. Have you not understood? Theornn was a dragon, the first ruler of Thrymhaiam. He instituted law among the dwarves to protect their value as workers and slaves. For a long age, while the other great dragons of the north could obtain wealth only by stealing it, Theornn's slaves made him new things of wealth and beauty every day. Until, at last, Theornn's servants rose up and killed him and his companions while they lay sleeping. So the good righteous dwarves of Thrymhaiam bought their freedom with the murder of their prophet, and the Longest War began with the treachery of a slave!"

Morlock, spellbound by the terrible revelations, did not have the strength to speak. He hardly had the strength to move. Dimly he remembered his former sense of power, and dimly wondered at the memory. He glanced back at the dwarvish image that had spoken so many words with his voice. Its light was brighter, its features stronger and more noble than ever. He began to understand that power was still passing from himself to the image. And if the image were but an extension of the Dead Cor . . .

He turned back. The greenish lumen woven through the Dead Cor's form shone like a lamp. The break at its shoulder had knitted; it seemed to grow brighter as he looked at it. Then he guessed that all this talk, true or false, was simply a ploy to keep him still while the life drained from him. He picked up his feet and ran to the edge of the grave. As he turned away the silver serpentine dwarf vanished like a blown flame and he felt strength well up within him.

He halted at the grave's edge. What, he wondered, was the source of the strange bodiless strength sustaining him? Part, indeed, came from within. But that was intensified and added to by the power-focus that lay through the grave itself. Could he use it against the Dead Cor, even destroy his enemy so?

It seemed unlikely. As he turned, he saw the other standing just beyond reach, waiting. Why should it wait, unless waiting was to its advantage? It would have never brought him here if there were even a chance he might use the focus to destroy it. He guessed that everything he did within the grave caused power to transfer from himself to the dead one. Outside the grave he might die; inside he was certainly doomed, and each long moment he stayed there brought that doom nearer.

But even the thought of recrossing the threshold was a painful one. Beyond the grave, the Dead Cor seemed even stronger than it was here. The strength the grave-spell provided might be an illusion, but it was a very pleasant illusion. Perhaps he should wait a while. . . .

Every instant he watched, though, the Dead Cor's image grew clearer and brighter upon its object. It had a face now. Morlock did not wish to see that face. He turned and crossed the threshold, feeling the lightless weight of his flesh descend on him; the black-and-white flames wrapping him vanished.

The Dead Cor was upon him at once, all light extinguished, a corrupt deadly weight heavier than stone. The monochrome shield of Ambrose glinted mockingly on its shoulder. His strength began to fail as the sharp fleshless hands forced him back toward the banefire. He tried to dig in his feet, but the ground crumbled beneath them and he was forced closer and closer to the zone of deadly light.

At the brink he finally caught his feet on a ridge of stone and turned. They struggled with the banefire burning at their side. Morlock saw the wild torn outline of his enemy, black against the blue blaze of the undying fire his father had set. The Dead Cor raised the dead weight of its arms and struck him repeatedly on the face. He saw the shield of Ambrose fly up and down on its shoulder, like a single wing, as he vainly tried to protect his head.

Groggily, Morlock realized he was about to lose consciousness and, with it, his life. With the last of his strength he seized his enemy by the bare bone of its arms and they fell together into the banefire.

The cold lightning-bright agony of the blue flames lanced through him. But he held, like death itself, his enemy by its arms. He dragged it farther back, toward the coldest heart of the flames. For endless freezing moments it fought him, the fire, the corruption in its own flesh.

Suddenly there was darkness. The undying flames were dead. Morlock cried out involuntarily in pain and fear. He had never seen anything as terrifying as that empty dark. He was alone; his hands were empty. His father's spell was broken, and that could only mean the Dead Cor was free.

Dazed with pain and fear he turned back and forth in the darkness, seeking to face his death as it came to him. It was not until he looked down and saw the skeleton and the shield of Ambrose, gleaming in the moonlight, at his feet that he realized the truth. He was the victor; Gryregaest, the sword-scepter, the prize of Tunglskin, was his.

That morning a storm came out of the mountains by way of the Hill of Storms. The snow rode bitter winds from the Whitethorn slopes; the storm struck lightning like sparks from the flinty gray hills. The Arbiter of the Peace waited it out stoically, standing inside Morlock's breach in the wooden wall, which she had reopened last night in the hour when the banefire failed.

It shocked her servants when she broke the wall. They had taken it, she guessed, as an act of despair. They thought, clearly, that it pleased her to make her final stand against the ancient horror at such a place.

In a way, of course, they were right. Things might end that way. But she did not feel they would. There was something else in the air. It went with the storm, with the clean cold winds the storm brought, with the sudden shocking light of thunderbolts in the snow.

The snow now covered the crooked black hill like a veil. As she waited for dawn in the storm, she wondered at the mysterious beauty of the hated hill in the rising light. The storm broke just before dawn, when there was still a dark blue brightness to the clearing sky.

In dawn's light Tunglskin was more beautiful yet: a crooked white outline against the straight high peaks beyond. For long moments the Arbiter simply looked at it, then had to look away.

Not long after dawn the watchers' horns began to sound. The first one sounded not twenty paces from her. Looking to the top of the hill, she saw that a figure was indeed making its way down the slope. She raised her own horn and sounded it, silencing the watchers. She sounded it again with a different call, telling her servants to stay at their posts at the base of the hill. Then she picked five to accompany her and began to climb toward the descending figure.

It was Morlock. They met about halfway up the hill. His face was like a muddy footprint in a field of snow.

He clearly had been through a mortal combat. There were black blisters and deepening bruises on his face. But beyond these he had a lost tormented look. The Arbiter heard her servants muttering ominously at her back, and not without cause; she had seen corpses dead from banefire that looked less damaged than Morlock did now. Nevertheless she was tolerably sure this was the man himself, not merely a new avatar for the Dead Cor. He carried the shield of Ambrose on his arm—and who but Morlock would look so dismayed at a legendary victory?

"Thain Morlock," she said, "what's wrong?"

He stared at her blankly, and when he answered it seemed no answer. "It's dark," he muttered. "Broken and dark."

"But it's not dark now," she said. "The sun has risen. Look! All around. Light."

He looked at her in astonishment and shook his head.

"How fares the Dead Cor?" she asked.

He laughed, and for a moment she looked away. But she found she must look back; his unhappiness fascinated her.

"Regin and Fafnir were brothers!" He shouted it in her face and rushed by.

She nodded to herself. She remembered Morlock crying this aloud in trance some days ago. Whatever it meant (and she had no idea; the names were gibberish to her, perhaps some wormhugger thing), this was surely the other side of Morlock's vision.

Some of her servants would have gone after Morlock, but she stopped them. If he had destroyed the Dead Cor, he would make short work of them, or so she guessed. And, if he hadn't, she would need them here.

At the summit they found the Dead Cor's grave still open to the sky, as if it were midnight instead of newest day. The veil of snow was humped in strange shapes within the grave, and the Arbiter forbid her people to enter there, lest they be snared by some lingering spell. She commanded them to sweep the rest of the area clear, hoping to find the remains of the Dead Cor.

Not long afterward one of her servants called her to the Broken Altar. "He left the sword," the servant told her.

"Gryregaest?" she said. "I wonder why." She looked down on the sword-scepter, glittering like graven ice on the dark stone surface of the altar. The blade's surface was bright, but there was none of that inner light the songs spoke of. There was no trace of snow on stone or sword.

"It's broken," the servant answered. "Look!"

With courage too reckless to be called commendable, he reached down and pressed the edge of the blade with his thumb. Then she saw that what she had thought to be a design engraved on the crystalline sword was in fact a pattern of fracture lines. The sword had been shattered, then the pieces put together like a puzzle. The sword was useless; it wasn't even a sword.

"Odd they don't mention it in the songs," the servant said.

"Maybe they will in the next one," the Arbiter replied. "Look, Bren, collect the pieces and tend to them. They'll be wanting every last sliver in Thrymhaiam or I don't know dwarves."

At that point another one of the servants cried out that the Dead Cor had been found in the banefire circle. She went over to take charge of burning its bones.

Morlock stole a horse from the Arbiter's stables and rode it at a cruel pace back to Thrymhaiam. Stealing was nothing to him, now—he knew why the dwarves feared it. Cruelty was nothing to him, now—he knew who had taught them to refrain. He would ride up and tell them, *I stole this horse. Take it.* He would . . . He would . . .

He was furious. How they had lied to him, all his life, teaching him a way to live but not telling him the evil that lay behind it. They were just like Merlin. *Harven* Tyr was no better than *ruthen* Merlin. In fact, he was worse. There had been a boldness, an openness to Merlin's evil. He was what he was and he didn't try to pretend virtue. Tyr was otherwise: timid, crawling in his cave, speaking wise words of caution, while all the time there was a serpent in him, rearing to strike.

He reached the ruins of Southgate well before noon. He dismounted the horse and challenged the watch in Dwarvish. "Take me to the Eldest!" he said. "Wherever he is, there I will go."

They sent a guide with him. It was past noon before they reached a chamber that was sealed in white wax: the sign of the Elders' assembly. Outside the door stood no guard; by dwarvish custom the chamber stood inviolate until the seal was broken from within.

Morlock laughed bitterly. Dwarvish custom! What was it to him, an Ambrosius? With a defiant glance at his guide, who was openmouthed with astonishment, he lifted the Ambrosian shield and crushed the wax seal. Then he opened the door and entered, a shout of furious defiance ready on his tongue.

Faces looked at him in surprise, seven blunt bearded faces. They were the Elders of the Seven Clans under Thrymhaiam, the heirs of the dragon Theornn. In the center should have been Tyr, their chief, as Eldest of the eldest clan. There was no better place for the inevitable confrontation. He would tell them all, tell them he knew everything, tell them he knew what they were at last.

But Tyr was not present. Vetr sat in his place.

"I beg your pardon, Elder Brother," said Morlock. He had no quarrel with Vetr. "I have words for Tyr. Some fool told me he was here."

Vetr rose to his feet. "He is not. You had better tell your words to me."

Morlock shook his head. "No. Where is he?"

"You have not understood, Brother. He is *not*. Your guide brought you, I guess, where you asked to go. Old Father Tyr has gone with the summoner Earno to his last combat. I am the Eldest of Theorn Clan."

CHAPTER SEVENTEEN

Under the Mountains

The nest that Vendas had fashioned out of his ruined bed was beginning to rot. This had something to do with the fluid being secreted under the scales that now covered his skin. A number of his guards had tried to buy the bed from him, as that was the only way he would even discuss parting with it. But he kept raising the price. Finally one of the guards brought in a small sum of gold, supposing the captive would, as the proverb had it, prefer real gold to talked-about jewels. But Vendas had simply killed him and taken his money. Now the guards sat their watches in pairs, wore armor, and did not talk to the prisoner.

He was unconscious when Vyrlaeth, the snakelike master of healing, brought Deor and Morlock in to view him. Smoke trailed from his distended nostrils.

"He's been asleep now for two days," Vyrlaeth told Morlock. "See how long and sharp his head is getting? We think the jaws will open up there, at the top of his head."

"What about his face?"

"Perhaps it will just wear away. He will never have wings. But: you see how low his shoulders are getting? Perhaps his legs and arms will fuse into his body and he will become a fire-breathing serpent. There are such in Tychar, they say. It's most interesting. I almost wish we had more like Ven to study."

"It is terrible to see." Morlock's tone was distant, as if he were remembering something.

"I've seen nothing worse," Deor agreed, scowling at Vyrlaeth. "Nor had Eldest Tyr; he told me as much." Deor paused, then added impulsively, "We are all like Ven, these days."

Morlock looked at him without expression. "What do you mean?"

Deor knew well enough what he meant, but it was difficult to say. Ven represented to him everything that had changed when the dragons came. The familiar had become strange, then horrible, without ceasing to be familiar. He stood there, talking to Morlock, as he had countless times before. But it was different—he could not speak freely, and Morlock seemed to have the same problem. Conversation had a tendency to flicker and go out. It was not because they could not think of anything to say—who cared for silence then? No: it was because they were thinking constantly of what they could not say.

When Tyr had lost (or won) the coin toss, this moment became inevitable. Someday Morlock would return to Thrymhaiam. It was the lot of one of his *harven* kin to go with Earno, to protect Morlock from exile. It was the lot of the other to stay behind and tell him the truth of these events, when he was ready to hear it. "Yours is the harder task, Deortheorn," said the Eldest, after the coin chose him. Deor had not believed it, and still did not. But it was hard enough. He knew that he could not tell Morlock the whole truth in his present strange mood. (What had he seen on Tunglskin? What had the Dead Cor, perhaps, told him?) But Deor refused to lie to him; that would do no one any good. So they ended up suffering through long silences—like this one.

"Never mind!" he said impatiently, brushing the matter away.

Morlock nodded. He, too, had something too dangerous to say. He was thinking how, in his insane anger, he had been ready to taunt Tyr with the twisted serpentine skeleton he had seen on Tunglskin. But he was not angry now. He felt only an emptiness that was not even grief or guilt. "I wish Old Father Tyr had not gone," he said.

Deor shrugged. "You'll get no argument from me. Vetr is a good enough fellow, but no one can pretend we ever saw eye to eye."

The dwarves on guard looked at each other nervously after this comment. "Deor!" said Vyrlaeth warningly.

Deor's impatience boiled over again. "Come along; let's get out of here and breathe some air."

In the corridor outside he resumed, "Nevertheless, Tyr had his reasons for going. I don't think you're . . . considering everything."

"Have I ever?"

"Quit that moaning. Think like one of us. You've brought more honor to Thrymhaiam in three days than I will in my whole life. That's not worthless."

"It is, though. Honor is no use to dead dwarves."

"Those-who-watch are 'dead dwarves.' You never understood about honor. A dwarf would never say that."

"Then."

"A very stupid dwarf might. You see, I correct myself. You do the same. Why else did Tyr go under the mountains? He went for honor."

Deor held his breath as he waited for Morlock to speak. He had privately resolved to tell Morlock the whole truth if he even seemed to ask about it. This situation was intolerable.

But Morlock said only, "I understand."

As they walked down the corridor Deor felt a kind of disappointment. He didn't know what Morlock knew, or thought he knew. But it could be nothing like the truth that Deor knew. Perhaps he should go on and speak out anyway. But the moment had passed.

As he walked next to Morlock he thought of how the crime he had committed along with Tyr was destroying them. Those-who-watch were already exacting their punishment.

Suddenly he thought of a way to say something. He said, "About Vendas . . ."

"Yes?"

"What I meant—Ven was no one out of the ordinary. All of us have felt what he must feel: arrogance that ends in the abasement of greed, anger that clouds even self-interest. We are taught from birth to overcome these things. That is what the customs are for; that is what hospitality means. The fact that we need them proves that the other things are there. They are always there. Ven's shame is Tyr's, and mine."

Morlock nodded, and then he said an odd thing, in an odd tone of voice, "Regin and Fafnir were brothers." It wasn't clear that he even intended for Deor to hear him, and when he met his kin's astonished eye he added, "And what's yours is mine. We are kin, *harven coruthen*."

"Hmph. *I'll* try to keep it in mind."

Morlock smiled, and they walked together in silence. But it was an easier silence. Morlock no longer seemed so troubled; he seemed to have made a decision of some kind. Not until later did Deor realize what it was.

The names Regin and Fafnir stuck in Deor's mind; he wondered what Morlock's murmured comment meant, but somehow was reluctant to track him down and ask him. Deor himself talked a good deal more than he was aware of, and he was sometimes embarrassed when someone asked him what he was talking about.

Late that night, he was leaving his workroom and ran into Vyrlaeth, outside the Chambers of Healing.

"Listen, Vyrlaeth," he said, on impulse, "have you ever heard of Regin and Fafnir?"

Vyrlaeth's long gray lips twisted in humorous chagrin. "Not before this afternoon, when I heard Morlock mention them to you."

"Oh, then—Hey! Were you spying on us?"

"Naturally, naturally," said the beardless shameless dwarf. "Morlock is an interesting study; I have often found him so. More interesting than Vendas, in some specific ways."

"Eh," said Deor—at a loss, and not for the first time, by the healer's frosty interest in his fellow beings.

"I consulted a few onomastica this evening, after my late rounds," Vyrlaeth continued, noting Deor's dismay with cold amused eyes. "Would you like to know what I learned?"

"Naturally, naturally."

Vyrlaeth nodded to acknowledge Deor's mimicry and said, "The names come from an ancient Coranian legend of dragonkilling. The story has attached to several heroes in Laent and elsewhere. But the tale tells of two monsters: a gifted maker named Regin and a great seer named Fafnir. They were brothers, and their father was rich, but the treasure was cursed. The father died because of the curse, and Fafnir stole the treasure. He turned into a dragon, the better to defend his stolen hoard. Regin recruits a hero to slay the dragon, offering to split the treasure. But he secretly plans to betray the hero and murder him, once the dragon is slain. The hero is warned in the nick of time, you'll be glad to hear, and kills both brothers, so getting the treasure for himself. I suppose it's a happy ending, of a sort."

"Urr." This was giving Deor a lot to think about. "What happens to the hero?"

"Nothing good. Heroes don't live happily ever after in these sorts of stories. Do you know what this means, Deor?"

"I'm pretty sure Morlock has figured out that dragons and dwarves are akin, at least. I was trying to tell him that myself, by showing him what Vendas had become."

"Too late, I think. I warned Old Father Tyr not to hide this knowledge from Morlock—if it came to him too late, it might destroy the trust that should obtain between *harven* kin. But I think Old Father Tyr was ashamed, and saw little reason to mention something so shameful and so unlikely to be relevant. Or so it would have seemed before this year."

Deor wished that Vyrlaeth would shut up. He had some thinking to do, and the snakelike healer's babbling wasn't helping him do it.

"It will be interesting to see what Morlock's behavior will be once he begins to assimilate this new knowledge," the healer remarked.

"I suppose so." Deor realized he had not seen Morlock for hours. He wondered idly where his *harven* kin was. Then he did not wonder; he knew.

He turned away from Vyrlaeth and ran all the way to the Helgrind Gate. By the time he had reached there a group of kin-councillors (Vetr's counsellors, that is, among whom Deor was conspicuously not included) were milling around the guards. At their center was Vetr himself, speaking to the senior dwarf in the watch.

Deor shouldered his way into the center of the group. Vetrtheorn looked up at his approach. Their eyes met and Vetr nodded. "Morlock has been gone for many hours," the new Eldest said.

A senseless rage, born perhaps of frustration, kindled in Deor. "You!" he shouted. "You let him go! Old Father Tyr is dead and you let Morlock go under the mountains!"

Vetr fixed his eye on Deor and did not glance aside. But when he said, "Stand away," everyone but Deor did so at once.

"Deor," said Vetr, when they stood alone, "calm yourself. My command was that no one should leave Thrymhaiam, except by my word. But Morlock is not my subject; he is sworn to the Graith of Guardians. The watch had no power to stop him." Then Vetr smiled wryly. "Nor, I guess, would they have done so if they could. Is he not *rokhlan*? Is he not the victor of Tunglskin? This hour I have received the fragments of the sword Gryregaest from that bloodless creature who arbits the peace for Ranga's colony. Morlock's prestige alone would have overridden my express command."

"So you would have let him go anyway—to secure your own power."

Now Vetr himself grew angry. "I would have been tempted to do so. It is because of him that my father went to his death with Earno."

Deor stared sullenly at Vetr without answering. He did not know what Tyr had said to Vetr before he left with the spellbound summoner; it had not been, Deor felt, his place to ask. But he had the impression that Tyr had told his successor almost nothing.

"Hear me," Vetr said, apparently mistaking Deor's silence for disbelief. "Morlock dishonored his *ruthen* father; he served his *ruthen* father's worst enemy, Earno. Can there be a greater disgrace for a *harven* father? Tyr did not think so!"

"Bah," said Deor. Vetr had apparently been making deductions from separate things Tyr had said about Morlock, Merlin, and Earno. "You are madder than Morlock, Eldest Vetr, and that is saying something."

"Tyr was grateful to Earno. Do you understand? The Old Father believed that Earno had given Morlock cause to hate him. If Morlock could hate his *ruthen* father's enemy, he might be a step closer to showing that father lawful respect. Remember: he took the Ambrosian shield to Tunglskin."

"Hate against hate. This is gibberish. Old Father Tyr went under the mountains because he had a high heart, not because he was afraid of . . . of . . ."

"Of a *ruthen* father's curse?" said Vetr. "But he did fear it. Almost the last words he said to me were a warning that my rule as Elder might be burdened with a curse. 'Do the best you can,' he said, 'and do not blame yourself. The fault is mine.'"

Deor could think of nothing to say. He was aghast at the chasm between what Tyr had meant and what Vetr had understood. Could this stubborn, dull, determined rock-pounder truly be the son of Old Father Tyr, that wise old head? Yet he saw the kinship, too—in that harsh decency that would spare no one and nothing for what he believed was right. . . .

"And I believe that we are cursed," Vetr was continuing quietly. "Not just because of Morlock—for many things. We stand alone against the oldest enemy, yet our defeat will bring down the new realm we have joined.

I don't claim to understand. I don't see why we were chosen to suffer this defeat." He paused, and Deor saw Tyr's eldest son was tired and confused. "Do not be my enemy, Deor. I know I will never be Tyr's equal. That is why I am angry with Morlock, I guess. I still believe Tyr died for his sake. Yet, if Morlock were standing with us, I would keep him from going the same way, if I could."

"Because it would be *just?*" Deor could not help mocking him. How did he dare not to be Tyr? It was Tyr they needed, not this grieving shadow, this leftover.

"No," Vetr replied. "In spite of justice, in spite of anger. But perhaps Morlock himself prefers justice to mercy. . . ."

"Justice!" shouted Deor. "Morlock is guilty of nothing, except being as mad as a new moon. You *defame* him. You *slander* him." He was shouting in Vetr's face, more than loud enough for those standing by to hear.

Vetr put his hand on Deor's shoulder. "Deor, I see and share your double grief. I bear you no ill will. But you have said a word too many. Tomorrow, on the twentieth day of Borderer, I will hold my first judgement as Eldest. In the presence of these witnesses, I command you to present yourself before me then. And I will pass judgement on you for these words you have spoken. For, by the hands of my father who stands now with those-who-watch, I call you *liar*. Now leave me."

Deor walked alone down a long corridor.

Wild thoughts, like a whirlpool, spun in his mind—narrowing, like a whirlpool, to a single strand of thought: he would not flee Vetr's judgement. Neither would he defend himself.

If Thrymhaiam were really under a curse, it was Deor's fault, and Tyr's. Vetr was as innocent as Morlock. Yet Vetr, and all the Seven Clans he now ruled, might have to suffer for Deor's mistake.

He regretted now his harsh words to Vetr. Vetr was wrong about Morlock, about Tyr, about everything, it seemed. But he was the Eldest; Thrymhaiam needed him in this hour, with the Longest War returned in all its horror. And the Clans needed to believe in Old Father Tyr, standing with those-who-watch to protect Thrymhaiam's people from their enemies.

Deor could defend himself only by accusing Tyr and Vetr at once. That might be the end of his people. Fear could turn to despair, and despair to panic, all too easily. A single stone could start that avalanche. Deor swore he would not be that stone.

In an odd way, it restored his own faith in those-who-watch. They had taken care of things very neatly. Tyr and Deor had violated hospitality to protect Morlock. Now Morlock, as a direct result of this, had gone to his death and, shortly, Deor would go to his. Let it end there, he thought. With himself gone, perhaps those-who-watch would finally act on behalf of their people. Clenching and unclenching his fists, Deor walked back under the mountains where he had spent his whole life.

But at the appointed hour Deor came to the Underhall of Judgement to find the Eldest occupied in welcoming a new group of refugees. At least, that was what Deor took them for; they were Other Ilk, and ragged enough to be survivors from Ranga or Haukr. But they said they were from Westhold, and they wore the red and gray of Guardians.

Chapter Eighteen

Guile

The chasm was radiant with gray light when Morlock stepped out of the Helgrind Gate. It was hardly past noon, and the sun had just been eclipsed by the towering edge of the eastern wall. The narrow sky above him was a dark brilliant blue. A veil of snow and ice lay over the floor of the chasm, broken only by the sheer dark walls and the shallow stream that wound through the center of Helgrind from its source in the Coriam Lakes.

After crossing the stream, Morlock walked directly to the Runhaiar Gate. Before its yawning unbarred entrance he halted and looked back a last time at the peaks of Thrymhaiam, blazing with fierce white light. His eyes full of bright echoes, he lowered his gaze to the shadows of Helgrind, then turned to the utter darkness of the Runhaiar.

His astonished eyes painted the dark, like a canvas, with dimly glowing mountain peaks. He moved toward them. Something in them, some part of the light, moved forward to him. Startled, Morlock drew back. The sharp light still advanced and did not fade as his eyes became accustomed to the dimness. There was something there; it was coming out of the tunnel.

Morlock stepped back into the gray light of Helgrind. The shape followed him and Morlock relaxed in surprise and recognition as he saw it standing on the threshold of the Runhaiar. It was the black unicorn, its horn shedding light in the shadow. The horn was pointed at Morlock's chest.

Morlock frowned, remembering again the shattered corpse he had once seen in the Grartan Range. But he did not back away any farther, nor did he try to protect himself with the Ambrosian shield hung on his arm; there was no sense in that. Nor, upon a moment's thought, did he suppose the unicorn meant him harm. Its aim seemed simply to prevent him from entering the Runhaiar. Certainly it might have skewered him as he stood amazed in the darkness.

He wondered why it had come here. Surely it could not have known (or could it?) that he would follow Earno and Tyr into the Runhaiar. Its mysterious threatening benevolence intrigued him. He felt the unreasoned sense of communion, as strongly as he had the first time they met. But now, as then, he understood nothing of what he felt; their communion was not communication.

"Old . . ." said Morlock, and paused. He did not know the unicorn's name, or even if it had one. Even to speak aloud at it seemed strangely inappropriate. But need spurred him on. "Swift One, I must pass. My *harven* father has gone under these mountains."

The unicorn looked at him through its red irises. Its right ear bent back as he spoke, until it lay almost flat against the equine skull. Morlock watched in fascination, wondering what the reaction meant. After a moment of tense motionlessness, the unicorn bent its neck and pointed with its horn. It moved slowly and deliberately, like someone gesturing for the benefit of a sleepy child. The horn pointed north. Morlock looked north, but saw nothing other than the stream winding upward to the high notched horizon.

He looked back at the unicorn. It was watching him now, waiting for him to understand. He shook his head slowly and said, "I don't understand."

The unicorn stood there, waiting. Morlock wondered dimly what the gesture had meant. He thought of the dragon that had died in the Coriam Lakes, the Northtower, Trua and her people . . . Trua. That might be it. The old woman would have led her people into the maijarra forest by now. It would be safer than the tower, but there still must be great danger and hardship. Morlock thought of Trua in the storm that had just passed. She was brave, but too frail to live long unsheltered in winter.

But that was folly—who in the north would now live long? No one, was Morlock's guess. It only remained to choose the death that suited them.

The unicorn waited.

Morlock flushed. If there were anything he could do, it would be different. But it made no sense to simply go and die with them. Even as this thought formed it threw a shadow, a counterthought that said, *You are simply going to die anyway.* Who could say what would happen if he went to the Haukrull refugees? He felt the tug of the idea. They were no more unlike him than anyone else. While living there he had had a few troubled one-sided romances, as searing and brief as thunderbolts. He had lived among them. Why not die among them?

It was not enough to sway him, finally. It was simply a death with a halo of questions about it. Before him, certain, fire-etched in the darkness, was a death freighted with meaning. Tyr had gone under the mountains with Earno because of Morlock; that was clear. The reason was less so, but the fact spoke for itself: Tyr had gone in his place, as Earno's second. And at the very moment of Tyr's death, perhaps, Morlock had been cursing him as a liar. No one but Morlock knew that, but that made the guilt more inescapable, somehow. . . .

And, in fact, he still felt that Tyr had deceived him. He should have been trusted; he should have been told. He could not help but forgive his *harven* father; all he wanted was his father's forgiveness in turn. Since that was impossible, he would go under the mountains to seek vengeance or death, like a dwarf, or a dragon.

He said, "I am going under the mountains."

The unicorn simply turned its head and walked out of the tunnel. It headed north, swiftly but apparently without hurrying. Morlock was conscious of some disappointment. Had he been expecting the unicorn to try to talk him out of it? Morlock smiled ruefully, looking after the unicorn for a moment.

But his path lay clear before him. He shrugged and walked forward into the darkness. The mountains of light had long since disappeared. He walked forward anyway.

The air was strange in the Runhaiar. Morlock noted it immediately, but found it hard to put his finger on the change. The air was neither warmer nor moister than usual; it was not tainted with venom or smoke. But when he had walked for some hundreds of paces he realized that there was still a freshness to it; the air moved more freely than it had in the past. Morlock guessed this meant that the Runhaiar had been broken open, probably at more than one point.

He was still pondering what this might mean when he came across a collapsed tunnel.

The break was sudden; he literally walked into a wall where none should have been. Feeling it with his fingertips, he sensed the rough unworked surface of broken stone. It made him slightly ill, like touching a broken, exposed bone. It was not a mere qualm, though—he became suddenly conscious of the vast killing weight of the mountain above him. Violence was breaking loose in the Runhaiar; death, if not vengeance, would be easy to find.

The Pilgrims' Way to Haukrull, which he had intended to take, was plainly impassable now. He took the next right-hand turn—south and downward. This led him closer to Saijok's den, which he had hoped to avoid. But he had never really believed he would be able to avoid it.

When he felt he could go no farther that day he sat down in the tunnel and ate some bread, moistened by mouthfuls of water from his bottle. He unbelted the sword he had brought with him and laid it near at hand. Then he lay down by the wall, using the Ambrosian shield as a pillow, and went to sleep.

Awaking some hours later, he continued his journey. His second day in the Runhaiar resembled the first. Whenever he tried to turn east he was blocked by fallen stone. It was as if the tunnels leading toward Haukrull had been deliberately destroyed. The second night he ate less but slept longer—or so it seemed. He awoke to find the air dense and warm.

He felt he was somewhere near the Drowned Arches, but he was unsure. He went into a tunnel entrance to read the signs there. But as he lay his hands on the wall, he was overcome by a sense of blindness and a choking feeling of being closed in, trapped. The patterns of heat and cool were gone; the whole wall was warm as blood, blindingly warm.

Desperation came over him. He returned to his pack and struck a light. Holding the wavering flame over his head, he felt himself relax. He also felt the foolishness of his action, as he saw one stone-gray tunnel at a junction with another; both began and ended in darkness. The light showed him nothing but himself, and what he had brought with him. For a moment he had thought—he didn't know what he had thought. He put out the light and repacked his firebox, thinking calmly.

His food would not last more than a few days; he had not anticipated a long journey. He had to acknowledge the possibility that he might never find an eastward tunnel; they might all have been destroyed . . . so that travellers would have to take the unprotected route overland, of course. That, perhaps, was why the unicorn had warned him against entering here—if that was what it had done.

Morlock shook his head. The air was warm and heavy, but not totally motionless. Somewhere ahead of him was the exit he sought. But if he did not find it in another day's walk he would turn back and try the overland crossing.

He strapped the pack across his shoulders, slung the shield atop it, then stood up and walked on.

In the dark midday, he stumbled on a dragon's tail. It lay across the exit from a tunnel. As Morlock sprawled on the rocky ground, he saw the darkness was merely a red dimness in this open cavern between tunnels. The dragon's form was clearly visible, outlined in red light. He heard sounds of breathing in the gigantic echoing chamber.

Had he caught the dragon asleep? Rising slowly to his feet, he drew his sword and slipped the Ambrosian shield onto his left arm. He advanced stealthily along the side of the dragon. But he had not taken many steps before he saw that the dragon was not sleeping; it was dead. Its snakelike sides were breached and the body gutted. The dim red light and the sounds of breathing were coming from farther away in the cave. He turned now toward them.

Along the walls of the great cavern he found a double row of creatures standing, waist-deep, in the stone floor, for all the world like a rows of carrots waiting to be pulled. They were gray in color, with heavy platelike scales. Their common form was manlike, except for the blunt animal snouts that blotted out what would have been their faces. Their eyes were bright as blood, and when their mouths opened smoke and flame issued lazily into the echoing air. They moved strangely, with the plantlike undersea motions of sleeping animals. Their size varied, from a hand's-breadth to two or three feet in height, the tallest ones being in the middle with the shortest on either end of the parallel rows.

They were smaller, still-living images of the dead creature he had found floating in Saijok Mahr's subterranean pool. There was something else familiar in them, too. . . . They were greenish gray; the forms were sharp and jagged, but the rows they formed were regular. Like a saw-edge. Saw-toothed.

Teeth.

Morlock turned and walked back to the fallen dragon. Even in the dim light it was easy to see that the dragon was toothless. The jaws had crumbled from the extractions, and their collapse gave the dragon's face—at once wolflike and serpentine—a boneless empty look.

Now he understood why the dwarves had smashed the teeth of the dragon killed at Southgate. He understood, too, what the rebel master Saijok Mahr must have done to get the creature Morlock remembered, the creature floating dead in Saijok's subterranean pool. The dragon had pulled one of his own teeth so that it would grow into a mandrake . . . perhaps to do work that needed hands. (Morlock thought of the carven pillars where Saijok's den opened up in Haukrull valley.) Then Saijok had killed it. If the sowing of teeth was the way dragons gave birth to their young (the words of the Dead Cor recurred to him: "they gave birth only in death") Saijok's act showed signs of an ultimate unsparing ruthlessness.

Staring down at the fallen dragon, he recognized it. This was not Saijok Mahr: the scales gleamed gold in the red light, not greenish black. The Triple Collar was gone and the toothless face was distorted, but Morlock guessed this was Vild Kharum. Saijok had at last claimed his victory, then, and had gone out into Haukrull to establish his mastery over the guile of masters.

Morlock wondered what action the guile would take now, since all questions of leadership were finally resolved. He watched the red-gold gleams of light on the dead dragon's broken wings. In his mind each separate gleam took the form of a dragon settling in fire into one of the thousand valleys of the north. By the time winter ended they would be prepared to invade the southern holds. Who or what would stop them? There was no hope; the thing was ended. He had seen the future, growing like a patch of mushrooms in the dark under the mountains.

In the release that came with despair he gained new knowledge. He saw the chain of events he had participated in, now that they had come to an end, as an outsider. He saw, at last, the essential pattern. As Saijok had meant him to carry the challenge to Vild, so he must also have let Earno and Old Father Tyr pass. In Haukrull, they had either defeated Vild or been defeated by him—or their combat, perhaps, had been interrupted. In any case, at the suitable moment, Saijok Mahr intervened, defeated Vild (if he was not already slain), and drew him underground to reap the spoils of victory. Even as Morlock mourned for Tyr a part of his mind frankly admired Saijok's stratagem: it had the accidental irregular elegance of a candle flame; it was the opposite of Earno's obsessive and useless insistence on a fruitless course of action.

The guile might be far from here. They might even have moved their place of assembly from Haukrull. If that was so, Morlock was perhaps the safest person in the north, in this dark stone womb under the mountains. Yet he had come here seeking vengeance or death in fine epic fashion. . . . The irony sickened him. He felt as if he could not move, as if he were turned to stone. All he saw and heard made as little impression on him as if he had been stone. Standing there he was only conscious of the shudder of the dead stone heart of the mountains.

The light came then, and the noise, like the fall of a red thunderbolt. Morlock saw his own shadow, outlined in bright red light, crooked on the face of the dead dragon. Then the dimness returned, amid the echoes of the roar, and Morlock knew the master dragon had not yet departed to plunder the north. The stone floor shook as Saijok Mahr leapt toward him.

Morlock spun about, dark meditations evaporating in the moment of action. He raised the sword he still carried in his hand. He saw the dragon pause, stretch out its lizardlike neck and inhale. Morlock held the shield of Ambrose in front of his face and ran forward with a defiant shout as the dragon expelled a fiery breath.

The force of the breath was not itself enough to knock him down. But the fire was intensely hot; the agony of its passage, though brief, threw echoes of pain up and down his nerves. Fumes and smoke swept around him, blotting out the bloodred light. On impulse he fell heavily to the ground, then rolled into a crouch beneath the cover of smoke. His clothes were smoldering.

Almost immediately Morlock saw the glare of Saijok's fiery eyes sweeping back and forth, looking for the flaming corpse it supposed Morlock to be. They focused quickly on the smoke rising from Morlock's clothing, rising straight up from the heavy venom-laden fumes. The eyes stabbed forward. Morlock waited for agonizingly long instants until he could actually see the dragon's hungry yawning jaws through the thinning curtain of smoke. Then he leapt up and drove his sword home into Saijok's left eye, desperately hoping the dwarf-forged sword was long enough to reach the dragon's brain.

A chaos of fire and smoke erupted about him. He was struck away by the dragon's head and struck spinning in a new direction by one of the dragon's forelegs as it convulsed in agony.

But not death-agony. As Morlock finally landed on his side, he saw the dragon shake the sword out of the dark gleaming wreckage of its left eye. Then it began to search the gigantic smoke-filled cavern with its single eye, moving its head in swift birdlike glances.

Morlock struggled to his feet and shrugged the smoldering pack from his shoulders. The motion did not go unnoticed. The dark dragon's bright eye fastened on him immediately. Yet Saijok made no other move, standing almost amazed.

"Ambrosius!" Morlock shouted suddenly. It was explanation, defiance, and battle cry. He raised the black battered shield, with its white device of hawk and thorns. "Ambrose!" he shouted again, then paused. He felt as if he had uttered a blasphemy, or a slander—or a confession.

Then he realized he stood alone, unarmed, before a vindictive enemy he had terribly (but not mortally) wounded. If he sought vengeance or death . . . he need only stand and wait to die.

He decided he preferred vengeance. In the instant before the dragon moved, he turned and ran like a thief.

The dragon was after him before he could take three steps. But his fourth stride hurtled him over the threshold of a tunnel too narrow for the dragon to follow him. When Saijok reached the tunnel entrance a moment later he made the mistake of thrusting his head into it. He realized his mistake before he wasted more time throwing fire down the tunnel. But before he was able to withdraw his snout and reach blindly up the passage Morlock had fled beyond the reach of his claws.

Morlock heard them clash against the ceiling, walls, and floor of the corridor behind him. Then, without further display, the dragon was gone. Morlock ran on through the absolute darkness that reigns under the mountains. Visions were born in his blind eyes, as if his mind were struggling to blot out the dark with lies. He paid them no heed but ran on. Somewhere ahead, somewhere above, there was light and free air.

There was a cool draft in the passageway. He kept his face against it, moving upward. This led him on a fairly straight path through the tangling passages. Many of those off to his left seemed to have been ruined; he could tell they were closed by the echoes that rebounded to him as he passed, by the dead pockets of air within their entrances. But mostly he ran without thinking: there was no need for it.

Cries came from the mouths of various passages as he ran by them, the echoes of the master dragon roaring in pain and rage. Morlock never doubted that the other knew by heart what seemed to be his only route for escape and was hurtling toward the exit by those tunnels that were large enough to let him pass. But there were few such in the Runhaiar, Morlock knew, and those seemed to be carrying his enemy south and downward as Morlock ran north and east and upward. Then for a long time there was silence, except for himself and the sphere of echoes surrounding him in the dark.

Presently he saw a crooked line of light before him: grayish gold leavening the darkness at the end of the tunnel. He had been running for so long, he found he could not increase his speed. But he did not permit it to lessen as he entered the zone of shadows at the tunnel's end.

He jumped through the jagged mouth of the tunnel, and open space and light and cold air swirled about him. He landed on a hillside of gold pieces gleaming with expelled venom. His feet went out from under him and he fell.

Rising to his feet he knew he must be in the den of the master dragon. Of course: Saijok had moved the hoard from Vild's seat in the valley to his own cave. Morlock ran a cold eye over the hoard. It was not paltry, but it was nothing to content a dragon. Haukrull was fairly wealthy, as the oldest settlement of Other Ilk in the north. But its accumulated wealth (added to much that must have been stolen in Ranga í Rayal) did not compare with the fame of Thrymhaiam. And Morlock knew that the fame of Thrymhaiam fell short of the facts.

The thought nagged at him, when he wished to think of nothing. Across the echoing treasure-filled cave was a blindingly bright hole: the gate of the dragon's den, which he had seen from the outside. To his right, as he faced the gate, was the dark mouth of a vast tunnel, from which a fountain of cool steam was rising. With the steam, troubling echoes rose into the light. They grew slightly louder as he listened. Saijok Mahr was approaching.

Without willing it, he backed away from the cavernous tunnel. He tripped over something and fell on a pile of jewels, as sharp as humbler stones. He rolled over and saw what had caused him to fall.

It was a body. It was Tyr's body. It was not dead. And it was not alone.

They lay in a ragged row, like a rack of silver spears he saw beyond them in the imperfectly ordered hoard. He knew them all. Beyond Tyr, who wore the gray cape of a thain, was Earno. Next to him was Lernaion, like a gray-etched ebony statue in that place, pregnant with violence. Beyond Lernaion was a member of his faction: Rild of the Third Stone, a vocate from Easthold. Beyond him were more vocates, and a line of thains beyond them. He did not need to lift the lids of any of their eyes to know they were in dragonspell: he could see the blood-bright circles of their enchanted eyes through the thin translucent skin of their eyelids. This was the fate Almeijn had died to escape.

From the cave behind him, Morlock heard the sudden full-throated roar of Saijok Mahr.

Plunging into action, Morlock seized Earno and Tyr by their collars and began to haul them toward the bright gate. It stood with its threshold slightly above his line of sight. When he had dragged the two bodies up the glittering slope that led to the gate, he stood still for a moment to catch his breath.

As he paused, he heard something. He heard it not above the other sounds around him—the rattle of coins falling back down the slope, the repeated roar of the approaching dragon, the sound of his own labored breathing in the venom-laden air—but below these, on the level of the wind that hissed by the gateposts outside. The sound was directionless, dim, irregular in rhythm. He had heard it only once before, but that made it all the more impossible to mistake.

Beyond the curtain of light, there were dragons breathing.

Morlock retreated hastily down the slope, drawing the bodies of Tyr and Earno behind him. Of course: when the hoard had been moved to the new master's den, the guile must have followed it. They were in attendance outside. Plainly they would not hesitate to destroy anyone who stumbled into their midst, attempting to make off with any part of the hoard.

He wondered whether he should drag the spellbound captives into the tunnel from which he had come. Saijok would not be able to reach them there (though how they would ultimately escape Morlock could not imagine). But he had no sooner thought this when he knew it was impossible. He could hear Saijok approaching, like a storm rising out of the earth. He would be here in moments. Morlock could save two of the captives, perhaps, and himself.

Lernaion and Earno should be saved, he supposed. But, given this miraculous opportunity, he had no intention of leaving Tyr to die while saving the summoners. The safety of the Wardlands and his loyalty as a Guardian dictated that he sacrifice his *ruthen* blood, but there were deeper loyalties—and, besides, would the realm really be safer with Earno in charge of its defense? He had been willful and strange, lately. Lernaion, too, had been tested against the dragons and failed. And father Tyr was wise: he knew the enemy from within.

This thought, bearing the knowledge of the dwarf's kinship with dragons, threw a shadow of repugnance. Why save any of them? he wondered, looking down at them sleeping like lizards on a sunsweep of gold coins. In that instant, if he could have saved them all by lifting a finger they all would have died, each one. Except Tyr.

Morlock wondered a little that he still revered his *harven* father, when he knew every dwarf's blood was as poisonous as his own. Dwarves too had betrayed, murdered, rebelled. It was odd to look on Eldest Tyr, the authority he had admired all his life, and know him for a rebel, the desperate and crafty leader of an ancient rebellion. No wonder they called it the Longest War! It would never be over.

As he stood over the singed and torn sleepers, his hands stained with the dragon's venom and his own blood, his heart ached to be at peace with itself. He hated the shame that burned him, worse than fire, the guilt he suffered that was not his own. He wished he could be free of it, be washed clean of it. But there was nothing in the world that could free him of it: he was who he was. Whether he called himself Ambrosius or syr Theorn he was still Morlock. The guilt was not his, yet somehow he shared the burden.

But he could rebel. The current of his blood might carry him toward evil, but he could fight it. Then he knew that Tyr was truly his father, as much as Merlin was. As the dwarf had fought to keep faith with a destiny beyond his blood, so Morlock would. He was Morlock Ambrosius: he would deny it no longer. But in his heart he was Morlock syr Theorn, and he swore he would keep faith with everything that meant or could mean. And then he knew what he must do—what he would do.

He no longer felt inclined to move any of the Guardians, even Tyr, to safety. Had they sought safety for themselves? Besides, there was no time. Saijok Mahr's angry light was already leavening the cavernous tunnel's darkness. But he reached down, grabbed the flawed gem, and broke the pendant chain around Tyr's neck.

This emblem of shame and peril had hung about Tyr's neck since Morlock had been a boy. Now perhaps it would be of some use. If he could break the unstable pattern at its core and release an endothermia, he might use it as a weapon against the dragon. His craft might yet slay the guile master.

Leaving the captives, he hurled himself toward the row of spears. Seizing the longest, he ran on to the base of the golden hill. The cavern above it was already red-gold with reflected light. The roar of the dragon was like a barrage of thunder. Yet he had time to think, a little time. A moment, at most, to think and act.

He summoned a vision and ascended into the lowest realm of rapture. In the undreaming state of vision he directly apprehended the ur-shapes he had blindly woven into the gem's core long ago, precariously balancing the energies of that-which-utters-heat and that-which-devours-heat: a red dragon and a blue-black dragon devouring each other in the gem's heart.

He lifted the flawed stone with the black-and-white flames of his talhand, letting the hand of his fleshly body fall quiescent to his side. Then he slew the red dragon in the stone, releasing the blue shock of endothermic reaction.

He fit the now-gaping flaw in the stone into the point of a silver spear and banished the vision.

The spear was shuddering in his hands as if it were lodged in the heart of a wounded angry beast. He gripped it with both hands and waited in a haze of bitter blue air for the advent of his enemy.

The light in the cave-mouth before him brightened unbearably; he could hear the beat of the storm-swift dragon's wings; he could hear nothing else. Yet he watched and wondered, pointless thoughts oppressing him as he awaited the fate he had chosen. The dragon did not appear.

Then he was there, but Morlock never saw him, only the blast of fire and venom that swept down from the tunnel mouth. He longed to raise the Ambrosian shield, to protect his eyes and mouth from the venom and the heat. But he could not do that and also achieve what he had set himself here to do. He felt the angle at which the flames struck him changing rapidly. Then the zone of flames was passing from him as he stood half-crouched under the onslaught.

Desperately he straightened and leapt back into the sheath of flames, holding the spear and its zone of bitter frost between him and the dragon. He hurled the shaking spear with all his strength upward, seeking only to strike the heart of the fire, the source of the dark light blinding him. The flames and the frost passed from him as the dragon flew roaring overhead, and he fell to his knees in the smoke, blind for long moments from tears and poison.

He heard the dragon land on the far side of the cave. He groped on the cave floor for some sort of weapon, but found none. As his eyesight returned and the bank of fumes over him slowly dispersed, he saw Saijok Mahr glaring at him menacingly with one eye. There was not even the mark of a spear on the dragon.

Saijok Mahr roared. There were words in it, but Morlock could not make them out. He lurched defiantly to his feet. He thought of shouting in response, but could think of nothing to say. He contented himself with raising the Ambrosian shield high. Fire and venom had stained the black battered shield, but the silver falcon and thorns still glittered against the dark field.

Maddeningly, his mind would not give up. He kept thinking of wild and unworkable expedients for the moment when the dragon struck to kill. It was pointless and it lacked dignity. If some of them had been more likely . . .

The dragon's throat exploded in a jet of fire and ice.

The dragon spread its wings and began to fall forward through a cloud of flame and steam. Saijok continued to fall headfirst down to the hoard. The ground shook when he struck.

The master dragon lay among the gold and jewels, writhing feebly. The explosion had nearly severed his neck in two; from the wide gaping wound, fire-bright blood flowed in a torrent. And something else gleamed there, red and silver, drenched in burning draconic blood.

Morlock watched in weary triumph. The single eye of his enemy turned in the motionless head and fixed on him. The look of malice and suffering on the dragon's face moved Morlock with unexpected pity. He did not avoid the eye as it focused to fire-bright clarity. This last futile effort exhausted the dragon. The eye went dark, and the jaws issued a final stream of black smoke into the dense cloudy air of the cave. For long moments Morlock continued to stare at the motionless dragon until even the blood ceased to flow. Saijok Mahr was dead. Morlock was *rokhlan* indeed, at last.

He went to assure himself the dragon was dead and the endothermia quenched, as it seemed to be. He found what had been the wounded gemstone and the silver spear lodged in the wreckage of the dead dragon's neck.

The gem had healed through absorbing the dragon's fire, finding at last enough heat to satiate its dark blue hunger. It hung, flawless—blood-dark and clear—in a filigreed basket of silvery metal: the remains of the bright silver spear that had carried it into the dragon's gullet.

As he carried Tyr and the Guardians, one by one, back up to the safety of the narrow corridor, his thoughts were somber. The terrible sense of guilt he had felt before the dragon's death had not lessened, but it was different now. His fear of the dragon had died in pity—was it anything, after all, but an animal, unable to escape the destiny of its blood? This thought, though, led to others. If he had been born with Merlin's guilt on him, so Merlin had been born with the bright poison of Ambrosian inheritance in his veins. That did not excuse Merlin; it did not change what he had done. But it did somehow change Morlock's feelings about him.

When he had deposited the last Guardian, a thain whose name he did not know, in the corridor, he took the cape from her shoulders to replace the smoldering rag of his own. Then he returned to Saijok Mahr's corpse.

Taking a heavy cup carved out of a single gemstone, he deliberately smashed three of the dragon's teeth. Inside each one there was a reddish black fluid, within which embryonic forms were already taking shape: mandrakes, protodragons, Saijok's children. Would they live or die, now that he had cracked their shells? He neither knew nor cared.

He did not rest then, although he was tempted to. He had taken the full blast of the dragon's venomous breath twice; his eyes and mouth and the slight hurts he had sustained all burned from the poison they had drunk. If he paused in what he was about to do he might never complete it, and it was the most important task of all.

He found a knife in the hoard's precious weaponry; the blade had a silvery gleam, yet was hard as steel. He took it and cut the Triple Collar from the throat of the dead master dragon. It was easy to do. Half the collar was burst asunder by the explosion that had killed Saijok. For the rest: the lead-colored metal was not as soft as lead, but the linkages of the collar were subtle and easy to break with the hard glittering edge of the knife. When he had severed each of the three plated bands he drew the collar from the dragon's neck and dragged it toward the gate of the den. Reaching the threshold, he let the collar go and sat down for a moment. But when he felt himself losing consciousness he got up again and dragged the collar behind him as he went out to face the leaderless assembly of dragons.

The long arms of the mountain lay on either side of him. The sky above was a dome of thick bluish clouds, lit from within by the silver radiance of a cold afternoon. The valley before him was bright and blank with new-fallen snow, like a page on which the dark burning words of the dragons were written. In the dim wintry day their fires were almost invisible, but they sent up tall columns of smoke and steam from the clean snow.

They said nothing as he approached them, laboring through the deep snow. They made no move but watched him closely. They knew what he carried; they knew what it implied.

If they said nothing, neither did Morlock. Once he had stirred them with words; now he did not need to. He lurched to a halt some twenty paces from the edge of the assembly, where there was still a slope downward. Then he took the collar by its central band; with both hands he seized it and spun it around in a full circle. He swung it again, and a third time to build momentum. Then he let it go. It arced briefly in the air and went down, trailing severed bands. It fell downslope a little farther, flailing in the snow.

The nearest dragons did not move toward it, did not even seem to see it. But they saw it. For a moment everything was still, except the dragons' eyes. To Morlock it seemed as if there was no sound in the world but for the irregularly rhythmic sound of their massed breathing; he could not even hear his own.

He turned his back on the dragons and walked away, following the trail of his own footsteps back to the dead master's den.

After passing the threshold and entering the dim smoky cavern, his legs went out from under him. He never knew if he had simply misstepped in the hoard or whether his legs were truly too weak to support him. There was a roaring in his ears; he could not tell if it came from within or without. He tried to clamber across the hoard on his hands and knees. The roaring grew louder. The ground seemed to shake. He was not sure whether these things were happening within the cave of his failing mind or in the world outside. He struggled on and up as far as he could.

Deor was a condemned criminal, and he supposed he had no right to speak. But it was not as if any of his companions were dwarves, or even northerners. Besides, it was cold in the everlasting blizzard. Maybe shouting a few words would take his mind off it. Perhaps that was why these towering madpeople were content to stand here and talk and talk and talk.

"Look here!" he said in their speech, interrupting a long rambling monologue (with gestures!) by the tall fair-haired one they called Jordel.

They obeyed literally. Jordel fell silent, and all the Guardians looked to Deor.

"Guardians of the south!" he said. "I was sent with you as guide by the Eldest of the Seven Clans. Perhaps you did not know he considered it a sentence of death."

They did not speak, but waited for him to continue.

"Instead of accepting my guidance you chose to follow the black unicorn that appeared to us in the Helgrind Gate. Very well. We have followed it over the mountains, through two days of storm. We have not slept; we have met, fought, and killed dragons. Now the unicorn has disappeared, and you wonder what we are to do. At the beginning of our journey you did not listen to me. But now we are comrades: we are *rokhleni* together, eh? Perhaps you will listen to me now."

"I will listen, at least," said Illion. "Have we gone wrong, Deor?"

"You are about to do so," Deor said frankly. "You chose to follow the unicorn. So you did. It's too late to change your minds about that. If the unicorn's intent was to betray us to the guile, it has already done so and we have only to meet our doom. But if it has not, then it had some other purpose. It brought us here to show us something, or have us do something. We should look to that, Guardians. Since we have already given our trust to the unicorn we should not withdraw it now."

"Champion Deor!" cried Thain Aloê. He did not exactly understand her, but he gathered she approved.

"What are your thoughts, Deor?" asked the vocate Norcê.

Deor pointed north. "We are on the verge of Haukrull vale. Look! That shadow against the snow is the Pilgrims' Gate of the Runhaiar." He turned south. "Yonder somewhere is the entrance to the den of Saijok Mahr, the renegade master, as Morlock described it to Earno, Earno to Old Father Tyr, and Tyr to me. Now, every dragon we have met came up from the south and east, from this very direction."

Naevros nodded, dimly visible through the haze of wind-driven snow. "So the rivalry between the two masters has been settled," he guessed, "and the dragons we have met are refugees, adherents of the defeated master."

"It's likely," Deor said. "More likely than a unicorn shilling for dragons!"

Deor thought of the dragon he had killed. (He was a *rokhlan* now. It was strange.) He had spotted it in a ravine high among the Haukr. It was transporting a pile of gold and jewels up the ravine, bit by bit. Deor watched it return to the pile under the wall of the ravine again and again. Then he placed himself over the pile and, when the dragon returned, toppled over a pinnacle of rock, striking the dragon unconscious. Then he snuck down and stabbed it in the brain until it was dead.

It had been a sordid death. Such was not how legends were born. And the victory had given him no elation. There was a senselessness to the dragon's actions that spoke of a mind broken by panic. In fact, none of the dragons they had met had displayed the terrifying subtlety that was their legendary hallmark.

Deor expected more talk from the Guardians, but there was none. Their consensus was unanimous, immediate, silent. They moved together to negotiate the slope down into the valley. Deor led the way south from there.

Darkness fell swiftly in the unrelenting storm. Before it was completely dark the company spotted a dark red glow on the southern horizon. Before long they heard the roaring of dragons in combat. They climbed a snowy hill, dense with red reflected shadow, and on the height they found themselves looking down on a blasted landscape.

There were dragons, dead and dying, scattered through the narrow valley that led up to the mountain Gramer. Melted snow and torn earth had formed a mire in which bleeding dragons burned dimly, like the separate coals of a scattered fire. At the high end of the valley there was a gigantic double-pillared gateway, which could only be the entrance to Saijok Mahr's den. Before the threshold two dying dragons thrashed in combat, their jaws locked around each other's throats. After a long somber look at the swathe of hell the company descended back under the shadow of the slope.

Illion spoke. "The guile of masters is destroyed. But the danger to the Realm is not yet ended. Not all the dragons can have been killed here. We met many refugees; there will be others. How many there are, where they have gone, and how the guile was broken: these are the things we must discover."

There was no dissent. They decided to divide into four parties: Jordel and Baran to go back to the ruins of Haukrull town and the site of Vild Kharum's assembly; Naevros and Aloê would stay on the dragons' battlefield; Noreê and Thea would go to explore the Runhaiar, via the cave that led into the Drowned Arches. As for Saijok Mahr's den, Deor claimed that for himself, and Illion smilingly agreed to accompany him. They all agreed to meet or send word to the Pilgrims' Gate in two days, and parted.

It was an easy thing for Illion and Deor to make their way past the fighting dragons; these were concerned only with each other. Inside the den they found a chaos of dead dragons and half-melted treasure, layered over with dark venomous air. Deor took a coldlight from his pack and lit it. The light wore a dim blue halo; the air was denser than fog, warmer than summer.

Ominous sounds came from the cavernous dark tunnel entrance on their left. They glanced at each other, guessing that sooner or later they would have to go that way. But they decided to search the den as best they could first. Illion turned to the left, and Deor turned right; they both set out on a circuit of the cave.

They had almost met on the far side when Deor cried out some words in the Dwarvish language. Illion was not thirty paces away and he glanced around but saw nothing. He made his way to Deor and asked what he'd seen.

"Old Father Tyr," said Deor. "I saw his face through one of those cracks in the wall."

Illion looked where Tyr was pointing. There were many cracks, most of them no doubt opened by the heat and shocks of the dragons' conflict.

"Which one?" he asked.

Deor gestured again, impatiently. It was an opening like any of the others. Illion could see nothing. But that, perhaps, meant nothing.

They climbed up to the opening. Within, indeed, they found Tyr leaning against the wall, unable to speak. Beyond him lay a corridor along which lay a row of Guardians, still as effigies of the dead.

Deor immediately began to speak to Tyr in the Dwarvish tongue, but Illion put him firmly aside.

"Your Eldest had been poisoned, at least, and almost certainly spellbound. If he could have spoken, he would have called to you."

"Can you help him?"

"Yes. Bring me a cup of dragon's blood, Deor, and I promise you will see your Eldest preside again over the feast of Cymbals."

Deor asked no more but jumped down the steep slope and plunged into the hoard. When he returned, with a half-melted cup brimming with black tarry blood, Illion was examining the Guardians.

"Are they all in danger?" Deor asked.

"No," said Illion, returning to him. "I was very concerned at first. But most of them responded to the dragonspell by going into a trance of Withdrawal. This has protected their minds and kept the poison from working into their flesh. The trance is very deep by now, and it will take time to draw them from it. But there is no danger."

As he was speaking he tore three strips from his red cape and soaked them in the black tarry liquid Deor had brought back. Then he drew a knife from his belt and nicked a vein on Tyr's neck and one on each wrist. Then he bound the soaked strips of cloth around the Eldest's neck and wrists. Tyr's eyes were open, but he watched the acts without apparent comprehension.

"The blood will draw the venom out," Illion explained, when he had finished. Then he picked up the cup and inspected its contents. "There is enough," he said, cryptically. "Come."

He stood and led the way back down the row of Guardians. Deor followed more slowly, wondering if he should stand by the Eldest—until he saw the figure at the end of the row.

"Morlock!"

"Yes," Illion said. "You see he has been drawn up here after the others?" He indicated a trail of ashes and venom smeared on the floor of the corridor. "My idea is that Tyr drew him up; exhaustion in the wake of a dragonspell can bring about that empty state the Eldest is in. However, he himself will be able to tell us soon enough."

Deor hardly heard Illion, taking in the awful sight of his *harven* kin. Morlock's clothes, except for the gray cloak, were burned rags. His skin was covered with bruises and wounds. His eyes were open and glaring at nothing, his teeth bared in the fearful grin of rigor. His spine was arched; his arms and legs, even his feet were bending inward as the muscles tightened against the bone; his twisted shoulders were bent like a bow. Beside him on the corridor floor lay the shield of Ambrose, battered and blackened by fire and venom. The falcon and thorns glittered bright blue in the light of Deor's coldlamp.

"Poison has worked deep into his flesh," Illion remarked.

"Then there is no hope?"

"No bones have been broken," Illion observed, "and the skin is more or less whole. By Noreê's teaching, these mean his life may yet be saved."

"Then the poison hasn't reached his heart?" Deor asked.

Illion might have explained that Morlock's mortal danger would be from wounds caused by flesh contracting on a framework of broken bones. He might have explained that the venom was no real danger to Morlock's heart, which could expand and contract without taking harm. He might have explained that the heart is just a muscle.

But none of that, he guessed, was what Deor really wanted to know. "His heart is sound," said Illion the Wise, and wondered if it was true.

EPILOGUE

CYMBALS

Just now it seemed to me I stood
between the worlds of life and death
and everywhere about me
the fires were burning.

—*The Waking of Angantyr*

On the last day of the year, Nimue walked into the little house in the Lost Woods after a long absence. Here Merlin and their daughters lived, in what the wizard called his last redoubt, though it was really just a cottage with a remarkable number of basements. Although Nimue loved her daughters she was rarely in the house these days; her marriage with Merlin was wearing thin.

"Mama is home!" shrieked Hope Nimuelle, and went to hide under a couch. Her mother frightened her a little: Nimue read that clearly. Her father frightened her a little also. Her sister frightened her most of all. Hope thought of herself as a timid child, but Nimue knew the truth was that the girl spent most of her life surrounded by frightening people.

Merlin emerged from his study, accompanied by a cloud of sorcerous purple smoke.

"Good evening, my dear," the uxorious wizard greeted his witch-wife. "Where the devil are you coming from, if you don't mind my asking?"

"From going to and fro in the earth, and from walking up and down in it," Nimue replied.

"Oh, I've read that one," Merlin said, after a moment's thought.

"Rather flattering, the role you assign me by implication. I take it you were mindsharing with strangers again."

"With unicorns, mostly. It's an exhilarating experience. You should try it."

"I have. I gained no useful knowledge."

"Knowledge!" Nimue said scornfully. "Experience is the only knowledge that matters."

"You didn't used to talk that way," Merlin remarked ruefully.

"I know, I know. Whatever happened to the girl you married, eh?"

"She went swimming in the Sea of Worlds, so I'm told. Are you hungry, my dear? I believe the kitchen is working on something."

"As long as it's not those squeaky mushrooms you're so fond of. They give me the creeps."

"You can always pluck them out of the salad if you don't like them. It's good to have you back, my dear."

She knew that he really felt that way, even though he was thinking about killing her if she tried to harm one of the girls, as she had last time. (She loved the girls with a true, mad love. But the thoughts in her mind weren't always her own.) Yes, it was good to be home, as near to a home as she would ever have again. She would have told him so, but she saw in his mind that he already knew it.

Morlock awoke to see the last sunlight of the year on the sill of the open window of his room. From where he lay in bed he could see nothing but cloudless blue outside. From the moment he woke he knew he was in Thrymhaiam.

It was pleasant to breathe clean cold air, but he felt feverish and had no desire to move. So he didn't. He lay in bed and watched the light fade from the window.

He became aware that someone else was in the room, sitting against the wall opposite the window. When the sun had fully set she stood and, striking fire, lit an old-fashioned lamp that hung from the ceiling. Her shoulder-length hair was a dark gold; her skin was darker yet. She wore the gray cape of a thain. He had seen her before. He had seen her many times before. Each time it had seemed to him that she was the most beautiful woman alive, but he had never found occasion to tell her so. He sat up in bed.

She turned and met his eye. Her eyes were large and their irises golden, brighter than her hair. He saw on her neck the flaw-line of gills, the mark of a true southerner. It seemed to him, again, that she was the most beautiful woman alive.

"Morlock," she said, "I am Aloê Oaij. We've never met, exactly, but we've seen each other from time to time. Do you remember?"

"More or less," said Morlock thickly. "In A Thousand Towers." He wondered how long it had been since he last spoke. He coughed and cleared his throat.

"Please stand, Morlock."

He looked on her sourly. He had no intention of getting up. He didn't like her voice, either; souther accents irritated him. Not until he felt his bare feet hit the floor did he realize just how much they irritated him.

Fortunately she was unfurling a long cloak. But as soon as he saw it he began to wave it away. It was a vivid red, cut to resemble a vocate's cloak. In fact . . . His mind finally focused on the words she was speaking.

"Morlock Ambrosius, called syr Theorn," she said, following the form of a ritual that had been old when his father was born, "I bring you this token at the command of your peers, who stand among the Guardians. If you accept it, they will call for your counsel and comradeship."

There was no formally prescribed response. Astonished, Morlock said, "I accept it from them—and from you."

"All right. Stand still and stop twitching, then."

He stood still. Aloê came to him and put the cloak across his shoulders. The fresh warm scent of her hair mixed disturbingly with the wintry draft from the window. Her eyes met his again as she stepped back.

"It looks well," she said. "I borrowed it from Naevros, and I wasn't sure . . . well, if it would fit."

This was an oblique reference to his shoulders, Morlock supposed. The appraising look in her eyes bothered him; he was achingly conscious of his bare legs, exposed beneath the hem of his shirt. "It fits," he confirmed brusquely. "Thanks," he added, as her appraisal turned to surprise.

"You might need to grow into it, after all," she said, laughing. "You should see to that. Good fortune, Vocate Morlock. Maybe we'll meet again in A Thousand Towers, or elsewhere."

"It seems likely," he said to her back, and "Good fortune," to the closing door. He was sure she had meant something by that last remark, but he was unsure what it was.

"Why, you sorry piece of northern fungus," said Deor, when he and Tyr looked in a few moments later, trays of food and drink in their hands, "are you telling me you don't know what she meant?"

Morlock, who had just told him exactly that, lifted his crooked shoulders in a shrug.

"That was probably her last task as a thain. At the next Station of your Graith, she'll be a vocate, too—in the regular way. I take it there's some special procedure for hopeless cases like yourself."

"Stop barking at him, Deor. He's been unconscious for four days. And, Morlock, go back to bed before you fall down!"

In fact, Morlock did feel unsteady. He carefully took off his red cloak and climbed into bed. His *harven* kin came and sat at his bedside, and they talked for a long while as Morlock slowly but steadily ate and drank everything his kin had brought with them.

The two dwarves had been changed by their separate ordeals, Morlock noticed. Tyr looked a little withered, frailer than he had been. But Deor was one of the *rokhleni* and a companion of legends, as Morlock now heard.

After each of them had told his story, they exchanged general news. Tyr had been seated again in the Eldest's Chair, but he would not displace Vetr from authority. "It was long overdue that he take up the task. I have much to teach him, but there is more he must learn by himself. And—it will be good to have a rest."

And Deor was to join the Guardians. He announced this rather diffidently, when they were discussing Tyr's adventures. The Eldest had taken the gray cape as a formality when he followed Earno into Haukrull (it being a violation of the First Decree for Guardians to have authority over the Guarded). Morlock assumed that Tyr had been released from the obligation after returning from Haukrull, but then was told that Deor had assumed it instead.

"It was a way to solve certain problems," said Deor, looking wryly at Tyr, though speaking to Morlock. "As the Eldest is so gently reminding us, he won't live forever. And, although Vetr is a good fellow, no one can say we ever saw eye to eye."

"That passed," said Tyrtheorn, quoting the proverb, "and so may this."

"Wolves may eat onions," said Deor, quoting another.

Morlock was pleased to hear that Trua and her people had safely arrived at Thrymhaiam.

"She arrived yesterday," Deor said, "with that very strange vocate they call Jordel. Your friends, the thains of Northtower, were with them. Just think! Now you can give them orders."

Morlock found the prospect uninviting. It must have showed on his face, for Deor laughed and Tyr changed the subject.

"Most of your peers," his *harven* father said, "have already left Thrymhaiam. They are pursuing the remnants of the guile through the north. It's unfortunate, in a way; I'd gotten quite fond of some of them. Particularly Earno."

"Earno is a great partisan of yours, these days," Deor informed Morlock, "but he is mixed metal, in my opinion. Badly mixed metal."

"It would be a narrow mind," said Tyr, "that could be filled by a single thought. Or a narrow heart, that never had conflicting feelings. Earno has his weaknesses, but he is not narrow. He does not grudge."

"I do," said Deor. "But does anyone notice?"

When his kin had left him to go to the New Year's Night feast, Morlock stood for a long time at the open window. He watched the three moons, reddish and somber, set in the east, beyond Haukr's black outline. He listened to the sound of cymbals and bells, ringing out from every part of Thrymhaiam welcoming a new year and a winter season beyond hope. He breathed the bitter air and felt his mind grow clear and cold.

He no longer ached for vengeance or death. The terrible feelings that had driven him to the edge of destruction were still within him; they were part of living, just as death was part of life. But they would not rule him. He would live his life and die.

It was all one, brilliantly clear and simple in his mind. He thought of it as a single act, like crossing a room to open a door. Whatever Other Ilk or dwarves had done in their lives before him, all that was over and done. Whatever he bore from it was something other than guilt. He was not his father. He was not either of his fathers. He would live *his* life and die.

Deciding he was strong enough to join the feast, he shuttered the window and turned away. He crossed the room to open the door. The hall outside was lined with doors, and at either end were staircases, leading to other halls and other doorways still.

On the next day, the first day of the new year, the masked powers of Fate and Chaos, enthroned in the dark blue heart of the winterwood, reflected on the failure of their stratagem with the dragons. It had been such a clever plan; they both disagreed about that. But it had failed; the Guard was unbroken; the Wardlands were as much a threat as ever. There were many the Two Powers might blame for this, including each other, and they did, taking what angry pleasure they could in that. But one person was most guilty of thwarting their opposing wills. And he had named himself to their agent Saijok Mahr, just before he had killed the master of the guile and ruined their clever plan.

"Ambrosius," said Torlan, the power of Fate.

"Ambrosius," disagreed Zahkaar, the power of Chaos.

"We hate him," Torlan said.

"Hate," agreed Zahkaar reluctantly, then added, "I hated him first."

"Liar. Liar."

"You're the liar."

"All my decrees are true and eternal."

"True and eternal *lies*."

So the long day wore on.

Appendices

APPENDIX A

THE LANDS OF LAENT DURING THE ONTILIAN INTERREGNUM

Laent is a flat or shield shaped landmass bordered by ocean to the west and south and empty space to the east; north of Laent is a region of uninhabitable cold; south of Laent is a large and largely unexplored continent, Qajqapca. Beyond that is believed to be an impassable zone of fire.

Along the western edge of Laent lies the Wardlands, a highly developed but secretive culture. It has no government, as such, but its borders are protected by a small band of seers and warriors called the Graith of Guardians.

Dividing Laent into two unequal halves, north and south, are a pair of mountain ranges: the Whitethorn Range (running from the Western Ocean eastward) and the Blackthorn Range (running from the Eastern Edge westward). There is a pass between the two mountain ranges, the Dolich Kund (later the Kirach Kund). North of the Dolich Kund there are only two human cities of any note, Narkunden and Aflraun. The rest of the north is a heavily wooded and mountainous region, inhabited by humans and others of a more or less fabulous nature (e.g., the werewolf city of Wuruyaaria).

The Whitethorn Range, by custom, forms the northern border of the Wardlands. The Blackthorn Range is divided between the untamed dragons and the Heidhhaiar (Deep Kingdoms) of the dwarves.

Immediately south of the Whitethorn Range is the wreckage of the old Empire of Ontil, ruined by its rulers' ambitions, ineptitude, and misused powers. A period of general chaos and more or less continuous warfare obtained in these lands until the advent of the Vraidish tribes and the rise of the Second Empire of Ontil (some generations after the present story).

South of the former Empire of Ontil lay the so-called Kingdom of Kaen. The ancient cities of the Kaeniar considered themselves at perpetual war with the Wardlands, which lay just across the Narrow Sea. The Wardlands, however, took little notice of the Kaeniar, or any other domain of the unguarded lands.

The region between the Grartan Mountains and the Whitethorns was called the Gap of Lone by inhabitants of the unguarded lands. Inhabitants of (and exiles from) the Wardlands called it "the Maze," because of the magical protections placed on it.

Immediately south of the Blackthorns was a wooded region of extremely poor repute, Tychar. Farther south was the Anhikh Kômos of Cities, Ontil's great rival that unaccountably failed to take advantage of Ontil's fall to extend its domains. The largest Anhikh city, where the Kômarkh lives, is Vakhnhal, along the southern coast of Laent. Anhi may or may not extend its domain to the Eastern Edge of the world—accounts differ.

APPENDIX B

THE GODS OF LAENT

There is no universally accepted religious belief, except in Anhi, where the government enforces the worship of Torlan and Zahkaar (Fate and Chaos).

In Ontil an eclectic set of gods are worshipped or not worshipped, especially (under the influence of Coranian exiles from the Wardlands) the Strange Gods, including Death, Justice, Peace, Misery, Love, and Memory.

In the Wardlands at least three gods, or three aspects of one god, are worshipped: the Creator, the Sustainer, and the Avenger ("Creator, Keeper, and King").

The dwarves of the Wardlands evidently assent to these beliefs. (At any rate, they have been known to swear by these deities.) But they have another, perhaps an older, belief in immortal ancestor spirits who watch the world and judge it beyond the western edge of the world. The spirits of the virtuous dead collect in the west through the day and night, and pass through at the moment of dawn, when the sun enters the world and the gate in the west is opened. Spirits of the evil dead, or spirits that have been bound in some way, may not pass through the gate in the west. Hence, dwarves each day (at sunrise, or when they awake) praise the rising of the sun and the passage of the good ghosts to those-who-watch in the west.

APPENDIX C

CALENDAR AND ASTRONOMY

1. Astronomical Remarks

The sky of Laent has three moons: Chariot, Horseman, and Trumpeter (in descending order of size).

The year has 375 days. The months are marked by the rising or setting of the second moon, Horseman. So that, if Horseman sets on the first day of Bayring, the penultimate month, it rises again on the first of Borderer, the last month. It sets after sunset on the first day of Cymbals, the first month of the new year. All three moons set simultaneously on this occasion. The number of months are uneven—fifteen—so that Horseman rises or sets on the first morning of the year in alternating years. Years where Horseman sets on the first day of the Cymbals are, idiomatically, "bright years"; those where Horseman sets with Trumpeter and Chariot on the first night of Cymbals are known as "dark years."

The period of Chariot (the largest moon, whose rising and setting marks the seasons) is 187.5 days. (So a season is 93.75 days.)

The period of Horseman is 50 days.

The period of Trumpeter is 15 days. A half-cycle of Trumpeter is a "call." Calls are either "bright" or "dark" depending on whether Trumpeter is aloft or not. (Usage: "He doesn't expect to be back until next bright call.")

The seasons are not irregular, as on Earth. But the moons' motion is not uniform through the sky: motion is faster near the horizons, slowest at zenith. Astronomical objects are brighter in the west, dimmer in the east.

The three moons and the sun rise in the west and set in the east. The stars have a different motion entirely, rotating NWSE around a celestial pole. The pole points at a different constellation among a group of seven (the polar constellations) each year. (Hence, a different group of nonpolar constellations is visible near the horizons each year.) This seven-year cycle (the Ring) is the basis for dating, with individual years within it named for their particular polar constellations.

The polar constellations are: the Reaper, the Ship, the Hunter, the Door, the Kneeling Man, the River, the Wolf.

There is an intrapolar constellation, the Hands, within the space inscribed by the motion of the pole.

In the Wardlands, years are dated from the founding of New Moorhope, the center of learning. According to Professor Gabriel McNally, the "year of fire" when the Guile of Masters invaded the Wardlands was New Moorhope 2748, Year of the Hunter, in Ring 394—a "bright year." The year following was N.M. 2749, Year of the Door, Ring 394, a "dark year." I have generally followed Dr. McNally's reconstructions of Ambrosian legend, including dates, in composing the text above.

But the reader should know that Dr. McNally's views have been disputed, especially by Julian Emrys, grandson of the eminent Ambrosian scholar H. N. Emrys. Julian Emrys' own early reputation as a scholar was gradually obliterated by his bizarre claims to be one of "those-who-know" and (in his own words) "the last descendant of the ancient Ambrosian kings on Earth." But, as Dr. McNally conceded, in his fair-minded if blistering review of Emrys' *New Evidence of the Old Ambrosians*, "the fact that Mr. Emrys is crazy does not necessarily imply he is in error."

In any case, settling on a definite date for these events is a little like trying to decide in what year young Sigurd slew his dragon or old Beowulf faced his.

2. A "bright year" and a "dark year"

Bright:

1. Cymbals.

New Year. Winter begins.
1st: Chariot & Trumpeter set. Horseman rises.
8th & 23rd: Trumpeter rises.

2. Jaric.

1st: Horseman sets. 13th: Trumpeter rises.

3. Brenting.

1st: Horseman rises. 3rd & 18th: Trumpeter rises.

4. Drums.

1st: Horseman sets. 8th & 23rd: Trumpeter rises.
Midnight of 94th day of the year (19 Drums):
Chariot rises. Spring begins.

5. Rain.

1st: Horseman rises. 13th: Trumpeter rises.

6. Marrying.

1st: Horseman sets. 3rd & 18th: Trumpeter rises.

7. Ambrose.

1st: Horseman rises. 8th and 23rd: Trumpeter rises.

8. Harps.

1st: Horseman sets. 13th: Trumpeter rises.
Evening of the 188th day of year (19 Harps):
Chariot sets; Midyear—summer begins.

9. Tohrt.

1st: Horseman rises. 3rd & 18th: Trumpeter rises.

10. Remembering.

1st: Horseman sets. 8th & 23rd: Trumpeter rises.

11. Victory.

1st: Horseman rises. 13th: Trumpeter rises.

12. Harvesting.

1st: Horseman sets. 3rd & 18th: Trumpeter rises.
6th: Chariot rises, noon of 281st day of year. Fall begins.

13. Mother and Maiden.

1st: Horseman rises. 8th & 23rd: Trumpeter rises.

14. Bayring.

1st: Horseman sets. 13th: Trumpeter rises.

15. Borderer.

1st: Horseman rises. 3rd & 18th: Trumpeter rises.

Dark:

1. *Cymbals.*

New Year. Winter begins.
1st: Chariot, Horseman & Trumpeter all set.
8th & 23rd: Trumpeter rises.

2. *Jaric.*

1st: Horseman rises. 13th: Trumpeter rises.

3. *Brenting.*

1st: Horseman sets. 3rd & 18th: Trumpeter rises.

4. *Drums.*

1st: Horseman rises. 8th & 23rd: Trumpeter rises.
Midnight of 94th day of the year (19 Drums):
Chariot rises. Spring begins.

5. *Rain.*

1st: Horseman sets. 13th: Trumpeter rises.

6. *Marrying.*

1st: Horseman rises. 3rd & 18th: Trumpeter rises.

7. *Ambrose.*

1st: Horseman sets. 8th and 23rd: Trumpeter rises.

8. Harps.

1st: Horseman rises. 13th: Trumpeter rises.
Evening of the 188th day of year (19 Harps):
Chariot sets; Midyear—summer begins.

9. Tohrt.

1st: Horseman sets. 3rd & 18th: Trumpeter rises.

10. Remembering.

1st: Horseman rises. 8th & 23rd: Trumpeter rises.

11. Victory.

1st: Horseman sets. 13th: Trumpeter rises.

12. Harvesting.

1st: Horseman rises. 3rd & 18th: Trumpeter rises.
6th: Chariot rises, noon of 281st day of year. Fall begins.

13. Mother and Maiden.

1st: Horseman sets. 8th & 23rd: Trumpeter rises.

14. Bayring.

1st: Horseman rises. 13th: Trumpeter rises.

15. Borderer.

1st: Horseman sets. 3rd & 18th: Trumpeter rises.

APPENDIX D

The Wardlands and the Graith of Guardians

According to Gabriel McNally's reconstruction (generally accepted by scholars of Ambrosian legend, always excepting Julian Emrys), the Wardlands were an anarchy with no formal government at all. According to legend, the Wardlands had not been a kingdom since the golden age at the beginning of time, when the King (usually identified with the divine aspect known as God Avenger) ruled in person in Laent and elsewhere. Since then it has been considered blasphemous, or at least irrationally presumptuous, for any person to assert a claim to rule the Wardlands. Those who try to do so are exiled or (in extreme cases) killed.

What in other cultures would have been state functions (national defense, dispute resolution, even road building and repair, etc.) were carried on by voluntary cooperatives: the Arbiters of the Peace, the Guild of Silent Men, the League of Rhetors, etc. Most famous in the unguarded lands was the Graith of Guardians, sworn to maintain the Guard.

The Graith had three ranks of Guardian: the lowest and most numerous were the thains, wearing a gray cape of office. They were hardly more than candidates to the Graith proper, and they undertook to obey their seniors in the Graith, even more senior thains.

Vocates, in contrast, were full members of the Graith, privileged to stand and speak at the Graith's councils (known as Stations). Their only obligation was to defend the Guard, and the Guarded, as they saw fit. Their cloak of office was bloodred.

Most senior in the Graith were the Three Summoners. They had no power to command but were generally conceded the authority to lead the vocates of the Graith proper. The Summoner of the City convened and presided over Stations of the Graith. The Summoner of the Outer Lands was charged with watching for threats to the Guard from the unguarded lands. The Summoner of the Inner Lands was charged with watching for internal threats: those who would try to disrupt the fertile anarchy of the Wardlands and establish the sterility of political order.

The greatest danger to the anarchy of the Wardlands was obviously the Graith itself. Members of the Graith were pledged to abide by the First Decree, which forbade any acquisition of power or authority over those under the Guard. Nevertheless, Guardians were exiled more often than the Guarded for political aspirations to government (euphemistically referred to as "impairment of the Guard"). Power corrupts, and the Guardians wielded power more often than their peers among the Guarded.

About the Author

JAMES ENGE lives in northwest Ohio, where he teaches classics at a medium-sized public university. His short fiction has appeared in *Swords and Dark Magic* (Eos, 2010), in the magazine *Black Gate*, and elsewhere. His previous novels are *Blood of Ambrose* (Pyr, 2009), which was nominated for the World Fantasy Award in 2010; *This Crooked Way* (Pyr, 2009); and *The Wolf Age* (Pyr, 2010).